CITY OF A THOUSAND SPIES

KATHRYN GUARE

THE VIRTUOSIC SPY ○ BOOK 3

CITY OF A THOUSAND SPIES

KILTUMPER
CLOSE
PRESS

Published by

KILTUMPER
CLOSE
PRESS

PO Box 1175
Montpelier, VT 05601

Cover Design by Andrew Brown
Print Design by Chenile Keogh

When people say that they do not remember what they do in a fit of fury, they talk nonsense.
It is false. I remember everything.

— Leo Tolstoy, *The Kreutzer Sonata*

1

As soon as night falls, darkness becomes your weapon. Use it, or you'll find it used against you.

She scrambled up the steep incline, repeating the words to herself like a mantra, like a prayer she was trying to believe in, willing them to produce the effect she needed. Invisibility. Concealment.

When Conor had offered this advice—his face solemn, as if reciting a piece of ancient wisdom—she'd tried to match his mood, but ended up annoying him with an ill-timed giggle. Kate wasn't laughing now. The situation was more frightening than anything she'd prepared for, and her strategy was unraveling.

Instead of heading for the summit she should have taken the last side trail to slip back along a different route. She'd realized her mistake a few minutes earlier, when the forested mountainside began dropping away. It seemed as though the unseen hand of an artist was rubbing at the scenery, thinning the composition. The higher she climbed, the fewer the trees. Eventually, there would be none. She would emerge like wild game flushed from its cover—a solid, unobstructed target.

It was too late to double back now, but with the cloud cover of a March evening speeding its arrival, the weapon she'd been waiting for finally appeared. Darkness. It poured over the mountain, an inky tide arriving exactly on time. Within a shrinking sphere of visibility Kate paused to listen for a sign of pursuit.

Earlier, she'd been able to detect it—a distant thump of booted feet on the trail, more vibration than sound. Methodical. Relentless. The beat of it in the ground under her feet had unnerved her, but its absence was worse.

Pebbles from eroding stone shifted beneath her feet. She cringed at the rattle echoing through the otherwise silent forest. Scrambling up the final steep section of rock, she pulled herself onto an outcrop of ledge and stood motionless on the summit. At the corner of her eye something shivered in a thicket of evergreens, and she spun to face it. A bird? A rustle of wind? Something else? Kate focused on the indistinct shape of the trees, but the movement had subsided.

She relaxed and took a long breath, wiping the sweat from her forehead, but when she turned he was right there, his dark figure filling the space in front of her, extinguishing what light remained. She screamed and reflexively took a step away, then felt herself toppling back over the ledge. A hand shot out and yanked her forward. She heard him grunt as one of her windmilling arms connected with his chin. Off-balance himself, he slammed her onto the ground and fell on top of her. Kate landed hard, flat on her back, and felt the air explode from her lungs like a shot being fired.

In one fluid movement the figure rolled away and up onto his knees, then loomed so close she could feel his breath on her face.

"Kate? Are you all right? Did I hurt you?"

Trying to speak, she managed only an urgent hiccup and lay still, struggling not to panic at the clenched paralysis of her lungs.

"Damn. Sorry, love." Conor's dark eyes flashed, wide and startled. "The wind's knocked out of you. Try to relax. It won't last long."

It felt like hours, though it was probably no more than a few seconds before her diaphragm relaxed and Kate sucked a gulp of air past the pain in her chest. He waited until her breathing grew less desperate, and then in a manner more clinical than either one of them was used to, he slipped his hands beneath her fleece jacket, watching her face while he probed her ribs.

Once satisfied she wasn't seriously injured, Conor gave her a cheerful smile. "No bones broken."

Kate pushed his hands away and sat up. "No thanks to you. What the hell was that, anyway? You told me this was a *chase* exercise. You were supposed to be behind me—*chasing*. You told me to evade and listen for signs of pursuit."

"I also told you to stay alert—and I did chase you, but then I peeled away to the right and got ahead of you." Conor smiled. "I didn't think it was going to work so well."

"You're proud of yourself! For knocking me senseless!"

"Ah, go on, you know that's not true." His face sobered. "Listen, I'm sorry, but this is what it's like—and anyway, can I remind you that all this 'getting a jump start' business was your idea."

"I know, I know." Kate scowled. "I should have seen you. I was just distracted by something in that tree over there."

"Sure that was me as well. I threw a stone into it, and you stood staring like you thought it would get up and walk away. That's something to remember. You need to be able to look at more than one thing at a time."

"Okay, I want this lesson to be over now."

"But, you were the one who—"

"Over!"

"Right so." He ducked his head, hiding a grin as he shrugged a backpack from his shoulders. After pulling out a thermos and several plastic containers, he removed a small lantern clipped to the side of the pack. Turning it on, he placed it on the rock between them.

"What's all this?" Kate peered down at the display.

"Candlelight supper, courtesy of Chef Abigail. It's a long walk down and it's already dark, so we might as well eat first."

"My God, you're a genius." She leaned over to reward him with a kiss, running her fingers through his tousled black hair. "It was worth it, just for this."

"Well, let's see if you still think so by the time we get home."

He had a point. Table Rock, far from the highest mountain peak in Vermont, was not a difficult hike in daylight, but it was a precarious descent in the dark, even when wearing headlamps, and after reaching the parking lot they still had an hour's drive ahead of them. It was after nine o'clock when Conor turned the truck onto the driveway of the Rembrandt Inn.

Since purchasing the property six years earlier Kate had continued the tradition of closing the hotel for the months of March and April—the state's least photogenic period in the calendar year and a dormant time for tourism. Famous for playing cruel tricks with its weather patterns, Vermont served as a sort of proving ground in early spring in a way that even the heartiest natives found challenging. As a transplant from New York Kate had experienced her share of soul-testing moments, but she'd learned to cope and to appreciate anything that helped remind her why she'd fallen in love with the place. Like right now, for example. With a pale moon hanging in the sky over its roof and the porch light shining, the inn looked particularly charming as they pulled up in front of it.

Her legs sore and her back stiffening, Kate gathered her strength before sliding from the passenger seat while Conor stood holding the door for her, his face unreadable. He could be good at that trick—projecting a blank slate without visible effort. She'd first seen that polite, impenetrable mask when he showed up on an April evening almost a year ago, an emigrant Irishman burdened with a stash of secrets he was determined to keep hidden.

He'd arrived with an unconventional résumé—a farmer who'd stopped farming, a professional violinist who'd stopped playing. Once settled under her roof he'd begun applying himself to both again, and before the end of that year Kate had poked her way through all his cautious evasions and given up secrets of her own—and they'd discovered others together that neither could have imagined.

They'd suffered and healed together during that time as well, and now Conor's opaque facades were less effective with her. He couldn't often fool her—he didn't often try—but tonight Kate knew he was trying to hide his distress. His mission for the evening had been to stalk and terrify her. He'd done it well and had banged her up in the process, but any heartfelt apologies would defeat the ostensible purpose of the exercise—to prepare her for more of the same—as well as his unacknowledged objective, which was to put her off the project altogether.

Prodded by rebellious instinct, Kate shook off her weariness. She reached into the bed of the truck to lift the heavy backpack, but this effort to prove her resilience was too much for Conor. She wasn't surprised when he stepped forward to take it from her.

"Hot shower?" he said, casually throwing the pack over his shoulder.

She gave his hand a squeeze. "I like the way you think."

Conor knew it was coming; he could see it in the set of her chin. An argument was on the way, and twenty minutes together in her spacious, walk-in shower had postponed, but not preempted, it. While toweling off, he watched Kate with guarded suspicion.

Wrapped in a blue silk robe, she stood at the bathroom sink staring at her reflection and shedding water from her toothbrush with rhythmic taps against the porcelain. A "fate motif" worthy of Beethoven. It sent him scuttering into the adjoining bedroom in search of escape, but he'd mistimed the strike. She waited until they were lying in bed together, her head on his shoulder, one hand trailing over his chest.

Very clever, he thought. *Attack when I'm most vulnerable.*

It wasn't hard to put him off-balance in this room anyway. He'd been occupying the master suite for a while now, but during his first six months at the inn he'd stayed in a guest room down the hall. He occasionally felt nostalgic for its more modest proportions.

Not that Kate's room wasn't comfortable. Despite its size it was warm and intimate, its best feature an expanse of floor-to-ceiling windows offering a view of the pasture sloping down from the inn and the outline of Lake Rembrandt in the distance. Opposite the windows hung a set of three small canvases, miniatures of the landscape surrounding his farm in Ireland. Kate had painted them during their stay the previous fall, the result of an artistic rebirth after many years of creative paralysis. She'd unveiled them as a gift, saying it was to help him feel more at home in the space they now shared. It was exactly the right touch, helping to remind Conor that some things from his past life remained intact.

Kate's hand slid away and he pulled his attention back to her, steeling himself.

"I know you don't want me to do this, but you need to get on board. I think it's important for me to go through with it," she said.

"Why?" Conor kept his tone neutral, wary of aggravating her, but when she lifted her head, her eyes were sleepy and reassuring.

"It isn't because I want to do what you do. I'm not planning to be Frank Murdoch's latest unconventional recruit, but he's offered to have me trained as if I were, and if I don't accept it I might not get another chance. I can't always go with you, I know that; but at least you won't have to hide what you're doing from me. It wouldn't be good for either of us. Besides, if he knows I might be around, Frank may assign the dangerous jobs to someone else."

Conor gave a derisive snort. "You put entirely too much trust in him. Frank Murdoch will do as he pleases. He's an MI6 officer."

"So are you," Kate said softly.

"Non-official cover agent," he insisted. He was an Irishman, contracted to work for the British Secret Intelligence Service. It was important to keep the boundaries clear.

"I stand corrected. Anyway, that's one reason. The other involves something I don't think you've given much consideration—that I might not be any safer at home. The last six months are proof enough of that, and you won't always be around to protect me. I suppose you'd want to surround me with bodyguards and high-tech security, but I can't live like that. I need to learn how to protect myself."

Conor had actually given a great deal of consideration to the issue of Kate's safety, but she was correct in thinking most of it involved armed men and surveillance cameras. A recent threat to her life had been eliminated decisively, but given her unique background there was no guarantee it would be the last. The skills he'd learned at the Fort Monckton training site during his own MI6 initiation had served him well, and the modified program Frank suggested for Kate would likely do the same.

Conor couldn't argue with the logic of giving her the tools to defend herself. It was the idea of her ever needing to use them that terrified him. But maybe his fear was a sort of poetic justice. This debate—which he was losing and probably deserved to—wouldn't even be happening if he'd left Frank's bargain on the table and walked away.

Even now, he wasn't sure why he'd decided to remain an

undercover agent. Was it because the offer came linked with a chance to rebuild his musical career? Or was it because he couldn't resist the adrenaline rush of performance, the compulsion for total mastery of everything he was good at?

The compulsive instinct felt closer to a truth he wanted to shield from Kate, but for months she'd lobbied him for inclusion in the covert side of his life. Although he didn't entirely understand her motivation, his resistance was crumbling. The Prague assignment might be dangerous—as usual, Frank was being coy about the details, including a departure date—but if Conor was being honest, he didn't want her to stay home either. His mission included an opportunity to play in front of an audience again, to step onto a concert stage, tuck the violin beneath his chin, and fill the hall with sound. The prospect generated a certain amount of panic, but his anticipation was stronger and he couldn't imagine experiencing something so momentous without her.

Kate propped herself on one hand to look at him and Conor moved restlessly on his back, preparing for the *coup de grâce*. Meeting the gaze of her expressive blue eyes always spelled defeat, partly because she employed the tactic without realizing it. She had no idea how magnificent she was, how beautiful, in a mood of earnest determination.

She hooked a finger under his jaw and turned his head to face her. "We can't stay on opposite sides on this. Please. I need you to trust me. I need your support."

"I do. You have it. I promise." Conor sighed. "Ah, Kate. You're going to be good at this, you know."

"Really? I'm not so sure. I made a fool of myself tonight."

"No, you didn't. Far from it." He sat up, giving her a kiss, and drew her down with him as he lay back. "You did well. Sorry for not saying so earlier. I did lose you for a while when it got dark." Conor still remembered the anxiety he'd felt when he realized he'd lost track of her. "You melted away from me like a ghost.

It was a bit unnerving. I didn't think you were paying attention when I told you how to do that."

"I'm always paying attention to you."

She snuggled against him and a minute later was asleep—he could tell by the weight of her arm stretched across his stomach. In slumber, the laws of gravity seemed to double for Kate. She slept hard, and woke with a slow, seductive drowsiness, while he tended to bolt awake as though touched by a live current.

She also slept silently, which sometimes alarmed him. To ease his anxiety, he liked to have a hand resting on her somewhere, just as he did now, his palm flat against the warmth of her back. Once he felt the rise and fall of her breathing, he let his fingers wander through the dark copper curls of her hair, still damp from the shower. With his lips against her forehead, he whispered a promise:

"I'm always on your side. From this day forward, for better or worse …"

Noiselessly, she slept on, which was probably just as well. She wasn't ready to hear those lines yet, but he was.

2

The next day Conor rose before dawn—as he did every day—and headed across the road to the dairy barn and the herd of eighteen cows he'd been managing for almost a year now. After the milking and a quick clean-up, he spent the rest of the morning splitting logs at a neighbor's sugar house. His family had farmed in Ireland for generations, so managing Kate's modest operation held few surprises, but the workings of a traditional Vermont "sugarbush" farm was a whole new world. He was enjoying his education in maple syrup production, as well as the wisdom and raucous humor exchanged with neighbors around the smoking evaporator.

Back at the inn after three hours of stoking the fires, he stopped to check the iron mailbox on the front porch. It was a vintage model in keeping with the overall theme of the inn, but Conor hadn't purchased it for decorative effect. He'd just been looking for something that locked and was easy to bolt to the wall. In compliance with instructions from afar, collecting the mail had become a restricted task.

Today, the box was filled to capacity, mostly with résumés for a recently advertised job opening at the inn. Once the post was filled, a management transition that had been underway for several months would be complete.

After years of being unable to make any art at all, Kate was brimming with ideas and energy, and anxious to spend more time in her studio. She had a vocation to explore, but she also had an inn to run and a finite number of hours in the day, so something had to give. Several long conversations with Conor between the Christmas and New Year holidays led to further discussions with the inn's chef, Abigail Perini, and her husband Dominic who managed the restaurant, and at the end of February Kate had formally appointed Dominic to be the Rembrandt Inn's general manager.

This meant the inn was in the market for a new dining room manager, and the single advertisement posted several weeks earlier was still producing an impressive response. Shuffling through the letters, Conor was wondering why no one had thought to ask the candidates to send their résumés by email when he suddenly stopped halfway through the pile. It was a plain white envelope, like all the others, but addressed to him, and the return address in the corner was as expected.

"Madison, Wisconsin," he read aloud. Resisting the temptation to open it on the spot, he pulled the remaining flyers and magazines from the box and headed inside.

In the hall he circled around the reception desk to Kate's office behind it, which was even more cluttered than usual. She'd promised to put everything in order before turning the office over to Dominic. Conor, who had a natural instinct for making things tidy, thought her progress seemed painfully slow. She was on the phone when he came in, so he loitered for a minute, surveying the chaos and casting an eye on an enormous package from New York sitting on the desk. When it looked as though the call would go on for a while, he tucked the envelope in his back pocket and carried the rest of the mail into the kitchen.

"The post is here." He dropped the pile onto the prep counter in front of the inn's stout rosy-cheeked chef.

Abigail wiped her hands down her apron and reached across the counter. "I'll take it."

"Not so fast now. I'm not sure they're all for you. Some of them might be for Dominic." Conor scooped up the bundle before she could grab it. No one—least of all her husband—was under the illusion that his new job was anything other than a shared position with his wife, but Conor couldn't resist teasing her.

As Kate had once explained, Chef Abigail Perini "came with the place" when she bought it and had soon become more like a family member than an employee, although an obstreperous one. Abigail hectored and fussed over those she loved, and Conor had been a target for this kind of attention from the day he'd arrived. He countered it as any good Irishman would—with a combination of mischief and flirtatious charm.

"Uh-huh, yep." He flipped through the envelopes again. "It seems most of these are résumés addressed to Dominic. What's he got against email, I wonder? I should probably pop them into his mail tray."

"You just pop them right over here." Abigail flapped a hand at him. "If they came by email I'd never see them."

Conor grinned, sliding the mail across the counter. "I was under the impression your husband was in charge of staffing now."

"He is, officially." She was smiling as well. "I'm his secretary."

"Oh, I see. You're a great help to him. Dom must be grateful."

"He doesn't complain."

"No, I don't suppose he would." Conor sniffed the air. Something both vinegary and sweet was wafting from a pot bubbling on the stove.

Although the inn was closed, Abigail was in the kitchen almost every day, experimenting with menus, supervising Dominic, and ensuring to her own satisfaction that Kate and Conor didn't starve during the off-season. By their own admission both were hopeless in the kitchen, so the arrangement made everyone happy.

"What have we got on the menu?" he asked. "Smells good."

"Potato dumplings, pickled cabbage and roast pork. In brown gravy." Abigail headed for the stove. "Traditional Bohemian cuisine. You might as well get used to it." She assembled the meal without her usual attention to detail and thumped the plate on the counter in front of him, as if daring him to eat it.

Undaunted, Conor picked up a fork. "Meat, potato, and cabbage. I feel right at home."

Although he'd managed to keep the scarier aspects of his personal history from becoming common knowledge, Abigail was one of the few people who knew that the town of Hartsboro Bend harbored an undercover operative. She'd heard about the upcoming mission to Prague, and of the plan to have Kate trained in the basics of espionage, and she was not happy about it.

He ate his dinner under her challenging stare and meekly offered up the empty plate when he'd finished. "Better than home, actually."

Abigail relented, smiling. "I doctored it a little."

He laughed, but then his smile faded. "Abigail, I hope you realize I don't like this any more than you do, but she's determined to go through with it. It's not for me to tell her she can't."

"I know that, honey." She took the plate from him, giving his cheek an affectionate pat. "Kate's not the only one I worry about though. Where is she anyway? I made enough of this to punish her too."

"In her office. There was a bloody great box from the Zimmer House fellow in New York, so she's neck-deep in the paperwork I suppose." Conor pushed up from the counter. "I'm off, myself. I need to get in a few hours with the fiddle."

"Well, send her in here." Abigail frowned into the pot on

the stove and gave it a stir. "I've got all this cabbage, and I know Dom will never eat it."

During the summer, Conor had practiced at least three hours a day in an empty shed next to the dairy barn, but in the freezing weather it was no place for a violin, particularly an 1830 Pressenda worth a small fortune, and it was no place for him either, as Kate had noted. For both of them, the previous fall had been full of unwanted excitement. He had the long scar of a gunshot wound along his side as a memento from one of its unexpected events. At the same time as the bullet had been grazing his ribs he'd been hit with pneumonia for the second time in a year. As with the previous bout—which had come with its own complicating factors—he'd barely survived, so for the sake of his lungs and his instrument he'd used his former bedroom as a winter practice space.

Today the weather was mild enough to return to the better acoustics of his gambrel-roofed studio, but as he headed in that direction, Conor remembered the envelope in his back pocket. Making a detour, he again poked his head into Kate's office and found her sitting at her desk, hunched over a three-ring binder.

"How's yer man in New York? Seducing you with bank statements? Finding castles you didn't know you owned?"

She looked up at him, her face drained of color, and he stepped quickly into the room. "What's the matter? Is it bad news?"

"It's … I'm not sure. I just … I don't know." Kate gestured at the binder, speechless. "You're not far off," she finally added.

"About what, the castles? Jaysus, Kate, are you joking me?"

Conor dropped into a chair in front of the desk and stared at her, wondering what kind of revelation he should be preparing for now. When he'd met her, it had come as no surprise to learn the young widowed innkeeper of the Rembrandt Inn had money in her background. In some ways Kate was fairly transparent about it. From early conversations about her family and childhood it was clear she'd had a privileged upbringing, though not always a happy one. Her mother had died when she was a baby, and her father, an investment banker and pioneering hedge fund manager, had a taste for marrying often and for selecting ever-younger brides. Kate spent much of her childhood living with her grandmother.

Up to a point it wasn't an unusual story, but there were some pertinent details Kate failed to divulge. Conor eventually learned of them months later—under less than ideal conditions—and confronted two equally bewildering facts. The first was that Kate's grandmother, Sophia-Marie, was one of five children from the marriage of a Luxembourg princess and the Crown Prince of Bavaria. The second was that having just turned thirty, Kate was of age to assume control of a trust fund totaling forty million dollars. He had managed to fall in love with a royal heiress. Nearly six months later, he still felt disoriented.

Kate never acted the part of an entitled woman of wealth; quite the opposite in fact. At the moment, she looked so pale and frightened Conor thought she might faint.

"Okay." He leaned forward. "Take a deep breath and tell me. What does it say in those books?"

"It's more," Kate blurted out, her breath hitching. "More. It's way, way more."

"More than forty million? Right." He scrubbed his hands over his jeans, which were filthy with sawdust and pine pitch. The conversation was preposterous. "Well, how much more, for fuck's sake?"

"It's a hundred and eight-five million dollars. Not counting the real estate."

Conor sat back, feeling light-headed himself. "Holy mother

of God. Not counting the real estate. That would be the castles, I imagine."

"Not castles. At least I don't think so. There's land in Luxembourg and Germany, and a building in New York—and some kind of villa in Italy."

"How did all this happen?"

"It isn't just the trust fund. It's my grandmother's entire portfolio. She's turned everything over to me." She shook a few sheets of paper at him. "That was outlined in these two pages. All this other crap is just a client's guide to the 'Zimmer House Difference.' Do you know what an open architecture product platform is?"

Conor snorted. "Seriously?"

Kate looked miserable. "I'm supposed to go to New York on Monday to get a briefing from the advisors, and then have dinner with Oma. Actually, she wants to have dinner with both of us. What are we going to do?"

She picked up the binder and tossed it aside, threatening the equilibrium of the remaining stacks on her desk. Conor quickly steadied a pile near the edge before it could slide to the floor.

"What are *we* going to do?" he said. "Don't look at me—you're the heiress. I'm happy to have dinner with your grandmother, but beyond that I've nothing to do with it."

"That's not true!" Kate protested. "We're in this together. What's mine is yours. Or will be. Someday."

"No, sweetheart. It's not, and it never will be." He softened his tone, realizing how rattled and confused she was. "Even if I ever manage to get you to the altar, what's yours will stay yours."

"What if I don't want it?"

Conor shrugged. "Tell them so. I'm sure they'll find someone who does."

Kate propped a fist against her cheek and was silent for a long moment. "Would it bother you?" she asked, finally.

"If you give it all away?"

"Or keep it. Either case." More composed, she stood up and came around to lean against the desk in front of him. "In the circle I grew up in, there were good people completely unaffected by money and others who were made small by it, but I never saw it make anyone a better person. Right now you're being noble and I appreciate that, but how do you think you'll deal with this later, in the long term, I mean?"

Stung by the question and what it seemed to imply, a mask of indifference settled over Conor's face. "Feels like a test. If you're asking if I'd come to resent you for refusing a fortune, the answer is *No*. I wouldn't know what I was missing and wouldn't care much. If you're asking if I'd feel emasculated by your stupendous wealth, the answer is also *No*. I don't know what you expect me to say, Kate, and to be honest I'd have hoped you already knew the answers to those questions. As to whether being around money will make me petty, I guess I can't answer that, but if you don't trust me …"

She sprang forward and took his face in her hands. "Of course I trust you. I'm sorry. I'm not questioning your integrity, I hope with all my heart you believe that, but this is new territory for us both. It needs to be talked about, and you're part of the discussion because you're part of my life." Kate lowered her face to his.

After a brief resistance Conor pulled her down to straddle his lap, appeased. "I've no villa in Italy, but I'm not a pauper myself, you know." He fingered the top button of her blouse. "Plenty of women would think me a fine catch. I own two hundred acres of Irish farmland and a violin worth a quarter of a million dollars— and I've all my own teeth. I'd be a star at the matchmaking fairs back home."

"You're already a star right here." Laughing, Kate put her mouth to his ear. "I'll buy you a Stradivarius."

"You could do, but the Pressenda would never forgive me."
After a prolonged kiss Conor pulled back. "By the way, you're
not the only one with news today." To her questioning look he
offered a wink. "Back pocket."

Kate reached around and pulled the folded envelope from
his pocket. She stared at it, wide-eyed.

"Looks like we finally got our marching orders," he said.

"Madison, Wisconsin." She ran a finger over the address and
turned over the envelope. "You haven't opened it yet."

Conor smiled. "Not without you, partner."

Once they'd looked inside the envelope Kate realized it would be
foolish to drive to New York on Monday because now they were
scheduled to be there on Thursday. Frank's letter, exasperating in
its brevity, was written according to a coded framework:

Conor,
Confirming Gordon's visit with you. He's meeting a Chamber
of Commerce group on regional tourism on the 30th but should
reach you no later than four in the afternoon. I shall forward the
travel documents for his upcoming trip to you directly, as he'll not
be returning to the office before departure. He looks forward to it.
Regards,
Bill

"Gordon" was the code for the MI6 station at the British
Consulate in New York. Once deciphered (all dates mentioned
were to be moved ahead one day and all times back one hour),
the rest of the message instructed them to report there at three
in the afternoon on March 31. For purposes of the Consulate
visitor's log they were there as representatives from a Chamber
of Commerce group concerned with regional tourism. This

was a verifiable story because Kate did belong to such a group. The real objective was to receive their travel documents prior to departure for London.

"Travel documents," she said. They were sitting on the couch in her office now with the letter between them. They'd given it plenty of space, as though making room for Frank himself. "Does that mean our flight information?"

"Fake passports," Conor explained. "Credit cards, driver's license. Probably a whole wallet full of fabricated ephemera to make it seem more legit."

"Oh." She felt an odd little shudder in her midsection, something between excitement and apprehension.

"It's just for traveling, I suppose. As far as I know we're not using aliases in London or Prague."

"Sure." Kate nodded and picked up the letter again, aware of his eyes on her, watching for any sign of hesitation. "Who do you think Frank has in Wisconsin to send letters for him?"

"He said there's an honorary consulate there. I expect it's somebody connected to that."

"It hardly seems worth the effort. He hasn't even told us when we're leaving. Why is he giving us so little information?"

"Och, if I had a pint for every time I've asked that." Conor took the letter from her and slipped it back into the envelope. "We could look at it all day, but it won't give up any secrets. Anyway, we need to do something about this Zimmer House business. What are you going to tell them, and your grandmother?"

Kate shrugged. "I'll call and say I've got a stomach flu and ask them to push the meeting to Thursday at eleven. That should give us enough time before the meeting at the Consulate. After that we can have dinner with my grandmother."

He gave a low whistle. "Well, that's all worked out, then. Fair play."

"I do feel bad about lying to her," Kate said. "I guess that's something I'll have to get comfortable with, right?"

Conor fidgeted with the envelope before returning it to his pocket with a tight-lipped frown. "Not necessarily. I never have."

Kate winced at the gentle reproach, an important reminder that Conor was a reluctant recruit for the job he'd accepted. Intelligence work had not been a career move for him; he'd been drawn into its orbit by bizarre circumstance. She knew his decision to remain in it sat uneasily on his conscience, and that he'd been appalled at her rejection of the firewall he'd wanted to create between that choice and his life with her.

It took months to persuade him she was serious about playing a role. Because so much had been taken from him already, Conor's fear of loss was very real and Kate understood his anxiety, but she had fears as well. He was good at this business. She could vouch for his skills because she'd seen them in action and they'd saved her life, but a man could become haunted by the things he's good at. Kate knew the weight of guilt Conor carried into each day, and the memories that could occasionally—even a year later—propel him from sleep into breathless, sweating panic. He wasn't far removed from the risk of losing himself, and the fear knotted at the root of her resolve was that if she let him begin this journey alone, they might lose each other.

3

Before sunrise on Thursday, still half asleep, Kate stepped out to greet a cold, dark morning and two inches of fresh snow. Conor had already been up for a while. He'd started the chores before handing them off to his assistant, Nate Percy, and was sweeping the snow off Kate's Subaru, his face comical in its disbelief.

"What the hell is all *this* about? It was sixty degrees a few days ago."

"Which you thought meant it was spring? That's cute." She tossed her overnight bag into the car. "I think that's probably good enough."

"Yeah, nearly there. Hop inside. Should be warm by now."

Kate groaned and fell into the front seat, closing the door with a shiver. "Neat freak," she said, when he finally climbed in beside her.

"Good morning to you as well, oh pulse of my heart."

"Five o'clock is too early to call it good." She opened her mouth in a jaw-cracking yawn.

Conor fastened his seatbelt and gave her a sidelong look. "How late were you painting last night?"

"When I left the studio it was a little after midnight."

"Hmm. No wonder you're grumpy."

Kate put on a peacemaking smile and handed him the travel mug she was cradling between her knees. "I made tea for you."

"Thank you." He accepted the mug. "Now, take a nap."

When she woke two hours later the sky had grown brighter, the car wasn't moving, and she was alone. It took a few woozy seconds to work out that they'd stopped at a McDonald's. Kate could see Conor inside having an animated conversation with the young woman behind the counter. No doubt he was sweet-talking his way to an early batch of french fries. She took a bracing walk around the parking lot and was in the driver's seat when he returned. He raised an eyebrow as he offered her a cup of coffee.

"I was getting a little antsy," she said.

"In your sleep?" Conor adjusted the passenger seat for his longer legs. "I didn't think we were behind schedule."

"We're not, but I'm afraid we will be. You drive like an old man."

He opened the bag, filling the car with the smell of bacon and french fries. "That's quite a feeble dig. You're no good with insults. You should give them up."

"You drive like a nervous goose."

"Also weak. Geese are mean, not nervous." He passed her a breakfast sandwich.

"Okay. Let's hear yours. How do I drive?"

"You drive like a ..." Conor grinned and shook his head. "Can't do it. It's against the law."

"Another one of Bobby's rules?" Kate rolled her eyes and drove back onto the highway. Bobby Gilligan was her friend Yvette's longtime partner. He and Conor had been sharing relationship survival rules, looking for cultural differences. Apparently, there were very few.

"You scoff, but they're around for a reason."

"So this one says to let me make fun of the way you drive?" Ahead of them, a tractor trailer was kicking a spray of dirty road slush onto the windshield. Hitting the accelerator, she shifted lanes.

Conor took back the sandwich and nudged her empty hand towards the steering wheel. "In a manner of speaking. You could also comment on my expanding gut."

"That one's definitely from Bobby. Yvette is always harassing him about his." Kate eased back into the travel lane and glanced at Conor as he placed the sandwich back in her hand. "Yours never expands at all, despite the amount that goes into it."

"Ah, see? You can say that, but I couldn't say it to you."

"Are you implying I eat too much?"

"I'm not, and you know that." He pointed an accusing fry at her. "Do you see, now? How quickly it all goes downhill? You follow the rules and it balances out, like an exchange."

"Where's the exchange part? What do men get out of these rules?"

"Television."

She laughed. "I'm glad we had this chat."

"Me, too. You drive slower when you're talking." He popped a french fry into her mouth. "Get that into you. You're too skinny."

Conor stood with his back to her in front of the gilt-framed portraits of Johan and Ludwig, the Munich-based founders of Zimmer House. Their bank—the second oldest in the world— had managed the private wealth of the European aristocracy since 1695. Kate thought the Zimmer brothers looked rather complacent, as if their seventeenth-century eyes could see across the years to the comfortable niche they would occupy in the New World.

The New York branch, wholly dedicated to private banking, was in a 1960s-style skyscraper on Maiden Lane, in the heart of the Financial District. They had arrived with fifteen minutes to spare and were waiting in the empty reception area, which Kate noted was a homage to Bauhaus design. Its sparse collection of furniture was made of tubular steel and glass, giving the large room an even greater sense of space. Conor, who'd made it clear he'd rather not be in the room at all, had just finished a restless tour of its perimeter. Understandably, he'd been drawn to the portraits. The dark tones of the late-Renaissance paintings added some warmth to the otherwise chilly atmosphere.

"I should have worn a suit," he said.

"You look fine," Kate said. "Especially from this angle." In chinos and a lightweight navy sweater—both a deliciously perfect fit against his lean frame—he was more than fine as far as she was concerned.

Conor shot her a glance full of tantalizing potential. "I'm only saying, if I'd known I was coming in here with you I would have worn a suit."

He turned as an elevator chimed the arrival of a group of well-tailored men. They spilled into the lobby and disappeared down the hall in loping strides, as though conquering new territory with every step. Conor crossed the room to where she was sitting on the couch, and after pushing aside their coats, he sat down next to her.

"Everyone else here is wearing a suit."

"So what? You don't work here. You're fine," she said again, resting a hand on his thigh.

The elevator trilled again, and this time the sliding doors revealed the advisor Kate was scheduled to meet—a man with the improbable name of Guido Brottman. Tall, blond, and solidly built, he seemed like an extension of the Bauhaus theme. His high forehead formed the top of a rectangular face, which extended down to join a wide, u-shaped chin.

As he advanced to greet them with the same confident gait as the other suited men, Kate realized she hadn't thought this moment all the way through. With little time to address the lapse, she looked at Conor.

"How should I introduce you?"

"Just tell him I'm the hired man." With an enigmatic smile, he slipped her hand away and they rose from the couch.

"Guido Brottman," the advisor said in a generic European accent. He took her hand in both his own. "Such a pleasure to meet you, Mrs. Fitzpatrick. So sorry to have kept you waiting."

"It's Chatham, actually," Kate said. "I've gone back to my maiden name, but call me Kate. I'd like to introduce Conor McBride, my … fiancé."

Conor's surprise registered with only a shiver along his jawline, but Guido Brottman was not so unflappable. Still gripping her hand, his thin lips parted in shock. "Fiancé? I wasn't aware, or rather I wasn't told … forgive me." Collecting himself, he stepped over to extend a hand to Conor. "Pleased to meet you, Mr. McBride."

"Mr. Brottman." Conor offered an amiable smile as the two shook hands, but to Kate the gesture looked like the opening move in a wrestling match. Even in the stylish lobby of one of the oldest banks in the world, ritual male instinct trumped the pull of evolution.

"Well, yes," said Brottman. Her announcement had clearly thrown him off his game. After an uncertain pause he appeared to reach a decision. "I've asked a few associates to join us, but they need a bit of time to assemble. In the meantime, shall we have coffee in my office?"

They took the elevator one flight up and followed him down a hallway that opened into a large suite. He ushered them ahead into his office, pausing outside to speak with his assistant. The office was much like the reception area—spare design, functional but elegant. An assortment of sturdy leather couches and chairs were arranged around a glass table in front of the window. The assistant brought in coffee, serving it in a stunning German porcelain service. Brottman poured, and after several minutes of small talk he appeared to get his wind back.

"Now I come to think of it, I do remember hearing about you, Conor. From the princess—that is, Kate's grandmother, Sophia-Marie."

Conor nodded. "I had the pleasure of meeting her last fall."

"You originally came to do a bit of farming for Kate, yes? And I believe you play on a fiddle?"

"That's right, Guido."

Detecting the ice beneath his easygoing lilt, Kate tried to catch Conor's eye, but he was avoiding her face.

"I started managing Kate's farm a little under a year ago, and yes, I do play on a fiddle."

"How wonderful." Brottman sat back, rubbing the knuckle of his index finger against his lip. "And you came here originally from—?"

"Ireland."

"I see, and your family are—?"

"Dead."

"Oh, indeed. I'm sorry."

"Thank you. So am I."

Brottman seemed momentarily flustered and Kate took the opportunity to interrupt their verbal fencing match. "Conor does more than just 'play on a fiddle.' He's a talented classical violinist. He's going to be playing—"

"It's just a little recital." Conor took her hand and gave it a firm squeeze. "For a local church back in Vermont. Celebration of spring and all that."

Brottman's perfunctory smile warmed several degrees as he

turned back to Kate. "Might I enquire as to the wedding date?"

She felt her face growing hot. "We haven't set a date yet."

"Aha. I see."

"No, but we're dead keen on it, so I suppose it'll be soon. Right, darlin'?" Placing his cup on the table, Conor got to his feet. "Your mates will be wondering what's become of you, Guido. I'd best get out of here so you can get down to business."

The banker's features softened in relief, and Kate leapt to her feet. "Wait. Where are you going?"

"I've a few errands to run," Conor said, still addressing Brottman. "How long do you expect you'll need?"

"I think ninety minutes at most. It was good meeting you."

"Likewise," said Conor, shaking Brottman's proffered hand.

Kate grabbed Conor's arm. "Dammit, wait a minute."

He leaned in to kiss her and hissed against her ear. "Kate, for God's sake. Don't. Please. And say nothing about Prague." He stepped back and touched a finger to her cheek. "I'll meet you in the plaza outside. Okay?"

Unnerved by the anger in Conor's eyes, Kate nodded, and before she could say another word he was gone.

He tried to think of something to keep himself busy for ninety minutes, something besides pummeling the smug, boxy face of Guido Brottman. Walking seemed the best option to cool off his steaming anger, so Conor set off across town in no particular direction, adopting the urban quick-step of the pedestrians crowded around him.

At first, he was equally furious with Kate. This was her world—her "circle" as she'd called it. She might disdain its shallow materialism but she was still more comfortable in it than he was. She knew how it operated, yet she'd thoughtlessly subjected him to an Armani-wearing bean counter who regarded him as some dodgy immigrant gigolo.

After covering several blocks, Conor calmed down enough to recognize his anger was misplaced. Kate wanted to involve him in her life. It wasn't her fault the details of it were so bloody outlandish, and on that score he had no right to complain. He lived in a glass house himself.

She'd wanted him there for moral support, but Brottman clearly had no intention of including him in a discussion of Kate's finances, and he couldn't entirely fault the advisor's motives. He was protecting the interests of his client, and Kate was indeed vulnerable. No one had prepared her for dealing with wealth at this level. Conor knew she felt overwhelmed; he just wasn't sure ninety minutes in a room full of Zimmer House gits was likely to help much.

The last of his irritation vanished when, without planning on it, his walk brought him to the vast, enclosed footprint of 9/11's Ground Zero. He spent twenty minutes walking its borders, shocked by the scale of it.

Watching from an ocean away, he'd had no concept of the sheer size of the World Trade Center, or of the vacuum created when it was gone. That afternoon in September he'd driven into Dingle to buy a pair of boots and had been getting into his truck when a tourist flew out of Murphy's, roaring that America was under attack. Conor had piled into the pub with everyone else and gathered around a television someone had brought in from the back. When the first tower went down it was like the air had been sucked from the room. If their own town had burned to the ground, the horror could not have been greater. No Irishman in the bar that day had ever been to New York, but all of them knew someone there.

Thinking now about friends who had emigrated, Conor wondered if his roommate from the Dublin Conservatory still lived in the city. That thought prompted another, about a memorial he'd heard of a few years ago. He made several inquiries and took a few wrong turns, but eventually he found himself at the end of Vesey Street, facing the memorial to Ireland's famine—*An Gorta Mór*, as it was called where he grew up. The "Great Hunger" had hollowed out the country's soul along with its population, and even now it lingered in the Irish psyche.

The memorial was a huge sloping plinth that replicated an Irish hillside. It jutted up and out towards the Hudson River, and stretching the length of its surface was a grassy field scattered with rocks. Its focal point was a roofless stone ruin—a "famine cottage"—with a mass of brambles creeping over its crumbling walls. It had a breathtaking authenticity, and its symbolism was poignant—a field gone fallow, a generation lost.

Along with a few other tourists Conor entered at the back through a corridor, which passed under the plinth and led into the roofless cottage, then on to a path winding up through the pasture. It was lined on one side by a dry stone wall and on the other by the field of rocks, each named for one of Ireland's counties. Near the top he found the one for Kerry and crouched next to it, then looked back over the tableau below him. He was astonished by a talent which could so capture the wild, forlorn beauty of his world, the one he knew better than any other, a place where he'd been known and understood. He raised his eyes from the small patch to its incongruous surroundings. The office buildings and hotels, the yellow cabs and honking delivery trucks, and—irony of ironies—the yeasty aroma of baking bread. There was a bakery on the side street next to the memorial.

In a mood more subdued than when he'd started Conor returned to Maiden Lane. Kate wasn't in sight, so he wandered into an upscale grocery store at the corner of the plaza, one floor below street level. It seemed to go on forever with buffets, sushi bars and delis sprinkled among endless shelves of high-end dry goods. After circling it once he'd had enough. He saw Kate waiting above as he climbed the stairs and gave her a wistful smile once he'd reached the top.

"Was that any way to propose to a man?"

Kate closed her eyes as if in pain. "Conor, I'm so sorry. I didn't even think about how he'd react. It was just the first thing that popped out of my mouth." She opened her eyes again, looking nervous. "That wasn't—I mean, I wasn't really—"

"I know. Relax." Conor drew her aside, away from the people streaming in to pay more for a bento box than some people spent on a week's worth of bag lunches. "He seemed to take against me awfully fast. Is Brottman in love with you?"

"I've never met him before!" Kate protested.

Conor nodded. "He's had a long relationship with your money though. I expect he's in love with that. I wish you'd stuck with the 'hired man' suggestion. He's bound to start looking for dirt on me, and we know what he'll find."

"Oh God—your arrest record!" She slumped against him. "Why don't I ever see these things coming?"

"Because you're kind and straightforward, and you think the best of people. Never mind about it. He can only get at the public records, and those are flagged. Frank will take care of it."

Conor spoke as if it meant little to him, but while it was true Frank would intercept anyone displaying unusual curiosity about him, it rankled that the arrest record—for a crime he hadn't committed—would plague him for the rest of his life. Anyone could dig it up and think they'd learned something about him.

Kate was still berating herself. "I always seem to cause you trouble. I don't know why you'd want to be my fiancé anyway."

"Because you're kind and straightforward, and you think the best of people. Did you think it was only the great sex?" Conor bumped her shoulder with his own, making her smile at last. "So, how was the meeting after all that? What went on?"

"I have no clue. There were seven of them—all men. I know

they were speaking English, but it was like a weird sports lingo. 'Auto switches' and 'swap spreads.' It felt like I was in a locker room." She shuddered. "I don't want to think about it anymore right now. Maybe Oma can help me understand it. Do you want to get some lunch?"

He looked back down at the hall of food. "Believe it or not I don't feel like eating, but if you're hungry, this store has a cafe— maybe two or three of them."

Following his gaze, Kate pursed her lips in distaste. "No, I don't want to go in there." She turned back to him and laid a hand against his face. "Are you all right? You have that 'astral traveling' look in your eyes."

"Do I? Well, it's been a funny old morning, but I'm okay. How about you?"

"Better now. Do you want to take a walk? I can show you the city."

"Yeah, let's do that."

Conor took her hand and looped it around his arm, feeling the relief of connecting with something familiar. Of coming home.

4

Another skyscraper, another chilly reception area, and now another oil painting.

As instructed, they'd arrived at the British Consulate at three o'clock, but as soon as Kate had signed the visitor's log and offered up her Chamber of Commerce credentials, a pin-striped intern sitting next to the receptionist popped to his feet and walked them out the door again. The meeting location had been changed, he explained. It would now take place at the residence of the British consul general a few blocks away.

Chatting all the while about his love for skiing and admiration for Vermont, he escorted them through the midtown traffic to the Beekman Regent apartment building. They passed through a marble-floored lobby and took the elevator up to a penthouse residence, where the young man ushered them into a conference room and departed without further explanation.

The room, long and narrow, smelled of furniture polish, and its atmosphere was muted by plush carpeting. The walls were painted a deep cardinal red and lined with artwork, the largest identified as a portrait of King William III, dressed for battle. Centered above the conference table, the monarch presided over the room like a board chairman, eyes fixed on the doorway, military baton resting lightly in his hands.

After pausing at a window to look at the view Conor joined Kate in front of the painting. "William of Orange. That figures." Seeing her questioning look he added, "King Billy wasn't universally loved in Ireland."

"Oh dear. Have I given offense before we've even started?"

The voice behind them, high, reedy, and unnaturally loud in the otherwise hushed apartment, made Kate jump like a burglar caught in the act. Conor grabbed her elbow to prevent her lurching against an antique side table and they turned to face a pudgy figure not much more than five feet tall, who stood in the doorway holding a tea tray.

"If you're that sort of Irishman, perhaps I should have draped a cloth over it." He came into the room and set the tray on the table. Then with hands clasped behind his back he peered at Conor through round, wire-rimmed glasses. "*Are* you that sort of Irishman?"

"Not really," Conor admitted, amused by his earnest curiosity. "I do love a good rebel song though."

"Indeed. A man steeped in music after all." He turned his attention to Kate, who was gaping in open astonishment.

"Are you Reginald Effingham?"

Looking pleased, he briefly rocked up onto his toes. "Ah, I expect you recognized my voice? Just so. 'Reg' will do nicely for me, and it's Ms. Chatham now, I believe? What a treat to meet you in person. Our first conversation was terribly strained, I'm afraid. I do hope you'll forgive me. I'm not sure your friend Abigail ever will."

Kate appeared too stunned to speak and his smile faded to a worried frown. "Sorry, were you expecting someone else?"

"We weren't told who to expect," Conor replied for her.

While the statement was accurate, in truth Reginald Effingham was exactly who they'd expected, but not looking like this. Kate had been introduced to the MI6 staff officer by phone six months earlier. He'd been at the inn, sweeping the property in search of listening devices while she was at a New Hampshire medical center waiting for news about Conor, who'd arrived bleeding from a gunshot wound and sizzling with fever. It had been a hectic night. From Kate's description, Conor got the impression the call had indeed been strained, and that Effingham's encounter with Abigail had fallen just short of violence.

With other priorities to tackle they'd never questioned Abigail about the man's physical appearance, but during the drive that morning Kate had offered her vision of a willowy, towheaded sycophant in his early twenties, puffed with an attitude of self-importance. "Puffed" seemed to be the one feature she'd nailed, Conor thought, watching the portly little man shift a plate of cake and biscuits onto the table.

"Milk. I've forgotten it." Effingham headed back through the doorway. "Back in a jiff. Do help yourselves to the biscuits."

Conor popped one into his mouth, grinning at Kate. "I hate to be the one telling you, but you are not magnificent at profiling. We should work on your poker face as well. You're about as opaque as a spit-shone window pane."

"His voice sounded so much younger on the phone," Kate whispered. "He must be at least fifty, and he looks like Alfred Hitchcock!"

"Younger version, maybe. He's got a bit more hair."

She clapped a hand to her mouth, muffling a burst of laughter, but recovered by the time their host returned. Effingham took a seat at the head of the table with Kate and Conor on either side of him.

"Apologies for changing the location of our meeting today," he said, after tea had been poured and cake distributed. "The consul general is out of town, but he's hosting a back-channel meeting here tomorrow evening. The TSCM team finished earlier today, so I thought why not get the benefit of their work?"

"What's TSCM?" Kate asked.

"Technical Surveillance Counter Measures—a joint effort with the Americans, so no expense spared. This is possibly the cleanest, most private room in all New York at the minute."

"Are there ordinarily a lot of bugs planted around the city?"

"Oh, quite." Effingham warbled a high-pitched laugh. "They spring up like mold, especially in the consulates and around the UN. Most of it's rubbish that doesn't even work—gimcracks from developing world networks—but we scrub them out anyway."

With a faraway smile he stared down at his teacup, as though recalling TSCM adventures not suitable for sharing, and then gave the table a light slap. "Well, to business, shall we? I've information and other treasures to dole out for the first leg that will deliver you safely into Frank's hands. You'll spend the first few nights at his home in Windsor, did he mention that?"

Conor was surprised by the news. He'd assumed they'd be staying either in London or Portsmouth, near Fort Monckton. "I haven't talked with Frank since Christmas, and as you're no doubt aware he's skimpy with information. I'm hoping you'll shed some light on this whole business. What's the agenda, and what can you tell us about the assignment?"

Effingham sighed. "As to the first question, there's not much light to shed. Ms. Chatham, you'll go from Windsor to Fort Monckton for three weeks of operational training, and I'm afraid that's something of a black hole. They play it all quite close to their chests down there. You're prepared for the odd surprise, I hope?"

Kate smiled. "I think so. Conor has given me hints about what to expect."

"Splendid. Yes. You seem like the sort who can put up with a bit of adventure." He lapsed into another reverie, beaming and squinting at her before switching his myopic gaze to

Conor's fingers discreetly drumming on the table. "Mr. McBride, meanwhile, will be busy preparing for Prague. You've met Maestro Eckhard, I believe?"

"I have, briefly," Conor said. Dr. C Eckhard von Hahnemann, the conductor for the Salzburg Philharmonic, had spent a night at the inn the previous summer. At the time, he'd been acting in a role he clearly found distasteful—serving as a courier for Frank—and he'd hinted at a desire for some future collaboration with Conor "*on the concert stage, a milieu I believe we each feel more suitable to our talents.*"

"Of course he'll be at the house in Windsor also," Effingham said. "My understanding is that he's to bring a chamber group to Prague for an event being sponsored by the Austrian Embassy. You'll get more detail on performance arrangements from him, I expect. I've no idea what he has in mind." He took a slow, contemplative sip from his teacup and placed it back in the saucer, now sitting level with his chest.

In the silence that followed, Conor could hear the methodical tick of a grandfather clock in the adjacent foyer. He exchanged a glance of weary impatience with Kate and pushed his own cup to the middle of the table. "Information and treasures, you said. Will we be getting to those any time soon, Reg?"

"Certainly. Yes, I beg your pardon. I so rarely get to spend a quiet half-hour with a cup of tea." Effingham put his cup down and folded his hands on the table, suddenly looking fully awake and alert. "First, to be clear: apart from facilitating the connection, British Intelligence has nothing to do with the Philharmonic, its agenda in Prague or its performance contract with you. It's an entirely separate matter from our interests."

"Understood," Conor said, pleased by the delineation. The wider the gulf between his artistic life and any clandestine activity the better.

"Your assignment for us is simple. You'll be facilitating the defection of a double agent who is a high-ranking officer with the Iranian intelligence service. We've been working with him for years."

Kate took in a sharp breath. "That doesn't sound very simple to me."

"Nor to me," Conor agreed.

"It's absolutely straightforward," Effingham said. "Little more than the work of an evening. His superiors have already sent him to Prague on assignment. You've only to make contact with him at an agreed location and drive him north to the Czech-German border. It's a place called Hřensko—glorious scenery, I'm told. The Elbe River, sandstone canyons, rock bridges—"

"What happens at the border?" Conor interrupted, anxious to prevent another whimsical detour.

"Oh, you'll just hand the chap off to our staff from the Dresden station. They'll drive down and collect him from you at the Hotel Labe in the middle of town, and that's the entire mission—done and dusted."

"Don't you already have people in Prague who could do this?" Kate asked. "Or couldn't your staff in Dresden go there to get him?"

"Yes, that's a good question, isn't it?" Effingham nodded approval at her. "Why on earth should we need you? To answer I must remove the veil, as it were, and share some of the dysfunctional politics and petty feuds often raging below the surface among intelligence networks. It's not a pretty picture, I'm afraid."

"I think we can handle it," Conor said. He was still waiting for a pinch of evidence that intelligence networks were anything *but* petty and dysfunctional.

"You see, we've recently had a disastrous falling out with the BIS—the Czech counter-intelligence service. Someone in their ranks leaked information of a similar defection operation we were running last year. When MI6 complained, the head of BIS got sacked, but next thing we knew, the Czech Republic's leading media outlet was broadcasting the name of our head of station on television and had camera crews surrounding his house in Prague. As you can imagine, the station is in disarray. It's impossible to involve them in this operation so soon after that debacle, and we dare not cast any Dresden staff into the soup until it's sorted, so someone new to the theater, without baggage or profile, perfectly fits the bill for this assignment."

"What happened to your station chief?" Conor asked.

"Still in Prague, poor fellow. Low profile and all that. But I doubt he'll stay much longer. I mean, really. What's the point?" Effingham shook his head sadly. "I'm afraid that's all the information I have—London is working out more precise logistics—so let's move on to the treasure, shall we?"

He leaned forward and removed a thick zippered bank bag from the tea tray. "I have passports for you. You'll be traveling as …" He removed the booklets from the pouch and squinted inside the front covers. "… Malcolm and Barbara Alder. Wretched names. They don't suit you at all. No matter. It's only to obscure your movements in the Customs databases. You're booked as yourselves at the hotel in Prague, so your own passports and Conor's green card will be sent ahead for collection when you arrive, and please remember to post them home before you leave. It's irksome for us when agents get blown carrying more than one. You have two wallets here as well." He pulled them from the bag. "A few hundred dollars each, credit cards, photos of baby nephews and whatnot—choose names you'll remember. Ah, Mr. McBride, you've ticket stubs from a concert at Avery Fisher Hall. Nice touch, that. Let's see, what else? Oh, boarding passes—mustn't forget those."

He dove back into the bag like a boy rooting through his Christmas stocking. Conor sat back and returned Kate's smile of bemused wonder. Reg was obviously a man who relished the minutiae of his work.

"You haven't answered the most important question," Kate said. "When do we leave?"

Effingham pulled his head up and, blinking, looked from Kate to Conor and back to Kate again. "What an extraordinary question. You leave tonight, of course. Your flight departs JFK at nine o'clock."

"What?"

"Tonight?" They shouted at him in unison, which had little effect.

"It was perfectly clear in your letter of instruction," he said. "Unmistakable, really."

"It most certainly was not," Kate said. "We decoded the letter and there was nothing about a departure date."

"In the penultimate sentence," Effingham insisted. "*He'll not return to the office again before departure.*"

"Oh, for—you call that *unmistakable*?" Conor dismissed any reply with a wave of his hand. "It doesn't matter what you call it, we're not leaving tonight."

The MI6 officer's eyes held a gleam of amused pity before his face changed, smoothing to the flat indifference Conor had so often witnessed among his kind. "I'm afraid you'll do as you're told, Mr. McBride. I must remind you, your contract with the Salzburg Philharmonic is not the only document you put your name to when you signed up for this enterprise." He zipped the bag and slid it across the table. "Do keep track of expenses, and collect receipts for anything above ten pounds."

Conor stared at the bag for a long moment then rose from the table. From the corner of his eye he saw Kate stiffen in dismay as he picked it up. With a satisfied smile Effingham stood also, one hand extended at an ambiguous, crooked angle, as though inviting him to compound his humiliation by bowing over it.

Conor took the hand in a strong grip. Chubby and flaccid, it yielded under his fingers like a damp package of meat. He gave it a quick wrench, pinned Effingham's arm behind his back, and pushed him face down on the conference table. Conor leaned down to speak in his ear, his voice level and quiet.

"You all seem to think my name on a piece of paper gives you leave to take the piss out of me whenever you like, but I'm a little tired of it, so listen to me now. We are not flying to London tonight. I don't even have my violin with me, which is sort of an important prop in this so-called 'enterprise.'"

Effingham made a feeble attempt to shift Conor's hand from the back of his neck. "Are you aware of the penalty for assaulting an intelligence officer?" His high-pitched voice was muffled against the table. "I could have you ruined for this."

"Ruin what, now? Ask Frank if he thinks I've much left that's worth ruining. I'd suggest a better idea is for you to get busy re-booking our flights and tell him we'll be there in two days' time. You can send him the fucking receipt yourself, or you can shove it up your arse. Your choice."

Removing his hand, he gave Effingham's shoulder a clap for encouragement and turned to Kate, who looked taken aback, but also relieved.

"Right." Conor gave her a brisk nod. "What time is your gran expecting us? We don't want to be late; I'm trying to make a good impression."

5

Most of what Kate knew about Frank Emmons Murdoch came from their brief but intense encounters the previous fall. The rest came from Conor, who didn't know much more than she did, so between the two of them they had a synopsis of the man that would fit on an index card.

Noteworthy on the list of known items was that although Frank had perfected a mannered British persona, he'd apparently grown up in County Monaghan, Ireland, in humble conditions. As improbable as it seemed, he'd managed to reinvent himself and get a job with the British Secret Intelligence Service. How and—more importantly—why he'd done it was a riddle swaddled in mystery.

Facts about the man were thin on the ground. They didn't even know what place Frank occupied in the MI6 hierarchy, but they had an instinctive fondness for him and accepted him—cautiously, as they would an affectionate but feral animal.

Contrary to his hazy background, Frank's chosen identity mimicked that of the iconic English Gentleman, which came with all the predictable habits of the stereotype. He drove a Bentley, his hand-stitched suits were made to order, his sleek, silver hair was never out of place, and apart from its unexpected location, his house was exactly as Kate had imagined it.

She'd assumed it would be a gated estate tucked in an isolated part of the countryside, but instead the driver who met them at the airport brought them to a five-story Georgian home in the middle of town, not far from the High Street and the ramparts of Windsor Castle. It was fronted by a brick wall and courtyard on the street side, and had a charming walled garden at the back. Restored to eighteenth-century glory with twenty-first-century conveniences, its spacious rooms were tastefully decorated for both comfort and style.

The house was empty when Kate and Conor arrived, but the driver—a young Brazilian who seemed familiar with the house and the habits of its occupants—conducted a quick tour and led them two flights up the central staircase to their bedroom. He left them with a key to the front door and a promise that Frank would appear later in the afternoon.

With his jacket still on, hands in the pockets, Conor looked at the bed and then at her. "Are you sleepy?"

Understanding the question had not been posed with amorous intent and confident of the answer he was hoping for, Kate shook her head. "Not really. "I'd like to stretch my legs and get some breakfast. Aren't you hungry too?"

"Hungry? Jaysus, I'd eat the wing off a low-flying duck." He grabbed the key off the dresser. "Let's go."

After breakfast at a cafe on the High Street, they explored the town and strolled along a pedestrian path called the Long Walk, then returned to the house and napped for a few hours. By late afternoon they were showered and ready for the knock that came at four o'clock. Frank swept into the room with a smile of welcome and an immediate question.

"What on earth did you do to Reg Effingham? He's taking three days leave and demanding hardship pay, and he seems to want you thrown into the Tower."

"I didn't leave a mark on him," Conor said. "It was a small disagreement about the terms of my employment."

"Oh, really?" Frank's brow twitched in annoyance. "Hardly his place to comment on that. Nosy little man." His face brightened as he turned to Kate. "Kate. My dear, you look blooming as ever."

She took his outstretched hands and accepted the kiss on both cheeks. "And you are as charming as ever, and even more handsome."

"Conor. Wonderful to see you." Frank studied him as they shook hands. "Why are you so thin?"

Conor dropped his gaze, imitating Frank's scrutiny. "Am I?"

"Quite skinny. You've not been ill again?"

"Not a bit. I'm grand."

"That great, barrel-chested cook of yours—Agatha? Adelaide?—feeds you properly?"

"Abigail. Stuffs me like a Christmas goose." Conor's eyes narrowed. "I'm no skinnier than the last time you saw me, Frank."

"Hmm. I'm not convinced, but perhaps you're just in need of some conditioning." Frank offered an arch smile. "Drinks at six and dinner at seven, yes? I've a few hours of work left, but make yourselves at home. Diego showed you where to find cups and saucers and such? Marvelous. Until six, then."

"*Conditioning.*" Conor watched the door close then turned to Kate, hands on his hips. "Do I look skinny to you at all?"

Amused, she came and slid her hands under his shirt to press against the hard muscle of his stomach. "No, my dear. Far from it."

"What's he on about then?"

"He was teasing you, and I think he might be a little envious."

"Envious? Of what?"

"Of me."

"Oh." Conor looked startled, then laughed and rested his forehead against hers. "Maybe you're not such a lousy profiler after all. They're going to love you at the Fort."

Conor was itching to get at his violin and tweak anything that might have been disturbed after five hours at thirty thousand feet. Kate decided he and the Pressenda needed some time alone, so she took herself off for another wander around the house. She went first to the very top floor to look at the smallest bedrooms, which she assumed once housed butlers, cooks and housekeepers. On the ground floor she browsed through the light-filled library and formal dining room, both of them crammed with antiques and interesting works of art. Tucked in another wing she found a cozy room with a baby grand piano. Passing through, she reached a glass conservatory and continued out to the garden. Frank found her there a half-hour later, taking in the aroma of spring and green things growing.

"You've discovered my favorite spot." Cigarette in hand, he took a seat next to her on the wrought-iron bench and crossed his legs—an ordinary gesture made graceful by his languid elegance. "A bit of country in the middle of the city. Unless it's lashing rain, I spend a few quiet moments here every evening. To wash off the day, as it were."

Kate tried to picture Frank engaged in such a contemplative activity. "Do you meditate?" she asked.

He gave a short laugh. "God no, though perhaps I should. I could do with an emptier mind. For the most part, I just sit and smoke. Where is our fine Irish lad now? Sleeping off the jet lag?"

"No, he's with the other woman in his life … the Pressenda," she added, seeing Frank's confusion. "I'm sorry we missed your signal and had to reschedule the flight. We could have come without luggage, but there was no way Conor would make the trip without his own violin. We also had a dinner date with my grandmother. It would have been awkward to cancel."

"Ah, the princess Sophia-Marie," Frank said. "How I wish I could meet her. She's well, I hope?"

"She is, thank you. We had a nice evening together." Kate traced a finger over the filigreed pattern of the bench, remembering the secretive gleam in her grandmother's eyes when she'd greeted them at her Upper West Side apartment.

"I think, perhaps, you have something to tell me?" she'd said, once they were seated in a quiet corner of Café des Artistes with drinks in front of them. With her lovely silvered hair swept up and secured with jeweled combs, Sophia-Marie had a regal bearing softened by a warm demeanor, but she tended to be frank in her conversation and expected the same in return. Kate realized Guido Brottman had already contacted her with his concerns regarding her granddaughter's suitor. Once again, filled with horror and embarrassment, she had been rendered speechless, and once again Conor stepped into the breach.

"I expect Mr. Brottman rang you," he'd said. "It's a misunderstanding. We decided to have him on, just for the *craic*—a bit of goofing around. Silly of us really. I'm sorry if it's caused you trouble."

He'd looked at Kate with a rueful longing that made her feel like weeping, and if he'd said anything kind or gentle at that moment she would have, but he only winked and reached for her cocktail. "Can I try it? I've never had a dirty martini."

Her grandmother was anything but a fool, but she'd long ago mastered the art of a tactful retreat. She'd waited until after the meal—when they were together in the opulent salon of the ladies bathroom—before raising the subject again.

"My dear, I hope you didn't misunderstand me. Guido is beside himself, but I'm not. I like Conor. I liked him as soon as I met him last year. An instinctual response, I'll admit, but I do trust such impressions. In my experience they hold up as well as any others. Still, there would be papers drawn up and a tedious number of things for him to sign, but I can't see he's the sort who would mind very much. Do you *want* to marry him?"

Kate had twisted the paper towel in her hands, in no way prepared for this discussion. "I do. I think. I'm just not ready."

"Your husband has been dead for over six years, my dear."

Kate dropped her head, remaining silent, and her grandmother sighed. "Do you love him?"

"With all my heart," she had said, her voice trembling.

"Well. That's all right then. Ah, little mouse. Wipe your tears." Her grandmother had patted a tissue against her face. "It will all come right in the end. From the look in his eyes, he's certainly not going anywhere."

The sing-song blare of a police car beyond the garden wall shook Kate from her daydream and she looked back at Frank. "I'm so sorry. What were you saying?"

He smiled. "Nothing whatsoever. I was watching you drift. Are you nervous about the program we've cooked up to 'indoctrinate' you?"

"I guess I should be, but I'm not really. I'm curious and a little excited."

"Let's hope it won't disappoint. There's a great deal in this line of work that comes down to protocols and paperwork. You're more likely to hear the operatives down there whinging about their subsistence than reliving feats of valor." Frank cleared his throat and his tone grew more formal. "Along those lines, Kate, I have some documents for you to sign later confirming your status as a contractor. Much as I'd like to keep the arrangement casual, there is a bureaucratic beast to be fed and I am not immune to its requirements. Will this be a problem?"

"Not at all," Kate said. "I don't mind signing papers."

"Excellent." Frank relaxed, giving her a glance of appreciation. "Have you given any thought to what your role will be in this partnership?"

"To keep him sane. To prevent him from being any more damaged than he already has been, and if necessary, to protect him from you. I can't do any of that unless I can see it from the inside." She laid a hand on his arm. "Don't take it personally."

"Certainly not. It's rather what I had in mind as well, although I've an inkling you'll bring more to the table than that." Frank rose from the bench. "Speaking of tables, may I have the pleasure of taking you in to dinner? I'm gasping for a gin and tonic."

He extended his elbow to her. She stood up, and before taking his arm, impressed him with a perfectly executed curtsey, just as her grandmother had taught her.

The Pressenda had weathered the journey with a tolerance Conor had come to depend upon but tried never to take for granted. Responding beautifully to his attentions, she quickly recovered the rich, textured voice he knew so well. After laying the violin back in the case an hour later, he realized he was alone, and vaguely remembered Kate saying she was going to poke around the house. He now went through it himself from top to bottom without finding her, and ended up one floor below ground level, in the kitchen.

He assumed the basement level had once been the domain of the household staff. The stone flooring looked original, but the rest of the room was a modern work of wonder—the sort of kitchen Abigail would drool over, Conor thought, admiring the professional Aga range. At the granite-topped central island he discovered not Kate but Eckhard von Hahnemann, beating something in a bowl with fierce energy.

"Aha, at last." Eckhard greeted him with a warm smile and an apron. "There are vegetables to chop, and my sous-chef has deserted me."

Conor well-remembered the rumbling purr of the conductor's

voice and its soft, Austrian accent. He'd spent only one night at the inn the previous summer, delivering a message—or rather, a summons—from Frank, but he'd made a lasting impression. His physical presence alone was imposing. At a muscular six-feet four inches he was a square-jawed mountain of a man, but his dimple-cheeked smile and dark eyes full of impish good humor took the edge off his intimidating size. Like Frank, he presented himself with a sophisticated panache, and his dramatic hairstyle—a tangle of wiry dark curls streaked with gray—seemed as integral to his personality as Frank's sleek, silvered mane.

Eckhard poured him a pint of ale to compensate for his enlistment, but gave him little opportunity to drink it. Conor had worked up a sweat by the time Frank and Kate came in from the garden.

"I see I have been usurped," Frank said as they entered.

Conor raised his glass from the counter, saluting them. "I've flown across the Atlantic only to be bullied by another chef. Say the word and I'll gladly stand down."

"There is still plenty for Frank to do." Eckhard thumped his enormous hands on Conor's shoulders, pinning him in place before extending them to envelope Kate's. "First you must fix a cocktail for our Kate, and then I have saved the sole for you to fillet. It's on ice in the pantry."

"Splendid." Frank shot Conor and Kate a sly grin. "I do enjoy that."

Once he was relieved of his duties Conor joined Kate on an antique love seat placed against the wall. From there, he watched their hosts trading quiet instructions, working together with the ease of long habit. He saw Kate's face grow pensive and imagined her thoughts were similar to his.

This was the very heart of Frank's private life, unveiled without fanfare or drama, and Conor was moved by the trust such a gesture represented. Frank had chosen to include them in what must be a very small circle—those who got to see him this relaxed, enjoying a simple evening at home, preparing a meal with his partner and sharing it with friends.

Earlier in the day, Conor had expected a very different sort of evening. When he saw the formal dining room, he'd pictured a fussy dinner with too much cutlery and had glumly wondered if he'd need to unpack his tuxedo early. As it happened, dinner was a casual affair, served in a candlelit room off the kitchen, on a rustic oak table. There were only three utensils to keep track of and the freshly caught Dover sole, which he'd watched Frank gut and filet with frightening precision, was superb.

After dinner they remained at the table. Eckhard uncorked a honey-colored Sauterne and presented a selection of cheeses, then excused himself as the conversation turned to business.

The covert assignment Frank described was essentially a more detailed version of what Reg Effingham had already told them. For several years, an Iranian intelligence officer named Farid Ghorbani had been passing secrets that strengthened the hand of the UK, France and Germany in negotiations over Iran's nuclear program. But things had changed this year and Ghorbani expected the reformist insiders who'd protected him to be ousted in the Iranian summer election, and his treason to be exposed.

"He wants to defect, and if we don't bring him over now we'll not likely get another opportunity," Frank said. "He's on assignment in Prague, cultivating a network of extremists— white nationalists, to be precise—for various joint projects."

"Why would Iran want to work with white nationalists?" Kate asked.

"Terror makes for strange bedfellows, Kate." Frank crumbled some Stilton over a slice of apple and handed it to her. "Multiculturalism is the common enemy. God forbid we learn tolerance and begin to like each other. Ghorbani's been in the city for the past three months and his superiors expect him back in Tehran at the beginning of May. It's time to get him out, and the Prague station is in no position to take this on, for reasons I'm sure Reg made clear."

"And the joint projects?" Conor asked. "What happens with those when Ghorbani is gone?"

"We have other eyes on that—an agent who has already infiltrated the network. But none of that concerns you. Your task is simply to drive a car to the side entrance of the Mandarin Oriental's restaurant at eleven o'clock on the evening of April 23rd. Stop in front of the door and signal by rolling down the right rear window. Ghorbani will get in and you'll proceed ninety minutes north to the German border at Hřensko. One of our officers from Dresden will be waiting for you in Room 6 at the Hotel Labe. He'll be booked there under the name Marshall."

Conor had to admit it sounded dead simple, which only made him wary. "Does your embedded agent know about Ghorbani?"

"None of our people in Prague know about Ghorbani. Nor will they know anything about you."

"Really?" Kate looked startled by this revelation and the glimpse it offered of the shell games MI6 played with information, even with its own officers. Conor remembered when this perpetual deceit would have surprised him as well, but those days were long gone.

"We'll have a final briefing on this and provide all the paraphernalia just before you leave." Frank's tone, placid but conclusive, indicated further inquiry would be useless. He went to invite Eckhard to join them for a nightcap, and when the two of them returned he redirected the conversation. "I'd hoped to give you another day of leisure, Kate, but I'm afraid your training is scheduled to begin tomorrow afternoon. A car will be collecting you at eight in the morning."

"I'll be ready," Kate said, after a slight pause.

This was sooner than they'd expected, and for the first time

Conor saw a hint of uncertainty in her face. He reached under the table to take her hand. "Can I ride down with her?"

"Ah. Well." Frank shifted his gaze to Eckhard, who glared in warning. "Actually, no. Eckhard has a full schedule planned for you tomorrow as well."

"I've booked a pianist to arrive early and spend the day working with you," Eckhard said. "We have much to do to prepare for your performances."

Conor sat up straighter. "Performances? As in plural?"

"Yes, certainly," Eckhard said. "The Mozart and the Beethoven. You've had the scores for months. Surely you've been practicing them?"

"Of course I've been bloody practicing them, Eckhard, but I thought I'd be polishing only one of them. Are you saying I'm meant to play both?"

"Both, yes." The conductor's voice was as categorical as his partner's. "There is a five-day symposium with Ministers of Culture from Germany, Austria, and Hungary. The Austrian Embassy in Prague is underwriting the musical events. You are the soloist for the ceremonial opening program, and for the closing concert with the Czech Philharmonic at the Rudolfinum, which will be attended by the Czech president."

"The Rudolfinum." Conor felt a cold sweat blossom on the back of his neck. It was one of the oldest, most celebrated concert halls in Europe. Dvořák himself had conducted its first concert.

"I did try to tell you this would come as a surprise to him, Eckhard." Frank smiled and moved his glass in gentle circles on the table, keeping his eyes fixed on the wine swirling inside. He seemed delighted to see Conor's consternation directed at someone else for a change.

*

A few hours after bidding their hosts good night they gave up trying to sleep, and Conor allowed Kate to lead him on a midnight visit to the conservatory. They gathered a few cushions and sat on the floor, Conor with his back against a wicker sofa and Kate seated in front of him. The house was quiet, and the occasional street sounds beyond the garden wall outside seemed far away. He circled his arms around her waist, looking up through the glass roof at the sky.

"How did you know the stars were out?"

"I didn't. We got lucky." She was quiet for a moment, then sighed. "Three weeks."

"I know."

"For three weeks you'll be living here in pampered splendor while I shiver in a Fort Monckton dorm room."

Conor laughed. "Losing your nerve? It's not too late to change your mind." He pushed aside the thin strap of her pajama top and put his lips to her shoulder. "You can stay here with me. I'll make it worth your while."

Kate tilted her head to one side as his mouth traveled up her neck. "Is this my first test?"

"It is." He moved to a spot behind her ear, knowing from experience it would draw a reaction. Her breath caught, as did his, feeling her stomach quiver beneath his hand.

"You secret agents are very sneaky."

"You don't know the half of it."

"No, but in three weeks I will." She peeked back at him, her eyes promising mischief, then rolled over to lie on top of him and wrapped a hand around his neck.

She kissed him, and as the motion of her hips grew less subtle Conor's response became more urgent. He pushed into her mouth, greedy for its heat, while his hand on the small of her back pulled her in more tightly. Her top inched higher, and Kate paused long enough to remove it along with his own dampening t-shirt. When her mouth moved from his lips to begin a wider exploration, he had little self-restraint remaining, but used the last shreds of it to question their judgment.

"Maybe we shouldn't do this here," he said, as the tip of her tongue slid along the scar at the base of his throat. Her low laughter blew hot against his neck.

"Losing your nerve?" Kate gave a playful tug at the drawstring of his light cotton pants and reached down farther. "Ah. No, I guess not. You relax now, McBride," she whispered, pushing him back. "I've got this."

Conor groaned as her fingers brushed lightly over him. The trail of kisses advanced down his stomach, and he dropped his head back against the sofa. How the hell was he going to get through the next three weeks?

6

She could end it with one phone call. Not that she had a phone, but surely someone had brought one, or a radio of some kind. Would they use it if she asked, or just laugh at her? She could try playing the "spoiled rich girl," say her father played golf with the Chair of the Foreign Relations Committee. She didn't know if the senior member from New York was even on that committee, but he'd been in the Senate for thirty years so he must be on something. They probably wouldn't know the difference … but then again, they might. They were the "Increment" after all, the Secret Intelligence Service's elite black ops unit, a perfect combination of brains and paramilitary brawn. Hard to fool, harder to kill.

Elbows to the ground, Kate wriggled a few more inches up the hillside on her stomach, holding the sniper rifle in front of her. She was trying to ignore how cold and wet she was as the rain pelted against her camouflage bush hat. The brim had tipped back, sending a stream of rainwater straight down her neck. She wanted to rip it off, but knew the excess movement would earn a rebuke from the hulking figure pressed against her shoulder. Lance Corporal Milbank angled his head at the pasture in front of them, misty and colorless under the first light of dawn.

"There—behind the gorse," he said, his voice pitched just above a whisper. "Do you see him? He's headed for the clearing. Wait until he gets there."

She nodded and shifted a few millimeters away from him. He reeked of campfire smoke and body odor, but Kate imagined she didn't smell any better. They'd all been in the same clothes for days. Fort Monckton felt like a place she'd visited in another lifetime, a continent away. In fact, she'd left it only four days ago for the three-hour drive to their present location in Herefordshire, camped on the edge of a forest in Brecon Beacons National Park.

The first few days of her MI6 training had been filled with lectures—the history of the service, the functions of each directorate, a thorough review of policies and protocol. The tedium of those lessons was relieved by a daily ninety-minute class in self-defense that left her bruised and aching, followed by a session on the firing range that made her hands tingle for hours afterwards. Things got more interesting at the end of the week when she began some of the covert exercises Conor had mentioned—gathering information from strangers, talking her way into private offices and coming out with photographs. These assignments required a glib tongue and an ability to slip into an alter ego—to become an actor playing a part. It was a lot harder than it sounded and she knew her performance had been uneven. It made her appreciate why Conor's trainers had been so dazzled by his skill in this area.

She wasn't a crack shot like him either, nor could she remember the names of the weapons she was directed to field strip and reassemble, but Kate was pleased—or, rather, relieved—to discover she excelled at a few things. Placed in a random setting, she could retain information and create a detailed sketch of the scene hours later. She was also good at absorbing data from maps and drawing them on her own, so she spent a few hours each day studying the streets of Prague. None of this was unusual, given her artistic interests, but her superior performance in one class—and the one she enjoyed most—caught the instructors by surprise: Vehicular Pursuit and Evasive Driving. At the end of her two-hour introduction to the slalom course they'd been sufficiently impressed to bump her up to an advanced level.

At times she felt the entire business was a mistake and that she had no business being there, taking up resources and rubbing shoulders with people more capable than her. When these thoughts intruded, Kate reminded herself that her objectives, while perhaps unorthodox, were still valid. She wasn't here to become a super spy, but to do her part to keep the one she loved whole, and human.

At the beginning of her third week, Kate appeared for a final check-in with her training coordinator, a petite, dark-haired woman with a severe expression and the physique of a bodybuilder. She'd displayed an attitude of bored contempt in all of their previous meetings, and the last was no different. As soon as Kate was inside the door, Joanna Patch dropped a pair of army boots on the floor in front of her.

"Right then, Chatham. Go fetch that rucksack in the corner. See if you can manage to get it off the floor and onto your back."

Sitting on the floor, the bulky pack reached as tall as her hip. It was like trying to wrestle a well-fed toddler onto her shoulders, but Kate managed it and braced herself for whatever was coming next. "Think you can hump that for twelve miles over rolling terrain?"

"I have no idea, Joanna, but I assume the point is to find out."

"It is, actually." The officer gave her a tight smile. "You're going on bivouac with a team from the Increment. They're testing some new field equipment. You won't be coming back here, so pack up your kit and leave it inside the door of your room. We'll send it back to Windsor by courier. A set of fatigues and everything else you'll need is in the rucksack. Go and change. Then meet Lance Corporal Milbank out front in an hour."

George Milbank and his colleagues were professionals accustomed to obeying orders. As he introduced her to the five other team members at the Brecon Beacons launch point they'd greeted Kate with jaded skepticism, but hid the disappointment they must have felt at having their camping lark disrupted by a female civilian.

When they got underway, Kate had done her best to keep up with the pace. She was in good physical shape and suspected the team members modified their stride to accommodate her, but after nine miles she'd been staggering under the weight of her pack. Milbank dropped back and removed it from her shoulders without comment.

"I'm sorry," Kate said. "Now you've got twice the load to carry."

"We'll share it out the rest of the way." He glanced at her before moving back to the front of the line. "To be honest, I thought we'd be carrying it a lot sooner."

She couldn't help thinking the intensity of this exercise was designed to humiliate her. Her companions appeared to share that opinion and over several days made it clear they didn't approve. They challenged her stamina in more ways than one and were far from gentle, but they were careful not to push her over the edge. Maybe it was out of kindness, but she thought it more likely that these battle-tested men were terrified of being stuck in the wilderness with a woman unraveling in hysterics. Kate had held up her end of the bargain, getting through each day by inventing color palettes in her head and then naming them—Christmas in Las Vegas, Campfire Nights, Bakery Case. She gave way to emotion only twice, and even then only after dark, when it could be smothered against her sleeping bag.

"Nearly there," Milbank said. "Get ready."

She pressed herself lower on the rain-soaked ground and put an eye to the scope, praying for it all to be over before her queasy stomach became a more active problem.

"Here we go. Clear shot. Take it." As her finger curled and flexed around the trigger he repeated the command. "As in, now. Take the shot." Getting no response he snapped around and hissed in exasperation. "For Christ's sake, Chatham. Take the fucking shot."

The rifle exploded and Kate absorbed the recoil with a grunt. Ahead she saw an eruption of mud and grass as the bullet tore into the ground, and ten yards in front of that the hare lifted its head and sprinted out of sight, without a glance in their direction.

Clearly disgusted, Milbank pushed himself into a sitting position and glared at her. "You did that on purpose."

"Yes, I guess I did." Kate sat up and pulled at the collar of her jacket, diverting the stream of water flowing down her spine.

"You're meant to take these exercises seriously, you know—preparation against the day when you might be out in a place like this living off your wits. That animal could represent the difference between surviving and starving to death."

"Believe me, I take them seriously." Kate offered him the rifle. "But, they're still exercises and I'm *not* starving, although I'm beginning to think I might die of hypothermia. Can we have a lesson on preparing against that?"

"Sure." Milbank smirked. "One pointer is to get the bloody rain poncho on before you're soaking wet." He offered a hand to pull her up, which she accepted without shame. "Let's get breakfast. You may not be starving, but I am."

It had stopped raining when they reached the campsite, but the men were not preparing breakfast. They appeared to be on edge. Their number had grown by one: a middle-aged officer who appeared to outrank everyone had arrived in an all-terrain vehicle. He approached Milbank with a casual salute, and a curt nod at Kate.

"I need a word in private, Milbank. New orders coming through."

They walked a short distance away for a huddled conversation while the rest of them silently watched. Milbank appeared to be resisting the new orders, until his superior officer lost patience and poked a finger at him, ending the argument. Kate looked to the rest of the team for explanation, but they avoided eye contact, with her as well as each other.

"Chatham." Milbank looked startled by the volume of his own voice. "Get over here," he added more quietly, waving her over. As she reached them, the new arrival turned on his heel and began walking back to the campsite.

"I guess this is where we say good-bye," Milbank said. "A transport helo is going to land here in ten minutes to pick you up."

"Why?" The Lance Corporal's obvious discomfort made Kate nervous. "Where are they taking me?"

"Sorry, I'm not at liberty to—" his eyes widened and in that same moment she felt an arm circle her neck and press against her windpipe. A test of her training, she thought. Alarming, but also extremely irritating. Kate recalled the tactics she'd learned to counter this line of attack and swiftly put them to use. She threw all her weight to the right and slammed a fist back into the groin of the man at her back. Gasping, his grip loosened as he doubled over in pain.

"Jesus fucking Christ," he panted. "Milbank, help me bring her down."

"For God's sake, sir, isn't there some other—"

"I said bring her the fuck down! Now!"

His shout rang in Kate's ear, matching her own as Milbank grabbed her and dragged her to the ground. The terror started when they blindfolded her, and then she heard the sound she could never forget—the long ragged rip of the tape they would use to cover her mouth. She'd been here before. It was happening again. The thought moved her panic to a level she could no longer control. Screaming, Kate thrashed on the ground while the two men struggled to hold her still. A pair of hands, and then a third, pinned her arm down. She felt the pinch of a needle—then nothing more.

7

When she finally stirred, Conor released his breath. He'd been holding it for uneven intervals during the last two hours, trying to hear hers. He remained quiet as Kate surfaced, watching her blink and struggle to focus.

"Your head?" he asked when she turned it and winced. She nodded, carefully. "They drugged you. I'm going to murder somebody for that."

"Where are we? What's going on?" She was groggy and sounded frightened.

"It's okay. We're in a barn—an abandoned one, I'd say—about an hour's drive from London. I couldn't tell which direction. Are you saying no one told you? It's a right stupid one, but I suppose you'd call it the spy's version of a final exam."

She sat up, rubbing her eyes. "Yours or mine?"

"Maybe both. I'm not sure it matters."

Kate seemed to register that he was sitting five feet away and had not come forward to snatch her into his arms. Conor leaned to one side, showing her the handcuffs behind his back. "They're looped around a chain that's padlocked to this post."

She moved over to him, crossing the floor on her knees. The barn was an ancient wreck and they were up in its loft, imprisoned behind a wall of square bales of hay. Conor's "captors" had stacked them, almost to the ceiling. Gray with age, they gave off a stale, sour odor. The single window, high up in the wall above them, had no glass, and a cold breeze wafted in, along with the weak morning sunlight.

Kate sat back on her heels next to him. "How long have we been here?"

"Me, since last night," Conor said. "You were supposed to get here straight after me. I was going mental until they brought you two hours ago. They must have bolloxed the timing."

"Are you sure this was MI6?"

"Positive. Sure I knew the two who came for me. I met them in the bar at the Fort last year. They showed up yesterday while I was rehearsing in London—at Wigmore Hall."

Conor was still irritated at their arrival. The rehearsal had been nearly finished, but he'd waited a long time to stand on the stage of Wigmore Hall. He didn't appreciate having that interrupted by a pair of goms from Vauxhall Cross.

"The cover story was they needed me for a meeting. After they loaded me into the back of a van and slapped a laundry bag over my head they let me know it was an exercise. I also knew one of the fellows who brought you here. He flies a helicopter for VIPs between London and the Fort. He said you were already knocked out when they picked you up. Away out in feckin' Herefordshire. Why bring you there and then give you the needle? What did they tell you was—Kate? What's the matter, are you sick?"

She'd curled forward, hugging herself. "I thought it was happening again. They held me down, blindfolded me, and I heard the tape." Her shoulders began trembling. "I thought it was real. I thought it was real."

"Oh, Jesus." He bent to kiss her head. "It's all right, love. You're okay. *A Thiarna, déan trócaire.*" *Lord, have mercy.* The whispered prayer helped him swallow a rage so intense it nauseated him.

For a long time Kate sobbed, compressed in a tight ball of tension, her face against his chest. He didn't try to stop her. She'd been through so much—threats, betrayals, and dangers a lot worse than the present situation in fact. She'd faced them with a courage Conor couldn't begin to understand or duplicate. Now, when MI6 with its bullshit games had shaken loose a demon, his hands were literally tied behind his back. In desperation, he pulled at the handcuffs until his wrists were numb, but in the end it was his voice that finally reached her. Since he'd begun in Irish he carried on with it, murmuring bits of old songs with his cheek on her head. Gradually, she grew quiet, and they sat together in silence.

"I think that had been coming for a while," Kate said at last.

"Yeah, I think so too."

"Not the best timing though. I'm not doing very well on my test."

"Stop. There's such a thing as taking courage too far. You don't have to be brave about everything."

She put her arms around his waist and he felt her relax. He thought she'd fallen asleep, but after a few minutes she reached up to kiss his neck.

"I'm sorry."

"Don't be."

"No." Kate sat up and looked down at herself. "I mean, I haven't had a bath in four days. I'm filthy."

"So dirty it's impressive," Conor agreed. "You'll turn the water black, so you will." He smiled. "If you're feeling better, maybe we could work on getting me out of these bloody handcuffs. How did you get on with your lock-picking class?"

"Not too bad, actually. I see they left my backpack. I'll bet I can find something that will work."

Her face brightened and Conor's heart lifted. He sometimes thought it should frighten him, the discovery that he could love someone so much, but he had a lot of things to be scared of—this didn't need to be one of them.

Using the hook and straight steel pin on an army knife, Kate got busy. While she worked, sitting cross-legged on the floor behind him, she described the details of her training at Fort Monckton and the grueling bivouac experience in Brecon Beacons. Conor was incredulous that she'd been sent out with the Increment. It was beyond the limits of her training brief as he'd understood it. He couldn't believe someone at the Fort would sanction it, let alone have the leverage to get the paramilitary unit's agreement.

He twisted around. "Did your training coordinator sign off on this?"

"I assume so. Try not to move around so much," Kate said, her voice distracted. She'd been able to spring the padlock after only a few minutes, but the handcuffs were giving her more trouble. "We didn't have much conversation about it—or about anything else, for that matter. I don't think she likes her job very much. Or maybe she just didn't like me."

"Your training coordinator was a woman?" He had a sudden intuition he didn't want to indulge, but did anyway. "What was her name?"

"Joanna Patch. Do you know her?"

"I do, yeah. She was my weapons instructor. How's it going back there?"

Conor knew how to evade, divert, and flat-out lie. He'd had practice and was good at it. The skill gave him no pride, but he used it now without compunction. He didn't intend to lie to Kate, but doubted there was any way to characterize a one-night stand that wouldn't make him sound like an asshole. He'd tell the truth. He'd just rather not be shackled while delivering it.

Kate continued tinkering with the handcuffs. "Oh, I see what I'm doing wrong. I think I've almost got it." Carefully, she moved his hands off her knee and scooted around to his side. Conor turned to look at her.

"What happened? I thought you were nearly there."

"Did you sleep with her?"

He sighed and dropped his head. "This isn't fair."

"You're right—it isn't. I'll look forward to hearing all about it another time." With a teasing smile she pecked him on the cheek. "Now, give me a hug. You're free."

Surprised, Conor pulled and one of his hands slipped from its cuff. Hissing from the pain in his stiffened muscles, he brought his arms forward and around her. Without leaving his embrace, Kate began working on the remaining cuff and popped it open a minute later. After she'd massaged his shoulders back to mobility, they tackled the bales, opening up a path of escape. Dust rose from the hay as they worked, and before they were done the loft was thick with it. Kate waved at the tiny particles floating in a beam of sunlight.

"This can't be good for your lungs. No wonder your doctor doesn't want you working in the barn."

"I'd like to think I keep ours a bit cleaner than this." Conor kicked aside the last bale and walked through the opening. Sweeping aside more loose hay, he lifted up the trap door. "At least they left us the ladder. Let's hope there's a car waiting outside, too."

The lower floor of the barn was darker than expected, and as his eyes adjusted, he saw the row of windows on each side of its long end had been sealed with cement. What the hell did that mean, he wondered uneasily. He paused on the ladder and as Kate started down he put a hand on her back.

"Wait a minute."

"What's wrong?" she asked.

"Sshhh." He stood motionless on the ladder, listening. He heard the faint drone of voices and then, also distant, a sharper, unmistakable series of clicks. "Shit. Go back up. Fast."

Pushing Kate ahead of him, Conor scrambled up behind her as an explosion of gunfire pounded against the wall.

When they reached the top of the ladder, Conor grabbed Kate around the waist. Roughly pulling her into the farthest corner of the loft, he pushed her down and dropped to the floor himself. Lying on top of her, he braced his elbows on either side of her head. Below them the bullets slammed into the barn, tearing through the wood, ricocheting off the cemented windows. It went on for a few minutes, then there was a pause before it erupted again.

"This isn't part of the exercise, is it?" Kate said.

"Strafing us with live fire? It can't be. I don't know what this is." Pressed against her so hard he could feel her racing pulse, Conor listened as the barrage again stopped and then resumed, always concentrated on the lower wall. When it repeated a third time, he understood the pattern. "Most of the bullets are hitting cement. They're not shooting at us; it's target practice—with assault rifles, by the sound of it. Whoever it is, I'm guessing they don't even know we're here."

Kate wriggled beneath him. "Does that mean it's safe to get up?"

"No. We don't know how good they are."

"I can't breathe."

"Sorry." Conor adjusted his position to take some of his weight off her.

A minute later, a poorly aimed shot came up through the floor and exited through the roof, validating his caution. During the next pause, he rolled away and jumped to his feet, telling Kate to stay put. Running across the loft and back through the opening they'd created, he jumped up to grab the windowsill and brought himself closer to the opening with a chin-up. There was nothing to see from this angle, but he yelled as loud as he could. From her corner, Kate was shouting too, but a few seconds later the firing resumed and Conor dropped down to take cover, calling for her to do the same.

"They're probably wearing ear plugs," he said, crossing back during the next break. "I guess we'll have to wait it out."

Following a few more volleys, the firing shifted elsewhere towards other targets. They remained huddled in place. After a while a longer silence gave way to the wail of a police siren, growing in volume as it got closer. It ended abruptly. A few minutes later they heard a car pulling up, and then the crash of something heavy against the door below them.

"McBride, are you in there?" The voice—loud, guttural, and carrying its habitual hint of irritation—was entirely familiar.

"Bloody hell." Conor offered a hand to pull Kate up from the floor. "Of all the people I'd want to rescue me, he's dead last on the list." Descending the ladder, he turned to face their champion.

"Ah, there you are, McBride. Warmer work than you expected, eh?" Lawrence Shelton's blunt, square-jawed face creased in a sarcastic grin. "Shit your knickers up there, did you?"

Conor waited for Kate to join him before speaking. "Kate, this is Special Branch Officer Lawrence Shelton, Scotland Yard's liaison to MI6. He ... ehm, helped Frank with my recruitment."

This euphemistic recasting of his limited but memorable interactions with the surly, short-tempered officer appeared to amuse Shelton, but his arrogant bravado evaporated when Kate came forward with a warm smile, her hand extended.

"Officer Shelton, I've never been so happy to see anyone in my life."

"Pleasure, M'um." Shelton took her hand, rubbing at the back of his neck with his other hand while his face turned crimson.

"Christ, what a cock-up." Frank stood silhouetted against the bright light in the doorway, then walked briskly over to join them. "You're both all right though?"

"Sure, Frank. We're both grand." Jaw clenched, Conor approached him, shaking off Kate's grip on his arm. "But we're after being shelled by assault rifles for forty-five minutes, so you'll understand we're a bit jumpy."

"Of course." Frank eyed him warily.

"Did you sign off on this exercise?"

"I did, but—"

Frank's reflexes were above average, but not fast enough to avoid the blow completely. Conor's fist landed hard, catching the edge of his mouth. He stumbled but recovered quickly as Shelton brought Conor down and dug a knee into his back.

"Oh let him up, Lawrence." Frank put a handkerchief to his mouth, dabbing at the blood already staining the lapel of his immaculate suit. "I didn't entirely deserve it, but I suppose I *am* ultimately responsible. I'm happy to explain, but may we first leave this ghastly barn? I imagine you're both hungry and thirsty, and the police cadets who've been 'shelling' you are eager to make amends by sharing their lunch."

Outside, Conor saw they'd been in the middle of a much larger training complex, with ramshackle buildings standing in a semicircle, all marked with targets. They got into the police car and drove a few hundred yards to where a group of men and women stood waiting, their postures anxious. Conor and Kate accepted the horrified apologies from the young cadets and followed them into the canteen, where Kate excused herself to go wash up. The rest went through the buffet line, and while Shelton stayed behind to eat with the cadets, Conor and Frank went to a private room in the back.

Once seated, Conor leaned across the table facing his boss, toying with the idea of taking another swing at him. "A simulated kidnapping? Do you have any idea what that did to her? What the fuck is wrong with you, or is it actually your intention to turn all your agents into basket cases?"

"I'd like to amend my earlier statement." Frank pressed a tea towel filled with ice to his mouth. "I did sign off on *an* exercise—I requested it in fact—but not *this* one. To begin with, the entire thing was supposed to happen yesterday, when this facility was closed. It was meant to be a final assignment for Kate, with you added in to see how the two of you would get on, working together. You arrived on schedule. Kate did not. We didn't realize she'd been sent off with the Increment. It wasn't part of the agreed curriculum. You were both to report back to Fort Monckton, and we only learned this morning that you hadn't."

Conor rose as Kate appeared and took the chair next to him. "I didn't know if you were still feeling queasy. Will I get you something?"

"No. Sit." Kate pulled him back down. "I'm okay, but I don't know how much I feel like eating. Can I just mooch some of yours?"

He pushed his plate over to her. "Mooch whatever you like."

Frank, watching them with a wistful smile, grew solemn as he addressed her. "Kate, I am deeply sorry for this. I hope you'll believe I would never have authorized exploiting your past experiences for the sake of a training exercise."

"I believe you. It seems pretty clear this was something Joanna did on her own. The question is why."

Both of them looked at Conor and he sat back, raising his hands in surrender. "Okay, yes. It happened. The day before I left Fort Monckton we ended up in her flat and I spent the night. I left for London the next morning, both of us thinking we'd probably never see each other again. And we haven't," he added, casting a glance at Kate, who looked amused by his defensive confession.

"Is that all you have to say on the matter?" Frank asked.

"To you, yes—except that we parted on friendly terms, so if she's got something against me, I can't imagine why."

"Well"—Frank took a sip of water before continuing—"Joanna Patch has a troubled past. Several years ago she lost an agent—apparently also her lover—while serving on the Johannesburg station. She was in hospital for a time, and then we posted her to Fort Monckton. It hasn't gone altogether well. She resented the assignment, and I understand she's also developed a serious problem with drink. Even before this incident there had been discussion about finding some other assignment for her."

"What will happen to her now?" Kate asked.

"Dismissal," Frank said immediately. "There's no question of it. It's unfortunate, but the Service doesn't have room for sentiment. As you've seen today, things go pear-shaped on a regular basis, which demands a certain psychological resilience. We senior officers have enough trouble keeping ourselves from going mad without worrying about potty juniors lapping up the sherry and fucking about with the recruits."

He lowered the ice pack and touched his lip. "I've staunched the bleeding, I believe. I'm grateful you didn't crack a tooth, Conor. I'm told my smile is one of my better features. All finished with lunch then? We've a lot to discuss and I'd like to get back before dark."

On the drive back to Windsor, Frank occupied himself with dossiers and phone calls while Conor sat in the back with Kate curled up next to him. She'd fallen asleep with her head on his lap before the car made the first turn onto the main road. He looked out the window, absentmindedly twirling a lock of her hair around his finger, then caught Shelton's cheeky wink in the rearview mirror.

"The reports came yesterday with her training scores," he said.

"And?"

"I wouldn't want her covering me in a shootout, but her numbers on the driving course were right through the bloody roof. Pursuit, evasion, cutouts—she aced them all. Nailed the one-eighty escape in one go. So if I were you, mate, I'd give her the wheel."

Conor smiled, watching the hedgerow expand into a smear of green as the car picked up speed. "Sure it's a good idea. I drive like an old man."

8

Back in their room in Windsor, Kate thought her first priority was a bath. Conor disagreed. Although skeptical of his insistence that the unwashed tang of her skin was intoxicating, she was persuaded by the evidence, and after her long soak in the tub he again convinced her the fresh-scented glow of it was just as alluring.

In truth, she needed little coaxing. Kate wanted to touch every muscle, find and kiss each remembered freckle, and feel the rough texture of his fingertips wandering over her. More than anything, she craved the music of his husky voice, and the simple contentment of having him near. For three weeks, she'd felt Conor's absence like the ache of a phantom limb, as if something too easily taken for granted had been suddenly removed, and it had shaken her.

He certainly isn't going anywhere. Her grandmother had assured her of this, and she knew it was true, but Kate also realized that, until now, she hadn't fully appreciated what Conor had trusted her enough to surrender. He'd given her his heart, as easily and generously as he'd offered his plate during lunch, and while she dithered he waited—hoping for the signal that would show she understood how special it was. His first proposal the previous

November had been only half-serious; they both sensed she wasn't ready for it. Since then he'd hinted at it but never pressed her—probably his above-average intuition told him she still wasn't ready. Kate knew her hesitation troubled Conor. She wished she could reassure him, but she didn't understand it herself.

He emerged from the shower with a towel around his waist, and seeing her still in bed, raised a questioning eyebrow. She stretched out an arm and lifted a corner of the duvet. "I'm not ready to get up yet."

Tossing aside the towel, he slipped in next to her. The caress of his mouth instantly raised a shiver, and to keep the tenderness from escalating into something unstoppable, Kate gently pushed against his shoulders. "I was actually thinking we could just talk for a while."

He groaned, laughing, and kissed her forehead before settling back on one elbow. "Go on, so. I'm mad for a bit of chat."

Kate shifted to face him. "Tell me what you've been doing for the past three weeks. I assume you've been practicing?"

"Jaysus, it's about *all* I've been doing—eight or nine hours a day—sometimes more."

"How do you think it's going?"

"Fairly well, in general."

"But?" Kate could tell there was a 'but' from the tension in his eyes. Rolling onto his back, Conor frowned at the ceiling.

"But … the Kreutzer is giving me the skitters. It's a sonata Beethoven wrote for violin and piano, but I'm to play it with a full orchestra. Exciting idea, but I hadn't expected it, and it's more nerve-wracking than dealing with just one other instrument. That's why I ended up at Wigmore Hall. He saw I was a bit twitchy over it, so Eckhard rounded up a chamber group to rehearse with me."

"Did that help?"

"It did, yeah. It'll be fine. I suppose." He sighed.

"It *will* be fine. I know it will."

"*How* do you know?" Conor's smile was half-hearted.

"Because I know you." She ran a finger over his dark eyebrows, and the furrowed line between them relaxed.

"True enough. Better than anyone else ever will."

He was quiet for a moment, then in a movement too quick to fend off he tipped Kate onto her back and burrowed under the covers.

They were a bit late getting downstairs for the cocktail hour. When they finally appeared in the conservatory, Frank was sitting with his feet up on a pillowed footstool, and a whiskey glass on the table next to him. Conor was surprised to see him again holding an ice pack to his lip.

"Sorry I lamped you so hard." He sat down next to Kate on the opposite couch. "Does it hurt that much?"

"It doesn't hurt at all," Frank assured him. "A concern was expressed about swelling. It seemed best to humor him."

His wisdom on that point became clear when the conductor entered. With a heavy-looking drinks tray in one hand and a bottle of whiskey in the other, his physical size seemed even more imposing than usual. Seeing the dark frown on his face, Conor cautiously got to his feet.

"Now where are you going?" Eckhard demanded, setting the tray on the coffee table in front of them.

"Nowhere," Conor said. "Only trying to be ready if you're planning to beat the shite out of me."

Eckhard exchanged a glance with Frank and the two erupted in laughter.

"I was in more danger of that than you," Frank said. "Bad enough Eckhard's rehearsal was cut short, but then came the news his soloist had spent the night with his hands pulled behind a post. If you hadn't split my lip already, he would have done it for you."

"And why not? *Mein Gott*, such foolishness. Conor, sit down, for heaven's sake."

He obeyed and accepted a glass of whiskey. "It's all right, Eckhard, I'm in great form. No tendons ripped."

"Even so, I've booked you for a massage tomorrow morning—for both of you, in fact." Eckhard poured a martini for Kate, and before retreating to the kitchen he set the bottle of Jameson's in front of Conor. "Probably you will need more of this." He hitched his head in Frank's direction as he departed.

Conor stopped with the glass halfway to his mouth and put it down again. "Oh? Why's that, now?"

Frank tossed the ice pack onto the table next to him. "There have been some unexpected developments in the past several days."

"Have there?" Conor looked at Kate. "This never happens."

She rolled her eyes at his feigned astonishment. "What kind of developments?"

"Stop a minute. Let me guess," Conor said. "'Developments that will almost certainly complicate the objectives of your mission.' That's the next line, right? Then we'll ask another question, and you'll give us some slippery rubbish and generally drag the arse out of it before we get to the point."

"Am I really so predictable?" Frank asked.

"Yes," Kate said. "So surprise us this time by skipping the rubbish. What, specifically, are the unexpected developments, and how do they affect us?"

Impressed by her smooth self-assurance Conor glanced at her in appreciation. He saw a flicker of the same in Frank's face before he swept his legs from the footstool and sat forward.

"Very well. As I explained before, we have an undercover agent who's already infiltrated the network Ghorbani has been working with, a group of white nationalists calling themselves the 'New Přemyslids.' The name goes back to the first ruling dynasty in ninth-century Bohemia. They've an agenda concerning racial purity and Bohemian ascendancy and a good deal of other dangerous nonsense. In their dreams, they hope to advance a program of ethnic cleansing, primarily aimed at the Jewish and Roma communities and anyone else they care to add to the list. Thankfully, they seem to be largely a collection of thickos and misfits with little political power and few champions, but two days ago our agent reported the group might be planning a disturbance during the ministerial symposium."

Conor gave a low whistle. "A 'disturbance.' That's fairly vague. Does he know what they have in mind?"

"It's 'she' actually, and no, she doesn't. In fact, there's a good chance they've nothing at all in mind. The whole thing might be cooked—disinformation planted by design."

"Why would they do that?" Kate asked.

"To trap her. She's indicated her colleagues in the network may have grown suspicious of her. If she's been fed disinformation it's not been communicated beyond a small circle, so if a rumor of it surfaces she'll be exposed as the only person who could have leaked it. It's a common ruse when an agent or source is suspected of playing a double game."

"But it might not be a ruse," Conor said. "This network might really be planning something. It's a credible threat—you can't just ignore it."

"Of course not," Frank said. "Under ordinary circumstances we'd pass the intel to the Czech security services for their action, but our relations with the BIS are strained and we can't rely on their discretion. Within the past year their blundering destroyed one of our operations and exposed our head of station. If they were to be careless with this information—"

"Your agent would be blown, I get that; but why don't you

just get her out of there now and then tell the BIS?"

"Because cultivating extremists within the Czech Republic is a pet project for both the Russians and Iranians. That agent has provided invaluable information about players and activities within the Russian GRU, and once Ghorbani is gone she'll be our best—perhaps only—source for a look inside Iranian intelligence."

"If she stays alive," Conor said. Impatient with the clinically impassive mood of the discussion, he shifted forward. "Jesus Christ, Frank, what if there's an attack and the Czechs find out MI6 had intel that wasn't shared?"

"It would destroy our relationship with all of Eastern Europe for years to come." Frank fixed him with one of his icy, professional stares. "I'm well aware of the stakes, Conor."

A misting drizzle had begun a few minutes earlier, fogging the glass walls of the conservatory. As Frank took a hooked pole to close the awning windows above them, Conor heard one of the "hammer blows" in Mahler's 6th Symphony coming from the kitchen. He hoped it was coincidence and not prophecy.

"So what will you do?" Kate asked, as Frank pulled the last window shut. "I mean, you must have a plan or you wouldn't be telling us all this, right?"

Instead of answering, Frank posed his own question. "Kate, how do you suppose the Czechs would react if they knew about this threat?"

"Cancel the symposium?"

"Extremely unlikely. Governments frown on allowing terrorists to control events. Capitulation sets a bad precedent."

"Okay. If they wouldn't cancel it, I'm sure they'd at least try to make it as safe as possible. More security? More screening? All those things you do on 'red alert' or 'DEF-CON 4' or whatever it's called these days."

"Indeed." Frank came to stand in front of them. "All

appropriate and precisely what we'd expect. The challenge is how best to elicit such a response."

"You want them at their highest level of readiness without disclosing a threat." Conor shrugged. "I don't see how you can do that."

Leaning on the window pole, Frank gazed down at him with a crafty smile, looking like the satirical version of a Bethlehem shepherd. "Do you know China Airlines is rated the most dangerous in the world? What would you suppose is the safest day to fly on it?"

When the answer occurred to him, Conor began feeling a prescient tingle of dread. "The day after they've crashed. I don't like where this is going."

"I don't even understand where it's going," Kate said. "What does China Airlines have to do with anything?"

"It's merely a metaphor to illustrate a universal truth," Frank said. "We are at our most vigilant just after a disaster."

"Frank, please tell me I've got this wrong," Conor begged. "Instead of warning them about a threat, you're going to engineer a disaster?"

Frank twirled the pole in his hand. "Not a disaster. A false flag operation. Our first option was to wait and see if the network followed up with specific information and a plan, but then our embedded agent suggested a different strategy. Instead of ceding the initiative she will bring a plan to them, and will request the honor of implementing it at the reception following the symposium's opening concert. It won't succeed, naturally, and it will have three desired outcomes." He tapped out each objective. "Our agent's credibility with the network will be reinforced. The group will likely not have enough time to plan a second attempt. Even if they do, the national police will react to the manufactured disturbance, so the security will be increased to the level it would have been had they known of a specific threat."

"Are you completely off your nut?" Conor shouted. "I'm playing the Mozart concerto at the opening concert. Kate and I will be at that reception."

"Of course. You'll have an additional assignment that evening—helping to ensure implementation of the plan and our agent's safe escape from the building." Frank smiled. "As you surmised earlier, your mission has become a bit more complicated."

"Sure I knew it sounded too easy. Bloody hell." Conor picked up the glass of whiskey, drained it, and reached for the bottle.

9

The plane had begun its final descent into Prague a few minutes earlier. Conor watched the cloud cover thinning to reveal the wide belt of farmland surrounding the city and then sat back to give Kate a better view.

"Makes me think of home," he said, admiring the artful geometry of the fields below.

"Which one?" She leaned across from the middle seat. "You have two homes, after all."

Not really, Conor thought. He didn't consider himself as having two homes or even one. The idea of home felt different to him, now. Limitless. The truth was, it existed wherever she was and nowhere she wasn't, but that sounded too corny to say out loud.

"I was thinking about the vegetable garden. I should have asked Nate to get it plowed and fertilized."

Kate straightened, smiling at him. "I love that you're thinking about gardening as we descend into unknown peril."

"Thanks for reminding me."

Against his will, and despite every effort he'd made for a different outcome, "home" was traveling with him on this trip. After Frank had outlined a mission significantly more dangerous than first presented, Conor's desire to have Kate as witness for his own artistic rebirth had been replaced by fear and a determination to put her on the next plane back to Vermont.

Not surprisingly, Kate had taken issue with this line of thinking, resulting in the longest, most heated quarrel they'd ever had. Behind their closed bedroom door he accused her of being foolish, petty, and insensitive, while she accused him of being chauvinistic and arrogant. At one point Kate appeared to yield, saying if he really thought her so weak and incapable she had no choice but to stay behind, but when Conor confirmed it was exactly what he wanted, the war was on again.

It ended in exhaustion, rather than agreement, and with the sheepish realization that they'd been screaming the house down for over an hour. The idea of having provided such a show for Frank and Eckhard brought on a fit of giggles, and when that was over they were too tired to fight anymore. She understood that he was not above using stealth to leave her behind, and he knew that she was not above chasing after him, so they reached a compromise: Conor agreed to accept her on the mission, and Kate agreed he was in charge of it. He'd treat her as a partner, but in any kind of crisis, she'd do what he told her.

After the plane had landed and they'd collected their luggage, they found the car rental office and Conor browsed a magazine rack while Kate, in her final task under the alias of Barbara Alder, dealt with the paperwork. He said it was only fair if she was to be the designated driver, but when they crossed the parking lot to the vehicle—a jet black BMW 7 Series—he gave her a mournful pout.

"Oh, here." Kate tossed him the keys. "I'm good with maps too. What should we do first? We're not supposed to be the Alders anymore, but we can't check in to the hotel without our own passports."

"Let's go there first anyway," Conor said. "They'll at least store our luggage, and I'd like to get the Pressenda into a safe before we do anything else."

Their drive from the airport began with a route through a landscape of construction sites and fast-food outlets giving way to a wasteland of cement-block apartment buildings. They lined the road for mile upon mile, and their grim Soviet-style design made the entrance into the city center feel all the more like stumbling into a fairy-tale village.

Conor had visited Prague ten years earlier at the age of twenty-three, having been offered the rare honor of joining his former teacher in a recording session with the Philharmonic. He'd fallen in love with the breathtaking beauty of the place— its architectural styles spanning eight centuries, its narrow cobblestone lanes, the great medieval-looking doors leading to cool stone courtyards. At the time, the country was five years beyond the Velvet Revolution that had peacefully ended forty years of Communist rule, and Prague was still coming to grips with democracy. In many ways the city looked as he remembered it, but from the abundance of cafes, restaurants and shops, it was clear capitalism had taken hold.

They drove down a long winding hill, the road banked on one side by the promontory which formed the base of Hradčany. The ninth-century castle complex, sitting high above the city, was Prague's most famous landmark.

Their hotel was at the edge of a district on the left bank of the Vltava River called Malá Strana, or "Little Quarter." The manager was dismayed at their early arrival, but relieved when Conor explained they didn't need to check in yet. He had their luggage stowed, and accepted the violin as though it were made of glass. After an early lunch in the restaurant they were ready to face their first official task: turning in their traveling aliases and collecting their own identities. As Reg Effingham had indicated, they'd been posted to an MI6 "asset" in a southeastern district of the city. Frank had provided the address and directions to a pub called the "Ram Gorse" in their final briefing before departure.

"If you've an asset over there, why can't he handle the rest of it?" Conor had asked, still looking for any means of escape.

"You'll see," Frank had responded, with a secretive smile.

Relaxed but beginning the switch to operational mode, Conor instinctively scanned the lobby as they walked through it, and from the corner of his eye saw something that ignited the nerves along his spine. He took Kate's hand as they continued out and across the street to the BMW. Just before reaching the car he glanced to his left, confirming that the man he'd seen in a shadowed corner of the lobby had also exited. He was moving towards a silver Hyundai. Conor stopped Kate just before they reached the car.

"Hang on. We forgot to pick up a street map."

"A street map? But we have—oh." At the urgent pressure of his hand, her puzzled frown gave way to startled comprehension. "Right. I think I saw some on the front desk."

Once inside, while leafing through a selection of tourist information Conor leaned in closer to her, speaking in a low voice. "We've got a tail." Kate stiffened and he put an arm around her waist. "Easy now. He's outside—short guy, bald on top with a curly fringe. I spotted him when we came through the lobby."

She unfolded one of the maps and spread it on the desk. "How do you know? Was he on our flight?"

"No, but I've seen him before. He's carrying the same copy of *The Economist* he had when he was three tables away from us in the Caffè Nero at Windsor. I'm guessing he was on an earlier flight and picked us up at the airport when we got here."

"What should we do?" Kate asked. "Confront him?"

Conor considered the idea, then folded the map and handed it to her. "Not yet, but we need to lose him before going to the Ram Gorse. He's got a silver Hyundai out in the car park. Let's walk for a while—make him follow us on foot."

When they exited again, the man was behind the wheel of his car, perusing his own map. Conor and Kate walked in the direction of the BMW, but continued past it to stroll over a stretch of green space in front of the hotel. It connected to a parallel street where electric tram tracks led over a bridge in one direction and uphill to the castle in the other. Before crossing, Conor risked a glance and saw the man was now a hundred yards to their left, reading the plaque below a sculpture in the middle of the green space. They started in the direction of the castle, and after a block, came alongside a high stone wall with an arched doorway.

"Stop here a minute," Conor said. "What's in there?"

Kate consulted the map. "It's one of the entrances to Wallenstein Palace."

"Tell me about it."

She pulled the guide book from her shoulder bag and began flipping through it. "Do you mean pretend to tell you about it?"

"No, really. I'm interested."

With one ear, Conor listened to her description of the grandiose gardens of Albrecht Wenceslas Eusebius of Wallenstein, whoever the hell he was. With the other ear, he listened for something else. When he heard it, he gently pulled Kate's arm and they walked back in the other direction.

"Don't hurry, and keep reading."

Their follower was keeping his distance, still ambling along the crushed stone pathways of the park, but when the tram passed them and pulled up at the bus shelter fifteen yards ahead, he walked more quickly and then began running.

Conor grabbed Kate's hand. They ran the final few yards and together jumped through the door of the tram just before it closed.

She fell into the seat next to him as the car lurched forward.

"Who do you think he is?"

"Haven't a clue." He watched the retreating figure race back in the direction of the Hyundai. An unknown enemy with an unknown objective, sent by God-knows-who. He could think of few worse ways to begin an operation.

In a transparent attempt to reassure her and deflate some of the tension, Conor had christened their stalker before he was even out of sight: Corner Boy—Irish slang for a loiterer on the street with no obvious purpose. Kate wondered if they should contact Frank or someone else at MI6, but before suggesting it she recalled a hypothetical situation presented to her during her training—what to do if a source didn't turn up for a scheduled meeting. Her proposed strategy of a phone call to headquarters was met with derision.

"We're not the bloody help desk, darling," the instructor sniffed. "Solving problems is the entire reason you're out there, isn't it? We don't sit waiting for you to give us a bell and dump them on us."

Reasoning that once in his car the man's only option would be to chase after their tram, they got off at the next stop and ducked into the nearest coffee shop. At a small table in the back Kate sat down—cheeks flushed, heart pounding. Realizing the adrenaline rush had little to do with fear she looked up at Conor … and laughed. His worried frown resolved to a faint smile.

"Do you want anything?"

"Just water," Kate said.

"Right." He tapped the map in front of her. "Figure out how we can get there by tram."

By the time he returned, she had the route planned. They were in a square called Malostranské Náměstí; they could take the number 22 almost to the end of the line and be within a block of the pub. She looked up from the map and stared at the enormous slice of apple strudel in front of Conor.

"What?" He filled her glass with water and set the bottle on the table. "Counter-surveillance is hungry work."

The tram took them through the main shopping streets of the New Town, and then once again to the land of block housing, more and more graffiti covering the walls the farther they went. Exiting onto a busy four-lane road, they crossed to a side street and walked the remaining block to the Ram Gorse pub. It was a smaller version of the prevailing cement architecture, painted a shade of absinthe green and sitting in the shadow of its five-story neighbor. Next to the front door, a Guinness logo appeared above the ubiquitous sign for Pilsner Urquell.

"Well, this looks promising," Conor quipped, holding the door open for her.

The interior was surprisingly upscale—all shining brass and dark wood—and immaculately clean. The walls were covered with photos and mementos of British sports, mostly the Premier League football clubs. The pub was empty except for a table of three men on their lunch break, and from the look of their dusty clothes Kate guessed they were probably construction workers. She and Conor sat at the bar and exchanged greetings with the bartender, and once they had two pints of Guinness in front of them Conor delivered his line as instructed.

"Will you have the next Liverpool match on the telly? A friend told me this was the best place to watch it."

The bartender, a heavyset man with deeply shadowed eyes and as much black hair in his ears as on his head, regarded them without expression. He nodded.

"You wish to see Harlow?" he asked in a thick Slavic accent.

"I do," Conor said.

The bartender reached below the counter and brought out a small crock with a wooden spreader and a basket of bread. He set them in front of Kate and Conor. "Greaves," he said. He lifted the hinged section of the bar and walked through, then plodded slowly to a door at the back of the pub.

"Greaves? What the hell is that, I wonder?" Conor sniffed at the greasy-looking mixture, then began spreading some of it onto a slice of bread.

Wrinkling her nose, Kate searched for an answer in the guide book and felt slightly sick when she found it. "It's the unmeltable sediment left after rendering pork fat." She looked up to see him taking a large bite.

"It's not bad. Want to try it?" He offered her the bread.

"I'll pass, thanks."

The bartender appeared from the door at the back of the pub and beckoned them forward. "Walk in this door." He pointed to the one straight ahead at the end of a hallway.

It led to a large, windowless one-room apartment. The only natural light came from a set of frosted skylights in the ceiling and the space was furnished simply—one wooden table with two chairs, one twin bed against the wall, one standing lamp in the corner. There were two exceptions to the utilitarian theme. The first was a traditional Russian samovar tea service sitting on a small table next to the lamp. It was made of gleaming bronze and looked to be about three feet tall, including the teapot on top. The second was a massive steel door built into the wall on the right side of the room. It was as high and wide as a standard doorway and had a five-pronged brass handle. Next to it, in a large alcove, a gray-haired woman in a wheelchair sat at a desk with her back to them, peering at a computer screen.

"Enter, enter," she sang out in a crisp British accent. "Bring the chairs along if you could, please."

They each picked up a chair, and when Conor looked at Kate, his widened eyes confirmed he was as surprised as she was. As they entered the alcove, the woman spun the chair to face them, and Kate saw why the MI6 asset in Prague couldn't do the job Conor had been assigned. She looked at least seventy years old, and although she was wearing a simple khaki skirt, the material lay almost flat against the chair, draping an empty space below it. Both of her legs had been amputated.

With an energetic movement, she pulled the glasses from her face and threw them on the desk, then extended a hand. "Conor McBride," she announced cheerfully. "Your legend precedes you. My God, you're gorgeous. The boys in London never give me the most important information."

"That's largely been my experience as well ... Harlow?" Conor still sounded uncertain as he took her hand.

"Harlow, that's right. Just today. Just for you."

"I see." He moved aside to give Kate room to step forward. "I'd like to introduce my partner, Kate Chatham."

Harlow took her hand, giving her a dazzling smile. "Yes, I assumed as much. Christ, even more gorgeous. They'll be wanting you both for the training videos. Please, sit down. Tell me how you're getting on so far."

They'd been told not to discuss the details of the mission, and Harlow seemed not to expect any, but as they chatted about Prague, where she'd lived for the past ten years, Conor occasionally darted a glance at Kate. She knew he was trying to decide whether to tell their contact about Corner Boy.

After a few minutes of conversation, Harlow took an envelope from the center drawer of the desk. "I hate rushing you out the door, but I've a Yank turning up any time now. You don't want to be crashing into each other in the hallway, I expect."

Kate handed over the belongings of Malcolm and Barbara Alder and accepted an envelope in exchange, which she placed in her bag. Conor waited for the completion of this transfer before speaking again.

"I realize this wasn't approved ahead of time, but there's

something else I need, and I'm guessing you're probably the right person to ask. We're under surveillance. Short, middle-aged male who looks like he's been sent by someone else. I don't know who, or why. As far as I can tell, he picked us up in London."

Harlow closed the desk drawer, her face suddenly sober. "Did he follow you here?"

"No," Conor said. "We ditched him, but he knows where we're staying. It's not a threat we planned for, so I'm hoping—"

"Yes, I know what you're hoping." She waved a hand and tapped a fingernail against the arm of the wheelchair, frowning in thought.

On the other side of the wall, Kate heard muffled voices and an occasional clatter of dishes coming from the pub's kitchen. She wondered what had happened to this woman and how she had come to be in this windowless room. Did she own the pub, or did MI6? Was the bartender also a spy, or was he a caretaker, or both?

Harlow gave Conor a firm nod. "All right then. Come along."

Wheeling from the alcove, she positioned herself in front of the vault door and placed her hand against a small square of glass next to the lock. Kate saw her palm briefly illuminated by an infrared flare. There was a low electronic hum and a click, and Harlow swung the door open to reveal a narrow room about twenty feet long. Its walls were lined with shelves stacked with boxes and bags of various sizes. She entered, flipping a light switch, and the room exploded into bright fluorescent light.

"There. On the top shelf." Rolling to a stop she pointed, and Conor reached up for the black plastic case. "I'm told you prefer the Walther," she said. "Are you an Ian Fleming fan?"

"No." He didn't return her smile. Bringing the case down to a middle shelf, he flipped up the lid and removed the gun and its accessories from the foam-molded interior.

As she watched Conor strip the gun and lay each part gently

in front of him, Kate was struck by the stillness of his face, the deft movement of his hands, and the absolute concentration that rated no detail too small for attention. She'd once told him the way he treated his violin seemed to mirror the approach he took with a gun. He'd been horrified by the comparison, but after reflection had admitted the truth in it. There was a similarity of method, he acknowledged, but his attitude to each was very different: he felt reverence for one and for the other, mistrust.

Conor reassembled the Walther, and after fitting it into a concealed holster under his waistband, he met Kate's eyes with a resigned shrug. She knew what the weapon represented for him—a painful combination of security, guilt, and shame— shame for a skill he'd never wanted to learn but now somehow felt compelled to perfect.

10

During the return journey, Kate sat with her shoulder bag on her lap, the weight of two eight-round magazines and a box of ammunition pressing against her knees. It didn't feel as bizarre as it would have a year ago—a good point of reference for how much her life had changed in the last twelve months.

The tram was nearly empty on the ride back, which allowed them to have a whispered conversation about the woman they'd just met, mostly driven by speculation about what calamity might have been responsible for the loss of her legs. By the time they reached the city center, they'd embroidered quite a colorful story for Harlow. Conor said their imaginations were probably still no match for reality.

Stepping off in front of the National Theatre they walked along the river's edge, but were reluctant to venture anywhere near the hotel just yet. Whatever his motive, their follower had lost them for the moment and they decided to enjoy the rest of the day—and their possibly short-lived freedom—by staying lost for as long as possible. This was achieved without much effort in the labyrinth of Staré Město, the "Old Town" neighborhood on the right bank. They wandered the streets until evening, along with successive waves of tour groups that swarmed up the lanes like Visigoths. The hordes were most easily avoided by stepping into the closest building, which more often than not was a church.

"City of a Thousand Spires," Conor said, as they ducked into another one. "I can see why they call it that."

Kate adored the elaborate Baroque interiors, taking particular delight in the statues of bishops and saints with writhing demons pinned under their croziers. Amused by her fascination, Conor searched out the most gruesome specimens for her appraisal.

They had dinner at a restaurant beneath Charles Bridge, watching swans and ducks coast along the river, and for a while the world of espionage and surveillance faded away. Instead of the mission, they talked about everything else, alternating between the silly and the serious. They prolonged it by making a bottle of Malbec last for more than two hours, while across the water the illuminated castle walls and cathedral spires grew ever more dramatic against the dark sky.

In some ways, Kate felt the setting was irrelevant. They'd often had the same sort of conversation in the kitchen back home, but the captivating atmosphere of an old-world city added a deeper air of enchantment to the evening. She'd traveled to beautiful cities all over Europe, but unlike Conor, Kate had never visited Prague. She thought it might be the most romantic city she'd ever been in, but she wondered how much of that feeling could be attributed to the city itself. Maybe romance was something people carried in with them, like an exotic invasive species, planting it on moonlit riverbanks, leaving it to grow and spread.

It was close to midnight when they crossed back over to the Little Quarter. Like the churches, the bridge had its own lineup of saints, snakes, and sinners perched along its fourteenth-century walls, but darkness obscured the details, softening the figures into two columns of benign sentinels with a procession of lovers strolling between them.

Halfway across, Conor led Kate to one side and pointed across the water to a Neo-Renaissance building. "That's the Rudolfinum," he said, resting his elbows on top of the wall.

Floodlit to spectacular effect, the bow-front facade of the concert hall and the verdigris patina of its roof seemed to be lit from within. Kate circled her arm around his and they looked at it together. The river was still busy with touring boats, and soaring above them a huge flock of singing gulls curled across the sky like the long white tail of a kite. She put her cheek on his shoulder.

"Tell me what you're thinking."

"That I'm an awful feckin' eejit," Conor replied promptly, then smiled. "But I'm excited, as well. One minute it can't come soon enough, and the next I just want to get the hell out of here."

Before they began walking again, she looked more closely at the iron grillwork mounted on top of the wall next to them. It had more than a dozen "love locks" attached—padlocks in all colors and sizes with writing on them. Kate wondered how many young couples had stood before them on this spot, filled with emotions they barely understood, honoring them with these symbols of permanence. She lifted one, angling it to catch the light from the street lamp. After reading its message she felt an unexpected sting in her eyes and looked up at Conor.

"*Never let me go.*"

He cradled her face and kissed the tears that had spilled with so little warning. "Don't worry."

He seemed unperturbed and unsurprised by her sudden emotion. Conor often had perceptions that transcended anything natural, an aptitude he believed he'd inherited from his psychic mother. Wrapped in his arms, Kate wondered if he could sense the power of her confused feelings—the frightening strength of all her love, hope, desire and fear. She wondered if perhaps he understood it better than she did herself.

*

The next morning Eckhard arrived along with the members of the Salzburg chamber group that would be playing throughout the symposium. The opening concert was scheduled for the following Tuesday evening, and Eckhard was known for meticulous preparation. He immediately called for a conference to review the rehearsal schedule and do a complete read-through of the program. Conor was the soloist for Mozart's Violin Concerto No. 5, which would be the final piece played, but the conductor wanted him for the entire meeting.

He was only too happy to comply, but it meant leaving Kate to explore on her own for several hours. This had always been part of the plan for the long stretches when he would be occupied either with practicing or formal rehearsals. She had her own objectives for making the most of that time, as evidenced by the French easel she'd brought along, a compact contraption that functioned as a traveling studio. He had too much respect for her—and art in general—to interfere with her work, but the surveillance added an element of risk they hadn't anticipated, and it would probably be more difficult to spot now.

They'd made their evasion the previous day look as natural as possible, but the man tailing them had to assume he'd been noticed. He'd likely step up his game and try harder to remain out of sight. This wasn't an immediate problem, since their clandestine activities were on hold for two days. If connected to their mission, the surveillance would likely be passive until the scheduled pick-up of Ghorbani on Saturday night. Apart from his intrinsic creepiness, Corner Boy might not be an immediate threat, but if he was, at least she had the Walther tucked next to her hip.

True, she wasn't a marksman, but Kate had been trained and was a harder target than she'd been three weeks ago. She knew how to use a gun and how to defend herself. Most importantly, she'd been taught how to think and react quickly to a threat. Conor tried soothing himself with all this calm logic, but watching as she checked her art supplies it was hard not to beg her to stay in the room and paint whatever she could see out the window.

"I'll be careful," she assured him, even though he hadn't said anything. "I'll keep my eyes open, I'll stay in crowds, and I won't talk to strangers."

"I believed you until the last bit," Conor said. "You talk to everyone."

They went together down to the lobby and then out onto the street.

"You're going to be late," Kate said. "I wouldn't keep Eckhard waiting, if I were you."

"I know, I know." Conor sent her away with a quick kiss. "I'll get better at this. I promise."

He wasn't sure how the other musicians felt about spending the whole afternoon in a hotel conference room with their conductor. Maybe they found it tedious. In pre-performance mode Eckhard certainly bore little resemblance to the genial host pouring drinks for his guests in Windsor. Maybe some day Conor would also come to view such a meeting as a necessary evil, but right now he couldn't get enough of it. He felt like the member who'd returned to a club he'd once been asked to leave. Wary of acting the brown nosing eejit he'd always detested, he mostly remained quiet, keeping his giddy enthusiasm in check, but he had more to say when they discussed the concerto and he could refer to comments he'd marked on his own copy of the score.

By the end, Eckhard seemed satisfied. As the others filed out of the room, he motioned for Conor to stay behind and the two sat together at the end of the long conference table. Once the room was empty his face relaxed into a smile.

"Very fine analysis, Conor. As though you'd never been away. Welcome home."

"Thank you, Maestro." Conor dipped his head in a gesture of sincere respect. "I wouldn't want to disappoint you. You can be fairly intimidating, Eckhard."

"I know. This is quite useful," he said. "A pity it doesn't work on everyone."

They discussed the upcoming rehearsal of the *Kreutzer Sonata* with the Czech Philharmonic and reviewed some final questions Conor had jotted down on the plane. When they were finished, the conductor dropped his bomb.

"There has been an addition to the schedule since we last spoke. You will be playing the Strauss sonata next Wednesday."

"Sorry, what?" Conor was sure he'd misunderstood.

"On Wednesday. The Strauss sonata for violin and—"

"No." Conor shook his head, and kept on shaking it. "I can't. I don't know it."

"Come now," Eckhard said. "I know you have played it before."

"I've played a lot of things before. That doesn't mean I know them now, and I certainly can't learn that sonata in less than a week."

The conductor poured himself a cup of coffee and stirred two sugar cubes into it. "This is a recital performance and there's no need to memorize. You are a masterful sight-reader. I believe you can do it."

"All right, let's just say I won't, then." Conor gathered his pages of sheet music and tapped the edges into an even pile. "You realize I've a few other things on my plate for this week, and they're all more complicated than they were supposed to be. I'm sorry, but if you added it to the schedule, you can take it off again."

"It wasn't me who added it," Eckhard said, frowning unhappily into his cup.

"Oh Christ." Conor had started to rise but now sat again,

dropping his hands on the table. "What is this about?"

"I realize this will seem to drift from the point, but it is connected: the threat to the symposium Frank learned of from his embedded agent has become more crystallized and he wishes to again expand your brief for the mission."

Conor was surprised, not so much at the news but at the fact the conductor seemed privy to quite a lot of MI6's "secret" intelligence. "Are you a spy as well, Eckhard?"

"No." His brief laugh sounded hollow. "Though I often think I may as well be. I have put my name to the Official Secrets Act. I don't listen—unless I am told I must—but even so, I know more than I should or ever wanted to. He has never trusted anyone else, but me he perhaps trusts too much."

"Everyone needs at least one person in their life they can trust," Conor said quietly. "I wouldn't want that burden, mate, listening to all Frank's secrets. He's a lucky man." He got up and gave Eckhard a thump on the back. "Come on. Let's hit the hotel bar. I've a feeling I'm going to need a drink for this one."

In the brightly lit cellar bar, happy hour had already started. It was noisy, filled with cigarette smoke, and jammed with a crowd Conor quickly pegged as elected officials. He thought this because they were within a few blocks of the Czech Parliament building, and because politicians looked the same all over the world. Little did they know they'd been infiltrated by an undercover agent. He enjoyed a rare subversive thrill at the thought, but figured there was a good chance he wasn't the only spy in the room.

Eckhard wondered if they should find a more private location, but noise was actually the best kind of cover, especially in an Eastern European city with a history of intrigue. After getting pints of beer they went to a table in the back, adjacent to a group of loud pontificators.

"Let's have it then," Conor said, after a long swallow from his glass. "Connect the dots—and will you ever stop running your eyes about the place. They'll think you're going to either shoot them or put them in the tabloids."

The conductor nervously lit a cigarette before beginning. "Frank's embedded agent reported in yesterday. She presented her plan to the leadership of the white nationalist network, the 'New Přemyslids' as they call themselves. They approved it but gave her a different objective. Instead of causing a general disturbance as she suggested, they've instructed her to assassinate the Czech Minister of Culture."

"And another 'false flag' operation spirals out of control." Conor watched a bead of moisture roll down the side of his glass and pressed a finger to it. "I can't say I'm surprised, but it seems like they're aiming low. Why would they give a shite about the Minister of Culture?"

"Their agenda focuses on racial purity," Eckhard said. "The minister is believed to favor leniency on migration policy, and he's an old and close friend of the president. They fear his influence."

A server who had threaded his way through the crowd approached their table to see if they wanted any food. They declined the menus, but since most of Conor's beer was already gone he ordered them another round and motioned for Eckhard to continue.

"Given the target, Frank acknowledges the threat is too serious not to communicate to the Czech BIS, but his embedded agent fears the information will be leaked back to the network, putting her life at risk. To insulate her, he's agreed to let her first proceed with a simulated attack at the opening reception. She's to prepare to return to London, but in the meantime will be protected against suspicion when MI6 communicates its intelligence to the security services. Frank said she will make contact with you regarding the details of your role in the operation."

"Since it's become more complicated," Conor observed.

Eckhard acknowledged the sarcasm with a sympathetic nod. "He indicated you should follow her lead on further developments."

"Right." He paused to let a burst of deafening laughter from the next table subside. "This is all fairly serious stuff, Eckhard, but I'm not seeing how it connects to an extra performance for me."

"Yes, I know." Eckhard raised his glass with a weary sigh. "This is how I have come to be involved."

As they started on their second beer, he connected the dots for Conor. Some months ago, the Minister of Culture, Martin Labut, had a member of his staff deliver a recording to the symposium organizers at the Austrian Embassy. It was a piece played by a young pianist who'd been living in the Labut household for some time. The minister hoped a place might be found for her to perform. The Embassy added her to the participant list and forwarded the recording to Eckhard, who rejected the idea of a performance in the official program. Although talented, she was not yet playing at the level required. As a goodwill gesture, he suggested featuring her in an auxiliary recital event and said a member of his chamber orchestra would be happy to perform with her.

"The Labuts offered to board the musician in their home to maximize rehearsal time," Eckhard explained. "Frank believes it would be useful if you and Kate were housed there instead, so he's asked me to substitute you for the musician I'd selected."

"I wasn't trained for personal security." Conor's objection was obligatory. He might as well save his breath. As usual, through cajoling and manipulation, Frank Murdoch had worked his magic, improvising a strategy as elegant as the man himself.

"Frank asks you to be watchful and alert. Nothing more."

"Except play a sonata I haven't looked at in years." Conor

rubbed his eyes, which were burning from all the cigarette smoke hanging in the room. At one time he wouldn't have noticed it. He would have been too busy inhaling his own. He'd been fourteen years old when he started on them and now, a year after quitting, he sometimes wanted a cigarette so bad he could eat one. Given his medical history, it would be safer than smoking it.

"What's her name, and what's her playing like?"

Eckhard looked relieved to move to another topic. "Sonia Kovac. I believe she is twenty-two years old. Her playing is quite good, but it depends too much on technique and not enough on a relationship with the music and the instrument. I think perhaps you will be good for her."

Conor smiled at this naked appeal to his ego. "Ah, go away with your fine talk and flattery. What's the minister like, Martin Labut?"

"We'll both discover this tomorrow evening. He's hosting a private program and dinner for the Austrian Embassy at the Clam-Gallas Palace—a special performance by the Opera Barocca. The chamber group is invited to attend along with their guests, so Kate is most welcome."

"Kate." Conor snapped to attention and looked at his watch. "Oh Jaysus, I was supposed to meet her back in the room at four o'clock."

"Then go, for God's sake." Eckhard waved at him. "I will pay the bill. This is the least I can do. I seem always to bring disturbing news to you."

"Never mind, Eckhard. Sure I wouldn't know what to do with good news." Conor worked his way through the bar but called back to the conductor before running up the stairs. "Don't worry about the Strauss either. It'll be fine. The piano does the heavy lifting in that sonata."

When he came through the door to their hotel room, Conor saw the anxiety in Kate's eyes turn to something ferocious in the space of an instant.

"You're late," she snapped.

He closed the door and stood next to it, thinking some distance might be safer. "I know. I'm sorry, I—"

"You follow me out the door like I'm a six-year-old going to her first day of kindergarten, but then leave me sitting here for an hour worrying what might have happened to you. How would you feel if I'd been late?"

"I'm sorry. I just—"

"My God, Conor." Her anger rose another notch. "Have you been *smoking?*"

"What? No. I'm about the only one who hasn't been." Ignoring the denial, she came forward and sniffed his shirt, clearly suspicious, and Conor jerked away with a flash of irritation. "For fuck's sake, Kate. I haven't been smoking, but if you can leave off chewing me to pieces I'll tell you what I have been doing."

She stepped back, startled, and he immediately regretted the outburst. "Sweetheart, I'm sorry." He pulled her back. "I just lost track of the time, but you're right. If I'd come back and you weren't here I'd have been up the wall."

"Where were you?" Kate asked.

"With Eckhard. We've got another 'development' to tackle." He rubbed at a smear of green paint on the back of her hand. "I'll tell you about it, but first show me what you did today."

11

～

"What do you play?"

The deep, raspy voice sounded close, but otherwise no different from all the other chatter going on behind him. The drawing room of the Clam-Gallas was filled with government officials and representatives from the Austrian Embassy, all enjoying some conversation and refreshment before the start of the opera. Conor didn't realize the question was meant for him until he turned and barely avoided dumping two glasses of champagne onto a petite woman in a skintight evening dress.

"Oh, I'm sorry." He swept the glasses away before they could spill and reversed a step, his back connecting with the bar. "I play violin. I'm one of the musicians with the Salzburg chamber group."

"How modest you are, Conor McBride. You are the soloist. As I've just learned from Maestro Eckhard." The woman's hazel-green eyes gleamed as she came forward another step. "I was curious as to the provenance of your ... instrument."

Her bosom, covered in a fabric studded with gold beading and sequins, inched closer to his chest, and an aura of smoke and perfume came with it. The low-cut dress looked like it could have been fashioned from bits of gilded stucco pulled from the walls around them.

"It's, ehm … an 1830 Pressenda. It was left to me by my teacher." Still pinned against the bar, he made his escape with a pivot to the left. "He was Czech, actually. From Brno."

"Ah, so you must know all about us. I am Petra Labut. My husband is Martin, the Minister of Culture." She took one of the glasses of champagne from him and held out a hand. "I believe you will be staying with us for the next week."

"Right, we're coming to you tomorrow I think. Really kind of you. We're looking forward to it." Conor already knew that was an outright lie as he shook her hand. The woman looked ready to swallow him whole.

"Yes, you and your friend—Kate, I believe it is?" Still holding his hand, she turned him slightly to the left and gestured with her glass. "That's my husband talking to her now. I wonder if he knows yet who she is? Or if merely by chance he's found himself speaking to the most beautiful person in the room—as he does. As we both do, I should say. Shall we join them? But you should bring her some champagne."

Frank, you bloody old son of a bitch. His boss never ran dry on ways to make his life difficult. Conor returned to the line at the bar as she walked away.

The introductions were quickly completed after he joined them and offered Kate a glass of champagne. She did look spectacular. She was wearing a strapless black gown that he alone knew she'd spent an hour ironing. The only jewelry she wore was a slim diamond bracelet with matching earrings, but despite the simplicity, or maybe because of it, there was something about her manner in a setting like this—her graceful posture, the lift of her face, the polite warmth of her conversation—that showed the influence of her grandmother. She was regal in the most genuine sense of the word, but the evidence of her straightforward spirit kept Conor from being altogether awestruck. She brushed a kiss against his cheek. ...

"They're both vampires," she whispered. "I'm going to kill Frank."

He covered his sputter of laughter with a cough. They were quite pretty vampires all the same, and unlike the undead they appeared to be sun-worshippers. Along with the killer green eyes and ample bosom, Petra had a lovely face with high cheekbones and a shapely figure, but her skin showed the effects of too much tanning—and probably too many cigarettes, judging from her voice. Her husband was also tanned, fit, and handsome. With shoulder-length salt-and-pepper hair and bangs sweeping across his brow, Martin looked like a gracefully aging hipster—the original Bohemian.

They chatted together until the signal came to move to the next room. The conversation was ordinary but their body language unsettling. Martin did most of the talking. Petra watched them with a lazy smile as she leaned back against him, stroking his arm while he gently massaged her stomach.

"Oh dear God," Kate said, when they'd finally moved away.

"Maybe we should pick up some garlic before moving in with them," Conor suggested.

"I doubt it would work. They'd just use it to marinate us."

The opera took place in the sort of intimate atmosphere Mozart might have played in; in fact it was possible he'd appeared in that very room—someone had mentioned to Kate earlier that both he and Beethoven had performed in the Clam-Gallas.

The audience was seated on three sides of the parquet floor, framing the low-hanging chandeliers in the middle of the room. When the orchestra appeared through a door at the back they were in period dress—powdered wigs, white stockings, and short breeches buttoned at the knee. As the audience applauded their arrival, Kate leaned over to Conor.

"I think you'd look good playing in a wig and knickers."

He made a face. "You'd have to get me good and drunk first."

The program was delightful, centering around the motif of Arcadia, which for the female singers meant elaborate hooped skirts covered in flowers and fruit. The men in the company took the form of mischievous, cavorting—and somewhat lascivious—fauns. When the performance was over, men and women in beautiful brocade costumes and decorative masks led the guests down the torch-lit central staircase to dinner.

Kate enjoyed every minute, but as the evening concluded with coffee and liqueurs in yet another candlelit drawing room, she reached the limit of her capacity for small talk. Conor, whose Irish "gift of the gab" ensured he would never run out of things to say, held up her end as well as his own, but when she felt the urge to yawn as they started another round with the Austrian ambassador, she politely excused herself.

After serving herself another cup of coffee from a silver urn, Kate drifted to an empty area of the room and observed the conversation from a distance. She liked to watch Conor when he wasn't aware of it, trying to see him as a stranger might—someone who didn't already know the entire geography of him. It was impossible. She couldn't look without seeing everything, all the little things a stranger wouldn't know. Right now, seeing his frequent sips from a glass of water, Kate could tell his voice was going. It was always a bit hoarse, damaged by an emergency tracheotomy performed with primitive tools during his first undercover mission. Pitching it to be heard in a noisy atmosphere for any sustained period strained it to the limit.

"I could have killed him easily tonight."

The voice at her ear made Kate jump, and when the chilling words registered she gasped. Before she could turn, she heard a soft rustle of fabric and one of the costumed staff members stepped forward carrying a tray of cordials. She made a slow pirouette in front of Kate, her dress flaring before settling back into perfectly arranged folds. She held out the tray with a smile.

"What did you say?" Kate stared. The woman's golden mask was sprinkled with rhinestones, and behind it her eyes were cool and ironic. She tilted her head to the left.

"Him. No screening, no security, but in a few days it will be quite different, won't it?"

Kate looked in the direction she'd indicated, and saw Martin Labut talking with musicians from the Salzburg chamber group. "Who are you?"

"You know that, of course. We recognize each other, yes? All of Frank's children?" She pushed the tray forward again. "Call me Greta. I've always liked that name. You must at least look interested in the cordials for us to continue speaking. Choose one, and I will describe it to you."

Lifting one of the small glasses from the tray, Kate held it up to her. "Why are you here, Greta? We weren't expecting you until the opening reception."

She bowed and smiled again. "A piece of urgent news concerning Frank's Iranian golden boy. He is blown."

Kate froze with the glass in her hand, but recovered quickly. She put it down and picked up another, sniffing it. "How do you know about him? Frank said the Prague station didn't know Ghorbani was a double agent."

"He has been careless. The New Přemyslids know he's a British agent and they think he's spying on them. It's amusing, yes?" Greta winked. "This is helpful to me, not so good for him."

"He's defecting. We're transporting him tomorrow night."

"Yes, I know. Did I not say he has been careless? But if you wait until tomorrow you will deliver a dead man to Hřensko. You must collect him tonight. Midnight. In the main square of

Pohořelec. You know this place?"

"Yes," Kate said, remembering it as a small neighborhood near the castle complex.

"There is a bar called Prašná Věž. In English it is Powder Tower. A picture is above the door. I promise you he will be there. I cannot promise he will be sober." Greta took the glass and placed it back on the tray. Kate put a hand on her arm as she turned away.

"How did they find out? How was Ghorbani exposed?"

Greta looked thoughtful. "Frank wants to pull me from this assignment and relocate me, but this is my home. The network has found its traitor. They won't look for another one. Do try to find him before they do."

Kate stood rooted in place as Greta walked away and when she finally turned, Conor was coming towards her.

"There you are. Had enough of the ball? You look fairly knackered. Will we head back to the hotel now?"

"What time is it?"

He looked at his watch. "Nearly half-eleven."

Eleven thirty. She visualized the route in her head and made a quick calculation of the travel time. "No." She sighed, looking down at her dress. "We're not going back just yet."

The BMW was parked nearby, in a reserved spot around the corner from the palace. Conor had the keys, and Kate was surprised when he tossed them to her as they raced down the dark central staircase. He pulled up short near the bottom.

"How long will it take to get there?"

"Maybe ten minutes?" Kate said. "Pohořelec is across the river in the Castle District, but there won't be much traffic at this hour."

"Right." Conor glanced at his watch again. "That should

leave us enough time. There's something else we need to take care of first. Corner Boy."

"Do you think he's still around? We haven't seen him since the first day."

"I'm almost positive he's around," he said. "I can feel him. I've got a theory, and anyway, we can't let him follow us, so now's the time to—Christ, Kate, mind your feet." She'd grabbed his arm as her heel caught in the hem of her evening gown. "I wish you had time to change. You're going to break your neck in that dress."

"I'll manage." She struggled with the slippery fabric and impatiently yanked a handful clear of her feet. "Do you want me to try losing him in the car?"

"No." He pulled at the iron ring on the door that led from the inner courtyard to the street. "We need something more aggressive, but we'll head for the car first. That's where he'll be waiting."

They turned right outside the palace and walked up to the square where the car was parked. Unlike Old Town Square, where tourists would be congregating in their hundreds, this was a quiet area without any entertainment to attract them. There were few cars remaining in the lot and no pedestrians in sight. Hand in hand they walked through the square and made another right turn onto a long, straight street.

"Good. Make him work for it," Conor said. "He'll wait until we turn the corner, and then he'll have to sprint after us."

They walked about a hundred feet after turning, and then Conor pulled her into the recessed opening of a small hotel entrance. Pressed against the wall in the shadows, Kate held her breath, feeling him turn rigid and withdraw into remote, operational readiness. They didn't need to wait long. In less than a minute she heard footsteps. As the short, thin figure passed them, she couldn't even be sure it was the man they'd seen before, but Conor had already surged forward. He slammed the man face down onto the paving stones, and by the time Kate had stepped from the hotel entrance he'd pulled him up again and was hustling the man across the street to a covered arcade. He dumped him over a low iron railing spanning one of the archways then vaulted over it. Dragging him farther into the shadows, Conor pinned the man on his stomach with one knee, and wrenched his arm back, all without making a sound. Panting heavily and with his face turned to one side, Kate could see the man was indeed none other than Corner Boy.

"Who sent you?" Conor's voice was eerily calm, almost conversational. Getting no reply, he grabbed the man's ring finger and pinky and bent them back. "You've ten seconds before I break them all and start on the other hand. Who do you work for and what do they want?" Stifling a yelp the man began to struggle, and Kate cringed as Conor pulled the fingers back harder. "Five seconds."

"Okay, okay. Ease up." The man groaned as Conor released his fingers. "Zimmer House."

"Bingo." Conor swung around to Kate, his smile at odds with the dark anger in his eyes. "That was my theory, but I couldn't figure out how they knew we were in London."

"They've got their own private investigator," the man said, and now Kate could hear his working-class British accent. "He tracked you to JFK before handing it off to me. He said you were a gold digger, that you'd been arrested for financial fraud, and you were traveling out of the country with one of their clients using fake passports. I picked you up in London."

"Shit." Conor's cold reserve finally cracked.

Kate's heart sank as he pulled his knee away from the man and leaned back on his heels, his head bowed. Other than the "gold digger" assumption, every word was true. Guido Brottman had not wasted a minute in putting his investigator on the case to root up Conor's past and reach all the wrong conclusions. She sat on the ground next to him as their stalker rolled away and sat up, looking surprised.

"What have you told them?" she asked.

"Sweet fuck-all, to be honest." He scuttled back against the wall as Conor's head jerked up. "I followed you both to Windsor, and then I followed her down to you-know-where. Once I saw where she was headed I hoofed it right back to Windsor and watched you muck about for three weeks. I just pretended she was with you. I'm not a complete moron, mate. It's good money, this gig, but I'd like to get out of it alive. I've been creeping about here like a little girl in a funhouse, scared shitless of walking into something. Which I guess I just did."

He drew up his knees and nervously watched them, massaging his fingers. Kate put a hand on Conor's back. "We're running out of time. What are we going to do?"

Conor shrugged. "Damned if I know. Ordinarily, I'd be dragging him to the head of station. They'd process him, make him sign his life away and send him home, but the bloody head of station doesn't know we're here." He went silent and for a long minute Kate stayed quiet while he thought. "What's your name?" he finally asked the little man, still cowering against the wall.

"Winnie."

Conor snorted. "You're joking me. Winnie?"

"Short for Winston. Me mum thought he was God."

"Jaysus." Conor looked at Kate. She bit her lip, but it didn't work. She broke into laughter and he joined her soon after. "Okay, Winnie." He got to his feet and gave Kate a hand up. "It's mad altogether, but what else is new? You'll have to come with us."

Kate thought they made an odd trio walking back to the car—two people in formal evening wear flanking a slight figure in jeans and a rumpled sports jacket, his chin bleeding slightly. When they reached the car, their captive moved towards one of the rear doors, but Conor stopped him.

"Look, I'm sorry, but we can't let you sit with us." He signaled for Kate to pop the trunk.

Winnie looked startled, but then shrugged. "All things considered, I think I'll be happier riding in the boot."

Conor waited until he'd settled himself as comfortably as possible and then closed the hood. He gave it a final glance, shaking his head.

"Next item," he said, sliding into the passenger seat.

"Will he be safe riding like that?" Kate asked.

"Sure why wouldn't he be. It's the boot of a luxurious BMW. Do you need me to read the map?"

"No."

She shifted the car into a quick reversing arc and they sped out of the square.

12

"This is actually better," Kate said. "We're closer to the highway from here."

"That's the spirit." Conor gave her a light punch on the knee. He was happy to hear of any silver lining in their position, perched on the lip of volcanic disaster. As always, Kate was putting up a brave front, but he could tell she was anxious. He removed his black tie and tailcoat.

"What's that building in front of us, do you know?"

"Believe it or not, it's the Ministry of Foreign Affairs," she said.

"Oh, I believe it." Conor finished rolling up the sleeves of his tuxedo shirt. He looked around the dark empty street in front of the Ministry. Not knowing who else might be lurking in the square outside the bar, it seemed safer to park a few blocks down the street, but he felt uneasy about leaving Kate alone—or almost alone. Wee Winnie didn't really count, although he was holding up well. He'd checked on him after they'd parked, and the little guy seemed to be weathering the ride just fine. Conor didn't know what the hell they were going to do with him. He pushed the problem and all its ancillary questions aside, until he could focus on it properly.

"You've got your phone on?" he asked Kate, holding up his own.

"I do, but it seems like we're never supposed to use them," she said.

"Except in dire emergency—important footnote." Conor got out of the car and came around to the driver's side, adjusting the concealed holster to fit more snugly against his back. Kate lowered the window and he spread his arms, inviting appraisal. "How do I look? Fit for a squalid evening on the piss?"

"Hardly." She managed a faint smile. "Be careful."

Conor leaned down and kissed her. "I always am."

He walked up the street to Pohořelec, a long square lined with historical buildings and divided by a parking island. With a few hotels and restaurants in the vicinity, the neighborhood was still active. He scanned the cars parked in a row along the island and saw one in the middle with a man sitting in the driver's seat. The battered Peugeot faced a bar that had a squat, round tower painted over the door and the name Prašná Věž inscribed above it. Conor went another block before crossing the street and approached the door from the opposite direction.

The place wasn't upscale, but it wasn't a dive either—just a typical, nondescript bar bathed in the ubiquitous fug of cigarette smoke. Most of the customers were jammed into a dimly lit room in the back, a stone-walled, barrel-vaulted space where a singer was belting out folk songs in an impassioned baritone. The front room Conor walked into was narrow, with just enough space for a row of tables running parallel with the long bar on the opposite wall. About a dozen people had gathered in this quieter area, and as promised, one of them was the man he'd come to collect.

Even if Conor hadn't already seen a photo of him, Farid Ghorbani would have been easy to spot. He was "outrageously handsome," as Kate had insisted on describing him. Tall, muscular, olive-skinned, with close-cropped black hair. In the photo his posture had appeared military-straight, but at the moment it was rather more relaxed because—as Conor quickly discerned—Ghorbani was "outrageously" drunk.

He also wasn't alone. The Iranian was slouched on a stool with his back against the bar and had four young women gathered around him. They weren't far behind on the blood alcohol content, and they appeared to be comforting him with the wobbling awkwardness unique to drunks and toddlers. Conor took a seat at the end of the bar and signaled for a drink. This wasn't going to be quick.

He eavesdropped on the conversation. It was as disjointed as one might expect from inebriates communicating in a second language, but he had no trouble following it. There was little variety in the discussion, and it played out as morosely as any "come-all-ye" ballad in the back room.

The gist was Ghorbani had been unlucky in love. He'd given his heart away (to a cold-hearted woman, his ladies assured him). He thought she wanted to be with him (who wouldn't, they exclaimed), but when he offered her a new life—a better life—she'd refused it (a chorus of unintelligible remarks, easily interpreted as unflattering). Before beginning again with some slight variation, Ghorbani ended his circular narration with a moan of self-pity.

"I don't understand. I don't understand."

Because you're a pure solid fuckwit, Conor thought, guessing who the woman in question must be. He was astonished by the Iranian agent's reckless behavior. The man had fallen for Frank's undercover agent, "Greta." Unaware her association with the New Přemyslids was a cover, he'd exposed his identity as a double agent and had tried to persuade her to defect with him. Her rejection had broken his heart. Ghorbani didn't realize it wasn't the worst thing she'd done to him. If not so angered by his lack of judgment, Conor might have felt sorry for the poor bastard.

After fifteen minutes there was still no sign of an end to the pity party—or of an opportunity for a discreet approach. Conor began preparing for a more abrupt extraction, but he'd waited one minute too long. As he pushed aside the beer he'd barely touched he heard the door open. He turned and recognized the man entering Plašná Věž as the one who'd been sitting in the Peugeot across the street.

He was a younger and much bigger man, filling the doorway with a size and shape Conor didn't relish the idea of confronting. He let his gaze fall away before their eyes connected, but not before noting the man's reaction as he took in the scene—a less disguised expression of his own disgust and impatience.

Entirely unconscious of the need for it, Ghorbani had tucked himself behind a human shield. A minute ago it had been an annoying obstacle, but now it looked like the path to salvation. Any doubt Conor had about the colossus standing in the doorway was settled by the murderous glare he directed at Ghorbani—who remained oblivious—but the hit man didn't have brains in proportion to his brawn. He hesitated inside the door, his concealed weapon rammed so hard against the fabric of his jacket that the muzzle threatened to poke through it. Taking out a mobile phone, he walked quickly through the bar to the next room.

As soon as he was out of sight Conor was in motion. He peeked around the corner in time to see the man disappear into the men's room—presumably to ring for instructions—then shouldered through the informal security detail, threw a bundle of Czech crowns on the bar and grabbed the Iranian by the arm.

"Sorry for the intrusion, ladies, but this fellow is late for an appointment. Let's go, mate. Frank is waiting."

The element of surprise bought him time. Ghorbani's entourage gaped as their hero lurched from his stool, and Conor had rushed him halfway to the door before he began resisting.

"No, no. What are you doing? It is for tomorrow night. At that hotel place. Chinese hotel place. Not for now. You are some kind of moron?" Off-balance, he staggered to keep his feet under him and Conor swung him around, using the momentum to carry them forward.

"I must be, risking my life to save your sorry arse."

They crashed out the door to the street, where Ghorbani abruptly lost his fight against gravity. For a second he danced over the block-patterned cobblestones, as though attempting a drunken game of hopscotch, then went down. Caught underneath, Conor hit the ground hard and felt the sharp edge of the curb smack against his ribs like a sledgehammer. Spitting obscenities he rolled to his feet and reached for the Iranian agent, but the fall seemed to have knocked him sober. He waved the hand away and got up on his own.

"Why are you here?" Ghorbani asked, giving him a wary but more focused stare. "What has happened?"

"You're burnt to a crisp, Farid. Your racist pals have turned on you, and—" Conor glanced through the bar's window and swiveled to look down the square. There was no chance of Kate reaching them in time. "There's a great ox of a man come to throw you in a landfill, and he's just out of the loo, so I'd say we should be on the move."

He hoped their enemy's shooting arm moved as slowly as his brain because the square didn't offer much in the way of cover, but as they raced down the sidewalk he caught a glimpse of an opening in the block of buildings on their right. Conor backtracked, redirecting Ghorbani with a hard shove, and they plunged into the darkness of a long, tunneled staircase.

The passageway smelled of damp stone and cat piss, and the faint gleam of the moon lit the arched opening at its opposite end. Now following the agent, Conor took the stairs two at a time, pulling out his phone as he climbed. He couldn't get a signal, but tried again once he'd reached the top and stumbled out of the tunnel. Kate picked up on the first ring and wasted no time on preliminaries.

"Tell me what you need."

"Orientation." Doubling over to catch his breath, Conor tried and failed to stifle a groan, which didn't escape notice.

"What's wrong? Are you all right?"

"I'm fine. I've got Ghorbani, but we had to leg it and now I don't know where the hell we are."

While the agent kept watch, he described their flight up through the tunnel and where it had led them—to a dark, quiet courtyard with a large Baroque-style building on one side. He waited for her to confirm their location.

"It looks like a church," Conor said. After a minute with only the rustling sound of a map on the line he added, "Fairly lively now, Kate."

"It must be Strahov Monastery. You're on Petrin Hill," she said. He heard the BMW's engine turn over. "There's a path from the courtyard to a street just below the Pohořelec main square; I'll be there in less than two minutes. The path should be on your left as you face the monastery. Can you see it?"

Conor walked farther into the courtyard and stopped. "Yeah. I can see it's behind a locked gate in a stone wall."

"Can you climb over it?"

Rubbing his side, Conor grimaced. "I guess we'll have to. See you in two minutes."

Ghorbani scaled the wall first—fresh air and fear acting as an antidote to intoxication—and leaned down to offer a hand. Conor stretched to grip it and scrambled up after him, gritting his teeth.

As Kate had promised, the path ended at a street no more than a hundred yards downhill. It was deserted in both directions, and they took cover in a graffiti-scarred stone shelter next to the road. A minute later Conor saw the headlights of the BMW coming up the hill.

*

As soon as they piled into the car, Kate smelled the air turning funky. Stretched on the back seat as instructed, the Iranian agent seemed to exude alcohol from every pore, while in the front Conor gave off a more natural odor of sweaty exertion. He was clearly in pain, but offered no explanations.

"I'm pretty sure we disappeared before he saw us," he said. "He's maybe already gone, or he's up in his car ringing for help again. I'll duck down, but just roll through the square like you're not bothered and we'll hope nobody cops on to us."

Kate watched as he gingerly moved to lower himself, but then he stopped with a sharp gasp. Worried and exasperated, she wrenched up the parking brake.

"We both know you're not fooling me, Conor, so you'd better just spit it out. What happened to you?"

He released his breath with a slow hiss. "I may have cracked a rib." He jabbed a thumb at Ghorbani, who seemed to be lapsing into a stupor. "Courtesy of the celebrated double agent. He was paralytic when I bounced him out of the bar and he fell on top of me."

"Oh, thank God. That's not so bad."

"Glad you see it that way," he muttered.

"I'm sorry. I didn't mean it the way it sounded." Surprised herself, Kate wondered at what point she'd come to view a cracked rib as something routine. She turned to look at the Iranian agent, then twisted back to face the road, confounded by the absurdity of it all. "He really is drunk, isn't he? This business isn't anything like I expected."

"Not really tracking with the brochure copy, is it?" Conor tensed and sat forward. "This, on the other hand …"

At the top of the street above them the darkness had paled, and headlights began swinging over the crest of the hill. As the car came around to face them, the driver snapped on the high beams.

"He's smarter than I'd hoped," Conor said, pulling his gun from its holster. "You said this was one-way."

"It is." Kate squinted against the intense light and took a centering breath. The time had come to find out what three weeks of training had accomplished, and whether she was going to be an asset or a liability. "Just keep an eye on him," she said, adjusting the rearview mirror.

"What are you going to do?"

"I'll keep an eye on the back." She shifted into reverse and floored the accelerator.

"Oh Jesus. Between us and all harm." Conor clutched the grab bar above him as the car rocketed down the hill backwards.

While steering in reverse at thirty miles an hour, Kate offered her own silent prayer. Her planned route would be viable only if the Castle Guard hadn't whistled the authorities into action.

To reach Conor quickly, she'd sped from the parking lot in front of the Ministry, following a road that ended in a wide, empty plaza at the gates of Hradčany. The castle complex attracted thousands of tourists, but it also housed the Czech Republic's president. The area was open to official cars only, and the palace had two guards at the gates around the clock. Hoping the imprimatur of a black BMW might carry some weight she'd flipped on the hazard lights and slowed to a crawl as she crossed the plaza past the gate. She'd watched the guards stir uneasily when they realized where she was headed. They had no doubt seen fancy black cars before at this hour, but not coasting down the pedestrian ramp that connected the castle to the street below. She hadn't dared to look back at their reaction, but Kate knew that even if they had only exchanged puzzled shrugs and logged it for someone else to figure out, she couldn't count on that kind of luck a second time.

Nearing the intersection where the pedestrian ramp ran

parallel with the road, Kate slowed their descent. As the pursuing car gained on them, Conor cleared his throat.

"Kate?"

"I just need him to come a little farther," she said. "This is going to be close."

"Does it have to be?"

"Yes. You'll see. I hope."

The car was coming fast, quickly catching up, and when it was within a hundred feet an arm appeared from the driver's side window.

"Gun," Conor said, his voice clipped. At the same time Kate threw the car into first gear.

The tires whined and spun against the cobblestones before getting traction, and she pulled the wheel hard to the right, sending them into a skidding u-turn as the car cornered the end of the ramp and started climbing. Behind her, she heard Ghorbani thump to the floor. Below, she saw the pursuing car had missed the turn and was squealing to a stop. Conor lowered his gun and stared at her.

"I think I'm done asking questions."

Kate smiled but stayed quiet, knowing what waited at the top of the hill. It was too risky to take it slow this time. She accelerated as they came around the corner at the top, racing over the plaza and back down the street to the place where she'd started.

"Are the guards moving?" she asked, her eyes fixed ahead while Conor looked out the rear.

"Oh, they're moving," he said. "Yer man nearly flattened them, coming around the corner. He's on his way now. That's some speedy class of Peugeot."

After a series of sharp turns in the Pohořelec neighborhood, Kate drove onto a wide main road with two lanes running in both directions and a tram track in the middle. She didn't stop for lights, and skipped back and forth between lanes, dodging cars, until they pulled onto the nearly deserted E55 highway. After several miles she was forced to slow down for a stretch of road under repair, and the Peugeot, still on their tail but unable to overtake, started to gain ground. Conor turned to face the rear, with one knee on the seat and a foot braced against the floor.

"Pull to the right," he commanded. Kate obeyed without question and a second later her side mirror blew apart. She kept it up, jinking left and right as clouds of road dust billowed around the car and bullets continued to slam against the metal.

"It is too straight, this road, and you drive too slow for going straight ahead. We must turn off this road." Ghorbani had surfaced again, clawing his way up from the floor and finding his voice at an inopportune time.

"Have you got a weapon at all?" Conor demanded.

"No. Gun is under front seat of my car outside Prašná Věž."

"Then shut the fuck up and get back on the floor. Kate, scoot down, and stay at this speed. Keep swerving until I tell you to stop."

Jaw clenched, she shimmied down until she could barely see over the dashboard. Conor swung his arms over the top of the seat to steady himself, and holding the Walther in a two-handed grip, went completely still. Kate waited for his signal, terrified by the silhouetted target he presented for the shooter.

"Hurry," she whimpered, unable to stop herself. Conor gave no sign of hearing her, but soon after, a loud explosion sounded inside the car and he turned, dropping back onto the seat. For a heart-stopping instant Kate thought he'd been shot, until she heard a scream of metal behind them.

"Okay," he said softly. "You're all right now."

Kate stretched up and looked in the rearview mirror. There was a bullet hole in the back window with cracks arranged like a starburst around it. Such a small hole, she thought, her head suddenly fuzzy and strange. Beyond that, she saw the Peugeot ricochet from the guardrail, and although the scene grew smaller with distance she watched long enough for it to veer back across the road and land nose down in a shallow ravine. She took a deep breath and began to shake, her hands jumping spastically on the wheel.

Conor reached over and rested a hand on her leg. "Let's get off the road for a while."

They left the highway at the next exit, which deposited them at a service area. Kate drove to a dark corner of the parking lot and stopped beneath a hundred-foot pole holding up the brightly lit "Golden Arches." A little piece of home.

She turned to look at Conor's expressionless profile. "There were no cars in front of us. What about behind us? Could you see if there was anyone else on the road when …" She trailed off, afraid of what naming the thing she'd seen might precipitate.

"When I shot him?" He completed the question without looking at her. "No. We're clear. No witnesses."

They sat without speaking—even their double agent sat quietly in a corner of the back seat. After several minutes Conor stirred and scrubbed his hands over his face, then looked at her with a faint, reassuring smile.

"Well, we can't just drop this car back at the airport. I guess I'm glad we're not the Alders right now. They just bought a bullet-riddled BMW."

Kate made a strangled sound, more sob than laugh. "It's a good thing nobody knows we once *were* the Alders."

They reflected on that, and then looked at each other.

"Oh, Christ." Conor fumbled with the doorknob as she popped the trunk.

They met each other at the rear of the car, which peppered with bullet holes. Kate shivered and looked away.

"You'll have to. I can't."

He raised the hood slowly. Kate darted a quick glance, and then a longer one. At first, the trunk looked empty, but as the hood rose higher she saw the small figure wedged into a tiny pocket of space at the very back of the trunk. Conor reached in and gently took hold of the crumpled sports jacket.

"Winnie?"

At the sound of his name, the little man rolled out of his hiding place like a hedgehog and landed in front of them.

"Fucking hell," he moaned, white-faced. "I'll sign whatever you like. You can even have me first-born. Just get me out of here."

Conor dropped his head and leaned on the lip of the trunk in relief. Behind her, Kate heard the scrape of a foot against the gravel and turned.

"Who is *he*?" Ghorbani asked.

13

It would have been inhuman to leave him in the trunk, so when they returned to the highway Winnie rode in the front seat while Conor sat in the back with Ghorbani, who immediately began firing questions. To keep him from hearing more than was good for him Kate tried distracting their docile prisoner by turning up the radio, which meant she couldn't hear anything either, but it was obvious when the message hit its mark. The agent erupted in a torrent of Persian—obscenities, she presumed—and repeatedly slammed his fist against the door next to him. Kate feared for their safety as the Iranian continued to roar, and was surprised but grateful when he rather abruptly burst into tears. It was hard to listen to, but better than his murderous rage.

Next to her, Winnie—eyes locked on the road, face frozen into a rictus of alarm—appeared to share her opinion. He gradually relaxed, shaking his head and wiping his palms against his legs. She gave what she hoped looked like a comforting smile, and turned off the radio. It hadn't been helping anyway.

"He's passed out," Conor said after an extended silence.

"Lucky him. I wish I could." Kate mentally kicked herself for the remark. She could predict his reaction, and he instantly proved her right.

"Why don't I take over the driving? You must be exhausted."

"I'm not really. It was just something to say. Anyway, I don't want to sit back there, and Winnie is sleeping now too. We shouldn't wake the poor guy." She looked at Conor in the rearview mirror. His face was hidden in the shadows and his voice—already waning at the beginning of this escapade—had become so fractured she could barely hear him. "How are you doing?"

"I'm okay." He said it too quickly to be convincing but redirected her before she could follow up. "I suppose you might call it karma. He betrayed his country. Maybe it's only fair for him to get the taste of it in his own mouth. Must be pretty bitter, finding out the woman you're having an affair with just informed on you."

"Aha. So that's why he was crying so hard."

Ghorbani's dramatic reaction made more sense to her now. Kate bumped up the heat to clear a patch of condensation from the windshield. The highway was cutting through some of the farmland she'd seen from the air as they'd landed in Prague, and they were surrounded by open fields as far as she could see, which wasn't very far. The night had grown even darker under gathering cloud cover.

"It sounds like he really loved her," she said.

"Seems like it," Conor agreed. "He's gutted."

"I feel sorry for him."

"Yeah, me too."

Even in the dark of night, the drive was scenic. After leaving the highway, their route matched the course of the Elbe River, winding through small, sleeping villages and a few larger towns, always with the water flowing next to them, first on their right, and then for the last leg of the journey on their left. The final ten miles passed along the edge of a forest with little to see on either side of the road, so when their destination appeared Kate nearly shot past the intersection before realizing they'd arrived.

The village of Hřensko was as charming as Reg Effingham had promised. It was perched at the mouth of a wide dramatic gorge that had two dome-shaped cliffs standing on either side of its entrance. The hulking shapes loomed over the town center like monolithic sentinels.

Connecting to the main route at a right angle, a secondary road wound farther into the gorge. It was lined with quaint, half-timbered buildings, and had a deep, stone-sided canal down the middle that carried a tributary from some interior source to its confluence with the Elbe. The Hotel Labe was the tallest of the half-timbered structures, but extremely narrow. It nestled under the immense overhanging cliff on the left side of the road, so close it looked as though the rest of its width might have been sucked into the rock. Kate hoped they wouldn't be given a room in the back.

She drove to a parking area down the road and backed the bullet-scarred BMW into a shallow alcove of the cliff face. They stripped out anything that might point back to them, and then Conor and Ghorbani, working together from front to back, carefully wiped it clean of fingerprints.

"Please God a boulder will fall on it," Conor said as they walked back to the hotel. He looked at their two companions and grinned at Kate. "An Iranian, a Brit, an American beauty in an evening dress, and a Paddy wearing a filthy tuxedo. I hope they get the joke."

The hotel's night manager was not amused, but accepted the explanation for their lack of luggage (car trouble while returning from a wedding) with an apathetic wave. Any dispute about sleeping arrangements was preempted by the news that only two rooms were available. Conor signed them in, and after tossing a room key at Ghorbani he took Kate's hand.

"Keep an eye on our friend," he told him, already leading her away.

"Don't you think Winnie will try to run?" Kate asked when they reached their room.

"Run where, now?" Conor inserted the key in the lock. "Up the gorge? Did you not see the look on his face? The poor little shite is terrified. If he's missing in the morning I expect we'll find him under the bed."

They entered the room, which was outdated and smelled strongly of the floral-scented air freshener on the dresser, but it was clean and spacious. Conor sat on the bed and started to sigh, but then grimaced and swore under his breath. After helping him remove the dress shirt, Kate carefully lifted up his t-shirt to see what kind of damage a curbstone could do.

"Oh, Conor." She stared, horrified. His entire left side looked like a dark and particularly brutal sky in a Turner landscape. "Sweetheart, I had no idea. We need to get you to a hospital and get it x-rayed."

"Wouldn't be any use. I don't think anything's broken, so they couldn't do much."

"But you can't be sure, and they could give you something for the pain. You must be in agony."

"I wouldn't go that far, but I'm thinking an ice pack wouldn't be a bad idea."

Glad to do something useful, Kate once more gathered up the hazardous folds of her gown and grabbed the ice bucket, sprinting from the room. Along with the ice and a liter of mineral water, she managed to pry a bottle of pain relievers out of the surly night manager. When she returned, Conor was standing bare-chested in front of the bathroom mirror with a folded hand towel between his teeth, his face running with sweat as he methodically probed each rib. Kate couldn't bear to watch. She sat in a chair with her face in her hands until he finally came out and stood in front of her, shaken but relieved.

"Like I said. Nothing broken." He tried to smile and nodded at the bottle in her hands. "Is that paracetamol? Brilliant. I'll have them all, please."

During the intermittent ice applications Kate asked for more details about his conversation with Ghorbani, hoping to distract him from the pain and satisfy her own curiosity.

"Did you tell him Greta was the one who contacted us?"

"God, no," Conor said. "I told him we just got word from London that he was blown and in trouble. He worked out on his own who'd done it. He kept asking me what she'd said about him, and I had to keep saying I'd no idea who she was. I can't tell if he knows I'm lying or thinks me a first-class eejit."

When they at last fell into bed an hour later Kate moved away to the edge, but Conor gave her arm a tug.

"Sure all we need is you cracking your head on the nightstand. Come over here."

"I don't want to hurt you," she said.

"You won't, if you stay this side of me."

They lay together, listening to the sounds outside the window. Kate had propped it open, hoping to dispel some of the air freshener fumes. She could hear the water streaming through the canal below them. It reminded her of the brook next to the inn, which made her think about all the people she missed, which made her ache to be home. Conor's mind was moving along a different track.

"That was the most amazing piece of driving I've ever seen."

"Why thank you." Kate raised her head to give him a kiss.

"I wonder why no one ever bothered to give me a course in evasive driving."

"It wasn't included in your training?"

"Nope." He pouted. "Eleven weeks I was there. Never had my hands on the wheel of a car. Not once."

"Huh." Kate ran a finger along his stubbled jaw. "Have I injured your tender male ego?"

"Are you joking? I was never so turned on in my life. It's a crime I'm too sore to do anything about it."

"I'll take a rain check."

She lay back, watching his profile. The last thing she saw before drifting to sleep was the flash of his smile in the dark.

When she woke several hours later Kate was alone, which was nothing new. She considered herself an early riser, but since Conor rarely stayed in bed past five o'clock she was never up before him. It stung a bit that he hadn't waited for her, but if he was motivated by a search for food it was probably a good sign.

A hot shower restored her spirits, but they deflated again as she considered her wardrobe options—or more accurately, her lack of options. It took a while, but she shook herself and the evening gown into respectable condition, and without a glance at the mirror descended to the lobby.

She wondered if their traveling companions were still asleep, or whether one had run away or been strangled by the other. At this point, nothing would surprise her. Her curiosity was partly satisfied when she peeked into the dining room and saw Conor and Winnie, sitting across from each other at one of the tables. Of course, they were as far away as they could possibly be, and naturally the dining room was crowded. Kate squared her shoulders and began the long walk over to them.

Conor looked up, eyes widening as he caught sight of her. He got up to hold a chair, and once she was seated, discreetly put his lips to her temple.

"Only you could pull that off."

"I look ridiculous."

"That's not the word I would have used."

"Bloody gorgeous," Winnie chimed in, gazing at her. "No disrespect intended," he added, seeing Conor's raised eyebrow.

"Easy there, tiger." Conor's movements were a little stiff as he sat down, but he looked remarkably rested for what little sleep he must have had, and his voice had returned to its usual husky pitch. He was like a quick-charging battery, Kate thought. Plug him in for a few hours and he was ready to go. She was happy to see him feeling better, but envious of his resilience. She felt like a foam-stuffed pillow, only less animated.

"I need coffee," she said. "Quarts of it."

"Allow me." Winnie hopped up and trotted across the room to the buffet and coffee station. Conor watched him go, looking thoughtful.

"Winston O'Shea. A widower, he tells me. He was a waiter at Rules in Covent Garden, and after twelve years of service they made him redundant. He got a job as a fraud investigator for an insurance firm and then a year ago started his own business. He's rethinking that now." Conor looked back at her with a bemused shrug. "I'm beginning to like the guy. I'm also thinking he's not our biggest worry."

"Ghorbani?" Kate asked. "Where is he?"

"Back in the bar, drinking away his grief. He may chuck himself in the Elbe before this fellow Marshall shows up from Dresden."

"Which won't be until late this evening, because we weren't supposed to get here until after midnight. Are we going to babysit him until then?"

"We can't," he said. "I've a rehearsal that I've no intention of missing, and the Labuts are expecting us to move in with them today."

Kate covered her eyes. "Oh, God. I'd forgotten about them. What are we going to do?"

"Strike a bargain." After a glance across the room, Conor

leaned over and lifted Winnie's sports jacket from the back of his chair. He pulled a passport from the inside pocket, hiding it in one hand under the table.

"What kind of bargain?" Kate asked as he quickly put the jacket back. Conor didn't answer, and before she could ask again, she felt the light tap of his foot against her shin.

"Look at this." He winked at her. "You're getting the royal treatment."

Winnie appeared at her elbow holding a coffee carafe and a large plate of fruit with a dish of yogurt in the middle.

"Thought you might enjoy a bit of fruit," he said, pouring coffee for her. "The eggs is swimming in grease and the sausage don't bear considering."

"He's right," Conor agreed. "Even I couldn't eat the sausage."

"Thank you, Winnie," Kate said. She wrapped both hands around the mug and breathed in the roasted aroma of the coffee, hoping an assault on all senses would accelerate its effect.

He took his seat, blushing at her smile of gratitude, but at the sight of his passport in Conor's hand Winnie fell back against his chair as though punched, his shoulders slumped in defeat. Feeling suddenly protective of the little man, Kate frowned at Conor and he rolled his eyes.

"Ah, get away, the pair of you." He put the passport on the table. "Hear me out, because it's the best I can do and it might work out for everyone."

Once explained, Kate admitted his proposition, though risky, was a generous one and probably the only practical solution to their dilemma. They could have tied Winnie up in his room for the agent from Dresden to deal with when he arrived. This would require cooperation and vigilance from Ghorbani, who couldn't be depended upon for either. Instead, Conor proposed putting their onetime captive in charge of the Iranian.

"I'm not saying stand guard over him," Conor explained,

keeping his voice low. Although still full of guests, the room wasn't noisy enough to mask a conversation at normal volume. "He knows what he's here for—he was the one who asked for it. Just keep him company and make sure he doesn't wander off to the woods or fall in the river. He'll be good and sozzled before midnight, so roll him back into his room and put a little something in his nightcap to help him sleep. I'll leave a coded message at the front desk for Marshall so he'll know where to find him, then you can get a train back to Prague in the morning. I'll give you an address where you can find us to pick up your passport and the score will be settled. No processing through MI6, no confiscating your first-born."

Leaving this as the last word, Conor dug into the bread basket next to him and started on a croissant—a demonstration of confidence Kate knew he didn't feel, any more than she did. It was a lot to ask, and they were asking it of someone who sat at the low end of the chutzpah scale.

A young woman came to clear away their dirty dishes. Once she'd moved on Conor shot Kate a furtive glance, which she interpreted as an order to say something.

"Yes, I think it sounds like a good plan." She gave a decisive nod. "What do you think, Winnie?"

Looking pensive, nervous, and hopeful all at the same time, he scratched a finger over the top of his head. "And after I put him to bed? It's no good staying in the room with him, is it? I've got no proper explanation for what I'm doing there. Where do I kip for the night?"

"You could have the room we slept in last night," Kate said, turning to Conor. "Couldn't he?"

"He could." Conor looked doubtful. "To be honest mate, if I were you I'd sleep in the train station. He may not have a lot of credibility, but we can't predict what Ghorbani will say. You might not want to be 'kipping' down the hall when he's telling

Marshall about the drinking buddy he first saw climbing out of the boot of our car."

"Crikey." Winnie stared down at his hands for a long moment and then seemed to pull himself together. "All right then. When do I start?"

"Right now," Conor said. "Go check on him in the bar. He's not had a feckin' thing to eat this morning so he's likely half cut already."

They watched him shuffle from the room, head bowed as though performing a slow march to his execution. Conor released a cautious sigh.

"Can we trust him?" Kate asked.

"Oh I think so, yeah. His father was a Kerry man. From Killorglin." He laughed at her withering skepticism. "Seriously, who the hell knows? We'll draw a line through it, hope for the best, and move on to the next item."

"Of course. The next item." She took a sip of coffee and glared into her cup. "When we first got into this, delivering Ghorbani was the entire mission—'done and dusted' Reg told us. It was supposed to be simple, but now for our next trick— we'll move in with the Minister of Culture to protect him against a threat he knows nothing about, and we're supposed to provide cover for Greta while she fakes an assassination attempt on him. We have no idea how to do that or what she's planning."

"Frank said she'd make contact with us," Conor said mildly.

"Like she did last night? Given her track record of making things harder for us, how's that likely to turn out?"

"Banjaxed, no doubt. Or 'pear-shaped' as Frank would say." He put a hand over hers and spoke more seriously. "It's no secret nothing in the field ever resembles what's drawn up by clever pricks in conference rooms. It turns to a pile of cack as soon as it hits the open air, and we deal with whatever's left to make it work."

Kate turned her hand over to let her palm rest against his. Warm, solid, and reassuring. "How are we getting back to Prague?"

"We're going by train as well. We leave in an hour." Conor reached over to the chair next to him and picked up a plastic bag. "I actually got you something to wear, too, at an open-air market around the corner. A sweater and some kind of … leggings, I guess the woman called them."

Grateful and annoyed, Kate snatched the bag from him. "You might have brought it up to me instead of letting me waltz down here and put on a show for everyone."

Conor grinned. "I didn't know you were going to, but I wouldn't have missed it for the world."

14

The train from Hřensko arrived back in Prague with enough time to change and collect the Pressenda from the hotel safe, but—to his enormous relief—not to join Kate for the welcome lunch at the home of Martin and Petra Labut. Conor decided it would be unwise to tease her about it.

He arrived at the rehearsal alone and a half-hour early, wanting to get a feel for the acoustics of the performance space. He also wanted privacy for determining what impact the bruised ribs would have on his range of movement.

It could have been worse. He might have broken a shoulder, or his wrist, or one of his fingers. Any of those injuries would have been catastrophic and impossible to hide from Eckhard, who would be understandably alarmed if he knew his soloist was in less than perfect condition. He wouldn't know it, though. Although Conor was black-and-blue from armpit to hip, as long as he could keep the pain under control there was no danger of discovery, or of recriminations from his conductor.

The symposium's opening concert was scheduled to take place in three days at five o'clock, and the rehearsal was at the venue itself—the Mirror Chapel, a resplendent vaulted hall in a sprawling complex called the Klementinum. Named for the oval mirrors embedded in the ceiling among elaborate frescoes, the chapel was like a lovely jewel box. Both the walls and ceiling were embellished with delicate patterns of gilded stucco, and the color scheme featured complementary shades of light rose and red ochre, right down to the geometric patterns in the marble-tiled floor. The space was glorious, the acoustics were perfect, and he was playing well. Conor felt the balance of his emotions shifting as nervousness gave way to confidence.

Eckhard and the members of the group arrived exactly on time. No one seemed surprised to see him already practicing, and he got through the rehearsal without incident, having front-loaded it with a generous dose of pain relievers. They weren't completely effective, but he could ignore the residual discomfort. Whether alone, with an orchestra, or in front of an audience, he could usually ignore everything that wasn't central to the immediate, precise execution of whatever piece he was playing.

Once the two-hour session had finished, he'd begun to register the throbbing pain shooting up his side and into his head when the mobile phone in his pocket began ringing. Conor removed it with a sinking feeling and looked at the screen, but saw the call was not coming from Kate's phone. They'd left it for Winnie to use if something went desperately wrong with his babysitting assignment. The message on the screen read "Unknown Caller." That could mean only one thing, and it did little to ease his nerves. Moving to a quiet corner of the chapel, Conor punched at the phone and observed the standard response protocol, even though he knew who it would be.

"Yes?"

"Who the bloody hell is Winnie?"

Shit. Conor closed his eyes and silently cursed the private eye he'd deputized. There were only two numbers coded into the feckin' phone and the twitchy little git had called the wrong one.

"What did he say?" he asked.

"He was asked for the password and he said, 'It's Winnie,'"

Frank snapped. In an office somewhere at the other end of Europe, his anger was burning hot enough for Conor to feel it sizzle down the line. "During the course of our acquaintance, I have given you secure numbers on three occasions, Conor, and not once has it been you on the line when we answer it. We get USAID doctors in Kashmir, your bellowing cook, and now some wretched creature called Winnie. Who is he, and what the hell is going on?"

"Frank, you've every right to be annoyed, but it's more important at the minute for me to know what else Winnie said instead of explaining who he is, which will take a bit of time."

"He said nothing else. The line is set to disengage at password failure, which as you most assuredly know, is not 'Winnie'."

"No, I realize that, but—hang on." Conor heard a beep on the line and quickly took the phone from his ear to look at the screen. "That's him. I'll ring you back." Without ceremony, he ended the discussion with Frank to take the second incoming call. "What's happened?"

"It's Winnie."

"I know who you are, for fuck's sake." The other musicians were waiting for him to go for a drink and Conor signaled them to go on without him. "Why are you calling?"

"He's done a runner, our Farid," Winnie said. "I only stepped away to take a leak, and when I come out of the gents he was gone."

"Did you search for him?"

"Did I search for him? Course I searched for him. It's my job, isn't it? Private detective? I hunted for an hour, but it's a small town, right? And it's just bloody forest everywhere you look. Then, I thought—"

"The car," Conor interrupted. "Did you look to see if the BMW was gone?"

"That's it," Winnie said, with greater energy. "That's what I thought, so I went to see, or rather not to see, because it wasn't there."

"Right." Having heard enough, Conor kneaded his eyelids with a thumb and forefinger. "You're drunk as well, aren't you?"

"I wouldn't say so," Winnie said in an injured tone. After a short silence he added, "But I wouldn't say I'm sober. He's a lot bigger than me. It was hard keeping up."

Conor instructed Winnie to sleep it off and take the morning train to Prague as planned, and reconfirmed the location for meeting him the following afternoon. After that, Conor thought it would be best to leave the chapel before ringing Frank. He packed up his violin and walked to Old Town Square, parking himself on a bench near the base of the Jan Hus Memorial. He sat with the phone in his hand, hoping some of the fortitude of Hussite warriors might flake off and settle on him; then he placed the call. The computerized voice was on the line before the phone had even rung.

"Welcome. Please speak or enter your password."

"Chaconne."

"Thank you."

After listening to the white noise of trans-continental static, Conor heard the line pop to life again.

"Is that you? What a surprise," Frank purred, oozing sarcasm.

The conversation remained chilly for a while, but when Conor finished his debrief Frank was forced to admit he was behaving better than the other wayward agents MI6 had in Prague. Ghorbani had been shockingly indiscreet and irresponsible, and Greta—equally indiscreet—had sold him out for her own benefit.

"What do you want me to do?" Conor asked, without great enthusiasm.

"Nothing for now, apart from your continuing assignment," Frank said. "I'll inform the Dresden station. If he's gone off the idea of defecting he's taking a hell of a risk, but he might simply be attending to unfinished business with Greta. Our best scenario is for him to surface again in Prague, seeking vengeance."

"That's our *best* scenario?"

"Preferable to the one that sees him surfacing from the bottom of a river, yes. As I've indicated, he's a valuable asset."

"Maybe you should pull her out now," Conor said, embarrassed that the idea of vengeance hadn't even occurred to him. He'd been so concerned about the Iranian doing himself an injury he'd given no thought to his more likely desire to confront the woman who'd exposed him.

"No," Frank replied, after a brief silence. "She lobbied me to do this job, and she can look after herself. That's apparently what she wants."

Following this icy remark, he rang off. Conor returned the phone to his pocket, thinking about the two enemies—Ghorbani, and now Frank—the woman had acquired over the past twenty-four hours. One might already be back in the city looking for her, but the one who remained a continent away was probably more dangerous.

Across the square, he saw tourists congregating under the Town Hall tower's astronomical clock. From his previous visit to Prague, he recalled that every hour, a procession of carved wooden apostles emerged from a door and revolved around a semi-circular track before disappearing again. As he stopped to watch, the minute hand advanced, and to the right of the clock a ghoulish mannequin was set in motion. The skeletal figure of Death pulled the bell and turned his hourglass, heralding that the new hour had begun, and that time was running out.

Conor returned to the Little Quarter via the Charles Bridge and arrived at the home of Martin and Petra Labut as dusk was falling. Their townhouse, only a short distance from where he and Kate had been staying, overlooked a plaza dominated by the curving, statue-studded facade of St. Nicholas Church.

Before heading over to their new quarters, Conor went to stand on the church steps. It offered a good vantage point for looking at all the entrance and exit points of the plaza, and for seeing if the people hanging around it looked like any kind of threat to the Minister of Culture.

They were mostly tourists, of course: strolling couples and roaming packs of college students. A few yards away from him a German tour group had gathered on the steps and were listening to their guide's final history lesson of the day. The city's residents were sprinkled throughout the plaza like sultanas in a seed cake, easily identified by their business attire and quick strides. They knew where they were going and had no interest in dawdling.

Turning his attention to the townhouse, he spent a few more minutes watching the bustling cafe on the ground floor and the small, quiet market next to it. Like so many other buildings in Prague, the townhouse was ornamented with pediments carved in elaborately decorative relief above each window. It looked warm and inviting, bathed in the soft violet hues of the setting sun, with a golden glow in all the lit windows of the upper floors.

Conor regarded it all with grim suspicion. He didn't like it—the Labuts, their home, the whole situation. His internal circuits were fizzing—a prescience forecasting trouble the way the scent of ozone heralds a storm. He'd been susceptible to auras like this his entire life. They were often impossible to interpret or immediately act on, but he'd learned not to ignore them.

After going through a central stone passageway and circling an interior courtyard, Conor had no further excuse for delay. At the gated staircase back in the passageway he tapped the intercom button. From the response he got, he assumed the unit must have some hidden camera technology.

"Ah, the delicious virtuoso. We have been waiting for you." Petra's throaty chuckle faded, but during the unusually long pause before the buzzer sounded, he got the impression she was still looking at him.

Delicious?

"Jaysus," he said under his breath.

The entire household—including an impossibly small black and tan dog—had assembled in the foyer by the time he reached the second floor. The Labuts greeted him with cries of welcome, and Kate with the silent, exhausted gratitude of a drowning woman. The only one missing from the group was Martin's protégé, Sonia Kovac, the gifted pianist Conor was to rehearse with for their recital together. When he inquired about her he saw Petra squint and pucker as though tasting something sour. He wondered if her irritation was because the young woman was absent or because he had asked about her.

"She's out for the evening," Martin explained. He was in jeans and a snug v-necked shirt and wore a thin gold chain around his neck. Ushering Kate ahead of him, he moved a hand down over her back—an overly familiar gesture, in Conor's opinion. "There is an elderly couple from her native town in Bosnia living somewhere near the botanical gardens. They are quite infirm, so she visits a few times each week to do cooking and cleaning and such. Sonia has a very tender heart."

"Tender. So tender," Petra echoed, a guttural Greek chorus.

"I didn't realize she was Bosnian," Conor said.

"Yes, she was orphaned in the war. Tragic."

He could hear the emphatic period at the end of Petra's one-word sentence. She was finished with the topic. She looped an arm around his and escorted him from the foyer.

They entered the first of three connecting rooms, all of them separated by white double-hung doors that were thrown open, allowing for a view from one end of the flat to the other.

Each featured tall windows facing the square. There was parquet flooring throughout, laid in a herringbone pattern with alternating shades of mahogany. The polished surface was gorgeous, but with no sound-dampening fabric, the high-ceilinged rooms felt like an art gallery—spare, hollow, and somehow unfinished despite the collection of beautiful artifacts in every corner.

They stopped in the first room; apparently the Labuts considered it their living area, but it was the size of a ballroom and hardly cozy. Martin finally took his hand from Kate's back to sweep it through his feathery long hair, revealing a loose gold chain on his wrist to match the one around his neck.

"Now. What can I fix you both to drink?"

Kate replied immediately. "I'd love a martini. Extra dry."

"Sounds good," Conor said. "Make it two."

He discreetly untangled himself from Petra. As though needing something else to fasten onto, she drifted over to her husband at the bar. With the two of them distracted, Conor crossed the room to Kate, concerned at her wan appearance. He circled an arm around her, pointedly running his palm down the length of her back, and felt her relax as he kissed her.

"You've gone a bit white. Are they sucking the life out of you?"

Smiling, she swatted his arm. "Quit it. How was your rehearsal?"

"Oh, the rehearsal. Yeah, it was good. I'll tell you about it later." He pulled away to look at her. "Honestly, though, you do look pale. Are you all right?"

"I'm just tired," Kate said. "They've actually been fine. It's just—excuse the pun, but they really are sort of draining, and there's a vibe in this place that's making me uncomfortable."

"What sort of vibe?" Conor was interested to hear he wasn't alone in his misgivings.

"You tell me. You're the one who gets them. If I can feel

something it'll probably hit you even harder. "

"What about Sonia? Did you meet her?"

"Not yet, but I've heard a few things. I'll tell you about it later." She turned him around to face Martin, advancing across the void with their drinks.

Conor nursed the martini little more than a glass of cold gin, really—while perched on the edge of an uncomfortable leather couch, and then later on the edge of an uncomfortable dining room chair. Their eccentricity aside, the Labuts did know how to entertain. The conversation meandered pleasantly over a number of topics, including the symposium, the upcoming concerts, and the cultural treasures of Prague. The meal was also excellent, right in the middle of his comfort zone: braised lamb with two kinds of potato, peas, and sweet red cabbage.

There was nothing the slightest bit tense or troubling about the evening. Their hosts were a relaxed, amiable couple, affectionate and solicitous with each other, and there was obviously a potent sexual chemistry between them. This overall impression made Conor's epiphany even more jarring when it came.

Kate's prediction was accurate. Although it took a while to reach him, it hit him hard—a toxic energy washing over him like a breaking wave. He wasn't surprised she hadn't known how to describe the thing she'd felt. It was incompatible with the surface atmospherics, but to Conor it could not have been more obvious if its name had been written on the tablecloth. Hatred. A noxious, virulent strain of it. These people despised each other with a malignant strength that frightened him, not least because the insatiable hunger pulling them together seemed just as strong. In the light of this awareness, he saw the Labuts as an appalling perversion of the yin and yang concept—fused together, but for all the wrong reasons.

Bone-weary and rattled by recent events, the prospect of bearing witness to a corrosive marriage for the next week made

Conor feel like he was long overdue for a lucky break, but it wasn't coming quickly. After coffee and dessert, Kate's transparent exhaustion was her ticket to an early night, but Conor had the additional duty of visiting Martin's study, ostensibly to review his collection of musical instruments. This turned out to be a cover story for an indirect conversation about partner swapping. Martin proposed it in coded language while Conor threw down shots of a fiery herbal liquor called Becherovka and pretended not to understand. Eventually he was allowed to leave with his stubborn naiveté intact, and pulled himself up the stairs—alone, thanks be to God—to the guest bedroom.

It was actually more like a one-room studio flat, with a fully equipped kitchenette lining the wall to the left of the door, and a bathroom in the corner to the right of it. Like every other room, it was enormous, had a bare parquet floor, and lacked any homely touches that might have given it warmth and character. The bed looked more like a piece of modern art than a place to sleep—he doubted they would even leave a dent in the severe rectangular mattress.

Kate was sitting on a sofa in one corner, awake and waiting for him. "Where have you been all this time?" she asked.

"His study." Conor sat down heavily on a wooden bench at the foot of the bed. "They're swingers. Fucking vampire sex fiend swingers, and they want to swing with us. Orgies and … like that."

Her mouth dropped open and remained that way for a good ten seconds before she spoke again. "What did you say?"

"Acted dumb—the thickest plonker he's ever met. It didn't fool him, but I think he got the message we won't be playing, so let's leave it at that."

He had no appetite for deconstructing the past half-hour. The conversation, the Becherovka and now this bloody soulless room had left him short-tempered. He moved on to give her a no-frills summary of the earlier events of the day—Winnie's failure, Ghorbani's disappearance, and his conversation with Frank—all of which did nothing to improve his mood.

"What will we do with Winnie when he gets here?" Kate asked.

"Give him his passport and send him home. Frank doesn't seem worried about him so neither am I."

She asked a few more questions, and finally bristled at his curt, monosyllabic answers. "I'd appreciate it if you didn't make me beg for every detail."

"Well it's no use begging for them, because I haven't many to give." Conor kicked off his shoes, one of which sailed far enough to thump against the opposite wall.

"Why are you so irritable all of a sudden?"

"Jesus, Kate, I don't know. Maybe because I'm after putting a bullet through a guy's forehead while the one I'd thrown in the boot was nearly shot full of holes. Or it could be I'm still a bit sore from popping myself in the ribs. Or maybe I'm reflecting on the fact I've bolloxed the defection of a high-level Iranian asset."

Instead of laying into him with the anger she had every right to, she sat quietly and didn't say a word.

"Or maybe I'm just being a miserable shit. Sorry." Conor rubbed at the back of his neck, thinking it an apt description: he did feel miserable and shitty.

Kate got up and went into the bathroom, returning with a small glass bottle. She climbed on the bed and settled down behind him, carefully lifting off his shirt. He heard her rubbing her hands together, and by the time she pressed them to the knotted muscles in his neck they were warm and soft. It felt so good he nearly wept.

"What is that?" he asked, detecting the peppery scent of sandalwood.

"Massage oil. I found it in the bathroom."

"Of course you did. So, what about Sonia, then? What's her story?"

"She's been living with them for a little over a year," Kate said. "The story is that Martin 'discovered' her at a student recital at the University of West Bohemia in Plzeň and brought her back to Prague. Petra said he wanted to help promote her career."

Conor snorted. "I'll bet."

"Hmm." Kate moved her hands down to his shoulders. "She's got a six-month-old baby. A little boy."

He twisted around to look at her. "His?"

"Apparently. Petra seems oddly philosophical about it, and she adores the baby. His name is Leo. They built a nursery for him inside the master suite down the hall. Oh, and Petra's got a lover as well. He's a member of the Castle Guard."

"Mother of God, and here's us, stuck in the middle of it for the next week." It felt like an eternity, given the level of activity they'd experienced in just three days. Conor sighed. "And here's me. What am I like? I volunteered us for this tower of shite."

Kate leaned forward and put her lips to his ear. "It's *absolutely* straightforward."

At this pitch-perfect imitation of Reg Effingham's plummy drawl, Conor burst out laughing.

"Little more than the work of an evening," she continued, her voice trembling with suppressed mirth.

"Stop." Still laughing, he pressed a hand to his aching side. "Ouch, ouch. Fuck."

"Ouch, ouch, fuck? Are you that sort of Irishman?"

Her bubbling, infectious giggle set him off again, and the harder he laughed, the less it hurt.

15

Conor shot up from his pillow with the scream still in his ears. Next to him, Kate was awake as well, her face white against the darkness.

"That wasn't me, was it?" He already knew it couldn't have been; his eyes were too clear. For him, nightmares didn't blink out like a television screen upon waking. They lingered like after-images—as though his retinas were saturated with them.

"No, that definitely wasn't you." She had the sheet clutched at her throat.

Hearing the soft thump of bare feet running down the hallway, Conor threw aside the covers and reached for the Walther stowed under his clothes on the floor. He didn't blame Kate for not wanting a loaded gun in bed with her, but unlike the hotel, the Labuts' guest room had no handy bedside drawer and he'd been too tired to come up with a better hiding place.

"Stay here," he whispered, buttoning his jeans as he moved to the door, but Kate had already pulled on some clothes and was at his side. Conor looked at her, exasperated. "We had an agreement you'd do what I say in these situations."

"Only in a crisis," she insisted. "This is a gray area."

"A gray area? It's two in the morning and I've a gun in my hand, so I'd say—" He stopped at the distant sound of something like a shelf of glassware hitting the floor. Kate flinched but stood firm, urging him forward.

"At least stay behind me."

"That I can do," she said.

Noiselessly, he turned the knob and passed through the doorway. He stepped carefully on the bare wooden floor, but it still sent up a crack that resonated down the hall. Conor back-pedaled into the bedroom, swearing softly.

"Echoes like a bleedin' football stadium. Would it kill them to throw down a few rugs?"

They stood inside the door, Kate gripping a handful of the back of his t-shirt while he listened. Hearing nothing, he tried again, this time more successfully, and she followed carefully in his steps. They moved in silence down the hall past a second door on the left—Sonia's room, he assumed—and then farther down past another on the right. This they could easily verify as the master suite because the door stood half open.

The room was lit by a pair of small ceramic table lamps on either side of a plump, cushiony sofa. It sat in the middle of the room with matching chairs around it, all of them more or less facing a flat screen mounted on the wall. There was a small bar in the corner next to it. The windows facing the square were covered with silk drapes in a dense purple-black that shimmered like the surface of a deep lake. In contrast to the rest of the house, this room exuded the profound hush of something smothered.

Peering through the crack on the hinged side of the door, he could see the king-sized bed at the opposite end of the room. The state of the bedcovers—in a style matching the drapes—showed it had recently been occupied, but the room was empty.

"Should we check the bathroom?" Kate whispered.

He shook his head. Unless absolutely necessary, Conor hoped never to cross the threshold of the Labuts' pleasure palace. He could hear the hollow sound of voices floating up the stairwell and began to feel confident the household was not being burgled or terrorized by white nationalists.

They started down the stairs and by the time they reached the second floor the voices had become louder and his hunch confirmed. Stepping into the foyer, Conor peeked around the doorway and lowered his gun, suddenly feeling foolish that he'd drawn on all his specialized skills to creep up on a couple in the midst of a domestic dispute.

"They must be in the kitchen," he said. "If they were in one of these rooms we'd hear them more clearly."

"I can hear them clearly enough. I'm just glad I can't understand them." Behind him, Kate sounded relieved and sad. She put her hands on his hips, resting her forehead between his shoulder blades.

The Labuts were arguing in Czech, if such a ferocious, hostile-sounding exchange could even be called an argument. The language was impenetrable, but the words were irrelevant. It was a vicious battle, its participants equally supplied with an arsenal of malice that needed no translation.

Conor stood transfixed with his arms slightly raised, half-consciously shielding Kate from a venom boiling too close to them. He finally shuddered and turned to face her.

"My mother was a great believer in holy water. She'd douse us every time it thundered, and I used to tease her about it. If I had some right now, I'd pour the bottle over both of us."

Kate took his hand. "Let's go to bed."

"I'm not sure I'll be able to stand this. What about you?"

"I don't know." She pulled him towards the stairs. "Let's see how we feel in the morning."

On the third floor, the hallway was darker than it had been earlier. The door to the master suite was now closed.

"Maybe the wind blew it shut," Kate suggested.

"Maybe." Conor didn't pause to ask "what wind?" or consider

other possibilities, but as soon as they'd passed it the door swung open and a figure stepped into the hall.

Conor pivoted, his hand flying back to where the Walther was tucked beneath his waistband, but he relaxed and left the gun where it was as the figure—a woman—leaned against the doorjamb and crossed her arms.

"I take it you didn't interrupt." Her soft, accented voice sounded amused. "That was wise. It's like a drug to them, punishing each other, and you know it can be dangerous to come between an addict and his fix."

She was a small woman, thin as a wraith. In the light coming from the bedroom Conor could see her skin was translucently pale, and there was a lot of it to see since she was wearing a black negligee and nothing else. In spite of this, the woman's most arresting feature was her hair. Long bangs swept low over her forehead to obscure one eye, but it appeared to be cut short at the back, and it was silver—not a naturally graying, old-lady silver, but an eye-popping, polished chrome, glow-in-the-dark sort of silver. Against this backdrop of white, black and metallic, her lips glistened, drenched in candy-apple red lipstick.

"I'm guessing you must be Sonia," he said.

She bowed her head and flicked the drooping strand of hair from her eye. "And I think you must be Conor and Kate. Sorry to have missed your welcome dinner."

"No bother." Conor cleared his throat, and stopped there. It seemed ridiculous to offer introductory platitudes as though they were meeting at a cocktail party. The woman was standing half-naked in front of them and he didn't know where to look. Next to him, Kate had gone as rigid as a wooden soldier, and just as silent.

Sonia's eyes traveled over him. "I'm looking forward to playing with you." After a pause, she added, "Would you like to come in for a drink?"

"Ehm, no. Thanks very much, but I think we're off to bed." Conor looked at Kate. "Right?"

"Right," she said mechanically, still staring at Sonia. "Thank you. We'll see you in the morning."

"Of course." Sonia's lip curled into a faint smile, her eyes sparkling with laughter.

Kate turned on her heel and headed down the hall. Conor followed, but they both stopped short as Sonia called after them.

"It will end with sex, you know. It always does for them."

"Is that what you're waiting for?" Conor said quietly.

She laughed. "I'm here for many reasons. Aren't you?"

With this cryptic remark she disappeared back into the master suite. Kate yanked on Conor's arm, pulling him towards their room. She gave him a shove through the doorway, and after staggering through, he turned and saw her alarm.

"What is it? What's the matter?"

Kate slammed the door shut and leaned against it. "That was Greta."

Conor's brain didn't process the statement with any sort of efficiency. As though mired in sludge, it spun uselessly on the name—*Greta. Greta who?*—and chugged slowly into comprehension.

"Sonia …"

"… is Greta," Kate prompted. "She had on a mask and wig when I saw her at the Clam-Gallas palace, but I recognize the voice. It's her." She threw herself on the bed and lay back, eyes to the ceiling. "I can't believe this is happening to us."

Catching up, Conor sat down beside her. "An MI6 agent, working undercover as a white nationalist named Greta, is pretending to be a Bosnian refugee pianist named Sonia." He immediately understood—and shared—Kate's aggrieved disbelief. "I've no patience for this triple identity horseshit."

"Tell me about it."

He lay back and joined her in a study of the ceiling. "What the hell is she playing at?"

They had no answers, but after climbing back into bed he and Kate talked for another hour, trying to explain the agent's behavior and how to respond to it. One obvious possibility was that she had been turned—or had never been loyal to MI6 in the first place. Instead of posing as a member of the organization she'd been assigned to infiltrate she might actually *be* one. Perhaps, acting on behalf of the New Přemyslids, she had worked her way into their enemy's home, and had invented the "false flag" scheme as a means of achieving the group's strategy. Of course, there was a hole in this hypothesis that Conor found hard to fill.

"Greta covered her ass by fingering Ghorbani as the traitor the New Přemyslids were looking for, but then she blew her own cover by telling you about it at the opera. At that point, she knew you'd eventually be introduced to her here as Sonia. She had to assume you'd recognize her, which suggests she doesn't care, and I wish to God I understood what that means."

"Frank said she was going to make contact with us," Kate said. "Maybe he knows she's here, and this is what he meant."

Conor considered the idea before rejecting it. "None of us even knew we'd be staying here until a few days ago. Frank got the idea to put us here after Greta told him Martin was a target for assassination."

"That's what he told you," Kate pointed out. "Or rather, that's what he told Eckhard to tell you."

Surprised he hadn't considered this angle, Conor bounced out of bed again. He flipped on the light and paced around the room, agitated, but finally shook his head.

"Not that I wouldn't put it past him, but what's the point in lying to us? I don't think Frank has a clue. She's playing a role that's different from the one he assigned her. I suppose the only way to find out why is to confront her with it. Let me have a go at her tomorrow when we're practicing. It's harder to lie when you're concentrating on something else."

Even with this strategy decided, Conor continued to pace, lost in thought. He didn't know how long he'd been at it when he heard Kate's voice again.

"Conor." She was sitting up in bed with her arms wrapped around her knees, watching him. He had a feeling it wasn't the first time she'd said his name.

"Sorry?"

"Shouldn't we tell Frank about this?"

It was the very question he'd been turning over in his mind as he circled the room, and he hadn't decided until that instant. "No. At least not yet," he added, seeing Kate's worried frown.

He remembered Frank's voice on the phone earlier—cold and merciless. Conor didn't know what sort of game this agent was playing, but he wanted some time to figure it out on his own. If it turned out to be a traitorous one, he dreaded the course of action his boss might demand of him.

With everyone guarding secrets and fearing the others knew more than they should, the breakfast table was a scene of subdued tension the following morning. The Labuts were especially considerate of their guests and each other, and when Sonia appeared—fully dressed—no one bothered to pretend introductions were needed.

Conor thought her more attractive with her clothes on, but she was oddly colorless; even her eyes were a washed out blue. It seemed as though the hair dye she'd used to achieve that striking shade of silver was also leeching the remaining pigment from her body.

She'd cultivated a youthful, avant-garde facade, probably to disguise the fact she was well beyond her declared age of twenty-two. A man twice her age probably wouldn't notice such a detail, but Conor imagined a woman like Petra would.

At the moment, Petra was feeding the baby, and he saw for himself Kate's assessment was dead-on—the woman was completely smitten with the child of her husband's mistress, and oddly possessive. When Sonia lifted him for a snuggle, Petra's face darkened into impatient resentment.

Leo was a jolly little snapper, with dark hair and hazel eyes, and his olive-tinted skin certainly took more from Martin than Sonia. Settled back in his highchair he held court at the head of the table, waving a hand and babbling amiably as if offering a toast to the company. The novelty of his presence helped relieve some of the awkwardness.

"When do you like to practice?" Sonia asked. "Morning? Afternoon?" She took a seat directly across from him.

He met her stare with an easy smile. "In general, whenever you like, but I need to schedule it around the practice for the concerto I'm playing on Tuesday night."

"Oh yes, the Mozart. I'm looking forward to hearing it. The Labuts have kindly included me on the guest list for the performance."

"Will you be at the welcome reception also?" Kate's contrived innocence was so persuasive Sonia looked puzzled.

"Also. Yes."

Sensing her temptation to further bait the woman, Conor asked Kate to pass the salt and shifted the conversation to safer ground. "Why don't we get started after breakfast? I haven't played the Strauss in years, so the sooner we crack on the better. I'll just pop upstairs for my violin."

Back in their room, he and Kate had a quick meeting to review their separate assignments for the day. While he worked to peel back the layers of Sonia's identities and pinpoint her loyalties, she would spend the morning sightseeing with Petra and collecting background on the Labuts.

"How will you get her to talk?" Conor asked.

Standing in front of the bathroom mirror, Kate glanced at him with affectionate pity. "Are you kidding? She's dying to talk. I'll say something like 'how did you and Martin meet?' I probably won't get another word in for the rest of the morning."

"Right so." He watched her from the end of the bed, happy to see the color back in her cheeks, grateful for her spirit. When she gathered up her hair to wind it into a bun, the lovely curving line of exposed skin was too much for him to resist. He felt her shiver as his breath stirred the soft curls at the nape of her neck.

"How are those aching ribs?" Kate asked.

"Remarkably better."

"Are you going downstairs?"

"In a minute." With the button already handled, Conor pulled gently at the zipper of her pants.

"Or maybe twenty?"

"Sounds about right."

When he made it back downstairs Conor went to the room he'd passed through but not yet spent any time in: the library. It was the middle of the three large salons on the second floor and was lined with ten-foot-tall shelves holding artfully arranged leather-bound books and pieces of Bohemian crystal. Even with the shelving on three sides, the room was still big enough to hold the concert grand Steinway that extended like a long, ebony thumb from one corner of it.

He found Sonia there with Martin, the two of them talking quietly near the windows with their backs to the door, their heads close together. Although Conor came in without a sound, Martin sensed his presence. His hand cupped Sonia's elbow as they both turned to him.

"So," Martin said. "The rehearsals commence."

Conor simply swung the violin case forward as confirmation. He noted the quality of Martin's smile—more forced than it had previously been—and Sonia's small frown of impatience as she moved away from him.

"I understand you'll be playing an orchestral version of the *Kreutzer Sonata* at the closing concert. A rare treat." Martin lifted his coffee cup from a side table and strolled after her, leaving a wafting scent of cologne in his wake. "Sonia is quite good with that piece also, but I expect it's as well you are playing the Strauss. Better not to tempt fate, hmm?"

Having no idea what he was on about, Conor placed his sheet music on a handsome wooden music stand next to the piano before facing Martin again. His wordless curiosity received a frown of disbelief.

"The Tolstoy novella, of course. You are not familiar with it?" Martin positioned himself behind Sonia as she sat at the piano, brushing his fingers over the back of her neck. Although both she and Petra seemed untroubled by it, Conor thought this constant touching, brushing, and fondling seemed less like affection and more like territorial marking.

"I've heard of it," he said, "but what's your point?"

Martin smiled. "My point is the theme, of course—a discourse on the perverse nature of conventional marital relations and their capacity to incite a jealous rage. As I'm sure you recall, the protagonist is married to a pianist. He murders her, as she and the man he perceives to be her lover—a violinist—are practicing the Kreutzer." Martin's smile broadened into a grin. "Fortunately for you, Conor, I am anything but conventional."

Conor returned the smile, suppressing a laugh at the scenery-chewing quality of his warning. "And fortunately, the pianist is not your wife."

Martin gave a shout of laughter and lowered his lips to Sonia. "I will be off to work now and leave you to yours."

She received his long kiss while regarding Conor with an open-eyed challenge. He dismissed it—bored with the theatrics—by bending to open his case. Once Martin had left she began playing, crouched over the piano as though near-sighted and running through scales at a pounding volume. After tuning the Pressenda Conor tucked the instrument under his arm and patiently waited for her.

"Don't you need time to get loose?" She barked the question without stopping, and he deliberately kept his response inaudible. Abruptly, she pulled her hands from the keyboard and sat upright.

"I didn't hear you."

"I said I got loose upstairs." Ignoring her facetious grunt he tapped his bow against the sheet music. "Will we take a run at it? I'd like to see where we stand."

Sonia nodded, clearly appreciating the layered meaning in his words. "You are the virtuoso. I look forward to learning from you."

"I think we'll be learning a lot from each other." He nodded for her to begin. She plunged into the opening fanfare of the Strauss sonata and Conor tucked the violin under his chin.

He lowered it at the end of the final movement a half-hour later and swiped at a line of perspiration above his lip. "About as bad as I expected—meaning me," he added, seeing Sonia's haughty glare. "You were fine."

"Kind of you. As I've been playing it for two months, I'm pleased you found it 'fine'."

"I meant 'brilliant.' You were dead brilliant."

"Now you're being sarcastic."

"Sorry." Hiding a grin, he removed the pencil he'd tucked behind his ear and bent over the sheet music.

Sonia shifted on the stool. "Obviously, in the second movement—"

"The mute. I know, I forgot it completely. I haven't needed it for a while so it's still in the case." He shuffled through the pages, scribbling notes. "Thoughts on the first? Don't hold back; I'm not as touchy as you are."

"To me, it sounded quite good."

"Did it? I thought my tempo was shite." Conor looked up and accidentally knocked a few pages from the stand. He made an awkward, twisting grab for them and yelped at the pain slicing through his side.

"What is it? You are hurt?"

"Thanks to your boyfriend," he said, straightening slowly. "Or maybe I should say your *other* boyfriend. Farid knocked me onto a curbstone when I hauled him out of the Prašná Věž two nights ago." She held his gaze then dropped her head with a faint smile. "You played a dangerous game with him, Sonia. Or would you rather be called Greta?"

"I prefer 'Sonia' now." She looked up again, amused. "At least you got him out."

"We did, but he disappeared in Hřensko. I've no idea where he is now, which is a problem for me but a bigger one for you. You'd better prepare for him looking you up again. I don't think he'll be asking you to run away with him this time."

It wasn't possible for her face to lose any more color, but it certainly lost its lighthearted smirk. For a moment, the tense silence was broken only by a yap from the microscopic dog in a room above them. Conor came forward and leaned against the piano.

"What have you been getting up to? This would be a good time to tell me."

"Does Frank know?"

"That you burned an MI6 asset and nearly got him killed? I told him that, yeah, but unless I'm wrong and Frank put you here, he doesn't know about this *ménage à trois* sideshow. What about Ghorbani? I'd be a little more concerned about him at the minute. Does he know you're living here?"

Sonia shook her head. "No, Frank didn't put me here, and Farid only knows of my flat near the botanical gardens. I leased it to be able to offer the New Přemyslids a place to hold their meetings."

"So, what's all this about, then?"

She put a hand over her face and took a deep breath. "It's about love."

"Rubbish," Conor said. "There's something nesting in the rafters of this house all right, but it sure as hell isn't love. I can't feel a hint of it in a single one of you."

"Yes, it's true. We have none for each other," she said quietly. "It's all for Leo."

"Your son."

"Yes."

"And Martin's."

She nodded. "Of course."

"Why is his nursery in the master suite? Do the three of you sleep together every night?"

"No." After a long silence, she rose. "I would like a cigarette. Do you mind?"

Apparently, the house rules prohibited smoking inside on the main floor. Conor found that ironic, since Petra seemed about one-third human and two-thirds tobacco, but he followed Sonia through the French doors at the front of the room out to a semicircular balcony. It felt like walking onto a stage; it was only one level above the street, but no one in the square below paid them the slightest attention.

"Right," he said. "Whatever story you're about to tell, I'm guessing by the end you'll want me believing it's pure coincidence that you're having an affair with the man the New Přemyslids have decided they want to kill."

"Sometimes the simplest explanation is the truth," Sonia said.

"Sometimes. Not often, in my experience."

She blew a stream of smoke out over the balcony. "You may not wish to believe it, but what choice do you have?"

That's what worries me, Conor thought.

Looking across to St. Nicholas Church, he peered at a shallow niche near the pinnacle of the facade. A statue of the saint himself stood there in glorious isolation—a melancholy figure, bent under the weight of what he saw beneath him: the persistent, banal idiocy of mankind.

16

Although a city of legendary beauty, with every vista begging to be captured on canvas, Prague also had its share of oddities and this was the oddest Kate had seen yet.

She stood in the open doorway to the chapel of Our Lady of Sorrows, trying to understand what she was looking at while Petra urged her to lean in for a better view. The tiny room was tucked into a corner of the Loreto, a shrine that had been a place of pilgrimage since the seventeenth century. It was also only yards away from the Ministry of Foreign Affairs parking lot, where she'd sat waiting for Conor two nights ago.

In the shrine's cloister, several chapels were arranged along the shaded colonnade, but visitors weren't allowed to enter them. They were obliged to stand or kneel behind a railing that spanned the doorway. This seemed a pity because Kate would have liked a closer look at the disturbing crucified effigy mounted on the chapel's side wall. It was a life-sized figure—more like a mannequin than a statue—clothed in a fringed shawl and full-length gown.

"You're telling me that's a woman?"

"A woman, yes," Petra assured her. "St. Wilgefortis."

"She has a beard," Kate said, stating the obvious. The thick brown facial hair looked exceptionally real, and in combination with the delicate features, decidedly creepy.

"Her affliction, her salvation, and her doom," Petra said. "It is a very strange legend."

"Which you absolutely have to tell me."

Kate moved away from the colonnade to join her. Petra stood on the grass, soaking in the sunlight and gently rocking the carriage where baby Leo was enjoying a late-morning nap. In her shoulder bag the tiny dog, Algernon, was also dozing. Only his ears were visible, standing at attention even in sleep. They were each half the size of his head and looked like two sculpted leaves of radicchio rising above the edge of the bag.

"Certainly, I will tell you." Petra smiled. "Come, let's sit for a while."

They walked to the opposite side of the cloister, and after positioning the carriage a few yards away, Petra sat on a stone wall surrounding an ancient cistern and lit a cigarette. Kate nervously glanced around to see if someone would challenge this, but there were no authorities in sight and the tourists were oblivious. She sat down and watched—fascinated—as Petra tilted her head back and dragged on the cigarette. She was a human backdraft, pulling the smoke down her throat until it disappeared, and just when it seemed every molecule had been absorbed without a trace, it came pouring out again as if belched from a refinery.

"As the story goes, Wilgefortis was a devout virgin who wished to remain so." Small puffs continued emerging from Petra's mouth as she spoke. "Her father cared nothing for what she wanted. He promised her to a rich man, a heathen, and so Wilgefortis prayed. She was a very pretty woman but perhaps not so wise. She asked God to make her face repulsive, and so ..." She trailed off with a wave in the direction of the chapel. "The fiancé rejected her, and her spiteful father had her crucified. As though she were to blame for the jokes of God and the cruelty of men. Now she is patron saint for women in difficult marriages." Petra sniffed, tapping her cigarette against the iron grate covering the cistern. A fragment of ash broke away and fell into the darkness. "It is absurd, of course—this legend. Quite comical."

"I wouldn't call it that," Kate said, not fooled by her breezy dismissal.

She wondered how often Petra came to lay her own grievances before the martyred saint, and found it only further muddied her efforts to form an objective opinion of the Labuts. The couple shocked and disgusted her, but Kate also pitied them. They had twisted love into something more vicious than tender and seemed unable to recognize the difference.

Above them, the sun emerged from a thin patch of cloud. The unfiltered light flooding the cloister accentuated the thin lines around Petra's mouth, making her face appear older.

"Sonia was not the first," she said abruptly, without turning. "There were others before her, but this time Martin preferred not to share. At least, not right away. What matter though? I took a lover as well … and did not share."

Petra absently fingered the amber pendant she was wearing. Lying below the hollow of her throat on a black cord, it glowed like honey with inclusions of fossilized insect wings frozen inside.

"Sonia was different," she continued. "More like us. She knew how to manipulate, but he and I have been doing that for so much longer. There were threats and tears, but in the end we all got what we wanted, or thought we did. At least we got Leo."

Kate glanced at the carriage, afraid the baby might wake at the sound of his name. "Leo was an arrangement between the three of you?"

"An arrangement, yes. This is a nice word for it. So delicate and well-bred." Petra's sardonic smile faded. "I am barren. An ugly word, no? Uglier than a bearded wife to a man who wants a child. I wanted one too. Sonia did not but became pregnant anyway. She thought it was checkmate, but she didn't realize what game she was playing, or that we had invented it."

She paused as a lean, middle-aged couple in cycling gear strolled up to a sculpture a few feet away from them.

"It's a depiction of the resurrection of Christ," Petra explained to them, gesturing at the statue with her cigarette.

The man nodded and offered an impersonal smile. "We're not religious."

She looked puzzled, watching them walk away. "What difference does he think that makes?" She tossed the exhausted cigarette butt through the grate and shrugged. "Americans."

Kate gently nudged the conversation back on track. "So Sonia agreed to give up the baby?" She felt uncomfortable prying into such a personal story, but as she'd expected, Petra was eager to share it.

"For a sum, yes, although smaller than she'd planned. When she moved in it was understood she would leave after the baby was born, but when she saw him—when we all saw him—there was nothing to do but fall in love. She refused the money and refused to leave." Petra frowned. "Martin agreed to let her stay. He has many secrets and I know them all, but now my threats have no power. Sonia has some stronger hold on him I don't understand." She turned to Kate and with a resigned, half-hearted motion flicked her hands as though waving off a fly. "Now my fear that she will never leave is nothing to the terror of her disappearing some day and taking my Leo with her."

Kate nodded, but said nothing. She'd expected something bizarre, considering what she and Conor already knew of the Labuts, but the tale left her stunned. What could she possibly offer for a response? It was a poisonous existence for all three of them. The only one she truly felt sorry for was the baby.

She was spared the challenge of offering sympathy she didn't feel by a sudden movement from the shoulder bag Petra had placed on the ground. With a whimper and an enormous yawn Algernon emerged. He leapt daintily from the bag onto the lawn and gave a violent shake of his head—which he couldn't do without violently shaking the rest of his tiny body. Petra looked affectionately down at him and rose as the dog fixed her with a look of bright expectation.

"One is awake and the other will follow soon. Shall we go back to the house for some lunch? You've had enough of legends and scandalous stories, I think."

"I'll walk down the hill with you," Kate said, "but I'm having lunch with Conor at the Café de Paris. I'm meeting him there."

This wasn't a complete lie, since they were in fact having lunch at the restaurant with Eckhard, but first she was meeting Conor at the address he'd given Winnie for their final rendezvous. He'd thought it safer for her to hold on to the private investigator's passport, and she was carrying it now in her purse.

"Excellent choice. The steak au poivre is divine, and the place is of course romantic." Petra scooped the dog back into her bag. She pushed the carriage onto the cement walkway but then stopped to look at Kate, her brow furrowed in warning. "He is too handsome and too charming. You realize this? You must see how women respond to him."

"I've seen how *you* respond to him." Kate kept her voice light and teasing to soften the sarcasm.

Petra bent her head to nuzzle the dog, avoiding Kate's eyes. "But this is just for playing. Some enjoyment. A little attention even."

"I didn't mean to scold you."

"No. I am so much older. It is not me to be worried about, but there will be others who are younger. There always are, and he will break your heart."

Hiding her astonishment at the woman's presumption—that her warped experiences offered useful insights into other people's relationships—Kate smiled. "How do you know I won't break his?"

"If you have the power you should do it. Break it now, while you have the chance, because some day you will wish you had, but too late. All that power will be gone, and you will never have it again."

Kate was startled by the vehemence of Petra's response and suddenly had an insight, but not the one Petra had hoped to encourage. It explained a paradox she'd been trying to understand. Her love for Conor had no limits. That it would grow every day felt as certain as the steady expansion of the universe, but still she couldn't seem to invite the proposal she knew he longed to offer. Until that moment she hadn't understood her hesitation.

All that power.

Kate already knew her power wasn't strong enough—not to break his heart, but to mend it. As much as she had, she would give, but what if it wasn't enough? She couldn't fix everything in him that had been broken, fill every place that was empty. He would realize that eventually, and ... what then? Her eyes brimmed, and Petra saw her exhortation was not having the intended effect. She growled a husky laugh and brought a packet of tissues from the side pocket of her bag.

"This is a hopeless case, I see. You are too much in love already. Such a pity."

Coming in from the bright midday heat, Kate let her eyes adjust to the dim interior before making her way down the aisle of yet another church. There was no end to them, it seemed, but Conor had been especially interested in visiting this one—the Church of Our Lady Victorious. Its main attraction was the iconic Infant

Jesus of Prague, a small wooden figure coated in wax and clothed in royal attire. Apparently there was a reproduction of the doll on just about every mantelpiece in Ireland.

The original was in a glass case in a side chapel, difficult to see in the midst of its gold encrusted surroundings. She found Conor standing in front of it, reading a brochure. Heedless of the setting, Kate greeted him with even more ardor than usual, which surprised and delighted him.

"How long have you been waiting?" she asked, finally pulling away to look at him.

"Not long. I just finished having a look round the museum out the back. It's full of all his little robes. He's got about a hundred."

"There are some rather odd things in this town."

"Too right." Conor put the flyer in his pocket. "Not just here though. A woman back in Dingle owns a pub with one of these behind the bar. A long line of whiskey bottles with the Child of Prague in the middle."

"Did your mantelpiece have one?"

"Actually it didn't. We were the exception. My mother wasn't keen on knickknacks. She was all for holy wells and passage tombs and monastic ruins." He smiled wistfully. "She was like St. Kevin—she'd let a bird build a nest in her hand."

"I wish I could have known her," Kate said. "Do you think she would have liked me?"

"She does like you." He turned away from the doll-like figure and took her hand. "Sure I'd say she's stone mad about you."

Kate accepted the present tense construction without trying to rationalize it. It was one of those things she just trusted him to know.

"Come on," he said. "Winnie should be here in half an hour. Let's go sit on the steps and debrief the morning."

The main staircase was already crowded with people who had

the same idea, so they went to the more secluded side steps that connected to an adjoining building. They sat huddled together, speaking quietly, and when Kate finished the narration of her morning and its revelations, Conor whistled.

"Hard to decide who's using who, isn't it?"

"I think they all use each other as it suits them," she said. "How does Petra's story stack up against Sonia's?"

"Fairly well, but they're not a dead spit. Sonia admits Martin didn't meet her at a recital in Plzeň. She says it was a jazz bar where she was playing here in Prague, but I'm not swallowing that either. Nobody is coming clean about how they really connected, which might be important. She says her colleagues in the New Přemyslids group don't know about her and the Labuts. I can't decide if she's telling the truth, but I find it hard to believe she's been turned and planted there by the network. She just doesn't strike me as a white nationalist."

There was also a discrepancy in the baby daddy tale. As Sonia told it, the pregnancy was an accident and she'd planned to get an abortion, but Martin begged her to have the baby. He promised to leave his wife, but then it became clear Petra had known about the affair and the pregnancy from the beginning. They offered to adopt the child, and expected her to move out once it was born.

"She thought it might be a solution, although she didn't mention money had been offered," Conor said. "She couldn't tell Frank. The relationship violates every MI6 regulation in the book, and she wasn't sure she wanted a baby anyway. She says she didn't turn them down but never actually agreed to it either, and once she'd laid eyes on Leo she couldn't bear to leave him. Now she's never allowed to be alone with the baby. They ship him off somewhere when they need a babysitter, and Petra keeps the nursery locked when he's in it. Sonia says she's afraid of what they'd do if she tried to take him away with her, so she's been placating them with sexual favors until she gets a better idea."

Conor stood up to give passage to a troop of foot-dragging teenagers, all wearing the universal adolescent expression of bored exhaustion. He earned a grateful smile and a longer, backward glance from the female guide leading them.

"Catholic school trip," he explained. Kate squinted at their retreating backs, wondering what clues he'd seen that eluded her. "I saw them doing the rosary inside," he added, reading her mind and grinning as she yanked him down next to her.

"So we've got competing story lines. Who do you think is lying?"

"Everybody." He grew serious again. "The one thing I do believe is they genuinely love Leo, or at least the women do. Martin probably thinks a baby is only something else to collect. I don't really understand why Sonia is so paralyzed. She's a spy, for fuck's sake. I would have thought she'd been trained to crack harder nuts than this, and what could they do if she ran off with Leo? The Minister of Culture is going to sue his mistress for paternity rights?"

"This is a mess," Kate said, after a short silence. "Even if she hasn't been turned by this white nationalist group, it seems like she still might have a motive for wanting the Labuts dead. Maybe the New Přemyslids weren't planning to disrupt the symposium or assassinate Martin until she gave them the idea for it. Sonia could be using it to give herself an opportunity to get rid of both of them. Maybe that's her 'better idea.'"

"Yeah, I've thought about that." Conor sighed. "The problem is we can't be sure, and this operation is happening in two days."

"And we're supposed to be helping her with it." Kate turned to him as a new thought occurred to her. "How, by the way? Has she told you what we're supposed to do?"

He confirmed that she had, and Kate was relieved to hear their role was limited. Sonia would attend the concert but beg off the reception by claiming the onset of a migraine, an excuse she'd apparently used in the past. She'd stop at the market on the ground floor and buy medicine to make sure someone had seen her, go up to the apartment for twenty minutes, and then sneak back to the reception at Old Town Hall.

"She's got an accomplice from the network who will already be inside," Conor said. "Some guy named Karl. He's posing as a server from the catering company."

He paused and shifted to let a few more tourists file past—Italians this time. "The entrance and escape route is through the basement and up the back stairwell to a balcony overlooking the hall. He's making sure all the doors are unlocked for her, and our job is to make sure her way out is clear when the time comes. Her plan—as she describes it—is to fire a few random shots. She told us to hang about near a door leading to the back stairwell. If people panic and head for it, we're meant to make a show of pulling at it and shouting at anyone who comes near that it's locked so they'll head in another direction. She says she only needs thirty seconds once she's finished shooting up the windows or whatever the hell she has in mind."

"What if she shoots up the Labuts instead?" Kate asked.

"Well, exactly. Then we've a different problem altogether."

They reviewed their options and agreed none were good. Whatever her motive, Sonia might have fabricated the threat, and if the plan she'd presented to Frank was a cover for actually killing the minister and his wife so she could escape with her baby, they obviously needed to stop it from happening. That would ensure the safety of the Labuts, but if they were wrong the consequences for Sonia could be severe.

"This is her loyalty test," Conor said. "If nothing happens she's failed it and will be back under suspicion."

Their other option was to assume Sonia had been honest in sharing the plot against the minister. If the simulated attack came off as planned she'd take flak for botching it, but her cover with the nationalist network would remain intact with no harm done to Martin. If they guessed wrong in this scenario both Labuts could wind up dead.

"How likely is that, though?" Kate reasoned. "She knows we're going to be there. We're supposed to be helping her, and if she blew off somebody's head we'd obviously do the opposite. She'd be arrested and maybe even shot herself. Doesn't that prove she must be on the level?"

Conor hesitated. He'd grown unusually tense over the past few minutes and now began rubbing a thumb over the calloused fingertips of his hand. Kate recognized it—a habitual, brooding gesture—and anticipated he was about to tell her something she wouldn't like.

"It doesn't prove she's on the level," he said, "but it might prove she's too clever by half. Whatever she does, we'll still have to help her because MI6 can't afford to have her caught. Imagine the Czech police uncovering the fact that their Minister of Culture was assassinated by a British intelligence agent, and that she'd submitted the plan directly to MI6 ahead of time."

"Oh God." Deflated, Kate was out of ideas. She put a hand on his knee and spoke gently. "This is beyond us, Conor. It isn't just 'help desk' territory. It's Frank's decision. We have to tell him."

"No."

"That's crazy. Why not? We can't—" She snatched her hand away as he turned to her, his eyes stripped of all expression.

"Because I said so. I'm in charge of this mission. I decide what's beyond us, and I'm telling you *No*—so deal with it."

She jumped to her feet and Conor quickly stood up as well. Muffled by the churn of blood rushing to her head, his voice sounded distant and weak as he reached for her.

"Kate, I'm sorry—"

"Don't touch me." She slapped his arm away and stumbled

up the stairs, then whirled back to him. "How are you going to *deal* with me if I disagree? Use your 'skills' on me? Throw me face down in the street maybe? I've seen how good you are at that."

He looked up at her, his face stricken. "You can't believe that. Please, tell me you don't."

Kate remained quiet, but finally shook her head. She took a deep breath. Releasing it, she turned away from Conor and walked back towards the church. "Don't follow me."

Back inside she roamed up and down the aisles under the eyes of leering cherubs, drawing in air thick with the smell of damp plaster and candle wax, agonizing over how to face a crisis that wasn't the kind she'd ever expected.

She'd seen it happen before: she'd watched the light in Conor's eyes fade into a dangerous stare of detachment; she'd heard his lilting voice grow flat and cutting—she'd seen him turn into someone deadly. But Kate had never experienced it directed at her, and the impact of it rocked her like a physical blow. She knew he hadn't meant to hurt her, but she wondered how much that really mattered.

She ended up at the side chapel of Teresa of Avila, studying a painting of the saint with her arms stretched out, reclining in the embrace of an angel while he, with tender serenity, prepared to thrust a needle-like spear through her chest. Kate read the inscription beneath the painting. *Pierced by the Lance of God's Love.*

"Nope." She swiveled away and marched towards the door. "Hell, no."

Conor was on the steps where she'd left him, sitting with his back against the wall, knees raised, arms crossed over them and his head bowed over both. Forgetting how he reacted when startled, she touched his shoulder and he predictably shot up, nearly on his feet before he saw her. He fell back, regarding her sadly. Kate crouched in front of him, her voice low and fierce.

"I recognize your authority, but not your right to treat me like that. You can yell, whine, argue—you can tell me to shut the hell up, if you want. But if you ever want"—she faltered before continuing—"If you want a future with me, you need to always remember who I am, and you can't ever do that again. You can't talk to me, or look at me, like a   a …"

"Like a spy," he said. "Like a fucked-up operative with blood on his hands."

Seeing his misery, Kate softened her tone but nodded. "It's hard enough when you do it to someone else—hearing your voice, watching you change—but I can tolerate it. When you direct all that at me, though … no. I won't put up with that."

"Jesus. Of course not. Why should you?" He rested his head against the wall and closed his eyes. "I'm so sorry, Kate."

"I know you are, but saying you're sorry doesn't mean enough. You can't ever do it again."

"I won't. I promise."

"Is it a promise you can keep?"

"Easily."

Satisfied, Kate relented. "You may think I'm through with this, but I'm not. This is not our last mission together." She gave his chin a light pinch. So deal with it."

Conor opened his eyes, and Kate welcomed the return of their familiar gleam. So dark and beautiful. So crowded with painful memories and mystic glimpses. With a smile he seemed afraid to trust, he nodded.

"I'm glad."

17

For a minute, he'd lost her. Conor knew that's how he would always remember it, like a person remembers the moment of death after being revived. Not as a narrow escape, or as something that almost or could have happened, but as something that did. She didn't *stay* lost—unbelievably, miraculously—but it didn't change the essential truth of the event. For a minute—a minute that lasted years—he'd felt her absence, complete and indelible. He would cut off his own arm to avoid feeling anything like it ever again.

Sitting next to Kate on the steps again, Conor began to recover an awareness of his surroundings. He heard the rumble of traffic and watched a tram roll to a stop in front of the church. It released a bundle of humanity and sucked in another before trundling down the street. The world was turning again—or at least he noticed it again—and he realized Kate was speaking to him.

"Why don't you want to tell Frank?"

He fingered the edge of the step next to his knee, advancing the erosion of its cement repair work. "Because I know what he'll do."

"Call off the operation?"

"Not only that. Our first mission here was to help with a defection. I made a mess of it, but Sonia is really the one responsible for its failure. She burned her bridges with Frank when she exposed Ghorbani. If he thought he couldn't trust her for this operation either, I've no doubt he'd return the favor by burning her."

Kate looked confused. "You said MI6 couldn't afford to have the Czechs know about her."

"He wouldn't give her to the police. Frank will blow her cover with the New Přemyslids and let them take care of her."

"Would he really do that?" Her question came after a long, shocked silence and Conor didn't answer. The truth was, his greater fear was that Frank would expect him to take care of Sonia. "So, you're going to let her go through with it," Kate said.

"I can't do that either. She can't be trusted."

"What other choice do you have?"

Continuing to rub at the crumbling stone, he avoided her eyes. "To do it myself. It's only a matter of making a big enough noise, which I can do as well as she can. Her network colleagues won't know it wasn't her making it, so the operation works the way it should. She gets her cover, and everyone stays safe."

Conor waited for the objections, which weren't long in coming, but he could tell Kate was trying to remain dispassionate.

"You'd need a weapon. You can't risk bringing the Walther in through the front door, so it would have to be hers. Even if she's innocent I doubt she'll want to just turn the whole operation over to you."

"There are some loose ends, but I'll work them out." He brushed his dusty fingers against his jeans and finally looked at her. "Unless you can think of something else?"

He asked in all sincerity and Kate took it that way, but after some reflection she gave it up. "Nothing that seems any better. Or safer," she added unhappily.

Hesitantly, Conor slipped an arm around her waist, relaxing as she shifted closer. "It'll be all right, love. Trust me."

"I do." She leaned her head against his shoulder. "On top of all this drama, you're performing the day after tomorrow and we haven't even talked about that. How will you manage it? You were already nervous and this can't have helped."

"Oddly enough, it has. I think the nerves have been knocked clean out of me. I was never concerned about the Mozart, and I'm not worried about the Kreutzer anymore either. I'm more bothered about this damned recital with Sonia, assuming she's still around by Wednesday to perform it."

"Why? Doesn't she play well?"

"Her playing is gorgeous, but the sonata we're doing is meant to be romantic—Strauss was in love when he wrote it—and her interpretation is a bit over the top. She's not finding the right sort of passion to fit the mood."

"How ironic," Kate remarked. "So unlike her accompanist." She lifted her lips to him and Conor gave them a timid kiss, still inhibited by his earlier behavior, but she drew him closer.

"Don't be afraid anymore," she said softly. "This means I've forgiven you."

A minute later, they separated at the sound of a slight cough behind them.

"Sorry for interrupting, only I didn't want to leave the impression of being late."

Conor sat back on the steps and looked up at Winnie, surprised by how pleased he was to see him. Even now, after he'd bungled the assignment of watching Ghorbani—a basic task for someone in the business of surveillance—it was hard not to like the guy and feel some protective concern for his hapless vulnerability.

Their onetime stalker appeared weary and rumpled but otherwise unscathed by the adventure in Hřensko. He seemed pleased to see them as well—particularly Kate. He shyly bowed his head to her and she returned his greeting with an affectionate smile.

"How are you then, Winnie?" Conor asked. "Bit of a head this morning?"

Obviously still smarting from his failure, the man's pale cheeks colored. "I won't deny it. I should have known the schnapps would be a mistake." He gave a rueful shrug. "I've let me self down as well as you, and I'm ashamed of it."

"Don't take it so hard," Kate said. "You did your best. None of us expected him to disappear."

Conor smiled at her tenderhearted absolution, but added his own reassurance. "You're not the only one to blame either. I gave him too much information and he reacted badly to it. Lesson learned for all of us." He gave the strap of Kate's shoulder bag a gentle tug. "I vote we let him go home. What do you say?"

"I think he's earned it."

They rose together, and when she presented his passport Winnie hesitated, appearing oddly reluctant to accept it, but then he took it from her hands with another bob of gratitude, and handed back Kate's phone.

"I suppose the arsehole's still missing? He's not turned up in the meantime?"

"No sign of him yet," Conor confirmed.

Winnie's face grew thoughtful as he fanned the pages of the passport. "You're decent people, not a bit how the Zimmer House bloke described you, and not up to anything like the things he was expecting. I'm to send him a report of all the money you've spent over here—liquor tabs from restaurants and nightclubs, lists of the shops you've visited and the price paid for all the fancy rubbish you buy—room service bills, that sort of thing."

"Room service," Kate echoed. "It sounds like a fantastic trip. I wish we were on it."

"So do I." Winnie gave her a dispirited glance and looked down at the ground. "The thing is, I don't feel happy about making trouble for you, but I can't tell him what you're really doing can I? When I got home, the black cars would be coming for me by the time I reached Cricklewood."

"They'd be waiting for you at the airport," Conor said. He thought it unlikely they'd be doing anything of the sort, but a healthy fear of consequences seemed important to reinforce and he was beginning to understand where all this was headed. "I get the drift. You're on the horns of a dilemma and you want us to help."

Winnie looked relieved. "I'd be grateful for assistance—if you're willing?"

"Sure why not? We've nothing else on our minds today, but let's walk for a bit." He looked at Kate. "I feel like we've been here long enough."

"Amen to that," she agreed immediately. "Which direction?"

"You're the one with the city map stitched inside your eyelids. We're following you."

As they descended the stairs with Winnie trailing after them, Conor swept a final gaze over the church, fixing it in his mind as the site of another lesson learned which would be painful to remember but too important to forget.

They walked in the direction of the restaurant where they were meeting Eckhard for lunch and ended up in a quiet park overlooking the river. It was close to one o'clock and the sun was hot and bright, sparkling on the water and winking off the windows of the Old Town buildings on the opposite bank.

Sitting on a park bench with Winnie sandwiched in the middle, they faced the river and Conor bluntly described the issue.

"Stop me if I go off track with this. I'd assumed Zimmer House hired you as a precaution to protect Kate's safety, which is insulting enough to both of us, but that wasn't even the point, was it? Guido Brottman wants hard evidence of my unscrupulous motives, and without it you're afraid of not being paid for the trouble you've taken."

Without denying the facts, Winnie quibbled with the characterization. "It's the expenses that mainly concern me, of course. Air tickets and hotels, car hire—it's not cheap, Prague, and I had to draw on funds not strictly my own. Funds that are expected back with interest. Within a strict timeframe."

"You're in trouble with a loan shark."

Perspiring lightly, Winnie loosened his collar and stretched his neck. "I engaged a firm which provides assistance on short notice."

Kate abruptly shifted on the bench with a choking grunt. Conor was tempted to continue on this farcical line to tickle an outright laugh out of her but decided to cut to the chase.

"So what are you suggesting here, Winnie—extortion? No. All right," he said, responding to the man's wordless horror. "Then I expect you're hoping to finish the job without staining our reputation, but I don't see how. We can't let you keep following us."

"Nor would I want to," Winnie quickly replied. "I've had my fill of that, but I was thinking perhaps I could offer my services, a sort of transferred allegiance, if you take my meaning."

"You want to work for *us*?" Kate's amazement was transparent and Conor chimed in, equally incredulous.

"Doing what, for fuck's sake?"

After turning his head back and forth between them with a force threatening whiplash, Winnie braced his hands on his thin knees. He stood up and turned to address them both at once.

"It's not only a matter of finances," he said with careful dignity. "It's a matter of pride, really. I know I've done nothing to impress, but I'm not half the dozy muppet you think and I'd like the chance to prove it."

"Fair enough," Conor conceded. "But again, by doing what?"

"By tracking down this bloke Farid. It seems he was important to you, but now he's done a runner and unless I'm wrong you've made no plan to find him."

Conor exchanged a long look with Kate. He was absolutely right. They hadn't forgotten about Ghorbani, but there were too many balls in the air at this point and he had pretty much tossed that one off to the side.

"How—" Kate stopped, apparently questioning her authority to pursue the idea, but Conor urged her to continue. He was game for a little more insanity if she was. "How would you go about it?"

"He left his jacket behind," Winnie said, pleased to be taken seriously. "I found a hotel room key in the pocket. No name or address, but there's the room number, and I thought I could poke around a bit, see if I could find the place."

Conor had to admit it was a solid idea. "He seemed to be a regular at the Prašná Věž. You might go there tonight and see whether the bartender or anyone else knows where he was staying."

"Protcha Veg is it? Crikey, you'll need to spell that one for me." Winnie removed a small pad and pen from the pocket of his sports jacket and grinned at them, his fingers poised over the paper. "It's agreed then? You'll have me on for the job?"

Conor moved down the bench to sit beside Kate and they studied the man before them. "What do you think?" he asked.

"We're probably crazy, but I say we do it. What could go wrong?" Her cheeks dimpled with the slow smile that had left him spellbound the first time he'd seen it.

"Okay, then. Contract accepted." He got up to shake Winnie's hand and squinted a warning at him. "Nothing fancy. If you find him, keep your distance and let us know. We don't want to scare him off again."

"How will I reach you?" Winnie asked. "Should I give you a bell if I've something to report?"

"Jaysus, no. Don't use the phone again." Conor thought for a minute. "I'll give you the address where we're staying. Buy a roll of white adhesive tape, and if you need to communicate put a strip of it on the lamppost in front of the building as a signal and leave the message for us at your hotel. If it's needed, we'll leave one for you, and we'll take it from there. Got it?"

Nodding vigorously, he wrung Conor's hand with surprising strength. "I'm chuffed, mate. Truly pleased, and I won't let you down again. I swear it."

They parted a few minutes later, Winnie towards his hotel to get some rest before his night shift, and Conor and Kate in the direction of the Café de Paris for their lunch date. Whenever possible, Eckhard made it a habit to have a meal with his soloist before a performance, believing the experience of sharing good food and wine in a convivial atmosphere helped strengthen the bond between conductor and artist.

Conor already shared a bond with his maestro that had a tensile strength it would be hard to break, but he was happy for any excuse for a hot meal, and the emotional strain of the morning had made him ravenous.

The restaurant he and Kate stepped into was small and unpretentious, and filled with a delicious meaty aroma. They found the conductor already seated near the window on a red-leather banquette. A sweating bottle of white wine sat in an ice bucket in front of him.

"No, you are not late." Eckhard waved off their apologies. "I was early. Come, this is a spectacular Sancerre. You must try it, both of you."

He was wearing a white shirt, open at the neck to reveal a triangle of wiry dark hair, and had rolled the sleeves up to his elbows. As he poured for them, Conor watched the muscles rippling in his powerful forearms, wondering how often the conductor had been pressed into service to advance one of Frank's covert objectives. This gave him an idea for dealing with one of the loose ends he was facing. He considered it as the meal proceeded, and by the time dessert arrived he'd reached a decision. After cracking the brittle surface of his crème brûlée, he set the spoon aside on the table.

"Eckhard, I think I'm going to need your help with something."

The smell of exertion. He'd forgotten about it, the scent that always wafted over him as he walked out to join the orchestra. Its character wasn't that of the locker room; no grassy smells of the outdoors or muzzy odors of athletic gear and gym socks. It was hot lights on dark suits growing damp with perspiration; it was the blend of overheated cologne and makeup, the spicy tang of rosin and old wood. It was heaven. He followed Eckhard, threading a path through the music stands, and after the ritual handshake with the concertmaster he took possession of the small pocket of space next to the conductor's podium.

There wasn't much time to look around, but in the few seconds before the opening Conor took in the shadowed elegance of the Mirror Chapel along with a sea of beautifully dressed strangers. These were the symposium's attendees— ministers, ambassadors, UNESCO representatives and curators of the arts, many accompanied by spouses—all with their faces turned to him, relaxed and expectant.

In the front row, Kate was sitting with the Labuts and Sonia. She was wearing a midnight blue dress, and both its scoop-necked bodice and three-quarter length sleeves were made entirely of lace. She'd been thrilled to learn a ball gown wasn't required for the evening. "I'll be able to run this time, if I need to," she'd observed earlier, laying the dress on the bed. Conor had taken one look at it and asked her to be sure not to sit next to Martin.

He saw she'd humored him. She was separated from the minister's wandering hands by both Sonia and Petra, who sat next to her husband with a hand on his thigh. Kate was sitting very straight, fingering a small diamond pendant and looking nervous on his behalf. Their eyes met for a second and he flashed her a smile. Then the audience faded from sight and Kate disappeared from his mind entirely as Eckhard picked up the baton, and Mozart's cheerful "Allegro aperto" filled the hall.

He waited calmly for his moment and thought it fitting to have his second debut begin with a solo entrance. As the theme exposition ended he lifted the violin to his shoulder, and when the music came to an abrupt halt he sent the first soaring notes of a six-measure adagio out into the silence. The melody hung in the air of the chapel like something ripe and sweet, and he savored it in a way he could not have if the entrance had been something more explosive. It was rich, expressive, and it was exactly right.

When the concerto and its ovations had ended, the chamber orchestra went to a large classroom to pack up their instruments. Conor thanked the musicians, shaking hands with each of them, and accepted his conductor's accolades. Then he retreated to a far corner of the room and sat on a folding chair, staring down at the violin lying across his knees. After a few minutes a shadow fell across the floor in front of him. He looked up at Eckhard, opened his mouth to speak, and failing closed it again.

"A performance like this takes something from you." The conductor removed his tailcoat and squatted down with his elbows on his knees, eye-to-eye with Conor. "From all musicians at times, but from you more often, I think." He ran a finger over the violin's scroll. "This has no life without yours. You drain your own to give her voice expression. In return, this Pressenda gives you a tone as complex as any I've heard from more famous instruments, but when the music stops everything must somehow be made to fit inside you again. It's the old feeling, yes? Intense, exhausting—and isn't it wonderful to have it back again?" He gave Conor's knee an affectionate slap and stood up. "If you think that was something, wait until the Kreutzer."

Conor smiled, then laughed softly, shaking his head. "You're a very wise man, Maestro."

"Good for many things, eh?" Eckhard gave him a wink.

"Right." Vaguely, he looked at the clock over the door and came to his senses with a jerk. "Oh, Jaysus. Right. We need to get going. This feckin' night is just beginning."

18

⌐

He left his violin with one of the orchestra members, all of whom were staying at the hotel he and Kate had left a few days earlier. The musician was storing his cello in the safe in the manager's office and had agreed to have the Pressenda placed there as well.

When Conor left the chapel with Eckhard, Kate and the Labuts were waiting outside along with straggling members of the audience. Sonia had disappeared, having already provided her migraine excuse, and Martin dismissed Conor's obligatory concern with a sniff. He took Petra's hand and gave it a gentle swing.

"It happens sometimes. She will be fine. Shall we go? It's only a short walk."

Exiting the complex, they made their way along the lanes of the Old Town pedestrian district, passing brightly lit shops and restaurant chalkboards promising traditional Czech meals. Eckhard strolled with the Labuts, still discussing the concert, while Conor and Kate followed several yards behind. As further proof her learning curve was shrinking, Kate had removed her heels for the trip over the cobblestones, replacing them with black satin shoes that looked like slippers.

"How did you even fit them in your purse?" Conor asked, digging in his pocket for the wristwatch he'd removed just before the performance.

"They're ballet flats. They fold."

"Folding shoes. That's brilliant." He checked the watch as he fastened the strap. "Are you following the time? How long has she been gone?"

"She left about five minutes before you came out, so if she's still planning for eight o'clock she'll be back in an hour." Kate looped an arm around his. "Can't we linger for at least a minute longer on how amazing you were tonight?"

"Since you put it that way ..." He laughed. "You enjoyed it, then?"

Kate stopped and pulled him around to face her. "You're special in so many ways, and tonight I got to see how other people look when they start to recognize it. You were magnificent, Conor. You could have gone on for another hour and nobody would have moved."

"Thank you." He wrapped an arm around her as they resumed walking. "That's better than a hundred curtain calls."

It wasn't quite dark when they reached the main square, but the large, open area was already assuming its nightly New Year's Eve atmosphere. Visitors were pouring in from the streets at the corners to sample the attractions, which included street music, fire-eating magicians and rotisseries spinning sides of ham. At Old Town Hall the seven o'clock performance of the astronomical clock had just ended. A traffic jam quickly formed as dispersing spectators tangled with symposium guests filing in for the reception.

Kate stopped to put her heels back on and Conor looked up ahead at Eckhard. He was easily visible, standing at least three inches above the next tallest man in the crowd. Before passing through the doorway, the conductor took a phone from his pocket and frowned in annoyance as he looked at it.

"I'm sorry," he said to the Labuts. "I've missed a call that's really quite important and I must return it. I'll step away and rejoin you shortly."

He slipped back through the crowd with surprising grace for a man so large and repeated the story to Conor and Kate. Promising to have a glass of wine waiting, they shared a conspiratorial smile with him before he disappeared around the corner.

Do you think he'll be okay?" Kate asked.

Eckhard had readily agreed to the role he'd been asked to take on that evening. His assignment was to double back to the Charles Bridge and wait for Sonia to appear, then use his phone to signal updates as he followed her to the Town Hall. At first, Conor was surprised by his composed acceptance, but after giving it some thought realized he shouldn't be.

"I think he'll be fine. I've an idea it isn't the first time he's done this kind of thing."

The reception was on an upper floor in a two-storied ceremonial hall once used as the city's assembly room. The ubiquitous parquet here was laid in a square-basket pattern, and apart from two monumental wall paintings facing each other, the room had a simple, understated style. The lights had been dimmed, giving greater effect to the votive candles scattered around on high cocktail tables. The only other lighting came from two spotlights trained on a podium standing in front of a set of windows with a mirrored panel between them.

The balcony was on the opposite wall, facing the podium. Once the room had reached critical mass and the reception was underway, Conor ran his eyes over it with greater attention. The entire area was obscured by dark velvet drapes from end to end, just as Sonia had described it. Apparently, the heavy curtains had been put up to hide extensive renovation work from tour groups.

"She was right about the security as well," Conor said as they browsed the buffet table. "There isn't any in here at all."

Kate stayed focused on the skewer of prosciutto and melon she was adding to her plate. "I guess cultural ministers and UN officers don't rate much protection."

At first, a steady stream of guests approached to express admiration for Conor's performance. Gratifying, but also alarming. He hadn't anticipated being the center of attention, and was relieved when it finally subsided. After spending a few more minutes discussing the art of Alfons Mucha with the director of Prague's National Museum—an exchange he was happy to let Kate handle for both of them—they retreated to a table in the corner. He noted the Labuts were at a comfortable distance, conversing with another group of guests near the windows.

"I need to do a little reconnaissance," he said. "It's getting late."

Looking worried but resigned, Kate nodded. "Should I wait for you here?"

Conor poured the rest of his wine into her glass. "No, move around a little. Remember Sonia said someone from the network is disguised as a server? Have a look without seeming keen about it; see if you can spot which one is a fascist. I won't be more than five minutes."

He left through the door they'd been standing near, which led directly into a second ceremonial room, with another door on the right leading into a stairwell. This was the door Sonia had instructed them to guard. Moving up the stairs he arrived in a foyer—empty except for a coat rack in one corner—and found the door to the balcony propped open with a gallon can of primer. He made a quick inspection of the area—tricky in a darkness made even deeper by the heavy drapes. Although the seats had all been removed the floor was littered with drop cloths, tools and more paint cans. It smelled faintly of turpentine.

Careful not to disturb any items that would clatter, he picked up one of the folded cloths and made a mental note to stay well away from everything else. With one finger he moved the drapes aside, exposing a sliver of light from the reception hall, which seemed bright by comparison. He surveyed the activity below and saw Martin standing near the buffet table talking to Kate.

"Oh, feck off," Conor breathed. In a moment of solidarity, he forgave Sonia for wanting to do away with the promiscuous Minister of Culture—if, indeed, she did.

As if hearing Conor's command, Martin gave Kate's shoulder a caressing squeeze and walked away. He disappeared through a door in the far corner of the room, and at the same time Conor's phone began to vibrate: Eckhard's alert that Sonia was coming over the Charles Bridge. It lasted the length of one ring and stopped.

Conor went back into the foyer and hung the drop cloth over the coat rack, then tested the carpeted floor for any random creaks before hurrying downstairs to Kate.

"The first signal came through. I'd say she'll be here in about ten minutes. What's wrong? You look agitated."

"We have a small complication," Kate said. "The president is here."

"The president?"

She nodded. "Of the Czech Republic."

"Jaysus. No one said he was coming."

"Nobody thought he would. He was invited but his scheduler only confirmed him for the closing dinner and final concert. The organizers are trying to figure out how to entertain him and Martin wants to introduce you. You're the closest thing they have to a celebrity, since Eckhard isn't here."

"Bloody hell." Conor scanned the room. "Well, it has to be now and quick, so where is he?"

Kate indicated the door Martin had disappeared through a

minute earlier. They went to it, announcing themselves to the security officer guarding the threshold. As he escorted them through, Conor noted that even the president's security detail was light, at least by western standards—one at the door and two inside it. The muted atmosphere was in sharp contrast to the noisy chatter in the spacious hall next to it, and the room itself was the most ornate Conor had seen yet. Decorated in a Gothic style and with heraldic insignia lining the walls, it was lit by chandeliers hanging from a painted coffered ceiling. In the middle, Martin stood with the Czech president, a burly man with a drooping white mustache that gave him a permanent frown. Around them, a knot of government functionaries anxiously hovered. They seemed to be feeling the strain of amusing a man who looked impervious to any such effort.

Unlike them, Martin seemed at ease. It reminded Conor of earlier information Eckhard had provided—that Martin was an old and close friend of the president, and that the minister's influence on migration policy had made him a target for the white nationalists. Conor wasn't convinced their fears were valid—the president didn't look like he would be easily influenced.

Since other guests had also been invited for presentation they waited inside the door for their introduction, Conor impatiently fiddling with the phone in his left hand. At last, Martin beckoned them forward with a smile.

"Here is our very talented virtuoso, Mr. President. This is Conor McBride and his lovely lady, Kate Chatham. You are in for a treat at the Rudolfinum this Saturday."

The president looked dubious but extended a hand, his lips barely moving in response to Conor's greeting and expressions of deep honor.

"A British musician? We rarely see them at the Rudolfinum."

"You won't on Saturday either, sir. I'm Irish." He produced his best artificial smile, and kept it glued in place while his left hand jumped as though electrified. The second signal, meaning Sonia had reached the square outside. Conor smoothly passed the vibrating phone over to Kate.

"Oh?" The president's small eyes brightened. "We have many Irish pubs here in Prague."

"You have. Unfortunately, I've only seen them from the outside."

While the assembled company chuckled at his incomparable wit he darted a glance at Kate, begging her to think of something as she stood staring at the phone.

"I enjoy a glass of Irish whiskey at times," the president droned on, and then launched into an oration on the "Troubles" of Northern Ireland while Conor squirmed. Even without a ticking clock he would have despised this conversational sinkhole. More often than not it was informed by boozy romanticism instead of any practical knowledge of Irish history or current events.

"I wonder what has become of Maestro Eckhard," Martin cut in when his friend at last paused to draw breath. "He has been very long with his phone call. I hope he won't miss my public words of welcome."

Conor fastened on the comment like a man grabbing a lifeboat. "Sure look, I think he's back now." He turned to Kate. "Wasn't that him at the bar? Just as we came in here?" Without waiting for her reply he swung back to the president. "Will I track him down for you, Mr. President? He'll be delighted to meet you." He offered an obsequious bow and took Kate's arm, already turning away. "It's been such an honor, sir. I look forward to playing for you on Saturday."

They were almost clear when, on the way out the door, they nearly collided with Petra coming in the opposite direction. She looked flushed and happy and was on the arm of a ruddy-cheeked soldier.

"I see you've met the 'Old Stick.'" She flashed her wide,

suggestive smile. "Only my nickname for him, of course. This is my friend Lukas Hasek of the Castle Guard. He's on leave from the motorcycle unit." She gave the man's hand a firm pat. "I'm afraid he speaks no English. He doesn't speak much at all, but this is not a problem."

Nodding a quick greeting, Conor explained his obligation to find Eckhard and abruptly walked away, leaving Kate on the hook with the vampire and her paramour. He'd be paying for that, later.

Although tempted to sprint, he doggedly kept an even pace while crossing the room, but after passing through the door in the rear corner he did begin to run, noiselessly. As he stepped into the foyer adjacent to the balcony, Conor heard a rhythmic swish of fabric echoing in the stairwell below him. Moving from the stairs, he pressed himself into a shadowed corner behind the coat rack.

When she appeared, Sonia turned to the left and continued on through the balcony door without glancing in his direction. Conor watched her examine the platform in the darkness as he'd done earlier, and when she parted the velvet drapes an inch-wide shaft of light illuminated both her face and her remarkable, chrome-plated hair. Still dressed as she'd been at the concert—a sleeveless black gown in a billowing pleated fabric reaching down to her calves—she managed to look like the perfect assassin and at the same time the farthest thing from it.

He'd allowed Kate to think he would try gaining Sonia's cooperation, but in fact conversational debate formed no part of Conor's strategy. Whether from pride or ill-intent, the woman wasn't about to be persuaded. A session of hand-to-hand combat was too risky for both of them—neither could afford to cause a racket—so he'd placed his hopes on an unconventional tactic. If it didn't work, he'd try debate.

Still watching her, Conor carefully took the drop cloth from the coat rack where he'd left it earlier and silently inched along the wall to the right of the door. Stepping into the opening, he whispered urgently.

"Sonia, we've got a problem."

It worked better than he'd dared to hope. She gave a start at the sound of his voice, but didn't register the threat until she'd turned to face him, and by then it was too late. Before she could recover, or even raise her arms, Conor stepped forward, enveloping her with the cloth as through taking her into a protective embrace. By the time her shock had transitioned to rage he had it snugly twisted around her from shoulders to thighs—a makeshift, paint-spattered cocoon.

"What the fuck are you doing?" Her whispering scream blew against his ear, which she then tried to bite as Conor scooped an arm around her waist.

"Relieving you of duty."

He lifted Sonia, struggling not to drop her while she kicked and thrashed, and set her down in the foyer, amazed that an old farming trick he used for transporting calves could work so well on a human being. After making certain the wrapping job would hold, Conor lowered her as gently as he could manage and she would allow, and propped her against the wall. He went back to close the door, then hit the switch next to it. Returning, he squatted in front of her, and under the weak yellow light filling the foyer, turned her face to him.

"Look me in the eye and tell me you weren't planning to kill someone here tonight."

She met his eyes without flinching. "This is insane, Conor. Of course not. For God's sake, let me out of this thing and go back downstairs. Go down and do what you were assigned to do."

Conor bowed his head and stared at the floor between his

knees, realizing how much he'd wanted to be wrong, shaken by the implication of being right. "You've misplayed it, Sonia. You were supposed to look surprised."

She did look startled then, but in the next instant exploded in quiet fury. "It is my operation. Frank assigned it to me, not you, yes? I could do it alone but he told you to help me. To help me," she said again, spitting the words at him. "It's not for you to do. You don't understand. You're not capable."

"You think I'm not capable of making a little harmless noise? Because that's what Frank is expecting. This is a simulation. You remember that, right?" Conor took a deep breath, dreading what he needed to do next. "I'm going to take the gun from you, now."

He knew it was in a holster on her thigh; she'd told him about that earlier in the day. As soon as his fingers touched the edge of her dress, Sonia launched a new strategy.

"Does it make you feel like a strong man? To tie up a woman and put your hands up her dress?" She spread her legs apart, her eyes mocking and hard, daring him to continue.

Conor sighed, lowering his hands. Beyond the closed balcony door he heard the sound of an amplified voice and of the reception crowd gradually settling down to listen. The speaker was introducing Martin. "I'm going to take the gun from you now," he repeated quietly. "You can do as you like, but you'll only make it worse for both of us."

He tried to keep his hand from touching her as he searched for the gun, swearing under his breath when he didn't find it on her right leg. Switching sides, Conor repeated the motion and connected with the holster halfway up the inside of her left thigh. After some awkward fumbling, he realized the complicated construction was necessary to handle not only the weight of the gun, but also that of a silencer and tactical light, tucked into adjoining slots.

"You weren't intending to make much noise at all, were you?"

He removed the Ruger and its various attachments. Looking at Sonia, he saw her face had lost its jeering scowl. She looked terrified.

"Please. I will end up dead because of you."

Her genuine fear unsettled Conor. "Listen. I'll make it look convincing—a solid near miss, I promise. Sure I'll even keep the silencer, and they'll never know it wasn't you. The point was to prove your loyalty by planning the job and making the attempt. That can still work."

"My loyalty was never in question, but it will be now. Farid was the only threat. He suspected I was with MI6, he hinted at it. It's why I exposed him first—to guarantee he would only appear vindictive if he tried later to do the same to me."

He put the weapon's attachments in his pockets and helplessly spread his hands. "This is the plan you designed, Sonia. You told Frank you needed this operation, and it isn't my fault you lied about it. We can call the whole thing off, if you like, but I can't let you kill the guy, for fuck's sake. You must understand that?"

She closed her eyes, shaking her head. "It's you who doesn't understand."

"Right," Conor said, heading for the balcony door. He knew he was missing something but had no alternative.

"Wait. Please," Sonia called, panicking now. "It's not Martin. He's not the target."

He froze with his hand on the wall switch, and slowly turned to stare at her. "Who is the target then?"

"The president," she said, avoiding his eyes. "He was my assignment."

"Your assignment was the president?" Conor let the news sink in, and then was back across the foyer in two long strides. He wrenched her head up to look at him. "Are you insane? Did you think we were going to make the road clear and all the lights green for you after you'd assassinated a head of state?"

"No? What would you have done, then?" She sounded tired now. "Turn your MI6 colleague over to the Czech police? Kill me yourself? It doesn't matter. I wasn't going to shoot him, but I don't expect you to believe it."

"How can I?"

"Yes, it's impossible," she agreed listlessly. "Only, if it is to be a near miss, make sure to aim carefully and miss the correct target. This is all I meant." Sonia nodded at the door. "You should go now."

Straightening, Conor stood looking down at her for several seconds, then reached around to loosen the wrapping at her back. "Start working your way out now. By the time it's off I'll be done and we'll both get the hell out of here."

He walked away and hit the lights, looking back at her. Sonia lay slumped against the wall in the darkness, limp and motionless, not even trying to get free.

19

Once on the balcony, Conor eased the door shut behind him and put his back against it, wary of moving in any direction until his eyes adjusted and his stress level settled. In the hall below, the introductory remarks continued, and for once he was thankful for long-winded bureaucrats. He took the silencer from his pocket and screwed it in place, making sure the fit was airtight while listening to the speaker alternate between Czech and English in a sonorous tenor.

When he felt confident of his footing and his nerves, he moved forward and put an eye to the thin crack between the drapes. Apart from the man at the podium the scene hadn't changed much since the last time he'd looked. People were still where they'd been standing when called to order, bunched together in small groups. They were listening quietly but showing signs of restlessness; one bejeweled woman at the front was trying—unsuccessfully—to stifle an emphysemic cough.

Methodically scanning the room, Conor allowed himself to sink into the mentality of an assassin, trying to visualize what Sonia had been planning, knowing he didn't have the whole story. He didn't doubt what she'd told him; frankly it made more sense. The New Přemyslids wanted a bigger disruption than could be achieved by killing a minor official in an obscure ministry. Whether she'd have gone through with the assassination or not was an open question, but whatever her intentions towards the Czech president, Conor remained convinced Sonia had been planning to kill Martin.

Looking down, he studied the minister's chiseled profile. He was standing near the wall with the same officials Conor had seen earlier with the president. They hadn't strayed far from the room where he'd met them, and since the security officer hadn't left his post by the door he assumed the president was still inside—no doubt preparing for his dramatic, surprise entrance.

Surprise entrance.

With vivid comprehension, Conor realized the piece he'd been missing. He jerked back from the curtain, barely avoiding a collision with a toolbox on the floor.

The president wasn't on the guest list. His arrival had been unexpected. How could the New Přemyslids have planned on assassinating the man at an event no one knew he would attend? Obviously because somebody did know he'd be there, and knew he would arrive with a nominal security detail to retain the charm of an unplanned appearance.

The president of the Czech Republic—a man who looked incapable of whimsy—had not concocted this bit of showmanship on his own. Someone had done it for him.

The speaker finally concluded his introduction. A swell of relieved applause filled the hall, and under its cover Conor slammed back through the door into the foyer.

"Who told you to kill the president?"

Sitting exactly as he'd left her, Sonia refused to meet his eyes. "It was the network."

"The network, the network." Conor reached down, pulling her up from the floor. "I'm after gettin' thick from all the bullshit, Sonia. A network isn't a person. Who gave you the order? The racist, neo-Nazi fecker leading it, I suppose? The top Přemyslid. And who's he, I wonder?" He took her by the shoulders, pinning them to the wall as she tried to twist away. "I'm guessing his name is Martin Labut. Have I got it right, now?"

She tensed, but then relaxed as though exhausted. "Yes. You've got it right."

"You infiltrated the network by sleeping with the leader, got closer by getting pregnant and moving in with him, and now you want to kill him before he discovers his handpicked assassin is an MI6 agent." He gave her shoulders a small shake. "Have I got that right, as well?"

"In a general sense, yes, but it's not only to save myself. I want to kill him before he discovers his son is half-Jewish." Even with the cloth imprisoning her like a strait-jacket Sonia looked defiant. "Imagine a man who has created a path for himself to become president as soon as the murdered one is buried, who looks forward to the day when he will have the power to force ethnic minorities out of the country and create a 'pure' Bohemian society. Will such a man have tender feelings for the offspring of his Jewish mistress? No. He is a monster. He will act as monsters do. Maybe you can't believe that either, but it's true."

Releasing her arms Conor stepped back, and in the background heard Martin beginning his "words of welcome" to mark the formal opening of the symposium. The strange language made no impression, but the words weren't as important as the character of the minister's voice. Like the proverbial wizard behind the curtain it sounded larger than life—forceful, charismatic, and cheerfully confident—a voice suggesting its owner expected something momentous from the evening.

"I believe you."

Hoping he wasn't inviting a different kind of struggle, Conor turned Sonia around and began pulling at the cloth he'd wound around her. He didn't trust her, but she wasn't the enemy, and he couldn't tolerate arguing with the woman when she was wrapped up like a mummy. When she was free, he threw the cloth into the corner.

"What about Ghorbani? And the others in the network? Do they know their colleague Greta has been leading a double life as mistress to their leader?"

"Of course not," she said, wrapping her arms around herself, as if the cloth had been keeping her warm. "Farid only knew of my flat near the botanical gardens. And he's never met Martin. The circle of people who know he is the leader of the New Přemyslids is quite small. Karl—the man who let me in the building tonight—he plays that role, allowing Martin to remain hidden."

Conor nodded. "Well, at least that makes sense, but why have you been lying to me and Kate, for the love of God? We're your partners on this operation."

"And you have been here for less than a week." Sonia glared at him. "Not for the past year, watching British intelligence officers and their Czech counterparts behaving like clowns, feuding with each other, leaking information, and risking the lives of their agents. How could I trust anyone in MI6, much less the Czech BIS? They care nothing for me or my son, only for their childish rivalries. Can you imagine how it feels, to be a pawn in this kind of game?"

"I can, actually," Conor said, empathizing with her helpless desperation. He'd had a bellyful himself not so very long ago. "It doesn't mean I'm going to murder a man in cold blood, or let you do it either."

"So noble," she jeered. "I will be sure to tell Gustav's widow that the man who killed her husband on the E55 highway is quite a sensitive creature."

Her derisive smile faltered as she looked at his face. He let the glacial silence answer for him, and it lengthened until they heard

Martin transitioning to his special announcement. First in Czech, and then in English, he described the pleasure of introducing the evening's final speaker and honored guest. Conor reached back to the inside pocket of his tailcoat and removed the gun.

"It seems you've forgotten the sensitive creature has your weapon and could end this operation without firing a shot. I assume you'd prefer otherwise."

"Of course." Sonia frowned, absently smoothing the pleats in her dress. "Although I wonder, will it make a difference? Either way he will live through the night, and I will have failed, in all respects. Still, a near miss would be easier to explain to him."

He left her sitting on the stairs with her back to the door. Once on the other side of it he shot the vertical locking bolt into place as an added precaution against interference. Taking up his position behind the drapes, Conor found it more comfortable to watch Martin by eyeing him down the length of his gun barrel. He had a more complete explanation now for the animus he'd felt saturating the atmosphere in the Labut household, and an even better reason to loathe the man responsible for it.

Like a consummate spy, the Minister of Culture had devised a clever legend for himself—the urbane intellectual and libertine, his vices an open secret but limited to an unapologetic lifestyle. Who would expect a man of sophistication and liberal tastes had darker secrets to protect, or that he could be a cultivator of ignorance, bigotry, and hatred? It was the sort of hoax that had supported the rise of nationalist despots down through history, and it sickened Conor to think how easily Martin made use of it.

He kept the Ruger trained on the minister. A thin stream of sweat ran down the side of his face as he alternated his aim between the man's head and the more challenging heart-and-lung circle below it.

"Wrap it up, for Jesus' sake," he said through gritted teeth, disturbed by the strength of his temptation to take the short cut.

With some effort, he shifted his attention to the area around and behind the podium, looking for a more appropriate target, and settled on something just as Martin finally roared his exultant invitation for the crowd to join him in welcoming the leader of the republic.

The president emerged from the door in the corner and the room erupted in applause. From the corner of his eye Conor watched his progress across the room, and with his knee he edged the gap in the curtain a little wider. His mark briefly disappeared when the two men at the podium came together in a close embrace, but reappeared again as they began to separate. He waited only for a few inches of daylight to appear between them before firing two quick shots.

On the table behind the president and the minister, a large crystal pitcher of water exploded, and an instant later the mirrored panel between the windows shattered with a deafening crash. Its pieces cascaded to the floor like a sheet of falling ice. Conor quickly stepped back from the curtain, and the last thing he saw before its dark folds wiped the scene from view was the incredulous, enraged expression of Martin Labut.

Racing to the stairs, Conor noted the uproar had already risen to a level one might expect from sending a few gunshots into a packed room. Ahead of him Sonia was halfway down the first flight, but he quickly caught up and urged her to move faster.

"Step on it, now. You said we only needed thirty seconds to get out of this place."

As they passed the first landing Conor tried listening for Kate. He pictured her, stationed with Eckhard on the other side of the door, but couldn't distinguish any voices in the general pandemonium.

At the bottom of the next flight they emerged from the

stairwell into a stone-vaulted hall. It was filled with the display panels of a photo exhibition, but the space was dark now, lit only by the glowing red emergency lights near the exits. Moving at a dead run, Conor followed Sonia to another staircase. She started down, and as he grabbed at the slender metal railing to corner the turn he glanced up and saw a tiny light appear at the end of the corridor. It blinked unevenly, and began moving forward. A man was coming towards them, also moving fast, and the blue-white flicker coming with him was unmistakable. It was the tactical light on a handgun.

Conor plunged down the steps into a low-ceilinged stone tunnel, which took a turn to the right before descending again. Sonia was waiting at the bottom, but started moving when she saw him appear. Even in the dark, which was nearly absolute, he could see they were in a large open space, vaulted like the floor above them, but more ancient.

"Be careful," she called back to him. "The ground is uneven and it's easy to get turned in the wrong direction."

"Good," Conor said, slapping his own tactical light on the Ruger. "Let's hope the fellow chasing after us trips on it, because he's got a gun." Sonia abruptly stopped and swung around to him but he nudged her forward. "Go. He's right behind us."

They traveled quietly over a surface that seemed like the worn, cobbled street of an earlier era rather than the floor of a basement. Through a series of rooms they passed over thresholds and under wide Romanesque arches, and Conor noted there were passages leading to other rooms on both the right and left.

He kept a hand over the light, allowing only a faint glimmer to guide them, wondering who the man behind them might be.

"What are the odds it's your man from the network?"

Ahead of him, he saw Sonia shake her head. "No. Karl's assignment was only to make sure I got inside. He let me in through the door at the end of this passage and then left through it."

That meant it had to be a member of the president's security detail, and Conor didn't think they were going to lose him. They needed a different strategy. Coming through another doorway into a smaller room he saw the rough contours of a solid wall ahead of them, indicating they'd reached the end of this odd, subterranean village. He could hear the heavy tread of the man searching through the rooms behind them, and as Sonia started up a short flight of stairs leading to a closed door, Conor made an instinctive decision. He took her arm and pulled her back.

"We can't let him chase both of us out of here. What was your original plan once you were clear?"

Sonia gave a wry shrug. "Go home, drink a glass of Scotch, wait for all of you to return with the news of Martin's tragic murder."

"Christ. Sorry to ruin your evening." After quickly removing the silencer Conor swung the gun in a circle around them. The beam of its light landed on an old wooden cupboard, sitting against the wall with a display of clay pots on top of it.

"What are you doing?" she whispered.

"Buying you some time," he said, and fired a round. The shot echoed off the surrounding rock and the cupboard jumped away from the wall, spilling the pots onto the floor. Conor added to the racket by pulling it over and gave a loud, pained cry as it landed with a crash. He held out the Ruger to Sonia.

"Take it and run."

She accepted it, but stood frozen in place. "This is madness. He could kill you."

"Sure why would he? I'm their only witness, an heroic eejit who chased a killer through the basement and nearly got my head blown off for it. What about you? Will you be safe at home?"

"He doesn't kill with his own hands." Sonia looked down at the Ruger. "And I'm the one with the gun. I will be safe."

Settling on the floor among the pot shards he waved her away.

"Fine. Hurry up, then." He didn't have to wait long once she'd left. Within seconds he heard the man rushing forward through the last few rooms. When the moment seemed right, he groaned loudly and stretched his leg out across the door, and then yelled again as a booted foot connected with it. The man contributed his own startled shout as he tripped into the room. He dropped the gun while going down, its light flashing in all directions as it spun on the floor. Conor resisted an instinct to break his cover and dive for it. Looking at the man at his feet, he saw the dim gleam of gold buttons, and a colorful braided cord strung across the man's chest.

It was Petra's special friend: Lukas Hasek of the Castle Guard.

He scrambled to his feet almost as quickly as he went down, retrieving the gun as he rose. He took a few steps towards the stairs and stopped.

"Shit." He turned the gun on Conor, shining the light into his eyes. "Clever move. You're not even really hurt, are you?"

"She took a shot at me, but missed." The guard grunted his disbelief and Conor regarded him warily, waiting for a clue as to what his presence signified.

"She missed, huh? At fifty yards she put a shot between the minister and the president like she was threading a fucking needle, but four feet away from you she missed?" He sighed and leaned down, offering his hand. "Anyway, you did your part. She got away."

Conor ignored his extended hand. "Petra said you didn't speak any English."

"Don't tell her." Hasek grinned. "It's more useful if people think I don't."

"Who are you? You sound like an American."

"I know. I'm not, but it's a long story. Come on. Let's get going. I told Kate you wouldn't be long."

At the mention of Kate's name Conor sprang to his feet.

"Where is she? What the hell is going on?"

Hasek had holstered his weapon but at the sudden movement he drew it and took a step back. "Relax." He shot a hand forward, a signal both of warning and reassurance. "I'm on assignment, and I thought I might need your help, so I told Kate to wait for you at the Hotel U Prince. It's just down the street."

"What kind of assignment?" Conor demanded, still suspicious.

"I was supposed to extract an MI6 agent and send her back to the mother ship, but it doesn't look like that's going to happen tonight." He sighed and again tucked the gun away. "I'd better come with you and explain the rest of it, because I'm definitely going to need your help now."

"MI6 sent you here? Are you working for Frank?"

"No, I don't work for MI6." Hasek smiled. "I work for someone you call Harlow. She sent me."

20

Kate was waiting as directed in the Terrace Bar, an open-air lounge on the roof of the Hotel U Prince. It directly faced the tower of Old Town Hall, bathed now in a golden light that accented the freckled appearance of its brickwork. Behind it stood the Church of Our Lady Below Tyne, illuminated against the night sky as if captured in a camera flash, and to the left a softer glow lit the dome and twin steeples of another church dedicated to St. Nicholas.

City of a Thousand Spires.

More like a thousand spies, Kate thought, reflecting on the latest one she'd met. Sitting in a quiet corner bordered on two sides by the roof's balustrade, she turned her back on the scenic view, preferring to focus instead on the terrace entrance. If Conor didn't walk through it in the next few minutes she was going after him.

After he'd disappeared back at the reception, she'd been left standing with Lukas Hasek and Petra, until Martin summoned his wife for an audience with the president. Although clearly resentful, even Petra knew some protocols couldn't be ignored. As soon as she was out of earshot the member of the Castle

Guard had begun speaking to Kate. At first she'd only smiled and nodded, preoccupied by the goal of connecting with Eckhard, who had indeed arrived in the hall and actually *was* standing near the bar, as if summoned by the power of Conor's suggestion. She'd started paying more attention to Lukas Hasek when she realized he was speaking in English and appeared to know a lot about them and what they were doing.

Without taking her eyes from the terrace door, Kate agonized as she sipped from her glass of hot cider. Her shoulders kept jumping in violent shivers, even though the patio had tall, propane heating lamps to warm the chilly night air. What if she'd done the wrong thing? In hindsight it felt unforgivably reckless to have confided in a Czech military officer she'd met only five minutes earlier, but he'd seemed so earnest and urgent, and when he'd thrown out Harlow's name it affected her like a magic password.

Remembering their meeting with that extraordinary woman at the Ram Gorse Pub, Kate had instinctively trusted Lukas and his assertion that MI6's embedded agent—whom he called "Greta"—was in danger. Since he apparently knew nothing of Greta's real identity, she'd only provided a summary of the operation as originally planned: a simulated assassination by MI6 that would sabotage any ideas the New Přemyslids had about staging a real one during the symposium.

Now she wondered if she should have kept her mouth shut about even that. She had no idea how an "agent extraction" worked, and unlike Conor, she had no track record when it came to acting on instinct.

Miserable from the growing fear that she'd made a horrible mistake, Kate's relief made her light-headed when Conor at last appeared in the doorway. Since Lukas was right beside him, she assumed something had gone wrong with his plan for Sonia.

"So, that went well," Conor said dryly when they reached the table. "Not quite pear-shaped, but near enough." He laid a hand on her arm as he kissed her cheek, then immediately pulled back and began shrugging off his tailcoat. "God almighty, Kate, you're freezing with cold. Why do you never bring something warm to put on?"

"Nothing matched." Kate gratefully accepted the coat, pulling it tightly around her shoulders before the warmth of his body could escape. She noticed it was covered in some kind of reddish dust, and wondered how many more times it would need to be dry cleaned before they got home.

Brushing at the sleeves, Kate looked curiously at Lukas. He was the same height as Conor, and they shared a further similarity in their lean, athletic frames, but the Czech officer was probably fifteen years older. His closely cropped rust-colored hair was feathered with gray, and a deeply etched network of crow's feet gave his eyes a look of weariness.

"What happened with Son—"she caught herself and switched gears. "You said I'd only see you again if something went wrong."

"Something did," Lukas said. "I didn't count on the heroic altruism of your partner, so Greta got away." He pulled one of the heaters closer to their table and frowned at it. "Sorry it took so long. Nearly everyone had run from the reception and they were standing around in the square, so we had to split up and mingle for a while. Should we try to find a place inside?"

"No," Kate said firmly. "I've waited long enough. Sit down, both of you, and start talking. The first thing I want to know is what happened to poor Eckhard. I didn't have much time to explain and I feel like I deserted him."

"Eckhard isn't looking for explanations," Conor said. "I spoke to him. He's not interested in adding anything to what he already knows, so he's heading back to the hotel with the other musicians. I'm wondering about the Labuts. I didn't see them in the square. What happened to them, do you know?" He directed this question to Lukas.

"They got swept up by the security guards. They'll assume the gunshots were aimed at the president, but the Labuts will likely be sent home with police protection as a precaution."

"It *was* you, wasn't it?" Kate looked at Conor. "I thought the plan was to shoot out a few lights. You came awfully close to hitting them, and I don't understand why you waited for the president to come out before firing."

"It's a bit complicated," he said.

"*You* took those shots? Did you happen to grab the casings?" Lukas grinned in admiration as Conor took them from his shirt pocket and laid them on the table. "Good for more than a Mozart tune, aren't you? Kudos. If she got away clean they won't have much to go on, and hopefully by the time they get a line on anything I'll have gotten her out of here."

Kate immediately jumped on this opening. "Which brings me to my second question. How did you get involved in all this, and what does Harlow have to do with it?"

"That's a little complicated, too." He stared into space, as if considering how to explain himself. "You know how airlines have hub cities?"

"Ah, Jaysus," Conor muttered. "An airline metaphor." He waved off the officer's confusion. "Keep going."

"Hubs," Lukas repeated. "It's not something they advertise, but intelligence networks have them, just like airlines. MI6, CIA, BND—all the agencies from the countries in the NATO Alliance have cooperated for decades on maintaining neutral stations in a dozen or so cities. They don't run operations, and they're agnostic—or at least they're supposed to be—when it comes to politics or national interests. Their main purpose is to support member state intelligence officers and agents in need. They manage identity documents, act as supply depots, and provide emergency response." He tapped each of his middle fingers on the table as he named the functions and drummed the last a few times for emphasis. "Emergency response. That's how I got involved in all this. MI6 requested help with an extraction."

"And they sent that request to Harlow?" Kate asked.

"They did. She's the head of the Prague Fermature. She's got a dotted-line relationship with MI6, but her primary duty is with the NATO Alliance and the Fermature network."

"What's that?" Conor frowned. "It sounds French."

"It is. When the system was set up, French was the ruling language of diplomacy. Literally translated, 'fermature' means 'closer' or 'fastener.'" Lukas shrugged. "Holding stuff together. The title applies to the hub itself as well as the person directing it."

Kate tried to think of a delicate way to phrase her next question. "It sounds like a pretty intense job for someone who's … nearing retirement?"

Lukas shifted in his chair and glanced away. "I'm not at liberty to discuss the profile of the Fermature."

"No? Why's that, now?" Conor sat forward, and his eyes narrowed as he studied the man's carefully blank face. "It's because she's not that old, isn't it? Does she have her legs as well?"

Kate gasped. She'd never considered this and was surprised Conor had never mentioned it, but as she remembered Harlow's alert eyes and energetic voice it seemed entirely possible the woman had disguised herself as an elderly invalid.

Lukas remained silent, but he didn't need to speak. The flush rising up from his neck made the answer clear.

"I'll be damned," Conor said softly.

"Look, I really can't talk about it. If you see her again, you can ask her yourself." He paused as a waiter approached their table. "What will you have? Wine, beer, something stronger?"

Conor quickly swept the bullet casings back into his pocket and took an experimental sip from Kate's glass. "That's quite good, actually. I'll have the cider as well."

On comfortable ground again, Lukas rattled off their order in Czech, and after the waiter retreated he continued. "As I was saying, MI6 needed help and they had intelligence to pass on regarding a threat to the Minister of Culture. I'm an officer in the Castle Guard, but I also hold an appointment with the BIS—the Czech security service—and *my* dotted-line relationship is with the Prague Fermature, so the director asked me to take care of the extraction. Usually it means an agent is in trouble, but in this case it looks like she's causing it. My understanding is Greta blew the cover of a fellow agent, and she's also been ignoring requests to contact London for instructions on reassignment."

At his mention of the name "Greta" again, Kate gave Conor a sidelong glance. Surely now was the time to reveal Greta was actually Sonia, especially since MI6 had formally handed over the threat intelligence? He nodded an affirmative to the unspoken question, and Kate released her breath in a sigh of gratitude.

"Right. About Greta." Conor cleared his throat. "There are few things MI6 doesn't know about her, and ..." He looked at Kate. "There are a few things I've learned tonight that even you don't know yet."

Kate felt sorry for their waiter, who arrived back at their table with three orders of hot cider only to find two of his customers rendered inanimate. Discreetly ignoring their paralysis, he arranged the glasses on the table, and nodded his understanding when Conor hinted they would need nothing else for quite a while.

Beyond astonishment, her immediate reaction to the news she'd just heard was revulsion. Kate found it hard to stomach the discovery that they were being hosted—and she was being flattered and provocatively touched—by the conniving leader of the New Přemyslids. The plot against the president didn't bother her as much as the prospect of continuing to accept hospitality from a man with genocidal tendencies.

Emerging from her daze, she noticed a different emotion on the face of Lukas Hasek. He was shocked, certainly, but for some reason he also looked deeply embarrassed. Conor saw it as well.

"Got something you'd like to share?"

The officer hesitated, then bowed his head in surrender. "There's nothing to like about it, but I suppose I should share it with you. I got this assignment because the Fermature knew I'd already be at the reception and in good position for an extraction after the incident. The BIS has been watching the Labuts for the last eight months."

"Eight months!" Kate exclaimed. "They've known the Czech Minister of Culture is a homicidal white nationalist for eight months and didn't do anything?"

"Um, no. That part comes as quite a surprise." Lukas looked sheepish. "Petra has been the primary focus. At several diplomatic events she'd made a point of bragging to the BIS director about the secrets she could tell. It's widely known she's slept with the president on more than one occasion, so there was some concern …"

"Ah, jayz. They pimped you out?"

Glaring at Conor, Lukas raised his steaming glass of cider. "That's one way of putting it. Thanks for casting it in the most professional light."

"Sorry, mate." Conor looked contrite, but Kate knew he was trying not to laugh. "Only, I wouldn't have thought you'd need eight months with Petra to work out what kind of pillow talk the president likes. Has she told you anything?"

"Nothing pertinent to national security, but now I'm realizing those weren't the kind of secrets she meant. Christ. I knew Labut was twisted, but I never imagined …" he trailed off, bowing his head before adding, "I've told her often enough to get away from him, but she can't seem to leave."

"You don't think she could be part of his network?" Kate asked.

"God, no. She's not that sort of person."

"But she's protecting his secrets," Conor pointed out.

"Seems to be, yeah."

Conor looked at Kate, all trace of laughter gone. She nodded and turned back to Lukas.

"You care for her," she said gently.

He raised his eyes to meet hers, his ruddy cheeks darkening further. "I know how she seems, but you need to understand, Petra's been damaged in a lot of ways. Her mother died when she was twelve and her father ... used her ... as a surrogate. Martin controls her with the same corrupted paternalism, I've seen that. I worry about her and ... yes, I've come to care for her. I'm sure she knows what he is, but I can't believe she's part of it." He lowered his eyes again. "I realize it's a biased opinion."

"It is, but I think you're right," Kate said. "I think the only person Petra really hates is Martin. And he hates her. They're both acting their parts, but they can barely keep the scenery from falling down. It's a gruesome relationship. Why do they keep at it?"

"It's an addiction," Conor said. "That's what Sonia called it."

"A good word for it," Lukas agreed. He rubbed his fingers against his eyes and looked even more tired when he was done. "I've met Sonia, by the way. I don't know what the hell I would have thought if I'd actually caught her tonight. And you're saying London hasn't been briefed on any of this, yet?"

Now it was Conor's turn to look uncomfortable. "Not exactly. Or, rather, not at all," he added, catching Kate's eye. "Look, okay, I agree. It's time to do that. Can you stand down and give me a chance to put them in the picture?"

"I'm not sure. I'm in an awkward position. I'm pledged to carry out this assignment, but in posing as a conspirator, this woman has the inside track on a man who represents a serious threat to the republic. I can't just put her on a plane and let her disappear. On the other hand, there's real danger for her in all this. I have until midnight to report back to the Permature on the results of tonight's operation. When MI6 requested help they indicated it might not be a friendly extraction, meaning she'd possibly resist or evade it. If she's not picked up quickly they intend to target her as a rogue, and that kind of thing generally ends badly for an agent."

Kate turned Conor's wrist to check his watch. "It's only nine o'clock. You have plenty of time to contact Frank before midnight."

"Right." He leaned across the table. "Just give me twenty-four hours to see if we can hash something out. Maybe this is an opportunity to patch up relations between MI6 and the BIS."

Lukas seemed dubious. "A nice thought, but I won't hold my breath. I'd think you were a wide-eyed innocent if I hadn't seen the shots you put under the nose of our president."

"I'd say innocence is something I left behind a long while ago. Do we have a deal?" Conor put out a hand to the officer, who grasped it after a few seconds of hesitation.

"Fine, twenty-four hours. No more."

"Good man. Let's drink to it. *Sláinte.*"

They all raised their glasses together. Looking at his bluff, apple-cheeked face Kate realized they'd learned almost nothing about Lukas Hasek, but she liked him very much all the same.

"You told me you aren't American, so why do you sound like you grew up a few blocks away from me?"

"I might have," he said, smiling. It was a nice smile, one that went all the way to his hazel eyes, making the lines around them seem more like creases etched by laughter.

"My Czech heritage dates back to the fourteenth century, but the government divested the family of its land and property in 1918, so my grandparents left Czechoslovakia. Both my father and I were born in New York. There was a brief restitution after the war, but then the communists took it all back again."

"Land that was yours since the fourteenth century? They took it from you?" Conor looked appalled. Kate remembered he'd once tried to explain to her the relationship between an Irishman and his land, and it was one of the few times she'd ever seen him struggling for words.

Lukas nodded. "It went along with a nullification of the nobility in Czechoslovakia. We finally got it back after the Velvet Revolution when the government returned most of it. That's when we came back. My family represents the Roudnice branch of the House of Lobkowicz."

"Oh!" Kate barely avoided knocking over her glass as she banged it on the table. "I've heard of that family."

"I thought perhaps you had." He looked pleased. "There were some marriages with the House of Nassau several centuries ago. It's likely we have a few ancestors in common."

"Yes, I guess so."

It wasn't the first time this had happened, but Kate never knew how to negotiate these chance interactions with the royal houses. It made her feel like a diplomat sent to a foreign land without training. She anxiously peeked at Conor, worried her own clumsiness about her lineage only made it harder for him to adjust to it. He was frowning down at the table, swiping a napkin over the cider she'd spilled, but he glanced up as if he'd sensed her eyes on him and his face softened into amused affection.

"Common ancestors a few centuries back. In Ireland that's enough to get you on the Christmas list. You'd best get his address."

Lukas laughed. "Don't quote me on it. I don't keep up on

the genealogy, I'm afraid. But then, I'm not the heir, so I don't have to. It's also uncomfortable walking around Prague with a name matching the most revered palace in the city. That's why I use 'Hasek'. Intelligence officers aren't supposed to have famous names, right?" He looked at Conor.

"That's no bother for me. If the McBrides have palaces somewhere I've certainly not been told about it."

"Maybe not, but a man who plays a violin with your sublime touch stands a good chance of getting his name recognized."

Conor smiled. "Thank you, but who's the wide-eyed innocent now?"

21

They talked for a few more minutes before Lukas departed, and to avoid being seen together Kate and Conor agreed to wait ten minutes before leaving.

When the officer was gone, Conor leaned back and rested an arm on her chair. "Cousin Lukas. Should I expect this to happen a lot, now? Your family were a fairly randy lot, back in the day?"

"Very funny."

"Ah go on, I'm only messin'," he chided. "If I can't tease you about it, I'll go mad. Seriously though, I'd like to know more about your ancestors."

"Well, I'm the wrong person to ask," Kate said. "I don't keep up with my genealogy any better than Lukas does with his."

"Why not? You should."

She was about to offer another tart reply when she realized Conor wasn't teasing any more. Flustered, and having no good answer, Kate stood up and leaned against the balustrade near their table. Every seat on the patio was occupied now, but their corner of it still felt secluded and private. Turning again from the picturesque view and the noise of the crowd she looked out on a quieter, darker section of the city. The waiter returned with their bill, which Conor paid before getting up to stand next to her.

"They're your family, Kate," he said quietly. "It doesn't matter if they were crown princes or Bavarian dirt farmers. Probably there are scoundrels and eejits in the mix, God knows we all have them, but they're your people. There must be a few that deserve to be remembered?"

"It isn't that." She laced her fingers through his, trying to think of how to explain something she'd never put into words. "I don't know how to do any of this. The money, the titles— I've run from it most of my life, and not because I'm a selfless humanitarian. The truth is, I just don't want the responsibility. How am I supposed to manage a fortune? How is a descendent of one of the great royal houses of Europe supposed to behave? My grandmother knows exactly what she's doing—she's telling me to grow up. I can't run from it anymore, but I'm afraid of turning into someone I don't want to be. I like myself the way I am."

"Me too." Following the direction of her gaze over the rooftops, Conor grasped her hand a little tighter. "And I'm not worried. You said you've seen people made small by money, but I don't really believe that. It's a fair bet they were small to begin with—money just gave them a better chance to show it. You're not shallow, Kate. You're about the farthest thing from it, and I'd say the least likely person to back off from a challenge. You're going to manage just fine."

"And you'll help me?"

"As much as I can, which is to say, as much as you'll let me." Conor turned to look at her. It seemed as though he wanted to say something else but then thought better of it. Instead, he changed the subject.

"I need to get on the phone to Frank." He swiveled to look at their surroundings. "I suppose I could do it here, but I've already paid the bill. We'd need to open a new tab."

Kate groaned. "I can't drink any more cider. Anyway, shouldn't we go somewhere quieter? Less crowded?"

"Not necessarily. Unless you're in an open space you're never as alone as you think you are, and the quieter it is the more your voice carries."

She digested this bit of tradecraft, wondering how much Conor had been taught, and how much he just seemed to instinctively know. "Okay. The square is a big open space, and it's noisy. Will that work?"

"It's already worked once. Let's try it."

If the rules called for crowds and noise, the main square was a perfect candidate. She and Conor skirted a large audience gathered around the stage of a raucous puppet show, and crossed to a more dimly lit area at the back of the square's large, oblong memorial. Sitting on a bench beneath the gaze of stern Hussites immortalized in stone, she waited while Conor placed the call. After giving the password he paced in front of her, evidently surprised by the length of the pause that followed. When Frank finally came on the line, the one-sided conversation was short, and not what Kate had expected to hear.

"What? ... Why not? I thought it was secure. ... Oh. Right. I did, yeah. ... Well, we've a few things on the boil, Frank, and I needed his help. Now we need to talk, so drop the feckin' attitude and tell me what to do. ... All right. I've got it. ... Yeah, ten minutes." Conor snapped the phone shut and sat down next to her. "Bollocks." After taking a quick glance around, he reached to the back of the stone bench and slammed the phone against it.

Alarmed by the uncharacteristic display of temper, Kate grabbed his arm. "What's wrong?"

"Sorry. It's okay." He held out a hand. "Let's have yours as well. We're not meant to use them anymore."

She took the phone from her purse and after turning it over to him winced at the sound of plastic shattering against stone.

"Well, it's not the first phone of mine you've smashed to pieces. What's the problem this time?"

"It's because I gave the number to Eckhard, but his phone wasn't registered as a safe one. I guess an alarm blew back at MI6 headquarters on the computer of some creepin' Jesus in the basement. When that happens they assume the phone is compromised and disable it. Frank was surprised it still worked." Conor stepped away to throw the electronic remains into a trash can. "He said we should go to the British Embassy across the river. He's calling the Prague head of station to get a secure line ready. I expect it'll be the first the poor bastard's heard about me or any of this, so he'll be good and stroppy." He sighed. "Ready? No, Kate. Keep the coat. It's chilly out here."

"Take it," Kate insisted, pushing the tailcoat at him. "It's dusty, but I don't want you showing up without a jacket. The British notice things like that."

Rolling his eyes, Conor pulled the coat on and allowed her to slap away some of the larger patches of grime. "We should grab a taxi. It's too far to walk in ten minutes, and I think it's going to rain."

Conor retreated into silence during the ride to the Embassy, no doubt bracing himself to meet an MI6 officer who had every right to be outraged. Kate left him alone and concentrated on what they'd need to do next. As much as she hated the idea, they'd have to return to the house at some point, and it might be better to do so sooner rather than later.

"Listen," she said, as the car stopped at the alley leading up to the British Embassy. "There's no point in my going in with you. I know the story already and you can tell me later what Frank says. Why don't I keep the taxi and go ahead to the house? Maybe the Labuts aren't back yet. We need to find out what Sonia is planning to do, and if I can talk to her before they get there it might be easier."

Conor gave the appearance of considering the idea, but she saw he was humoring her and wasn't surprised when he shook his head. "If they're aren't home already they will be soon enough. I don't want you in that house without me. The last time I saw Martin he was seething."

"So what? As you told us earlier, she's got a gun. And so do I, if it comes to that. The Walther is under the mattress."

"Kate—"

"Conor." She cocked an eyebrow at him. "It won't come to that. He doesn't know who Sonia really is, or who we are, for that matter. Why would he drop the masquerade now, right when he needs to double down on it? He's lived in the shadows for years and the last thing he wants is to draw attention to himself in his own house. That's why Sonia knows she's safe there, and we are too. Also, you're conveniently forgetting the other part of the agreement we had—that you'd treat me like a partner. Isn't this what you'd be asking any other partner to do right now?"

She knew she had him then. He had to dig deep, but he finally agreed and she was proud of him for it. "You're impossible to argue with," he muttered. He threw open the door but before getting out looked back and reached over to thread his fingers through her hair. "I love you."

Before she could respond he jumped out, slapping a hand on the roof as he closed the door, and the taxi sped away.

After getting what she'd asked for, Kate immediately began wondering why she'd lobbied so hard for it, since a conversation with Sonia was the last thing she really wanted at this stage of the evening. She also regretted giving up the tailcoat because now she was cold again, and her head was throbbing. The thing she most wanted was bed, and not the unyielding concrete slab waiting for her back in the guest room. Kate wanted the soft, enveloping comfort of her own bed at home, but pining for it only made its absence more painful. She put the thought aside as the car bumped over the tram tracks in Malostranské Náměstí, and a minute later the taxi turned onto the long plaza in front of the Church of St. Nicholas.

The Labuts' building stood at the far corner, and the headlights shining against its lilac-colored stone was the only illumination in evidence. The windows were dark on every level, suggesting Martin and Petra had not yet returned or else had gone straight to bed. As Conor predicted, it had begun drizzling. Kate leaned forward to pay the driver and looking between the slapping wipers saw the outline of a figure next to the lamp post. He was leaning forward as though praying or preparing to be sick, but Kate knew he was doing neither.

"Oh crap." She motioned for the driver to keep the change, and after leaving the taxi, hurried forward. When she was almost on top of him, Winnie looked up with a panicky twitch, but then his face relaxed.

"Lucky thing, you turning up just now." He held up a soggy length of tape, lip curled, as though he'd caught a rat by the tail. "It's rubbish, this tape. Won't even stick to itself. Thought I'd need to wrap it round the bloody post like a ribbon, but then I wondered would you know what it meant? Tying instead of taping?"

"Not quite so loud, Winnie," Kate whispered. Their corner of the plaza was dark and deserted, but the carrying power of his voice startled her. She darted a look around them, feeling greater respect for Conor's wisdom about conversations in quiet places. "What is it you wanted to tell us? Did you find Ghorbani?"

His face brightened. "That's right. Exactly that, and what's more, at this very minute our Farid's not three blocks from here. I tailed him by car to this part of town. For a minute I thought he was driving straight for this place, but then he turned down a different street and went into a restaurant. He was tucking into a large whiskey and a great platter of meat when I came away to fix a signal for the two of—" Winnie's smile faded as he finally noticed they were missing a team member. "Where's Conor, then?"

"He's at a meeting," Kate said. "Which direction is the restaurant?"

He jabbed a thumb over his shoulder. "Well, it's down the street a bit and then off to the left, but I suppose we ought to wait—"

"No, show me now. Let me just get rid of these heels." Ducking into the building's covered passage, Kate put on the ballet flats, and after placing her high heels next to the gated door she ran back to Winnie. "Let's go."

She passed him, still moving fast, but he immediately caught up and tugged her to a stop. "Best wait for Conor, I'd say. He's had me on the pavement once already. I don't care to think what he'd do if I drag you round the streets, running after this Iranian bloke."

"I'm the one dragging you, Winnie. Believe me, he won't doubt that for a minute." Seeing this didn't shift his reproachful pout, Kate decided to share a few details. She tried imitating the crisp, professional tone Conor used with such success when he wanted to end a discussion. "Farid is working for MI6, and he's supposed to be defecting. That's why we took him to Hřensko, but then he disappeared. I need to find out why before he does it again."

Her posturing failed to impress Winnie, nor did he seem to appreciate the trust implied by Kate's revelation. If anything his face grew longer, but he appeared resigned to being on the losing end of the argument.

"At least put on my jacket," he said morosely. "You're not properly dressed for walking about in the sodding rain. Not that you don't look lovely," he quickly added. "As always."

Although cleaner than the tailcoat, Winnie's sports jacket was remarkably ugly, but she accepted it as though it were made of sable. "I'm sure I look like a half-drowned castaway, but you are very sweet and a perfect gentleman."

The compliment and her smile went a long way towards improving Winnie's mood. He led the way across the plaza and down the steeply graded street on its opposite side, struggling to stay a few steps ahead of the pace she set while puffing out the tale of how he'd located their wayward double agent.

Prašná Věž, the bar Conor had suggested he visit, had turned out to be fertile ground. Winnie arrived late in the evening, presenting himself as a visitor who expected to meet his friend at the bar, and had expressed concern when Farid didn't appear. Once they knew who he was waiting for, he found both the bartender and several female patrons eager to talk. Ghorbani had been a loyal customer for months and was sadly missed. They told Winnie he hadn't returned since being hustled out the door several nights ago by a man they'd never seen before.

The witnesses presented a range of opinions about what had taken place—and violently disagreed as to the stranger's appearance—whether Conor was handsome or ugly, muscular or fat—but everyone agreed Ghorbani had been staying in a hotel somewhere near Wenceslas Square before he disappeared.

"They had me thinking I'd make a quick job of it until I got to see how many bleedin' hotels are on Wenceslas Square, never mind all the little streets and alleys around it. I mapped it out very methodical like," Winnie said, warming to his story as the sidewalk leveled off and he steered them into a smaller side street. "It took most of the next day, nosing around hotel lobbies trying to match up their keys with the one I had, but I finally found the right one. The Hotel Imperial. A bit worse for wear, to be honest, but I expected that from the key, didn't I? The flashier joints don't use real keys anymore. Anyway, it was a sweet moment when I finally got the chance to pop it into the keyhole of his room."

Kate came to an abrupt stop, and after a few more steps Winnie did as well, realizing he'd left her several yards behind. "You used the key to get into Ghorbani's room?"

"Well, not while he was in it, of course. I mooned about in a cafe across the street most of the evening yesterday, waiting to see if he'd show. He came out of the hotel around eight o'clock and I nipped over to have a look while he was gone."

"Conor told you not to do anything fancy."

Winnie waited for a few pedestrians to pass before walking back to her, looking wounded by her hard stare. "I wouldn't have called that fancy, taking a few minutes to peek around an empty hotel room as a matter of interest. I thought it might be helpful."

She wasn't sure she agreed with this liberal interpretation of his orders and was positive Conor wouldn't, but Kate had to admire the man's initiative. Taking him by the shoulders she turned him around and they continued walking. "What did you find in his room?"

"Close to bloody nothing. Literally." Winnie gave her a meaningful glance. "A bit queer, isn't it? He's been in Prague for months, living out of a duffel bag like a monk, with only one change of clothes? I'll wager the ladies at old Protcha Veg don't waste time on blokes who show up in the same suit every night. Where's all his clothes, then? And the rest of his kit? Laptop, magazines, Chinese take-away menus, the bits and bobs of rubbish you collect in your pockets and empty onto the dresser at night."

"That does seem odd," Kate agreed.

"From the looks of it, I'd say he's tidied up and is ready to travel. Might have sent his luggage ahead or chucked most of it. If he's not defecting, it still don't look like he'll be hanging about in Prague much longer."

It was a reasonable conclusion to draw from the evidence—Kate was beginning to think they'd underestimated the skills of their private eye—but she wondered where Ghorbani could be planning to go, since his documents were still waiting for him in Dresden. For all she knew he might have already contacted MI6 to schedule a new rendezvous, but maybe he really had changed his mind about defecting. He could have decided to risk the exposure of his treason back in Iran rather than leave his country forever. And what about Frank's theory—that he'd returned to Prague looking for the woman who'd betrayed him? Apart from tonight's excursion, Sonia hadn't left the Labuts' home since Ghorbani had disappeared, but maybe he hadn't even been looking for her.

"That's the place, up on the right," Winnie said. "It's connected to a hotel."

He pointed ahead to a quaint-looking restaurant with large windows on two sides of a quiet corner. The awnings covering an empty outdoor seating area were dripping with rain, but the scene still looked inviting. The light from two gas lamps attached to the building gave definition to its decorative friezes and a shining iridescence to the sidewalk around it.

"I parked the Hyundai around the corner and stood over here to watch him," Winnie said as they stepped into the shelter of one of the city's many covered arcades. It was directly across from the restaurant, its Roman arches stretching down the street for more than a block. Grateful to be out of the rain, Kate swept the wet hair from her face and peered in the direction he indicated. When her eyes had adjusted, she saw Ghorbani was still inside, sitting at a table wedged into the corner next to a brick fireplace.

"He was alone earlier," Winnie said mildly. "Any idea who the other bloke is? Kate? Something wrong? You know him, do you?"

"Dammit, be quiet for a minute," she said sharply.

Withdrawing into the darkness, Kate pressed her back against the stone pier of the arch. Her mind riffed on a dozen thoughts at once, hoping for one that would offer an alternative to the most likely, most disastrous interpretation for why Ghorbani was sitting across a table from Martin Labut.

22

~

The British staff member who met Conor at the door was a bony young man well suited for night duty at a sleepy embassy in Central Europe. He offered a fluttering handshake, his cold fingers more like a spectral encounter than a greeting, and walked him through several darkened drawing rooms. They were stuffed with antiques and he stepped along quickly, as though afraid anything slower would give Conor a chance to pocket a few knickknacks.

Once through the ceremonial rooms, they turned down a hallway with doors on either side. Near the end he opened one and invited Conor to walk into a shabby, sparsely furnished office where a battered mahogany desk occupied most of the space.

"This is the phone I should use?" Conor indicated the one sitting on the desk.

Alarmed, the staffer immediately placed a protective hand over it. "Oh no, no, sir, don't touch anything yet please. If you'll just have a seat, someone will be along shortly to assist you." He nodded at a chair in front of the desk and waited until Conor was safely settled before removing his hand from the phone.

"Could we have the lights on, do you suppose?"

"Certainly, sir." He reached forward and switched on the desk lamp. Together, they watched it struggle to cast a pitiful light through the nicotine-stained lampshade.

"I expect you need to tell someone I've arrived," Conor suggested.

"Yes, indeed. I shall do it straightaway." The young man reluctantly crossed the room and paused before leaving. "It will be no more than a moment."

"Sure I won't move a muscle."

He broke that promise as soon as the door closed but found nothing of interest to snoop over, so Conor moved to the window and opened a set of brittle venetian blinds. There wasn't much to see outside either, other than a dark garden, glistening now with the rain that had begun falling. As he looked at it, a tingling stirred at the base of his neck, moving up over his scalp like a fast burn, but then it moved out of him just as quickly, leaving nothing behind. He closed his eyes, letting the sensation pass, and then taking advantage of a calm moment with nothing to distract him, he rested his forehead against the glass, reflecting on the mounting chaos swirling around him.

He wondered how Sonia would explain the failed assassination attempt to Martin and whether he'd believe it. He also thought getting her safely out of the city would be trickier than Lukas anticipated. Now that she was again barricaded inside the Labut home there was no chance Sonia would leave Prague without her son. Given how tightly Martin controlled her access to Leo, Conor dreaded the possibility of a kidnapping stunt— mother, son or both together—getting thrown atop the pile of complications. Before he could tease out this disturbing train of thought, the room's overhead light snapped on, flooding the office with a fluorescent glare.

"Why the devil are you standing here in the dark?"

The venetian blinds came down with a crash as Conor jumped

away from them and spun to gape at the figure in the doorway.

"Apologies for the subterfuge, my boy. I only arrived from the airport an hour ago and wasn't expecting to speak with you so soon." Frank arched an eyebrow. "What a treat to see you dressed for work. You're quite handsome in a tuxedo, I must say, although it looks as though you've rolled on the floor in it."

"I did, actually."

"Well, I look forward to hearing about it. Shall we move to more comfortable quarters? Poor Bradford is still convinced we're here to pinch the silver but he's agreed to let us sit on the good furniture."

They returned to the first drawing room where Frank made a silent, lightning-quick raid on the liquor cabinet, coming away with two glasses of whiskey and a Cheshire-cat smile. Despite the droll humor, when they retreated to the sitting area Conor took note of his weariness and the uncharacteristic tension in his eyes.

"You're not here with tidings of great joy, I'm guessing."

"Am I ever?" Frank took a long sip from his glass. "Give me your report about tonight first—and where is Kate, by the way?"

"She went back to the Labuts' house. Martin Labut," Conor clarified. Sighing at Frank's squinting attempt to recollect the name he finally added, "The Minister of Culture?"

"Oh yes, of course. Lord, I'd quite forgotten you were staying there. What are they like?"

"What are they like." Conor nearly choked on the maniacal laugh rumbling in his throat. He hardly knew where to begin.

"He's trying to get even. He's blowing her cover."

"Who's … ah, bugger." Winnie gave her an apologetic glance and heaved a sigh. "I know. You don't have to tell me again. 'Shut it, Winnie.'"

"I'm sorry for snapping at you." Kate spoke without taking her eyes from the restaurant's window. "It's a long story, and it's probably better for you not to hear it."

She patted his arm and returned to concentrating on two men she'd never expected to see together. So it was true—Ghorbani had come back to Prague looking for vengeance, and he was getting it by doing to Sonia exactly what she'd done to him. Both had acted ruthlessly, but their mutual betrayals weren't mirror images. Before exposing Ghorbani, Sonia had waited until Kate and Conor arrived, providing him with an avenue of escape. Kate felt sure he had no intention of returning the favor, but she wondered how he'd discovered the Minister of Culture was the leader of the New Přemyslids. Sonia said Martin kept himself in the shadows, letting his second-in-command serve as the network's public face. She believed Ghorbani didn't know his identity.

Kate strained for a better look at Martin, curious to see how he was coping with the news that his mistress—and the mother of his son—was an MI6 agent who'd been spying on him for almost two years. The distance was too far. His features were smudged and distorted by the rain spitting against the windows, but she could tell Martin was doing most of the talking at this point. Their meeting ended a few minutes later, when he picked up the glass in front of him and drained its contents in one swallow. He stood up, and after a parting remark that Ghorbani received with an apathetic shrug, Martin disappeared from the dining room.

She pulled Winnie back into the shadows and they waited for him to exit the restaurant, but after several minutes it became obvious he wasn't going to appear.

"Maybe he went out the back. What should we do now?" Winnie cast his eyes to the heavens, as though praying she'd give an answer that would please him.

"I'll let you know when I think of something," Kate said. She was focused on Ghorbani now, who had finished his drink and was signaling his server for the bill.

Their mission had been to facilitate the defection of an Iranian double agent and he was sitting less than a hundred yards away from her. Now that he'd planted the seed of his revenge he might re-establish contact with MI6, but it was equally possible he would disappear again. If he'd decided not to defect this might be the last chance anyone would get to convince him otherwise.

More than all the simulated nonsense she'd endured at Fort Monckton, Kate realized this was truly her final exam. It didn't matter what she thought about Farid Ghorbani and the decisions he'd made. He was a vital intelligence asset and she had an obligation to bring him over, or at least try.

In Hřensko, Conor had assured her nothing would go according to plan, but with a little improvisation they could still accomplish something. The time had come to test that theory.

"We deal with whatever's left to make it work." She watched Ghorbani get up from the table and head for the door. Quickly, she stripped off Winnie's sports jacket and thrust it into his arms. Startled, he nearly dropped it before catching it by one sleeve.

"What's this now? What are you doing?"

"Improvising. His car. Where is it? Where did he park?"

"It's that black Honda up there."

"Good. Go get in yours now, Winnie. Hurry, before he gets out of here. I'll see you back at your hotel."

After giving him a firm push Kate took off, running in the opposite direction. She stayed close to the wall beneath the arcade, forming a plan she hoped would work as she raced from one archway to the next. Up ahead, the Honda—parked a few hundred feet beyond the end of the arcade—suddenly flashed to life. The interior lamp and headlights snapped on, and Kate heard the high-pitched chirp signaling Ghorbani had pressed the remote on his key ring. She stopped at the last archway, watching him approach through the rain, half-running himself. He passed where she stood without seeing her, and when he reached the car Kate ran into the street, waving at him.

"Farid! Wait!"

Immediately, Ghorbani tensed and half-crouched beside the car like a cornered animal, one hand moving to his back in an unmistakable gesture, but when she shouted again he recognized her and slowly straightened. Reaching the car, Kate stopped and gazed at him over its roof, giving him her best smile in an effort to appear delighted.

"I can't believe it. We'd just about given up on you."

Wary and clearly suspicious, he scanned the wet, empty street around them before turning back to her. "What are you doing here?"

"Our hotel is only a few blocks away. I came out for a walk to clear my head. You're the last person I expected to run into, but I'm glad I did."

"You came out to walk in the rain?" Ghorbani snorted his disbelief.

Dropping her smile, Kate gave him a withering look. "Obviously it wasn't raining when I started. How about giving me a ride back? I'd say it's the least you could do, after the trouble you've caused us."

He seemed about to refuse, but then frowned, apparently considering the idea. After giving her a long appraising look he impatiently yanked the car door open and motioned for her to do the same.

As soon as she pulled hers shut Kate felt a claustrophobic discomfort and snuck a peek at Ghorbani while he started the car. He adjusted the rearview mirror, his thick eyebrows pulling together as he glared into it, still wary of an ambush. Unlike the first time she'd met him, he was clean-shaven and completely sober, and projected an aggressive, almost belligerent physicality. His wet leather jacket gave off a musky odor mingling with the stronger scent of men's cologne.

"Where is the other one? Conor?" He shot her a dismissive glance before pulling out onto the road.

"I left him at the hotel," she said. "He's probably snoring by now, although he could have used a little fresh air too. He's been drowning his humiliation in a few too many pints of Guinness."

Even though entirely fabricated, Kate regretted the snide remark, but it achieved the desired result. He said nothing, but the stiffness in Ghorbani's face subsided a little, and seeing a faint grin she struck while his guard was down.

"What happened, Farid?" she asked, softly. "You said you wanted to defect, and a lot of people put the effort into making it happen."

"Things have changed. It's not so simple."

He looked uncomfortable now rather than angry, which was probably a good sign. Kate let the response go unchallenged for the moment, hoping her patience might encourage him to add something to it. She directed him through the streets to the hotel she and Conor had stayed in for their first three nights in Prague before prompting him again.

"I'm sure it isn't simple, but don't you think we deserve an explanation? What's changed? You said you're in danger of exposure if you go back to Iran. If you get caught, you'll have done all this for nothing. Do you really want to risk that?"

He pulled the wheel sharply for the wide turn around the green space in front of the hotel, but when he answered his voice was surprisingly mild and touched with a note of relief. "You don't understand, but it is not for you to know. Here is your hotel now. Go to your snoring man and don't think of these things any longer."

They pulled up to the front door, and Kate sat staring at

the rhythmic swish of the windshield wipers. Realizing she'd achieved little and her opportunity was slipping away, she risked a different, more dangerous tactic.

"Revenge. That's what you came back here for, isn't it? You have an opportunity to make a difference, isn't that why you started this in the first place? To contribute something that might help make the world a little more peaceful? Make us all less likely to bomb each other into atoms? Are you saying none of that is important now, and that all you want is to get back at one woman?"

Ghorbani took his hands from the wheel and rested them in his lap before turning to her, his expression blank. "I came back here for justice. You have no idea why I started all this, or what is important to me. "

"Justice," Kate snapped, angry now. "You want to send Sonia to her death and call that even, but it isn't."

"Sonia?" His eyes suddenly narrowed. "How do you know Greta by this name? I learned it myself only tonight. How do you know her at all, when Conor told me over and over that you didn't?"

"I don't. I mean—" Flustered, Kate tried desperately to recover from this catastrophic slip of the tongue, but her face gave her away. She popped the seat belt off and reached for the door handle, but she was a second too late. The automatic locks engaged with a definitive, hollow thunk.

"Put your seat belt on, Kate."

Slowly, she turned from the door to face his hard, angry eyes and the gun in his hand. At that moment, more than fear for herself, she felt an overwhelming sorrow for the mistake she'd made and the suffering it would cause someone else.

"I'm so sorry." She covered her face, whispering the apology into her hands. "Oh, Conor, I'm so sorry."

*

A security detail was stationed on the street outside the building when he arrived, although apparently the Labuts had not yet returned home. The police weren't inclined to allow Conor passage, so in a twist that moved the night one step closer to farce, Sonia was summoned to the intercom to vouch for his character. He moved off to one side, letting her disembodied voice persuade them of his honor, and saw Kate's shoes placed neatly next to the step. Amused that she'd forgotten them and the police hadn't noticed, he picked them up, looping a finger around the spiky heels as he climbed the stairs. Sonia came into the hall before he reached the apartment, looking down from the top of the staircase.

"They're still not back?" he asked, looking up at her.

She shook her head. "They heard there would be police all about the house and they didn't like the idea, so instead of coming here they've slipped away to a hotel nearby." She smiled. "The police are quite annoyed. At least they have me to protect, which is ironic, yes?"

Pulling himself up the final flight, Conor realized he was extremely tired. "You and Kate, I suppose. Did they give her the third degree as well, or did she charm them out of it?"

"Kate?" Sonia's eyes widened. "She's not here. Did you not meet her outside the Town Hall?"

Alarmed, he sprinted up the remaining steps and waved the shoes at her. "What do you mean she's not here? She left these down by the door. Are you sure she didn't come in earlier? Maybe she went up to our room."

"It's possible, but I've been waiting and listening for you both—"

Pushing past her, Conor went through the foyer and up the stairs, calling Kate's name as he ran down the hall to their room. He nearly broke the latch as he came through the door and ripped half the shower curtain down in a hasty search of the bathroom. He snatched the Walther and its holster from under the mattress and raced back out of the room, meeting Sonia in the hall.

"Where the fuck is she?"

"I don't know. I promise you, Conor—she hasn't been here. Is there someplace else she might have gone?"

"No. She was in a taxi coming straight here." He grabbed Sonia by the arm, pulling her back towards the stairs. "The police. Ask them if they've seen her."

They returned to the foyer and Sonia used the intercom again to call the men stationed at the front door. After several exchanges in Czech she turned back to him, her face troubled. "They haven't seen her."

"When did they get here?" Conor demanded.

"About forty-five minutes ago."

"And I left her an hour ago." Realizing he was still holding Kate's shoes he was about to toss them on the floor, but took a shuddering breath and clutched them more tightly instead. "I don't know where to look for her."

Sonia took his arm. "Come sit down in the living room. We must think this through before we can decide what to do."

He refused the drink she suggested and wandered across the parquet to the boxy leather couch. Removing his tailcoat, he lowered himself stiffly onto it, staring blankly at the windows while Sonia switched on a few table lamps. A strong wind was mingled with the rain now, throwing waves of accelerated drops at the windows like a handful of pebbles, or a hail of gunfire.

"She must have been here at some point," Sonia said, gesturing at the shoes he'd set on the cushion next to him. "And she knew this is where you expected her to be. Wouldn't Kate phone you if she needed to go somewhere else?"

"She couldn't. She didn't have a mobile." From the pocket of his trousers Conor pulled out the two new phones Frank had given him before he left the Embassy. He placed them on the glass coffee table, feeling helpless and terrified.

"Maybe if you think back to earlier in the evening." Sonia took a seat next to him. "Where did you go from the Town Hall? Did anything happen?"

This, of course, reminded Conor of all the things she didn't know yet. It made him weary thinking about it, but he knew he had to tell her. "Something happened, yeah. In fact, something's been happening every ten minutes tonight. I'll give you chapter and verse, but first let me change out of this feckin' tuxedo."

He stood and looked down at the shoes. If they were meant as a signal, he wasn't getting it. Where could she have gone, and why would she go anywhere without waiting for him? Gently, Conor scooped them up from the couch and carried them upstairs with him.

23

Under normal circumstances, Conor represented the orderly half of their relationship. It was a good indication of his state of mind that several islands of clothing littered the floor by the time he'd exchanged his tuxedo for jeans and a sweatshirt. Before returning downstairs, he went to the bathroom sink and popped his last three paracetamol tablets, chasing them down with a handful of water cupped in his palm. The two middle ribs on his left side were still painful enough to require more pain relievers than was probably good for him, and the bruise was still an impressive collage of color that Kate compared to the minimalist "Zorn palette", whatever that meant.

With the water still running, he stood with his hands braced on the sink, looking at his reflection. He replayed the last few minutes spent in the taxi with her, but there was too little material to draw on to be helpful. They'd said nothing during the ride; there had been nothing in the least suspicious about the driver. He remembered every word she'd said in persuading him to let her go ahead to the house. He recalled his agreement, and telling her he loved her … Conor cupped his hands under the faucet again, this time splashing the cold water onto his face.

That was all. There was nothing else. He remembered watching the taxi coast down the hill, and then getting spooked by a dark figure standing against the wall, until he realized it was a bust of Winston Churchill sitting atop a four-foot pillar. He walked up the alley to the Embassy door, and—

Winston Churchill.

"Oh, shit. Why didn't I think of that?" Conor snapped upright, his face dripping. Swiping at the water on his face he dropped the towel on the floor and ran from the bathroom.

Until now his nerves had been threatening to jump through his skin, but with a workable hypothesis and an immediate need for proof he felt a familiar process engage. Within seconds, every spiking nerve had flattened to something like the surface of a dead calm sea. Kate referred to it as his "Buddha mood." The assessment reports from Fort Monckton termed it an "extraordinary talent for repose." Sonia saw the change at once when he came into the living room and rose from the couch.

"You've thought of something."

"I have," he said, fitting the gun into the holster beneath the waistband of his jeans. "Get the police on the intercom, again. No, hang on a minute." Conor picked up one of the new phones and pocketed it. "On second thought, let's go down and talk to them this time."

Once in the passageway outside the door to the apartment, Sonia spoke to the police, asking if they'd seen a short, balding man in the area, while Conor continued out to the street. Although the rain had stopped the wind was still fierce, but on the curb next to the lamp post he found a mangled length of white tape too waterlogged to blow away. He picked it up as Sonia came hurrying from the passageway.

"He's been here," Conor said.

"Yes. They said he was here twenty minutes ago, standing in the parking area there in the middle of the plaza. When they challenged him he said he was waiting for a friend. He was a British tourist with a rented Hyundai and he looked harmless, so they politely asked him to leave. Who is he?"

"I'd need half the day to give you that story, but the abridged version is he's a private detective we hired to look for Ghorbani. This tape was his signal, so he'll have left a message at his hotel. That's probably where Kate went."

"But the police never saw her," Sonia reminded him.

His spirits deflated, remembering Kate had left again by the time the security detail arrived. She couldn't have been here to meet Winnie, but Conor had to believe his appearance was somehow connected. It was all he had. "Right. He'll still have left a message. I need to get another taxi."

He scanned the empty plaza, wondering if it might be more efficient to simply run to the hotel since it was less than a mile away. As he considered it, one of the stone pylons in the parking area caught his attention, and in that instant Conor became a true believer.

"Jesus, Winnie, you're right. You're nothing like a dozy muppet, are you?"

When Sonia caught up with him, he'd already pulled the ugly, rain-soaked blazer from the pylon and was searching through it. He feared whatever message Winnie had left would be unreadable by this time, but then found an empty cigarette package in one of the pockets. Fishing inside it, he pulled out a bone-dry slip of paper and unfolded it.

Hotel Imperial on Krakovska. Room 347.

"It's one of the streets off Wenceslas Square," Sonia said, reading it over his shoulder. "I'll get the Ruger and come with you. We can use my car."

"No. It's possible this isn't even related to Kate. I need you to stay here in case she comes back. I left the second mobile up on the coffee table. We'll stay in touch that way. Just get me your car keys and tell me how to get to the hotel."

"You think Ghorbani is there? That this private detective has found him?"

"If he has, it will be a real stunner for Frank. He thinks the guy is long gone." Seeing her confusion, Conor again recalled he was holding far more information than he'd shared, and there was no time for anything but the most perfunctory details. "Frank arrived in Prague tonight. I just came from meeting with him at the British Embassy. Things are fairly desperate inside MI6 just now because it looks like Ghorbani's made a holy show of them. He was never a double agent at all. He's a loyal Iranian agent, and he's been pulling their wire for years."

While driving towards the bridge that would take him from the atmospheric streets of the Little Quarter to the smooth asphalt of the New Town, he considered phoning Frank with an update but talked himself out of it, realizing it would mean disclosing Winnie's continued role in their operation. Until he had a better handle on the facts, Conor thought it a bad idea to test the patience of his boss, who was already under enormous pressure and operating on little sleep.

During their meeting at the Embassy, Frank had explained that the "Ghorbani affair"—as the chattering class inside MI6 was already calling it—was a full-blown fiasco gathering steam. Most grievously embarrassing to the Service was the fact that they would have gone on being duped if the Americans hadn't come to the rescue.

"The irony is that even they wouldn't have known anything had it not been for Greta—Sonia, whatever her bloody name is—exposing Ghorbani to the New Přemyslids." Frank had offered this remark while again plundering the liquor cabinet and skewering young Bradford—who hovered just out of earshot—

with a stare even Conor found hair-raising. "I was ready to drum her out of the service or hunt her down for a rogue, but now I suppose I shall have to pin a medal on her."

The source of his angst—and salvation—was a listening device the CIA had managed to plant in the Iranian Embassy in New York. A few days earlier it had captured a conversation between a junior officer and one of his colleagues, and after some bureaucratic throat-clearing the Americans had kindly passed it along to the British.

The transcript detailed the officers discussing an agent in Prague who'd been posing as a double agent with MI6. The Iranians had intended to insert him as a sleeper agent by letting the British bring him over as a defector, but only days before departure he'd contacted Tehran with the news that his assumed status as a British agent had been blown, and he couldn't be sure his deeper cover as a sleeper was intact. Iranian intelligence had pulled the plug on the operation, instructing the agent to lie low and wait for the travel documents he needed to return home.

In a dispirited tone entirely out of character for him, Frank said he'd come with no expectation of capturing Ghorbani, who he assumed was safely back in Iran, but with the Prague station essentially leaderless and the foreign minister spitting nails it was important to at least *seem* to be doing something.

"My sole consolation for being here is the opportunity to watch you in your glory at the Rudolfinum this Saturday."

"And see Maestro Eckhard in his," Conor added. This brought a wan smile and a little color to Frank's face.

"That as well, of course."

Conor might be offering further consolation if it turned out Farid Ghorbani was hunkered down at the Hotel Imperial, but as he pumped the accelerator and raced over the bridge to the New Town he knew the only person he really cared about finding was Kate.

At just after eleven o'clock, the night was still in its infancy as far as Prague was concerned. Coasting up Wenceslas Square, Conor saw it fill up with people, all of whom looked younger than him—and certainly quite a few who were drunker than him. The street called Krakovska ran in a perpendicular line from the southern end of the square, near the National Museum. The hotel was an ugly cement building with an off-centered front door, sandwiched between a Chinese restaurant and a jazz club. He parked and studied it from across the street, and seeing nothing remarkable, went into the garishly lit lobby.

Bypassing the front desk and elevator, Conor bolted up the staircase to the third floor. He listened at the door of Room 347 and after a single rap, drew the Walther and stepped aside. He heard footsteps approach and stop, and after a long pause the handle slowly dipped without a sound. When a crack of light appeared in the frame Conor threw his full weight against the door, which gave way without much resistance. Once inside he kicked it shut, pinning the room's occupant against the wall and fastening his hand around a spindly throat. Only then did he realize his gun was jammed against the ear of Winston O'Shea.

"Winnie." As soon as Conor stepped back the little man sagged against the wall like a rag doll, pale and bug-eyed. "What the hell are you doing in here? I swear to God, if I've raced all the way across town for—"

"He's got her in his room down the hall," Winnie interrupted, "And he's got a gun."

"Has he hurt her? Has he touched her at all?"

Winnie flinched at Conor's tone, quiet and lethal. "I don't think so. I can't quite tell, but it looks like he's just put her on the floor in a corner."

"What do you mean 'looks like'?" Conor demanded. "How can you tell?"

Maneuvering cautiously around him, Winnie went to the desk

and picked up a device that looked like a sawed off telescope, holding it up for inspection. "Peephole reverser. I booked this room as soon as they got here, and I've been sneaking down the hall to check on her every so often. I came away once to try finding you, but there's a squad of coppers at your place and they didn't want me hanging about. What's going on?"

"Plenty, but never mind about it. Let's have it, then—your reversing yoke." He plucked it away from Winnie and started for the door. "Which room?"

With the small brushed steel cylinder gripped in his hand, Conor walked swiftly down the hall. Outside Room 338, he could hear voices, and though the conversation was inaudible they sounded calm. Small comfort, but he took what he could get.

Carefully placing the device against the door's peephole, he put his eye to the lens and peered into the room. The scene inside translated as a blurry, fish-eyed image, but he could see Ghorbani sitting with his left arm thrown over the back of a chair. The gun in his right hand rested casually on the table next to him, pointed sideways into a corner across the room. Conor could just make out the shape of Kate on the floor next to the bed, but her head was bowed, her hair dropping down in a curtain that hid her face from him.

Barely breathing, he considered his next move. His heart urged him to kick down the door and rescue her, but his head was telling him such macho heroics could get her killed. He needed to retreat and form a better plan, but after several minutes he still couldn't bring himself to stop watching her and walk away. The decision was made for him when a loud metallic ding sounded from the elevator down the hall. Before an older couple stepped out into the hallway, he jumped away from the door and walked back to the room. Winnie—massaging his throat—answered his knock again.

"Sorry for throttling you like that." Conor settled glumly at the foot of the bed.

Winnie joined him. "Understandable, given the circumstances. I expect I'd have done the same in your situation."

Conor shot a skeptical glance at his pint-sized companion but let the comment go unchallenged. "You'd better give me the story from the beginning."

He listened to the account of Winnie's discovery of Ghorbani, raised an eyebrow at his confession about sneaking into the man's hotel room, and stiffened at his description of the scene inside the restaurant. He could imagine Kate's shock, since none of them had realized Martin and Ghorbani knew each other.

"I was nervous about her going with him, but Kate didn't think she'd be in any danger. I followed in the Hyundai and thought it would be all right when they headed for the hotel, but after pulling up in front of the door he peeled off again with her inside the bloody car, and I tailed them back here." Winnie looked downcast. "Should have done more to keep her safe. I'm sorry."

"No apologies," Conor said, and meant it. The man had shown more brains and ingenuity—and chutzpah—than he ever would have expected. "I'd have no idea where she'd gone to if it weren't for you. I'm grateful."

Winnie brightened a little and nodded proudly at the cylinder he was still fretfully rolling between his fingers. "It's a top brand—made by the Germans. I threw down fifty quid for it, but it's paid off handsome, hasn't it?" He frowned. "I'm afraid I've mislaid the receipt in all the excitement."

"I'm good for it. Add it to the list." Conor turned as another thought occurred to him. He narrowed his eyes and Winnie began to look nervous. "I suppose you bought it to use on Kate and I, though. Did you, those first few days when we were still at the hotel?"

"Should have done, if I was going about the job properly, but I couldn't do it." The corners of his mouth dipped low and Winnie's chin crumpled into a landscape of dents and wrinkles. "I saw the whole thing was rubbish from the start. Most freeloaders give themselves away, if you pay attention. When they get a minute with nobody watching, their faces take a break and you see what they really look like. Mate of mine taught me how to notice when that happens. Sometimes they just look bored—sick of the game and what they're puttin' up with—but some, as soon as the other one's back is turned, you see the greed, and how they just want to get the goods and run off with them. Those are the worst, because they're maybe not just spongers. They could be thieves, or even killers. So, I watched you, waited to see how you'd look when Kate wasn't paying attention."

In spite of his frantic state of mind, Conor found himself drawn in by Winnie's method of profiling and was curious to know his conclusions. "Go on, so. What did you see when my face took a break?"

Winnie gave him a smile of sympathy. "Christ, mate. I saw the only thing you're hiding from her is you love her twice as much as she thinks, and you're afraid it's still not enough. How's that then? Am I close?"

"You are. Pretty close, yeah." Conor's throat tightened, and it was another minute before he could speak again. He scrubbed a hand over his face and stood up. "I suppose I'd better call Frank."

"Are we going to sit like this all night?"

"You should be more grateful. If I become sleepy, I will be tying you to this radiator."

"Well, I'm freezing," Kate said. "You can tie me to it now if you'd only turn it on."

Ghorbani's nostrils flared in an arrogant sniff. "The

temperature is fine. You are cold from shock, and the fear. It will pass."

She bristled at the man's smug confidence. Of course she *was* frightened, there was no denying that. As he'd sped away from the hotel she hadn't looked back—hadn't dared to even peek in the side-view mirror—afraid of casting any suspicion on her story that she'd been caught out in the rain alone. Still, she'd tried to believe Winnie was in his Hyundai somewhere behind them. He might not have seen the car pull away or maybe hadn't understood what it meant, but surely he'd eventually realize something was wrong. A slender hope, but enough to give her the spirit to challenge Ghorbani's power to terrify her.

"Don't flatter yourself. I'm cold because my clothes are wet."

"Oh? Would you like me to help you out of them?"

Kate bit back a retort, realizing how dangerous it would be to anger him. She also recognized her predicament had quickly moved beyond the limits of her training. The three weeks at Fort Monckton had felt like an eternity, but now they seemed pitifully inadequate and she doubted any amount of training could overcome the problem of a gun pointed at her chest from ten feet away. She'd been taught how to disarm an enemy, but her instructor had also cautioned it was a bad idea to try it. He'd concentrated on teaching her how to avoid being disarmed herself.

"Don't worry." Ghorbani was sneering at her now. "I'm not going to touch you. I've had enough of women like you."

"What *are* you going to do with me?"

"Yes, it's a good question. I'm thinking about this. You are a problem I did not expect."

He was watching Kate as though she were an interesting species of wildlife he'd pinned into a corner, and in fact she did feel a bit like a cowering animal—a wet and shivering one. Having discarded her rain-soaked shoes, Kate tried to warm her bare feet by tucking them beneath her. She scraped her legs against the cheap, rough carpet in the process, stirring up the noxious odor of whatever chemical had been used to clean it. Her dress and hair were damp from the rain, her back against the wall was numb with cold, and she couldn't keep her teeth from chattering, but her captor ignored her discomfort.

"What about Sonia? What are you going to do with her?"

"She is no problem. Not any longer." He frowned. "Sonia. I don't like this name. Greta suited her. I expect both are false. Everything was a lie."

"But you lied to her too."

"Yes. As our jobs required, but I would not have betrayed her, and I knew she was an MI6 agent."

"How did you find out about that?"

He didn't answer. Staring at Kate, he remained quiet for a moment, and then looked away. "I also knew she was a Jew. I loved her anyway, and kept that secret also. I've known Minister Labut for some time, and we told each other many things tonight."

"What about us?" Kate asked. "Did you tell Martin he had a houseful of MI6 agents?"

"Of course not. I didn't know the two of you were staying in that place, or that you even knew the Labuts." His face soured. "Also I did not know, during these months and all the nights my Greta lay beside me, that she was his mistress and had borne him a son. Of all the things I told him, one enraged him most. More even than knowing his lover is a spy, he is nearly mad thinking his pure blood has mixed with hers to create a mongrel son. 'My son no longer.' This is what he said." Ghorbani shrugged. "What I think is, he will no longer want the child in his house. What I know is, he no longer wants Sonia alive. This is very clear. She is a problem for him now, but not for him to fix. Not by his hands, and not in his house. He is a cowardly man. He wishes someone else to make it go away—tomorrow night. She will be going out, and he knows where she will be."

"The recital." Kate clenched her teeth against another shiver. His casual, conversational tone horrified her as much as the words themselves. "How can you say you loved her?"

"It is the past." Ghorbani waved the gun, as though lazily swatting at a fly. "I was a fool, but I am not a fool any longer."

"No, now you're going to become a murderer." Closing her eyes, Kate rested her head against the wall. "That's not progress, Farid."

24

The hotel room wasn't big enough for the range of movement he needed. Conor prowled it like a caged tiger, grinding a path into the carpet around the bed with his phone still clutched in his hand while Winnie watched from a safe distance.

He should have trusted his intuition. *It's your pole star.* He knew that line well enough by now; his mother started saying it before he was out of the cradle. If his pole star offered something clear enough to act on he generally obeyed it, but this time he hadn't. When he'd reached for the phone to call Frank and felt a prickle of foreboding translate to a whisper—*Don't*—he'd hesitated, but placed the call anyway. Now he was suffering the consequences of not trusting his own instincts, and of allowing himself to forget that Frank Emmons Murdoch would always be—first and foremost—a calculating intelligence officer. In any situation, he could dump his humanity into a six-foot grave and walk away without so much as a prayer over the remains. Of course he'd expressed genuine concern over Kate's welfare, but it didn't diminish his astonished delight at hearing Ghorbani was not only still in Prague but also conveniently positioned, oblivious to his imminent danger.

After Conor had filled Frank in, he'd explained the course of action he intended to pursue. "We've the key to Ghorbani's room. All we need is a tactic to get him out for a few minutes to give us access."

"Agreed," Frank said crisply.

"We'll go in, Winnie will get Kate back to his room, and I'll stay behind, wait for Ghorbani to come back, and deal with him when he does. *He* can sit on the fucking floor for a change. Then we'll wait until you—and whatever friends you can round up— come get him."

There had been a short pause at the other end of the line before Frank offered a response. "I'm afraid I can't approve that hypothetical plan."

"Sorry? Can't approve what, now?" Conor wasn't conscious of offering anything hypothetical, or of asking permission.

"We've an opportunity for salvaging something from this fiasco. As soon as he's captured, Ghorbani will shut down. We'll get nothing out of him through ordinary interrogation methods. The enhanced measures are risky—they produce spotty results— but it's vital to get him to talk. He's had more than one British control officer handling him over the years and the devil only knows what he's learned from them."

"Fine. He can talk to me." He'd heard Frank draw a breath and release it in a patient sigh.

"You are being purposefully obtuse, and of course I understand, but we both know these are ideal conditions. Ghorbani is relaxed and unguarded, thinking he has thorough control over his prisoner and his situation. He'll talk to Kate. The only thing we need is a diversion long enough for you to get into that room. You'll explain the assignment, put a wire on her, and get out again."

At that, fear dropped down through Conor—a heavy stone falling through a bottomless void. "Jesus Christ, Frank. You can't seriously expect me to—"

"To be a professional. Yes, I do expect it of you. You're an intelligence operative, and your partner is well placed to exploit an opportunity that will help repair enormous damage, and possibly save lives. As I've said to you once before, Conor, I not only expect it of you—I require it. For now, you're to do nothing. I'll assemble what's needed on this end, and you'll be contacted again shortly."

A direct order. Had he been tempted to disobey it? Indeed he had—sorely, but he hadn't. Instead, he'd been wearing away the threads of the carpet for the past hour—in between trips down the hall with the magic spying cylinder—tortured by idleness, and by a recognition that Frank's logic was unassailable. The value of interrogating Ghorbani without seeming to was obvious, and if his partner in that room had been anyone else he would have thought of the idea himself.

"I don't suppose a drink would help at all?" Sitting next to it, Winnie circled his palm over the top of the refrigerated minibar.

"It would, but I'll pass on it. Have one yourself though. I think you're probably off the hook for whatever's left of this gammy production."

Winnie had no sooner cracked open a Pilsner Urquell when there were two heavy thumps on the door, startling both of them. They looked at it and then at each other while Conor picked up the Walther from the bed. After a wary check of the peephole he relaxed, lowered the gun, and swung the door open.

"Special delivery from your neighborhood supply depot." Lukas Hasek smiled, holding up a knapsack.

"I thought the Fermatures didn't get their hands dirty with national agency operations." Conor stepped aside, inviting him into the room. The officer, no longer in uniform, wore a gray fleece pullover and black jeans, topped by a New York Mets baseball cap that made him seem even more American.

"It's a stretch, but technically this could still fall under the category of aiding an agent in danger." Seeing the effect of his remark on Conor's face, Lukas immediately grew serious. "Is she all right?"

"As far as I can tell."

"Okay, we'll make sure she stays that way. I'm actually here in a different capacity, representing the full support and cooperation of the Czech BIS. It turns out you were prophetic, Conor. We've patched up our relations with the British. At least in this instance." Lukas turned and extended a hand to Winnie, who'd risen from his chair, beer can still in hand. "O'Shea, I think? A pleasure to meet you. The British Embassy sent a car for you that's waiting downstairs. I understand they'd like to help you collect your things from your hotel and then relocate you to the Embassy."

Winnie slowly put down his beer, his face distressed. "I was hoping to see it through with you, to be honest. Am I under arrest, now?"

"Of course not." Conor pivoted to Lukas. "Is he?"

"No idea. They just told me to send him down to the car."

"Look, I don't think you need to worry." Conor gripped Winnie's shoulder, trying to reassure him. "I hardly think of you this way now, but you're a civilian. They're only trying to clear the decks of any non-operatives. It's for your own safety really. Kate and I will catch up with you when it's over. I owe you a lot. I promise to make good on it."

"All right then. Good luck to you both." Winnie picked up his sports jacket, still too wet to wear, and solemnly shook hands with both of them. Before pulling the door shut behind him, he looked back at Conor with a faint smile. "You know, I was surprised you didn't ask me about her—what Kate's face looks like when *you're* not watching."

Swallowing, Conor nodded for him to continue.

"Same thing as you, mate. Exact same thing."

*

With Winnie out of the picture and on his way to the Embassy, Lukas turned to business, unzipping the knapsack and unloading its contents. When he'd finished, an array of electronics littered the top of the bed and he began a tutorial to explain each item.

The body wire, a compact arrangement of technology, was tucked into a wide strip of elastic fabric to be wrapped around the body like a sturdier form of ace bandage. A laptop and two sets of headphones would allow them to be networked to the same transmission going into the more elaborate system in the BIS van down the street. There were also radios to connect to other team members on the same secure channel. Conor was assigned *Radio 1*.

While Lukas brought the laptop online, Conor broached the topic of a plan for getting Ghorbani to leave his room. "I thought about pulling the fire alarm but that was rubbish. He'd have to bring Kate with him, and I'd be stuck with trying to get her away from him with a lot of other people around. I got stuck on the alarm idea though. His car is parked in front of the hotel. Winnie said the front desk took down his plate number when he checked in, so they must have Ghorbani's as well. I'm thinking if we can activate his car alarm, they'd probably call him to come down and turn it off."

Lukas didn't look up from the keyboard but he smiled, his fingers continuing to fly over the keys. "We can make sure they do, and we've got a few technicals in the van who will love this. It's like a practical joke. They can rig it up without breaking a sweat."

Within fifteen minutes, the technicals had done their work. When the alarm went off at high volume, they could hear it clearly, even three floors up, and Lukas let it go on for a minute before reaching for the phone. He dialed the front desk and unleashed a furious barrage of Czech on whomever answered. After listening briefly, he followed up with more outrage, slammed down the phone and grinned at Conor.

"They think the car belongs to a guest. They're searching their records as fast as they can. We've got an agent in the lobby ready to signal us when Ghorbani gets there, but would it buy more time if I go down the hall and wait for him? He doesn't know me. I could pretend I was getting off the elevator."

Although he liked the idea of having more time, Conor vetoed the suggestion. "Too risky. This is the only chance we'll get and I'm afraid of spooking him. Give him a clear road to the lobby."

Fitting his gun into its holster, he picked up the room key and the elastic fabric with its hidden electronics and went to stand by the door. The car alarm continued blaring. The minutes ticked by and the atmosphere in the room grew tense.

"He might have refused to go down," Lukas speculated. "If he does, it's possible he could still bring Kate with him."

Conor shook his head. "He'll go down. He doesn't want anyone to come bang on the door, and if he was going to take her along he'd have done it by now."

"Why this delay then?"

"He's tying her up."

"Of course." The officer ducked his head in apology for forcing him to name this disturbing reality. A second later he surged to his feet and Conor yanked the door open, both of them hearing the command from their earpieces.

"*Target acquired. Go, Radio 1.*"

He didn't consciously register his passage down the hall or the act of fitting the key into the lock. Conor's brain returned from oblivion only after he'd entered the room, which completely dark. He banged a fist on the light switch next to the door without effect. Moving forward, he had better luck with the bathroom switch. The slender tubes bracketing the mirror flashed before steadying, and its stark glare had enough wattage to cast a shadowed light into the rest of the space. Conor stared at the empty corner where he'd seen Kate previously, then realized Ghorbani had moved her. She was positioned awkwardly on the floor behind the chair, tied to the radiator.

Quickly crossing the room, he paid little attention to the radio traffic streaming in sporadic bursts into his ear. Some of it commented on the effort to keep Ghorbani distracted with the short-circuiting car alarm, but Conor finally noticed one of the repeating commands was meant for him.

"*Radio 1, report, please. Position and progress. Repeat, report your position and progress, Radio 1.*"

"Radio 1 is in the room. Now shut your fucking gobs for a minute, all of you, or I'll turn this bloody thing off."

"*All units. Hold traffic.*" Following Frank's curt order, the radio fell silent.

Motionless until now, Kate stirred, and he saw the explanation for why none of the lights worked. Ghorbani had cut the electrical cords from the lamps and used them to tie her.

"Conor?" Her voice caught, but although half-concealed behind her tangled hair, he could see Kate's incomparable smile. "I knew you'd find me."

There were few tears while he knelt on the floor, cradling her head against his neck. He couldn't tell if she was being impossibly brave, as usual, or if she was too tired for emotion. Passing his hands over her, Conor noted both her hair and dress were still damp from the rain. Her hands felt ice cold, bound tightly together and to the radiator with the translucent yellow lamp cord, but the rest of her seemed a little too warm. He worried Kate was becoming ill as well as exhausted and in that moment came close to weeping himself. He realized he could do nothing for her. Nothing to warm or console her, nothing to make her more comfortable. Absolutely nothing.

Kate sniffed and lifted her head. "Do you have a knife to cut these off? I think something happened to his car. Did you do that? Anyway, he'll be back soon, so we need to hurry."

He'd already considered ignoring his orders. Now Conor thought about throwing them over to her, giving her the choice to accept or refuse them, and was immediately disgusted by his own cowardice. He cupped her face in his hands—too flushed, definitely too warm—and forced himself to meet her eyes.

"Kate, there's something I need to ask you to do."

As soon as Lukas radioed with the news of his arrival back in the room, Conor's mobile phone rang. He picked it up from the desk, and seeing the number on the screen, almost dropped it again without answering.

"Conor, how is she?"

"Exhausted, and I think she's running a fever. I don't feel like talking to you, Frank. I'm not sure when I will." He rang off and hurled the phone against the wall. It didn't break, but he probably wouldn't have felt any better if it had.

"Have a seat." Lukas pushed a chair forward and tossed him an offering from the minibar. Conor caught it and dropped into the chair, peering at the ridiculous, elfin liquor bottle.

"Tia Maria. Are you having me on? Throw me the feckin' Crown Royal."

The whisky burned going down and hours later still smoldered in his hollow stomach like the embers of a fire, but had no other effect. Conor imagined he could have emptied the minibar without achieving the smallest buzz. He didn't test the theory, but sat instead in front of the laptop next to Lukas, holding the headphones tight to his ears. The transmission quality was fine, but he kept the cushion-rimmed cups jammed against his head like they were the only thing holding it together, as though releasing the pressure meant letting it split and fall to the floor in two neatly sliced halves.

There was no reason to be looking at the laptop either. There was nothing to see but spiky dancing lines against a black background and numbers that meant nothing to him. Yet Conor nearly sat on top of the thing, never taking his eyes from it. He couldn't have got any closer to the sound of Kate's voice.

She'd known immediately, probably from the look on his face, that what he needed her to do would be difficult, and that he was struggling to make the words come out of his mouth. When he'd finally managed it, Kate actually relaxed.

"I was afraid you were going to ask me to seduce him."

Conor sat back, slack-jawed, horrified. "Holy Mother of God, Kate. There is nothing ... *nothing* ... that would make me ask you to—"

"Okay, okay. I'm sorry, but that's all I was thinking about, so I missed half of what you said. Give it to me again."

They'd had only a few minutes for him to get the body wire fitted around her waist under her dress, and then to think through some strategies for getting Ghorbani to talk. Conor checked the minibar and saw a full-sized bottle of vodka inside, half-full. They agreed that exploiting the man's enormous arrogance and his weakness for alcohol might help loosen his lips, although he didn't love the idea of Kate being in close quarters with a drunkard holding a gun. With little time left, he'd spent a minute massaging her freezing hands, trying to get some circulation moving, while an agitated BIS agent yammered warnings in his ear.

"*Radio 1, confirm position. Target is moving to elevator. Confirm position, please. Radio 1.*"

"Jesus, all right. I'm going." He put his lips to her forehead. "I'm going. Make him untie you before anything else."

"I will. I'll be okay, Conor, and I'll do my best." She angled her face up to him, demanding a better kiss. "Whatever secrets he's holding, I'll try to get them out of him."

And she had. After convincing Ghorbani to give her a drink and encouraging him to have one as well, Kate spent the next two hours in a tour de force performance. It was a different sort of seduction, and a delicate balancing act, coaxing and cajoling the Iranian to dazzle her without rousing his suspicion. She began with skepticism, goading him to prove his brilliance, and then affected a growing interest and grudging admiration that kept him talking. All of it excited his conceit, and made him eager to confirm his greatness. So Ghorbani talked. And talked. And talked some more.

At one point, during one of his many long soliloquies, Lukas had removed his headphones and poked Conor on the shoulder, forcing him to tear his eyes from the laptop and lift one side of his own headphones.

"I know this is hard for you, but do you understand how much Kate has gotten out of him? She's amazing. Did you ever expect she would be so good at this?"

Conor raised an eyebrow at the officer, struck by the idiocy of his surprise. "Of course I knew she'd be good at it. She's a trained intelligence agent, you eejit."

At three in the morning, Ghorbani finally ran out of steam. Announcing he intended to go to bed, he moved closer to Kate, his voice growing louder, and Conor held himself very still. The body wire picked up his inebriated grunts and panting breath as he tied her up again.

"There." Conor and Lukas both jumped at the volume of his voice, indicating Ghorbani was inadvertently speaking directly into the wire's microphone. "That will hold you, I think. So, goodnight. I've enjoyed the conversation. It would be a pity to kill you. We'll see what tomorrow brings, shall we?"

"Yes." Unlike his, Kate's voice sounded small and weak, completely spent. "We will."

Within minutes Ghorbani was snoring, and she spoke again, to her larger audience this time. "I'm not sure what happens now. I guess I'll try to sleep."

Conor ripped off the headphones and bolted from his chair, drawing the Walther. "I know what happens now."

"Conor, wait." Lukas reached for his arm, grabbing only air. "We need to get people into position. I need to get clearance."

"You do that, Lukas. Tell them to get into position. Tell them to do it very fucking fast, because I'm not waiting."

He did pause for a minute outside the door of Ghorbani's room. Closing his eyes, he took a deep breath, and when he opened them he was calm again. The key slid soundlessly into the lock, and by slow, careful degrees, he pressed down the handle and entered the room. Inside, he removed his holster and wedged it under the door to keep it open. He heard it quietly swing inward again before he reached the bed, and glanced back to see Lukas coming through, gun drawn.

"Right," Conor said at a normal, conversational volume. "I've had about enough of this carry-on."

Moving to the bed, he stood over Ghorbani and slammed the side of his hand like a hatchet into his stomach. He jackknifed up from the bed with a choking gasp, his face caught in the blinding white beam of the flashlight Lukas trained on him. While he gagged and squinted against the brightness, Conor placed the muzzle of his gun against the Iranian agent's temple.

"Rise and shine, Farid."

It didn't take long for a BIS response team to arrive on the scene. They swarmed up the stairs and down the hall, rapid and silent. A few remained outside while others moved into the room, closely followed by Frank. Together with Lukas, one of the operatives took charge of Ghorbani, and before the agent could catch his breath they'd slapped a piece of tape over his mouth, a pair of zip-tie handcuffs on his wrists, and had hustled him out of the room.

"Can somebody give me a knife?" Conor worked at the loops of electrical cord wound through the fins of the radiator. Without a word, Frank approached and offered him his pocket knife. Conor accepted it, glancing up at him. "Thanks."

Once he'd freed her and guided Kate into a chair, Conor stripped the blanket from the bed and wrapped it around her. He crouched down, watching her face while he rubbed her wrists. "You were magnificent, love. Just bloody brilliant on every level. How do you feel?"

Although she looked pale and ready to drop, Kate seemed peacefully satisfied. "I'm all right." Her eyes widened a bit, seeing Frank, who'd moved several feet away and remained silent, not interfering. "Did you get all you needed?"

"All we needed and more," Frank said. "You did something extraordinary here tonight, Kate. The Service owes you a great debt of gratitude."

"And you, Frank?" Conor spoke without turning. "What would you say you owe her?"

As sometimes happened when overtired or deeply moved, the ironic British edge in Frank's voice dropped into the musical cadence of another man entirely, from another place altogether. "What I owe to you both is not easily put into words."

Conor pressed his lips together, refusing to let it soften him, but Kate rested a hand on his face. "Why should you be angry if I'm not? You know it was the right thing to do. Don't hate him for it."

He got to his feet, pulling her up with him. "I don't, sweetheart. It isn't about hate, or even anger, really. He knows that. It's about me being scared to death that I get a little more like him every day."

Leading her from the room he finally met Frank's eyes and nodded, a gesture his boss returned. They understood each other.

They would have preferred to go almost anywhere else, but duty and the continuing question of Sonia's safety demanded a return to the Labut home. Presumably the couple was only a few blocks away, in the hotel connected to the restaurant where Martin had met with Ghorbani, but the security detail was still guarding the door of their house. Since Conor had put in an appearance earlier, he talked the police into letting them in without waking Sonia. They tiptoed up the stairs and past her room into their own.

"What happened in here?" Kate, half asleep but still shaking like a leaf, became more alert at the sight of the clothes he'd scattered everywhere.

"Oh, right. I forgot about that." Conor kicked aside his tuxedo trousers and stopped her from gathering another pile from the floor. "Never mind, love. I'll get it later."

She collapsed onto the bed. "Can I have a few of your para-whatever-you-call-them? Acetaminophen, isn't it?"

"Shit. There aren't any left."

Kate sat up again, alarmed. "They're all gone? Conor, how many have you taken over the past three days? You can get liver damage."

"Can I? Christ. Well, anyway. I'll go find you something. Do you want to get in the shower? It will help you get warm."

Breaking his own promise to himself, he went into the Labuts' decadent master suite. As expected, he found a well-stocked medicine cabinet. Returning to the guest room he heard the shower running, but Kate was still fully clothed, flat on the bed.

"What happened to the shower curtain?"

Staggering with weariness himself, Conor put a hand over his eyes and laughed. "Jaysus. All right. Hang on a minute."

He did a makeshift repair job on the curtain he'd ripped then helped Kate off with her dress and put her under the hot spray. He stepped back and watched skeptically before shedding his own clothes and getting in the shower with her, afraid she'd tumble out of it.

After all that—dry, dosed with paracetamol, enveloped in sweatpants, a turtleneck, and a sweatshirt, and tucked into bed— Kate still couldn't stop shivering. Conor was out of ideas.

"You've no fever now, but maybe I should take you to the hospital. You might need electrolytes or something."

"I don't need electrolytes. I need you." Wriggling beneath the covers, Kate stripped off all the clothes she'd layered on, and after doing the same to Conor she shifted over. "Just hold me. I think that will work."

He pulled her close, wrapping his arms around her, and she pressed herself to him with a deep sigh. A few minutes later, the relentless trembling had stopped, and Kate was sound asleep.

"Good as a gas-fired boiler, so I am." He kissed the top of her head and closed his eyes.

25

They'd gone to bed at four in the morning and Conor wished he could sleep for a month, but at seven o'clock he came awake with a start, his brain tricking him into thinking he'd missed the morning milking.

"No cows here, ya feckin' eejit." He gazed at the ceiling, lingering over his self-pity before carefully sliding out from under Kate, who was lying in the same position she'd been in three hours earlier. While dressing he wondered what kind of scene might greet him on the floor below, but once downstairs Conor discovered only Sonia sitting at the breakfast table with a cup of black coffee in front of her. She rose when he entered the dining room, offering to bring him a *koláče* and some tea. He waved her back into her seat. He knew they had a lot to talk about and couldn't face the discussion with only a jam-filled pastry in his stomach.

"Would it be all right to nose about the kitchen a bit?"

"Certainly, yes." She sat down again. "Do you enjoy cooking?"

"In fairness, no, but I'll give it a lash. I can at least be trusted with a pan of eggs and bacon."

He explored the cupboards and the contents of the

refrigerator, and got a cooked breakfast together without any need for the fire brigade. He carried his plate and another for Sonia into the dining room, along with a half-loaf's worth of toast piled into a basket. Placing it all on the table, Conor nodded at the empty seats around it.

"Are they gone for good, do you suppose?" Her face froze at his casual wisecrack, and he belatedly realized the Labuts weren't the only ones missing from the flat. "The baby. I'm sorry, Sonia. Have you any idea at all where the sitter lives? Maybe we can find Leo ourselves."

She dismissed the suggestion with a tense shake of her head. "I wouldn't know where to begin to look."

Early the previous afternoon, Petra had packed a bag for Leo and taken him away, explaining he would be staying with a friend since they would all be out of the house for the next two evenings, first for the symposium's opening concert, and then for Sonia's recital the next evening.

"She always makes sure I can't follow," Sonia had remarked, watching from the library's balcony window until Petra's car had crossed the plaza and disappeared. "So crafty. A much better spy than I am."

They'd been practicing at the time, which Conor had viewed as a futile exercise, even then. He doubted they'd ever perform the sonata they were so diligently rehearsing. The recital was scheduled to take place in less than eight hours—ironically, in the Concert Hall at Lobkowicz Palace, Lukas Hasek's ancestral home. He considered calling Eckhard or Frank to suggest that something needed to be done about cancelling it, but then decided the two of them could sort the feckin' logistics on their own. He had his own plateful of tricky tasks, and the first was to bring Sonia up to date.

Of all that had happened, he knew one development would horrify her even more than the fact that Ghorbani had been contracted to kill her. Conor dreaded telling her about the Iranian agent's exposure of her Jewish ancestry and Martin's reaction. He delayed that piece of news for as long as he could, explaining the events in the order they'd happened after Sonia had left the Old Town Hall. When he got to Ghorbani's description of his conversation with Martin, she pushed her plate aside—barely touched—and rested her elbows on the table. Putting her hands over her face, she remained that way for the rest of his narration.

He finished with the obligatory delivery of a message he'd completely forgotten about until now. During their meeting at the Embassy, Frank had asked Conor to pass along instructions for Sonia to report to the Embassy, for her own safety. From there, she would fly to London and be processed into the UK as an asylum-seeker. With her hands still covering her face, Sonia began shaking her head, rejecting the orders before he'd even finished.

"Tell Frank I refuse to go. I won't leave here without Leo."

"No, of course not." Conor pushed a piece of sausage gristle around on his plate. "Tell me how you want to play this, Sonia. Whatever you want to do, Kate and I will help you with it, but we have to start trusting each other."

She dropped her hands, giving him a grateful smile. "We will be partners at last, yes? For now, I think we should carry on as we normally would."

"Meaning what?" Conor asked, grabbing the last piece of toast as she stood up and began clearing the dishes from the table.

"Meaning it is time for us to practice. Have you forgotten we are performing a recital tonight?"

He stopped with the toast halfway to his mouth. "Are you joking me? We can't play that recital. You can't even go out of the house. It's not safe."

"No, Conor. As you would say, this is 'rubbish.'" Sonia

looked pleased with herself for successfully mimicking him. "Martin thinks he knows things I don't. He doesn't realize the killer he hired has been captured. I will be safer now at the recital than anywhere else, and we need Martin to relax and enjoy his anticipation. If I refuse to perform, he would grow suspicious and might even change tactics. We would lose our advantage."

"Fair enough." Conor thought Sonia was finally starting to sound like a spy. "It's a good argument, but what's the end game? This masquerade is on its last legs. We can't go on with it much longer."

"Yes," Sonia agreed. "But we only need a little time. Petra said she would fetch Leo after the recital, and I believe she will, whether Martin wants him or not. She and I have been enemies— lovers and enemies at the same time, strangely enough—but we have also been mothers together. Leo's ancestry will change nothing for her. She will bring him home, and if you help me get him away, I will go to the British Embassy."

Instead of responding right away, Conor let his silence imply he was considering her argument, but actually, he was waiting for a warning to manifest. A sign of some kind—tingle, shiver, anything—any sort of whisper or signal that would point him in the right direction. Naturally, it didn't work that way.

His connection to the numinous was strong. Conor could close his eyes and with little effort connect to a pulsing energy that filled him with an awareness he could never adequately describe. The predictive bit was different though, its communication as tenuous as a beam of sunlight. At times it shone straight down on him without warning, and at others the ray struck at a distance, but he could see enough to walk into it. It was a different sort of energy, and it didn't obey a summons. He knew this, of course, but it didn't stop him from trying occasionally. It would make his life so much easier.

At last, reasoning that Sonia deserved to set the strategy she preferred where her son was concerned, Conor agreed to go forward with the recital and her larger plan. The only barrier was that he didn't have his violin.

"A member of the chamber group took the Pressenda back to his hotel after the concert last night," he explained. "He was going to leave it in the manager's safe for me, so I'll walk over and collect it. If Kate wakes up before—ah, no. Never mind. She won't wake up before I get back." He thought it possible she might not wake up in time for the recital.

She woke up knowing she was alone even before opening her eyes. Without Conor's ample metabolic heat, Kate couldn't keep the bed warm and after fifteen minutes abandoned it for the shower. A thaw gradually took hold as she let the water scald her for the better part of forty-five minutes. She looked irradiated from head to toe by the time she was done, but Kate felt human again, and not quite as inclined to rail at Conor for deserting her.

Her remaining irritation turned to worry when she went downstairs at eleven o'clock and learned from Sonia that he'd come down hours ago and had gone to pick up his violin. Had he slept at all? And exactly how many pain relievers had he been taking for those bruised ribs? Although tenderly attentive to her smallest twinge, Conor resisted having the same kind of scrutiny focused on him. His aversion to being fussed over made him unusually laconic when it came to his own aches and pains. Kate tried not to, but she did occasionally fuss and realized that in this instance she hadn't been paying enough attention.

The news that he and Sonia intended to go through with the recital further alarmed her, but she couldn't deny the logic in the plan. There was no possibility of Ghorbani being a threat to her now, and trying to manufacture an excuse for not performing would likely raise suspicion just when they needed to lull Martin into a sense of false security.

While waiting for Conor's return, they sat in the living room, wondering when the Labuts would turn up and discussing possible strategies for separating Leo from them—or more specifically, from Petra—with the least amount of trauma. In the back of her mind, Kate was also wondering what they'd do if the Labuts didn't come back at all. How would they find Leo if the two of them disappeared? Not wanting to upset Sonia, she tried to think of some delicate way of asking the question, but a minute later there was no need for it. Hearing footsteps on the stairs and recognizing the voices accompanying them, they turned to look at each other.

Martin walked through the door of the flat with Petra's hand under his arm, both of them still dressed like dissipated socialites who'd stayed out all night, moving from one after-party to the next.

"Well," he said with forced jocularity. "Do you know the saying they use in America, Kate? 'Other than that, Mrs. Lincoln, how was the play?' I never thought to use it in such a fitting circumstance. I hope you haven't been terribly concerned over our absence. After an exhausting interview with the national security officers, we slipped away to a hotel to avoid this business of having the police around our home. They've been withdrawn at last upon my request."

Forcing her weary mind into action, Kate produced a credible exclamation of relief. She got to her feet and hurried forward. "Of course, we've been concerned. What a frightening experience for you both. Everything happened at once, and the bodyguards took you away so fast I was afraid you'd been hurt."

"Yes," Sonia chimed in, joining Kate in the middle of the room. "It is such a relief to see you safe, Martin. I was terrified for you."

"Were you? Ah, Sonia. I am deeply touched." His smile was fixed and cold. "But there was really no cause for alarm, was there? As I insisted to the officers last night, I feel quite safe. Who would bother themselves to murder a lowly Minister of Culture? The assassin—some sort of terrorist, no doubt—was clearly intending to eliminate our dear president. How lucky we are this killer had such poor aim." Martin's eyes rested on Sonia for a long moment before shifting to Kate. "My dear Kate, I am sorry you've had to endure this horror. I would wish for you to have better memories of your visit."

Kate found the next few minutes particularly arduous, trading questions all of them could have answered, pretending surprise and horror about an incident they'd known about well in advance. During this ordeal, Petra stood at Martin's side not saying a word. Her hand hung limply on his arm and her eyes remained lowered. Kate thought she looked awful, haggard with exhaustion, and something else.

Finally, he brought the charade to a conclusion. "Well Sonia, I am anxious to spend some time with you. Perhaps you could wait for me in my study while I take Petra upstairs. As you can see, she is in great need of some peace and quiet." He lifted his wife's hand to his lips. "Isn't that right, my dear?"

At the sound of her name, Petra raised her head. Her eyes looked unnaturally bright, and turning them on her husband they filled with a wild, desperate hatred. "Peace." As though exhaling the word on a stream of smoke, her gravelly voice drew the single syllable to an extended length. "Yes. I am in great need of peace."

After accepting the Pressenda from the hotel manager, who treated it with as much reverence as he had on the day they'd arrived, Conor realized he should tell Eckhard about Sonia's decision to perform, to preempt any plans underway to cancel the recital. He rang the conductor's room from a hotel phone in the lobby and Eckhard answered in an irritated whisper before the first ring had finished.

"Sorry, Eckhard. Did I wake you?" Surprised, Conor looked at his watch. It was after ten o'clock.

"Not me, no," Eckhard hissed. "Is it important? Are people dying? Because he got here only an hour ago. If people are not dying I am not waking him."

"No, Jesus, don't wake him." Only an hour ago? Conor wondered what Frank had been doing with Ghorbani for the past six hours and decided he didn't want to know. "I was calling for you anyway. I'm in the lobby if you want to come down."

Eckhard arrived a few minutes later, crossing the lobby to where Conor sat on a window seat.

"You look exhausted," the conductor announced immediately and Conor smiled.

"Same to you, Maestro. I suppose none of us got any sleep last night. I thought Frank was staying at the Embassy."

"He was. More 'discreet' he said, but then here he comes to my room, and *mein Gott* he looked terrible." Eckhard shrugged a dismissal. "What to do? I should lock the door? I require no discretion, and I'd told him to stay here in the first place. It's nonsense, *ja*."

Despite his dry wit, Eckhard was clearly concerned about his partner and relieved to have him under his own supervision. For the first time Conor allowed himself to feel a little sympathy for his boss. "I imagine he knew he'd get a warmer welcome here. The Embassy doesn't lay on much hospitality, as far as I can tell. He's had a rough week, I'd say."

"Yes, I've heard." Eckhard nodded. "And for all of you, a rough night as well. How is Kate?"

"It was harder on her than she'll admit, but I think she'll be okay. Kate's not as neurotic as I am. She was still sleeping when I left."

"Are you staying here in the hotel, now?"

Conor sighed. "No, we're back at the Labuts, but there's still no sign of them. We're there with Sonia, and she's the reason I called you."

Eckhard insisted they talk while eating, so over a second breakfast in the hotel's restaurant Conor explained Sonia's intention to go through with the recital. He also explained the plan to get her baby away from the Labuts and his intention to help her regardless of what anyone might think of the idea. Before leaving, he asked the conductor to pass the news along to Frank once he was awake.

His errand had taken quite a bit longer than anticipated and the city's church bells were ringing out the noon hour when Conor returned to the Labuts' building. Entering the passageway he saw the security detail had disappeared. On the main floor he looked through the open doorways to the opposite end of the flat, and although it was empty, he sensed something had changed. Upstairs, he was surprised to see Kate awake and dressed, sitting on the bed with her back against the headboard and her hands wrapped around a mug of tea.

"They're back," she said, after he'd closed the door.

An important piece of news, but Conor initially ignored it. Putting his violin case on the floor he sat on the edge of the bed, assessing her appearance. She still looked a bit fragile, but the shivering, glassy-eyed exhaustion was thankfully gone, and her cheek felt cool and dry when he kissed it.

"I'm worried about you," Kate said, examining him just as closely. "You've had almost no sleep and you've been taking too many pills."

"No, you've scared me off them. I've not taken a single one today."

"Which means you're in pain. I'm worried about that, too."

"Right. You've enough strength for wittering on at me,

anyway. Slide over." Conor gave her leg a poke. Kate shifted sideways and he settled down beside her. Taking the mug out of her hand, he sipped from it and made a face. Chamomile. Not likely to help him stay awake. "So, they're back. Tell me about it, now."

At some point after Kate finished filling him in on the return of the Labuts, Conor did drift off, and strange, uncomfortable visions of Petra followed him into sleep. Awake, he'd taken no time to consider the effect losing the baby would have on her, but in a shallow dream her anguish was palpable, taking the shape of something that he couldn't quite see. He bounced awake and nearly off the bed when a sharp rap sounded on their door.

"Christ. That wasn't a bit helpful. How long?" he asked Kate, rubbing his eyes.

"Not long enough," she sighed. "Less than twenty minutes."

She got up and opened the door a crack before swinging it wider to show Sonia on the other side, standing uncertainly in the doorway.

Kate took her hand and drew her into the room. "Have you been in his study all this time?"

"Yes. May I have a glass of water, please?"

Conor vaulted from the bed to get it while Kate put an arm around Sonia and led her to the sofa in the corner of the room. She looked as though she'd been in a fight. Her silver hair, ordinarily smooth and flat as a polished helmet, stood up from her head in spiky peaks. The black cashmere sweater she was wearing had been twisted and stretched out of shape, and an angry, red welt had formed on her cheek.

"What happened?" He handed her the glass and remained standing to examine her more closely, flooded with a cold rage.

"We took turns telling lies." Sonia accepted the glass of water with both hands and drank half of it before continuing. "He asked what went wrong last night. I told him the gun jammed and then misfired. He pretended to believe me, and I pretended not to notice that he didn't. He wondered if I was still committed to the project and I assured him I was eager for an opportunity to make it up to him." She flicked a strand of hair from her eyes, trying to appear indifferent. "He said I could begin that part immediately."

"Sonia." Conor touched a finger to her cheek as a tear spilled down over it. "What happened?"

"No, he didn't strike me, Conor. He is more careful than that." She brushed at her cheek, frowning. "This is from the rug in front of his desk. What happened was no more than the usual. I'm used to it."

"No, you're not." Kate's grip on Sonia's shoulder tightened. "Don't ever say that again."

"You are both very kind. I hardly deserve it after the danger I've put you in, and the lies I've told."

"Rubbish."

Conor's light remark succeeded in bringing a smile to her face. "Thank you for that. It reminds me we still need to prepare for this evening. Will you practice with me for a little while?"

"Of course."

"I need to change first, but I can meet you in the library in fifteen minutes." Sonia winked at him. "It will give you some time to get loose up here."

26

It was his second performance in two days, so he thought it best to loosen up in more traditional fashion. He was running through a few of Rode's Études when Sonia joined him in the library. Instead of beginning her own routine she sat at the piano, listening to him.

"When did you first start playing?" she asked, when he stopped after the third caprice.

"When I was five. I started with traditional Irish music and switched to classical when I was ten. What about you?"

"I was twelve. My piano teacher lived next door to our flat in Sarajevo. I was sixteen when the war began. My parents were going to Israel, but he was coming here, and I chose to stay with him. Of course, at the time neither my parents nor myself realized he was a retired MI6 agent. He'd spied for the British in Prague and Budapest during the Communist years." She smiled. "My music teacher. My recruiter. Bizarre, yes?"

Conor shrugged. "No more than any other recruitment story I've heard. They all strike me as a bit bizarre."

"Yours as well?"

"Mine especially. I'll tell you about it over a beer some day."

He calibrated his bow, playing with the tension until satisfied, and took advantage of their new camaraderie to voice a concern he'd hesitated to raise earlier. "I think the second movement has the farthest to come. I'd say we should focus on it for an hour or so, and then run through the whole thing and call it a day. How do you feel about that?"

Sonia nodded. "I know the second has bothered you. I'm playing it badly and have been hoping you would tell me what's wrong."

"You're not playing it badly, Sonia." Conor pulled a chair over and sat in front of her. "It's just too aggressive. I may have misled you with what I said earlier about Strauss falling in love as he was writing this piece. You know as well as I do that passion has more than one face. If we were trying to capture something about the heat of it, the obsession—the side that's a bit mad, really—then we *should* have been doing the *Kreutzer Sonata*. The Strauss isn't like that, and the second movement particularly isn't. It's expressing a more complicated side of love, the sweetness and the pain of it—lost and hopeful at the same time. It's meant to sound improvisational, like you're making it up as you go, trusting it to turn out all right because you feel it so much. If you can get yourself into that space, we'll be killing it."

Turning to face the piano, she let her fingers travel over the keys without making a sound. "I think you are more familiar with this side of love than me. I've experienced its pain, of course, but never the painful sweetness of it."

"Of course you have." He stood up, moving aside the chair and pulling the music stand forward. "I'll wager my Pressenda against this piano that you felt it the minute you first held your baby in your arms."

After watching her for a moment, sitting motionless and staring at her hands, Conor reached his bow over the keys to press the end of it against the High C, releasing a light, pure sound. "I win," he said softly. "Now, let's get to work."

He was conscious of the obstacle they faced—and had faced from the beginning in that room. The destructive energy of the Labuts reached everywhere, a gelatinous hatred seeping into every open space and crevice. Summoning the right kind of emotion while suspended in it presented a musical challenge unlike any Conor had faced before, but in their final practice together, he and Sonia found the harmony they'd been missing. The finale achieved the heroic grandeur it was meant to, and when they'd finished he actually felt the atmosphere clear, as if they'd created a bubble of clean air to stand inside, allowing them to breathe more easily, if only for a minute.

"I don't care what it sounds like later. It was a pleasure playing that with you."

"I agree completely." Sonia was hugging herself, her eyes shining, happier than he'd ever seen her. It seemed cruelly unfair that they didn't get to enjoy it longer.

At the back of the library, the door to Martin's study opened and he entered, applauding.

"Sneaky, sleeveen bastard," Conor muttered.

"A spellbinding performance," Martin enthused. "I only hope you've saved something for the audience tonight."

With his back to the minister, Conor placed the Pressenda in its case before turning to him with a forced grin. "I won't speak for Sonia, but I can tell you a violinist always has a few tricks up his sleeve."

Lobkowicz Palace stood on a promontory high above the city, inside the castle walls of Hradčany and in good company with many of the most famous attractions in Prague, but it was easy to miss. In the narrow lanes behind St. Vitus Cathedral, an area closed to vehicular traffic, Kate and Conor had already strolled past its unassuming doorway when Sonia called them back.

"This is it? I thought it was a museum," Conor said.

"And I thought it was a restaurant," Kate added, finally seeing the name of the building on a banner next to the door, in print much smaller than the enormous word "Café" below it.

"It's both," Sonia said. "The family has put a great deal of money and effort into its renovation."

They'd arrived at the palace ninety minutes before the recital to ensure enough time for Sonia to get comfortable with the piano, and for Conor to get the Pressenda tuned to its particular tone. Kate's assignment during these preparations was to stay within the physical range of his comfort zone. If he couldn't keep her directly in his line of sight, Conor was apparently determined to at least keep her within shouting distance until they were safely back in Vermont. Assuming his mantle of authority as "agent in charge" (firmly, but gently—he'd learned his lesson in that department), he'd preempted any scheme she might have been entertaining about keeping an eye on the Labuts and coming to the palace with them later. In fact, Kate hadn't even considered the idea. Judging from their attitudes when Petra and Martin arrived home, further outbreaks of hostility seemed certain, and she had no intention of staying behind to witness the ongoing battle. She'd been relieved to leave the flat and shut the door behind them, only wishing it could have been for the last time.

The three of them had discussed Martin and Petra as they set out on foot for the palace, an uphill hike along Nerudova, a street lined with souvenir shops and restaurants.

"I wonder how much he's told her and what she's figured out on her own," Conor had mused.

"I believe she knows more than Martin realizes," Sonia said. "He's exploited her weaknesses, and in some ways Petra is in thrall to him, but she is not a stupid woman, nor an entirely helpless one."

Sonia theorized that by becoming the creature he controls, Petra had created a dependency in Martin as well. He needed her as confirmation of his own megalomania, which gave her leverage to manipulate him just as he did her. Sonia hadn't bothered to add what Kate knew they were all thinking as they continued up the steep incline. She hoped Petra's leverage would be enough to force Martin to accept his son, or at least to allow her to bring Leo home after the recital. If it wasn't, they were going to need a new strategy.

Passing through the doors of the palace, the first person they saw in the entrance hall was Lukas Hasek. He was again out of uniform, but stood at parade rest in a gray business suit, looking every inch the titled heir to the House of Lobkowicz—even if he wasn't.

Conor was wearing a darker version of the same suit—recitals were less formal affairs, which was just as well because his tuxedo was still in a heap on their bedroom floor. Switching the violin case to his left hand, he extended the other to Lukas.

"Thanks for having us over. Should we throw our coats in the bedroom?"

Lukas laughed. "My flat is more modest than this, but you are cordially invited to come for dinner one night before you leave Prague." He offered a hand to Kate, who pushed it aside to give him a hug instead.

"Thank you for your help last night." She stretched to reach her arms around his broad chest.

"You did all the work, Kate." He gave her a tight, bone-cracking hug and released her. "We just mopped up what was left."

"I think she's talking about me," Conor said. "Thank you for helping to stop her partner from going up the wall."

Kate confirmed his hunch with a smile.

"Who sent you this time?"

They all turned to look at Sonia, who'd reacted nervously at the sight of Lukas, reminding Kate that the officer's mission had formerly been to scoop her up and put her on a plane to London, whether she wanted to go or not.

"Good to see you, Sonia," Lukas said, unperturbed by her accusing tone. "Fancy you being a spy. Don't worry, I'm not here to grab you unless absolutely necessary. I met with Frank at his hotel a little while ago and he asked me to come here, in service to the belt-and-suspenders theory that you can't be too careful. I'm also looking forward to seeing Labut's face when he realizes his Iranian hit man isn't showing up."

His reassurance didn't diminish Sonia's suspicious glare, but he dismissed her concern with a shrug. "I assume you're armed?" He cocked an eyebrow as Sonia and Conor nodded in unison and then looked at each other, surprised. "Lord, what a duo. Let's hope you won't have to interrupt the music to draw down on anyone."

"Is Frank coming to the recital?" Kate asked.

"No. He's gone back for another chat with Ghorbani at the safe house we stuck him in, but Frank's friend, the conductor ... Eckhard? He'll be here." Lukas turned back to Conor. "I came straight from the hotel because he said you'd probably be here already, prowling around the corners of your performance space. Do you want to go up and have a look?"

He led them past the museum's ticket desk, up a red-carpeted staircase to the Concert Hall on the first floor. Contrary to the image its name implied, the space was not a large, intimidating chamber; it felt more like a formal drawing room. It had two ornate fireplaces at one end and a magnificent Baroque ceiling decorated with vibrant painted scenes trimmed in white stucco. The piano had been placed at the other end in front of three windows framed by lemon-chiffon drapes. With a seating capacity of just over a hundred, the hall promised an intimate musical experience for its guests.

Sonia sat at the piano and began experimenting with a loud flourish of scales, while Conor did indeed move into a far corner of the room to listen to the sound quality.

Lukas watched them, and then turned to Kate in mock alarm. "It's like watching sausage being made. I think we should get out of here until the finished product is ready. Would you like a tour of the family homestead? We have one or two rather good paintings in the galleries upstairs."

"I'd love to see them," she agreed immediately. "It would be a relief to act like a tourist for a change."

Approximately eight-five minutes later, Conor was sequestered with Sonia in a tiny room adjacent to the Concert Hall. It was a crimson-walled space that had once served as a family chapel, unfurnished except for two chairs brought in for their comfort. The events director for Lobkowicz Palace—a severely efficient woman whose sturdy black pumps braced a heavy stride—had placed them in this backstage area when the audience members had begun arriving. At the time, she'd acted breezy and self-assured, but now she was turning her elegant necklace into a string of worry beads. Conor watched her twist and rub at the pearls, which seemed in real danger of breaking and scattering, while she explained her predicament.

Close to one hundred invited guests were seated in the Concert Hall. Champagne and light refreshments were being prepared in the ornate Balcony Room for the post-performance reception, but the program's master of ceremonies was nowhere to be found. With five minutes to go, the Minister of Culture had not yet arrived.

Conor and Sonia exchanged a startled glance but offered only vague words of sympathy. When the events director marched out to make one last search through the hallways, Conor held the door open a crack and peered into the Concert Hall. Seeing Kate in the front row with Lukas and Eckhard, he motioned for all three to join them.

"They're not here," Kate said, coming in first.

"We heard." Conor closed the door when they were all gathered, and after a brief silence Eckhard ventured a question.

"You saw the Labuts before you left to come here?"

"We saw Martin," Conor said. "I told him we were coming over early, and he said they'd be along in another hour, which means they should have arrived a half-hour ago."

"I'll call the house." Sonia plucked her phone from the handbag next to her chair and went to stand near the window.

"Could be he thinks it's too big a risk," Lukas said. "Look at it from his perspective and what he's expecting to happen here. Within a twenty-four-hour period, he's on the scene of two separate shootings, both of them the result of a hit job he set up himself. Maybe he decided it would be better to stay away from the place."

"What's his excuse for not being here?" Kate asked. "He knows people are expecting him."

"Delayed trauma? Exhaustion? He did get shot at last night. Maybe he really is a little gun-shy."

"If that were the case he would have said something to us, or at least called to cancel." Staring absently at the chapel's altar painting, Conor bounced the strings of his bow lightly against his shoulder. He kept his expression impassive, but Kate picked up on his mood and moved closer to him.

"What is it?" she whispered.

Not looking at her, Conor responded with a barely perceptible shake of his head. He didn't know what it was, but it wasn't good.

Sonia returned, gesturing with the phone. "There's no answer."

"They could be on their way." Eckhard floated the idea without much conviction.

"Could be, yeah. Maybe they're stuck in traffic—sorry," Conor added, when the conductor scowled at his sarcasm. "Sure look, there are really only three scenarios and we can't do much about any of them right now. Either they're on their way, or they're at home and not answering the phone, or they're somewhere else altogether. Whichever it is, we've no actionable information."

He sympathized with Sonia's alarm at the possible implications of the third scenario, but Conor couldn't alter the facts, and although he was successfully hiding it from everyone but Kate, he also couldn't shake the sensitivity to something acting on him like a bad smell. He couldn't tell where it was coming from, or what it was.

"Maybe I could get some actionable information," Lukas suggested. "The house isn't far. Why don't I walk down and see if anyone's there?"

"To be honest, I'd rather have you here," Conor admitted. "The belt-and-suspenders theory is growing on me, and I don't think we've much choice but to carry on as planned at this point. Eckhard, you can stand in for Martin."

"I?" The conductor's eyes popped wide. "And I should say what? I've prepared no notes. I've not studied the sonata."

Amused in spite of his worry, Conor gave him a bracing clap on the shoulder. "It's an introduction, Eckhard, not a lecture, and if I could learn to play the bloody thing in less than a week, you should be able to spit out a few words about it."

When she returned, the events director accepted the substitution without hesitation and quickly ushered Kate and Lukas from the room so the program could begin immediately. Pausing by the door, Eckhard preened, snapping the lapels of his suit and flicking his wrists to display a set of black onyx cufflinks. After offering Conor a playful grin he strode into the Concert Hall to polite applause, and—as expected—proceeded to charm his audience with a warm and eloquent welcome.

Sonia went next to begin the recital with a series of short solo pieces she'd prepared. Alone now, Conor roamed the chapel with the violin under one arm, head lowered like a monk at his prayers. The air stirred a scent of sun-warmed muslin from the tightly drawn window shades, and the muffled sound of the piano did nothing to alter the room's thick, watchful silence He probed at the undefined thing tightening in his gut, hoping it would unfold and reveal itself. As a result, he nearly missed his stage cue. Racing back across the room, he paused with his hand on the doorknob, and then pulling the door open Conor walked out to join Sonia.

They got off to a good start with the sonata. The first movement had always been their strongest and it provided the confidence they needed for the second. Conor had suppressed any thoughts that would interfere with his concentration, but while adjusting his stance during a two-measure rest, a startled jump from Kate in the front row caught his eye. As a further disruption, the phone in his pocket came alive in two quick bursts of vibration just as he'd resumed playing. Someone had sent him a text message.

Sneaking another look at Kate, he saw she was discreetly handing her own phone to Lukas. The officer gave it a quick glance and a few seconds later left the room in the grip of a simulated coughing fit. Conor forced his gaze back to the music, but while delivering the final, extended note of the second movement he turned his full attention on Kate. She was staring at him, wide-eyed, tapping a finger against the phone she still held in her hand.

The pause before the start of the third and final movement generated the usual rustle of activity in the audience—the scrape of a chair, a few murmurs, some noisy throat-clearing. On the pretext of pocketing the cloth he'd used to wipe perspiration from the violin, he turned away and pulled his phone out far enough to see the screen. The message had come from Frank. Reading it, Conor felt his mouth go dry.

Recital threat active. Assassin still at large. Ghorbani says he refused the job.

In the few, brief seconds he had to consider options, Conor pushed aside the self-recrimination threatening to paralyze him. He'd allowed his empathy for Sonia to obstruct an assessment of the risk involved in her strategy, or any rigorous testing of the assumptions behind it. Questions regarding the specific details of Ghorbani's meeting with Martin should have come up a lot sooner than this, but until now none of them had thought to question the conclusions they'd already drawn. The Iranian agent had refused the contract to kill the woman he'd once loved, so Martin had found a substitute.

They'd walked into a trap thinking they were clever, thinking they were only pretending to be clueless, and it was all for the sake of biding their time until they could get their hands on a baby. Talk about mission creep. If lucky, Conor would get a chance to berate himself later, but right now the danger was imminent, and he had decisions to make.

Approaching the point at which the silence would become awkward, he bought himself a little more time by adjusting the music stand. Glancing up, he saw Lukas had slipped back into the room through a door in the rear and was standing next to it. Conor met his eye, hoping for a little helpful advice. Lukas made a lightly closed fist and moved it rhythmically in front of his chest, as though waving a baton.

Keep playing.

Conor gave a curt nod, grateful, because his own instincts suggested the same. Between the two of them they had the small room covered. If an unknown killer was lurking in it, he or she must be feeling confident. An assassin with a sense of control was preferable to one who felt panicky and desperate. Staying the course seemed safer than any improvised action, at least for now.

He straightened from the music stand and looked back to see Sonia watching him with impatient curiosity. Smiling an apology and praying it was the right decision, Conor nodded for her to begin.

During her solo opening of the finale, he had about forty seconds to focus on his audience. Dividing the room into quadrants he quickly examined each of them and concluded it was an entirely innocuous crowd. He reminded himself the recital had been scheduled as an auxiliary event to the ministerial symposium. Most of those present had familiar faces he'd already studied at the reception the previous evening, and those who weren't familiar appeared to be benefactors of the museum, seated in two rows of wider, more comfortable seats on the right side of the room.

There wasn't a single person who came anywhere close to matching the profile he was looking for, but when the door at the back next to Lukas opened, Conor realized his focus had been too narrow. The events director poked her head into the room, apparently to assess how much time remained in the recital, and before she retreated and closed the door Conor caught a glimpse of the Balcony Room behind her—of floral bouquets and white tablecloths, and figures moving through carrying dishes and glassware.

The catering staff. Why invent new tactics, when the old ones still worked so well?

27

It wasn't the most soulful interpretation of a sonata he'd ever given, but Conor held it together and did so while devising a post-performance plan, part of which—regrettably—again involved taking Sonia by surprise.

From the level of applause after the finale, he knew they'd get a curtain call. While escorting her from the stage, Conor communicated what he hoped was a clear signal, directing Lukas to head for the opposite door leading to the staircase.

When Sonia closed the door inside the small chapel and leaned against it, the happy look on her face indicated she had no idea what was happening. He felt miserable for deceiving her, and for what he was about to do, but he needed the reins back and couldn't waste any time struggling to get them.

"How long do you usually wait?" She was patting the door lightly, as though still hearing the music.

Conor smiled. "This is long enough. Let's go."

They swept back into the room on a wave of rising applause, a standing ovation, in fact. They might have easily coaxed a second curtain call out of the audience, but after their orchestrated bows—pulled off nicely, though they hadn't rehearsed them—he wrapped an arm around Sonia's waist and walked her quickly towards the exit.

"What's wrong?" she demanded, resisting his grasp. "Where are we going?"

"Frank sent a text message. It wasn't Ghorbani who accepted Martin's contract." He tightened his grip, forcing her forward. "I'm nearly certain it's your friend Karl from the network who's come to kill you, and that he's in the Balcony Room, waiting for you to walk in to the reception." In shock, Sonia briefly stopped struggling, which allowed him to rush her the remaining few steps to the staircase, where Lukas was waiting.

"It's one of the catering staff," Conor said to him. "You need to get her out of here. We don't know where Martin is or how many back-up plans he's got, and we can't arse around with this anymore. Take her to the Embassy, and tell them to keep her there until Frank can arrange to get her to London."

"What about you?" Lukas asked. "And what about the shooter?"

"I'll sort him on my own."

"Well, don't kill him. I need a witness to nail Labut for all this."

"I'll do my best. No promises," Conor added, grimly.

He expected Sonia to lash out at him as she'd done the last time he interfered with her plans, but when he cautiously loosened his grip to transfer custody to Lukas, he felt her muscles grow slack and saw her face turn hopeless. Lukas touched her arm and she nodded, allowing him to draw her forward without protest. Conor watched them move to the stairs, more disturbed by the listless surrender than he would have been by her fury.

"It's for your own safety, Sonia."

This was true, but they both knew he was also invoking operational procedure. Her cover was blown and her role was finished, and his own mission to assist the defection of a double agent had morphed into something unrecognizable. They'd become too deeply involved in a war that wasn't theirs to fight. It wasn't for MI6 to unravel how a government minister had plotted to assassinate his president through the auspices of a domestic terror network. That was a job for Lukas and his colleagues. As far as Conor could see, the only bit of business he had left was to confront the bastard who'd intended to kill a fellow agent.

He was calling for a retreat from this battlefield, and he knew Sonia believed he was insensitive to what might get left behind. He winced at the despair in her eyes when she looked back at him.

"The sweetness and pain. I thought you understood. I trusted you," Sonia said.

"I do understand." He didn't bother trying to convince her; he simply made a promise. "We'll find your baby, I swear it. I won't leave this city until we do."

Watching them descend the staircase and disappear, he considered the weight of the pledge he'd just made. Foolish, reckless—all that and more, but it was one he intended to keep. Conor started to move away, but then looked back. Like an apparition, Frank had appeared at the bottom of the stairs and was bounding up to him, taking them two at a time. Following behind was a man dressed from head to toe in black nylon and Kevlar with a machine gun strapped to his chest.

"We just passed them in the hall," he said, reaching the top. "Thank God she's safely out the way at any rate." Frank gave a side nod at the officer next to him. "A detail from the anti-terrorism unit. There are four others in the courtyard, awaiting instructions from this chap. Brief us on your plan."

Flummoxed by the demand for a formal synopsis, Conor puffed out a sigh. "It's a pretty basic plan, Frank. We're going to stroll into the reception, have a glass of champagne, and look for the waiter with a gun. I don't think this 'chap' figures very comfortably into that strategy. Maybe he could stay here for a few minutes? See if we can do this without calling in an air strike?"

They secured the officer's reluctant agreement and returned to the Concert Hall. The rear door stood wide open now. All the guests had passed through and were gathered around the refreshments, leaving behind a few recital programs scattered on the floor, and one forgotten sweater on the back of a chair. Kate and Eckhard stood near the piano, anxious and confused, and relieved to see Conor and Frank when they appeared.

"I don't think Martin's hired assassin was here," Kate said. "Nobody even tried to follow you. As soon as you walked out everyone just piled into the reception room and—oh." She stopped as the thought occurred to her. "Do you think he was planning to do it at the reception?"

Conor nodded. "I do, and I've a fairly good idea who he is. Remember Karl? Martin's second-in-command? He was part of the catering staff at last night's reception. He let Sonia in through the basement and then left once she was inside. I'm guessing he's doing this gig as well."

"How will we know which one he is?" Eckhard asked.

"I'm counting on Kate for that." Conor took her hand and headed up the center aisle to the back door. "You were paying more attention to the staff than I was last night. Let's go see if there's anyone here you recognize."

With an even larger painted ceiling and twice as much decorative stucco, the Balcony Room was a grander version of the Concert Hall. In some ways, the scene they entered was much like a replay of the previous evening. More wine and canapés, more erudite chit-chat. Again Conor was beset with admirers, but he nudged Kate forward, urging her to continue circulating. He excused himself several times, maneuvering in stages around guests and a large table laden with finger foods before finally rejoining her at the far end of the room.

"Anything?"

"I'm afraid not," she said. "There are five servers and none look familiar. Maybe I didn't see him last night, or maybe he's already left."

"It's possible, but I'm more inclined to think he's hiding and doesn't realize yet that Sonia isn't here. If it's Karl, he knows she'd recognize him. He can't afford to be swanning around the room serving hors d'oeuvres. Where are Frank and Eckhard?"

"Frank thought they should cover the exits."

"Ah. Good point." Conor swiveled to examine the crowded room again.

Before the recital, he'd taken an abbreviated tour after Lukas had returned from showing Kate the galleries upstairs, and had noted the palace was laid out in a square pattern around a central courtyard. The Concert Hall and Balcony Room comprised one side of the square, and directly ahead he saw Eckhard standing close to the doorway between these two rooms. In the middle of the wall to Conor's left, another doorway led to a series of connecting salons, stretching one after the other for close to a hundred yards. Frank stood next to it, pretending to be engrossed by a landscape painting on the wall.

There was a third door on the right-hand wall, leading to the staging area for the catering staff. The servers bustled through it, emerging with trays of food in one direction and whisking used plates and glasses from sight in the other. Conor watched them moving among the guests and concluded none could be Karl. The extended visibility in the open room would be more than he could afford.

"I don't think our assassin is one of these five—hang on, make that six. Check out the incoming waiter." Taking her elbow, Conor turned Kate slightly to the left. Next to Frank, a stocky man with a blond buzz cut had appeared who, like the catering staff, was wearing a black tie and vest over a white dress shirt. She gave him a quick glance and looked away, taking a sip from her glass.

"Yes. I recognize that one. It's him."

He stood a few feet behind the threshold of the door, and although holding a bundle of napkins in his hands he appeared to have no particular task to complete. As if on sentry duty, he swept his eyes back and forth over the packed room. After taking a step forward he hesitated, then walked quickly to the buffet table and began arranging the napkins on it.

Frank had given no sign that he'd noticed the man standing less than a yard from him, but now he slowly pivoted to face them, raising an eyebrow. Conor nodded and looked at Kate, who mercifully relieved him of the burden of giving a direct order.

"I'll stay right here, boss. I promise not to move an inch."

"Thank you. No 'burning deck' heroics, though. You've permission to move as needed."

He gestured to Frank, a scooping hand signal indicating they should begin converging on their target, but after only a few steps Conor stopped, hearing a startled shriek, followed by more exclamations from the guests at the front of the room. He couldn't tell what had happened. He saw Eckhard, head and shoulders above the crowd, speaking urgently to someone a good deal shorter, but the group gathered around him blocked any further view. They'd surged towards the conductor, but then just as suddenly reversed like a retreating wave, shrinking from whatever had drawn them forward. As they drew back the crowd thinned, and across a widening buffer zone Conor could now see Petra.

Wrapped in a green leather coat that reached below her knees, she slapped at Eckhard's tentative hand on her shoulder and slowly walked into the no-man's-land in front of her. The wooden floor popped with the sound of her heels in the sudden silence. She was bent forward in an awkward crouch as she moved, her hands balled into fists at her side. After a few steps she stopped and Conor heard a collective murmur as her coat dropped to the floor.

"Oh my God, what happened to her?" Kate had come forward to stand next to Conor. "Is that …?" Her breath hitched in a shudder before she could finish.

"Blood. Yes." He stared, appalled at Petra's appearance. Her hair hung around her face in wild, sweat-soaked ropes, and her face—drained of color—was twisted into a mask of anguished madness. From neck to waist, the front of her sleeveless gray dress was soaked in blood. More of it was smeared over her arms in varying degrees of thickness, creating a gruesome palette of color against her bone-white skin. He started forward but stopped again at the sound of her voice. Loud and guttural, it echoed through the high-ceilinged room.

"Where is he?"

At first, Conor thought she was looking for Martin, but then realized her eyes had already fastened on someone else.

"Where is he, Karl?" Petra spat the question at the uniformed server at the buffet table, who was now backing away. "A superior race? You are nothing. You are ignorant savages. What have you done with him, you animal?" Her voice rising to a scream, she launched herself forward. "What have you done with my son?"

The next three seconds seemed to advance slowly, like still images from a stop-motion video. Eckhard ran forward to sweep an arm around Petra's waist while Conor made a running dive at Karl, who continued backing away as he drew a gun from the holster at his back. The shot exploded an instant before Conor connected with him, and as they went down he saw Eckhard drop to the floor and lie motionless. Flinching in horror, he mastered an instinct to rush across the room and forced his concentration back to the thrashing figure beneath him. Prying the gun from Karl's hand he batted it aside, hoping Kate would pick it up, but the weapon skated across the floor and under the skirted banquet table. The move caused a shift in their relative positions, allowing his prisoner to escape.

With pandemonium reigning inside the room and guests surging in a panic through the Concert Hall doorway, Karl headed for the side exit. Frank had been covering that door, but now, understandably, he was sprinting across the room to where Eckhard lay, still not moving. Scrambling to his feet, Conor saw Kate had already retrieved the gun from under the table. She stood poised but uncertain, ready to run in any direction.

"Stay here," he shouted, running after Karl. "Stay with Eckhard."

He pursued the retreating figure down the corridor of rooms—a hundred-yard dash over a terrain of bare parquet alternating with thick Oriental carpets—drawing frozen stares from the tourists throughout who'd clearly heard the gunshot. Conor hoped to chase him right around the square floor plan and into the arms of the officer at the main staircase, but at the end, instead of taking a right turn into the next series of rooms, Karl ran straight through the double doors ahead of him. These led to a private staircase, where Conor made up some ground by sliding down the banister—a skill he'd acquired long before anything he'd learned at Fort Monckton. Emerging from the stairwell he found himself in the palace cafe, where a tour group was filing through to the entrance hall, blocking the exit. Ahead of him Karl veered to the right, making straight for the open-air terrace. A few seconds later he swung himself over the stone balustrade and abruptly disappeared.

"Ah, bollocks."

Praying that he remembered how to do it properly and that

it wasn't the stupidest—and possibly last—move he'd ever make, Conor accelerated to the balustrade. "Knees up," he muttered as he vaulted over, bringing them to his chest while the forward movement carried him away from the wall. It was a twenty-five-foot drop to a grass verge at the edge of a long promenade next to the castle wall. He landed on the balls of his feet and rotated into a shoulder roll, then bounced back up and kept running, grateful to be alive, and to not have cracked any ribs on his right side. The burning ache on his left was beginning to take its toll.

Karl was fifteen yards ahead and pulling away again in a sprint. The promenade was deserted, but at the end of it they would merge with the walkway leading to the main gates of the castle complex, where visitors would be collecting for the hourly changing of the guard ceremony. This was Conor's only chance to end the footrace and make a capture. He pulled out the Walther and dropped to one knee. Aiming as carefully as his heaving chest would allow he pulled the trigger. Watching Karl go down in a heap he raced the remaining yards separating them and slammed him back to the ground as was struggling to rise.

Conor dug a knee into his spine, struggling to steady his breathing, and angled the gun's muzzle for a snug fit against the base of the man's skull.

"Listen very carefully, Karl, because so help me God, I will only ask this question once. What have you done with the baby?"

Since he'd incapacitated the man by firing a bullet through his leg, Conor had no choice but to drag his captive to a park bench and remain there until help arrived. He shoved Karl down and moved to the other end of the bench, unwilling to share more air space than necessary with a fascist murderer, and climbed up to sit on its vertical edge. Planting his feet on the narrow wooden slats, he took out his phone and rang Kate. By a fortunate coincidence, she was already downstairs with the anti-terrorist detail. She'd been chasing Petra, who'd run from the room in the confusion following the gunfire.

"I couldn't catch her," Kate said. "She's gone."

"What about Eckhard?" Conor asked, tightening his grip on the bench to prepare for the reply.

"He's alive. I know," she added gently, when he released an explosive breath of relief. "I thought he was gone too, when I saw him go down. He's unconscious but he's breathing, and it doesn't look as though he's badly wounded, although it's hard to tell how much blood is his own and how much had transferred from Petra. The ambulance is just getting here now. Should I go with them to the hospital?"

"If Frank doesn't mind, I'd rather have you with me. I'm going to need your help with something." Conor shot a black look at Karl, who sat grimacing with his eyes averted, haughty and uncommunicative since giving up a secret in exchange for his life. "Ask the police to let you ride down here with them."

Almost as soon as he ended that call his phone rang. Seeing the number was one he didn't recognize, he answered in silence, waiting for the caller to speak first.

"Conor? Are you there?"

He relaxed. "How did you get this number, Lukas?"

"Frank gave it to me earlier today. What's going on at your end? Are you clear yet?"

"Not exactly. Things got fairly complicated. I've kept your witness intact for you, but he'll be limping for a while."

"Yeah, good." Lukas cleared his throat before continuing and Conor detected the strain in his voice. "I brought Sonia over to the Labuts so she could pack a bag to bring to the Embassy. I need you to get over here."

Conor stood up on the bench and hopped to the ground. "What is it?"

"It's … Christ. Just get over here. As soon as you can."

He continued holding the phone to his ear after the line went dead, sensing events beginning to clarify, moving through a curtain of mist to merge with his shapeless premonitions. He didn't need any extra senses to spell it out for him, now.

"*The blood-dimmed tide is loosed, and everywhere the ceremony of innocence is drowned.*" Yeats, at his most morbid.

The winking blue light on the approaching Humvee pulled Conor from his moment of pensive kinship with the poet. The vehicle stopped in front of him, and the officers poured out in an overwhelming show of force that quickly wiped the arrogance from Karl's face. Conor accepted a card from the officer-in-charge, promising to make an appointment to be interviewed about the incident, and then faced Kate, who'd exited the Humvee more slowly.

"That all didn't go the way I expected," she said.

"No. I had something else in mind as well." He lifted his arm to scrub a hand through his hair, only at that moment realizing he'd torn the seam out of the right shoulder of his suit. "Lukas called from the Labuts' flat. We need to get over there."

"What's happened?" The look on her face told him her thoughts were similar to his own.

"He didn't say, Kate." Conor put a hand against her back as they started up the promenade. "He didn't need to."

Lukas and Sonia met them on the stairs outside the flat. Their reluctance to stay inside it gave Conor a warning of what lay in store for him, but he was still unprepared for the strength of his sensitivity. As soon as they walked through the door it was like piercing the membrane of a protective barrier. He felt as if somebody had begun screaming directly into his ear.

From the beginning, he'd felt the waves of hostility and suppressed violence generated by Martin and Petra, but there had been something else lurking in the flat as well. It felt related but separate from them, a dark malevolence that absorbed everything while remaining hidden. Its presence now was so alive and overpowering it literally knocked him back a step.

"Conor, are you all right?" Kate steadied the wall mirror he'd bumped into and grabbed his arm.

"Sorry. Fine, yeah." He calmed himself, slipping on his customary layer of ice. "Upstairs?" he asked Lukas.

The powerful, ruddy-cheeked officer of the Castle Guard looked unnerved. He nodded. "Yes. Upstairs." He turned to Sonia, who not only looked unnerved but ill. "Do you want to wait here?"

"If you don't mind, I would like to wait downstairs." Sonia's voice faltered. "I promise not to run away."

Conor touched Kate's hand, still resting on his arm. "Maybe you should wait downstairs as well."

She gripped him more tightly. "Let's go."

The smell reached them when they were only halfway up the stairs, a thick, iron tang that snagged at the back of Conor's throat and remained there. It mingled with odors still less pleasant, the source of which he didn't want to consider but soon enough could no longer avoid. Stepping ahead of both Lukas and Kate, he approached the closed door to the master suite, and after a slight hesitation swung it open to the width of his own body.

"God help us," he whispered. Behind him, he heard a strangled moan from Kate and she sagged against his back. Conor spun around, scooping her into his arms and away from the door. He braced his back against the wall, cupping her head with one hand while her face rested against him. "Don't look at it, love. Don't look at it anymore." There seemed no way to describe what they'd seen as anything other than "it", but he felt a stab of remorse for the dehumanizing reference.

Butchered. There was no other word for that either, no other word that could capture the scene of carnage Petra had left behind. The master suite, with its silk curtains and sheets shaded the color of midnight, had become little more than a slaughterhouse, and lying on top of the bed, in a form rendered grotesque, Martin Labut had become something less than human.

28

For the next several hours, the flat was full of people—military police, crime scene investigators, and more than a few dark-suited intelligence officers from the Czech BIS. It was ironic to think the procedural commotion of a homicide could be soothing, but since they weren't allowed to leave, Kate found it a relief to have the ghoulish atmosphere moderated by a buzz of purposeful activity.

Throughout most of it, the four of them sat in the living room, answering questions posed by a revolving cast of professionals, and when the connecting pieces of the story began to emerge, the officer Conor had spoken with earlier arrived to interview them about the incident at the palace. Karl had already identified Sonia as an MI6 agent, but Conor's cover had not been blown, and after a side conversation Lukas had with his superior, it was allowed to remain intact.

All of them were eager to leave the place, but Sonia was especially wild with impatience, anxious to be out and on her way to Leo. The information Conor had "persuaded" Karl to share indicated Martin had instructed him to get the baby from the sitter's house and take him to an orphanage in Klánovice, a municipal district on the eastern-most edge of Prague.

Restless herself from the wait, Kate went to stand at the window, staring down at the plaza while conversations continued behind her. Two of the forensic analysts were discussing preliminary findings. Kate listened and began to form a picture of how Petra had taken her revenge with the eight-inch chef's knife found in the bedroom.

Martin had most likely delivered the news to her about Leo in the kitchen, because the analysts had determined the samples there represented the first blood shed. Judging from the battle she and Conor had heard on their first night in the flat, that seemed to be a pattern for them. The bedroom was for pleasure, if what the Labuts took from and gave to each other could be called that. The kitchen was for fighting. Small amounts of blood had been found there, but in the library, a much larger amount was discovered, smeared in a trail across the wall.

Martin had fought with Petra and probably struggled to take the knife from her, but at some point he'd realized he was no match for her desperate, adrenalized strength. He'd fled from her, with Petra giving chase, and once she had him cornered, she'd hacked him to pieces.

The jokes of God, and the cruelty of men.

Kate remembered Petra's comment after she'd recounted the legend of Wilgefortis, and how she seemed to identify with the martyred saint whose wishful prayers and passive resistance had hastened her death. How long might she have remained shackled to the sinister relationship corrupting her, covering for the sins of a monster in exchange for the love of a child? By arriving on the scene, Kate and Conor had innocently precipitated a chain of events, culminating in the grisly scene on the floor above them. She couldn't condone the violence, the wild, mindless savagery of it, but searching deep in her heart, Kate discovered she had no appetite for condemnation. Petra might go to jail for the rest of her life, but she was finally free.

"Kate? They're saying we can leave now. Let's pack up and get the hell out of here."

She turned from the window, sighing in relief, as much for Conor as for herself. If even she could feel the oppressive undercurrents of the flat, she could only imagine the job they were doing on all his susceptible sensors.

"Do we need to go with Sonia to Klánovice?" Kate asked.

"No," he said. "Lukas will drive her and then drop both her and Leo back at the Embassy. He said he'd take the dog home with him."

"Oh, good. Poor little thing." Tiny Algernon might have been easily overlooked if she hadn't discovered him hiding in the bathroom on the main floor. "Have you been keeping Frank updated on all this?"

Conor shook his head. "I figured he's enough to worry about without getting the story in bits and pieces, but I just phoned him at the hospital. Eckhard is conscious. The bullet only grazed him, so it looks like he suffered no more than a concussion from the fall, but they'll be running tests to be sure for the next few hours. I told Frank we'd be there in half an hour. If you're up for it?" He looked at his watch. "It's nearly eleven."

"I'm up for anything you are," Kate said.

He gave her a weary smile. "Of course you are. I should know that by now, shouldn't I."

At the Military University Hospital, they found Frank in the crowded emergency room waiting area. With his tailored suit and handmade English dress shoes he stood out among the more modestly dressed population around him. He was thumbing through a Czech celebrity magazine, his posture expressing a languid boredom that Conor interpreted as a good sign Eckhard must be doing all right. His face lit up in relief when he saw them come through the door.

"Can you read Czech?" Conor asked, dropping into one of the plastic chairs across from him.

"No, of course not." Frank tossed the magazine aside. "But in this instance I find it's no impediment to comprehension."

Kate bent to give him a kiss on the cheek before taking the empty seat next to him. "How's the maestro?"

"Well enough to become cranky. Eckhard prefers to be in charge of fussing, and he grows impatient rather quickly when the roles are reversed."

"Aha. Another one," Kate said.

Conor ignored her ironic gaze and leaned forward, elbows on his knees. "I never got a chance to ask before now, but what have you done with Winnie? Is he a prisoner in the Embassy?"

"Quite the contrary. I've given him a job. We've a small matter with a loan shark to tidy up, but assuming an otherwise clean background check, he'll report to Vauxhall Cross for orientation in three weeks." Frank smiled at Conor's open-mouthed astonishment. "You didn't tell me he was a waiter at Rules. They're legendary for their discretion, and I've been looking for a personal assistant since Gavin retired three months ago. We had a chat early this morning and I concluded we'd get on well, although I refuse to call him 'Winnie.' It's too ridiculous."

His expression changed as a young, harried-looking woman took a seat next to Conor. Pulling her toddler onto her lap she positioned a small plastic bucket under his chin. Frank regarded them with alarm.

"Perhaps we might find a more suitable venue for your briefing, Conor. I could do with a bit of fresh air."

Although Conor thought he looked fit to collapse from exhaustion, Frank wanted to walk, so Kate agreed to remain behind and wait for further word about Eckhard. The two of them strolled out into the empty, darkened streets of a not particularly handsome suburb of Prague and wandered off in a random direction. Conor delivered a detailed briefing and Frank questioned him closely, but during the walk back they spoke little. Within a few blocks of the hospital they came to an elevated bluff with a staircase leading down a hundred feet to another street below. Frank went to stand at the railing and braced his hands against it.

"I owe you an apology, Conor."

"An apology?" Startled, Conor turned his gaze from the view, a sea of nondescript apartment buildings as far as the eye could see. "What for?"

"For failing to provide back-up. If I'd remained where I should have been, we'd have kept Karl in the room, possibly Petra as well."

Conor suppressed a bemused laugh. Of all the things Frank might have apologized for—and he could think of a few—this was a transgression that didn't require it. "Maybe," he said, opting for a light tone, "but then I'd never have had the fun of throwing myself off a balcony."

"You might easily have been killed."

"Thanks for the vote of confidence." Conor put his back against the railing and crossed his arms, studying the stark expression on his boss's face. "Ah go on, for fuck's sake. The person you love took a bullet and hit the floor like he was dead. If you'd ignored him to do your job I could never have looked you in the eye again. It made me think there's hope for you after all. Don't apologize for it."

Frank's jaw clenched and it was a long time before he spoke again. "The bullet barely grazed his face. Hardly more than a paper cut. I keep saying it to myself and wondering how it's even possible he's alive. Something so deadly, so close, when only a millimeter in the other direction, the smallest change in angle …" He trailed off and glanced at Conor with the hint of a smile. "I wonder am I getting too old for this? I know you think the ice gets thicker and harder over time, but you're quite wrong. It thins, becomes brittle. It cracks open, and things you never expected to see begin to slip through."

"And that's all right." Conor put an arm around his shoulders, pulling him from the railing and steering him back towards the hospital. "You know, Frank, in Vermont they've a word for that. They call it 'spring.'"

It was small and humble, and the heating vent rattled, but to Kate their modest little hotel room felt like the sanctified antechamber of heaven. Before falling asleep she'd extracted a promise from Conor that he wouldn't abandon her at some ungodly hour of the morning. She got her wish, but it came at a price. Earlier than she was ready for, Kate felt his lips moving over her, coaxing her awake. Lying with her back to him, she stretched and responded with a less than amorous groan.

"Does that mean stop?" Conor paused, resting his chin on her shoulder.

"I'm not sure. What time is it?"

"It's nearly eight o'clock, Kate. The day's half gone, so it is."

"Good heavens, eight o'clock." She gasped in mock horror then fell stubbornly silent. He gave her a minute before venturing another tentative kiss on the back of her neck.

Kate surrendered and rolled over to him. "You are hopelessly diurnal."

He grinned and slid a hand between her legs. "Jayz, I love it when you talk dirty."

Her snort of laughter sent them into successive fits of it, but eventually Conor got back to more serious business, putting to good use the hour of sleep he'd robbed from her.

Later, while she was getting her breath back, he leaned on one elbow next to her and wiped a bead of perspiration from her forehead with his thumb.

"Will I need a tetanus shot, do you suppose?" he asked.

Lying on her back and massaging an area near his neck, Kate lifted her head to give it a closer look. "The skin's not broken. I think it's going to be bruised though. God, I'm so sorry. Does it hurt?"

"Ah, will you ever stop now. Of course it doesn't hurt, I was only having you on. But I don't understand why you were so worried."

"A woman screaming in a hotel room can mean a lot of things. I didn't want anyone to get the wrong idea."

He considered this, lips pursed. "Okay. Fair enough."

Kate gave his shoulder a final rub and ran her fingers down over his chest. "What are we going to do today?"

Conor looked surprised, then thoughtful. "Good question."

It could have been a joke, but as she'd intended, he took it seriously. Although she felt a nagging sense of incompletion, it seemed the covert aspect of their trip had ended. They'd fulfilled their contract—in a manner of speaking—and the mission was over. Ghorbani would eventually be allowed to go home—Frank couldn't hold him indefinitely—and MI6 would lick its wounds before moving on to some dubious new project. Their "enhanced" mission to help Sonia, with all its twists and turns, was also finished. She was safe at the British Embassy with Leo, and only Frank knew whether she'd soon be on her way to London or not.

As a bonus accomplishment, they'd helped to restore civility between the British and Czech intelligence services. Using information provided by Sonia, the BIS had already begun dismantling the New Přemyslids network. They'd arrested more than a dozen members in Prague and surrounding cities as part of their investigation into further plots against government figures.

At the tangled center of it all, the scandalous story of the Labuts—the murder and intrigue, the sheer depravity—would be fodder for the media for months to come. The only loose end remaining was Petra, still missing as far as they knew, but it wasn't their job to find her. That burden would fall on the police, and possibly on the shoulders of a friend.

"I wonder what Lukas is doing today," Conor said, as though reading her thoughts. "He was collecting intelligence on Petra, so I imagine he's under some obligation to help search for her. Maybe we should offer to help. What do you think?"

Kate had entertained the crazy notion they might spend the day like normal people—maybe visit a museum, have a long lunch, pass a few more luxurious hours in bed—but she shared Conor's sympathy for Lukas. He hadn't enjoyed the assignment of seducing Petra and had grown fond of her. She imagined he was feeling even more conflicted about it now.

"You should call him," Kate said. "I don't know how helpful we can be, but I'm sure he'd appreciate the moral support."

Conor placed the call while she was in the shower, and when she came out he had surprising news.

"He's heard from her. Petra rang him at five this morning."

"And?"

"He wouldn't talk about it on the phone, but you were right about the moral support. I'd say he nearly collapsed with relief when he heard my voice—said he'd thought about getting in touch but didn't want to drag us into the whole business in case it went badly."

"What whole business?"

"That's what he wouldn't talk about," Conor reminded her, patiently. "He's coming by in an hour. I told him we'd be in the dining room, if I don't fall down dead from hunger before we get there."

It was a beautiful, warm morning and Kate persuaded the restaurant manager to serve them an after-hours breakfast in a sunny corner of the terrace, where the Castle Guard officer found them an hour later. Looking haggard and subdued, he refused any food but drank several cups of coffee while they talked. Sitting with his arms on the table, Lukas wrapped his large hands around the fragile china cup, cradling it gently.

"I don't think she'd ever planned to kill him, but I think Petra had been thinking about escaping from her situation for a long time. She called me on a burner phone from a studio apartment she's been renting for months. She said it was in a city outside the Czech Republic, but who knows in what direction? There are five countries within a four-hour drive of Prague, and she's traveling under a different passport. Apparently, Martin had complete identities created for both of them a few years ago, in case his own went sour."

"Sounds like she won't be easy to track down," Conor said. "Have you any ideas for how to go about it?"

"Apparently, I don't need any." Lukas sat back in his chair, regarding them with his palms flat against the table. "She could probably stay under the radar and avoid capture for a while— years, maybe—but the longer I talked to her, the more I realized she doesn't want to get away with it. I think maybe Petra wants a chance to tell her story, and it's possible she might get some leniency from the court once her side of it is told. I've convinced her to turn herself in, but only if I promise to meet one condition."

"Leo?" Kate asked.

Lukas nodded. "She was relieved to hear he was safe with Sonia at the Embassy but wants to see him before she's arrested."

"No surprise there," Conor said. "Will the police go for it?"

"I don't know. That's why I wasn't intending to tell them about it." Kate and Conor exchanged an uneasy glance and the officer gave them a rueful smile. "You don't approve of that decision, I guess."

Before responding, Conor paused to thank their server and accept the bill. He scowled at it for a moment, then turned his attention back to Lukas. "We're only thinking it's a risky decision, mate. Risky for you, that is."

"Point taken, but I'm willing to accept the risk and the responsibility." Lukas sat forward again, appealing to them both. "Petra's not a terrorist or serial killer, but this a big case and the police will respond with everything they've got. I'd just like to bring her in peacefully, and this might be a way to do that. I could really use your help, if you're willing."

Conor shifted his eyes to Kate. He was giving her the opportunity to refuse for them both, knowing full well she'd do no such thing. They'd been running since the day they'd arrived, and there was no point in stopping now. That was the collateral effect when a mission grew complicated: there were no shortcuts to the finish line, and it wasn't always easy to know when you'd reached it.

29

In the opinion of both Conor and Lukas, Sonia presented the greatest obstacle to their plans. Getting her agreement to allow access to Leo seemed unlikely, especially since Petra had flatly refused to meet them at the British Embassy.

"She wants to name the location herself," Lukas had explained, "but she won't tell me where until I've confirmed Leo will be there."

Lingering at their table on the terrace he and Conor spent the better part of the next hour anticipating Sonia's arguments and coming up with ideas to counter them, while Kate listened with thinly veiled frustration. For all the virtues she had in abundance, patience was one she possessed in short supply. She was sitting with her legs crossed, one foot jiggling in midair, and Conor could see she'd grown restless with the discussion. When she adjusted her chair, irritably scraping it over the pavement, he looked at her in exasperation.

"Bloody hell, Kate. It's an open conversation. If you've something to add you needn't sit there looking fit to burst."

"You're making too much of this, and the clock is ticking." Kate uncrossed her leg and let her shoe hit the pavement with a slap.

"You think Sonia will cooperate?" Lukas asked.

"Yes, I do, but we'll never know if we just sit here wondering." Kate stood up and took her shoulder bag from the back of the chair. "I'm going to the British Embassy to ask her. Who's coming with me?"

They followed in meek obedience, and on the way to the Embassy Kate described the approach she thought would work. By the time they arrived, she'd convinced Conor and Lukas to let her conduct the meeting alone. While she waited for Sonia in the drawing room, the Embassy's day-time concierge—a matronly woman far more hospitable than the suspicious night manager— served glasses of lemonade and invited "the gentlemen" to enjoy theirs in the sunny back garden.

As soon as Conor stepped out the back door, he felt as if a beam of heat was moving up his back and over his neck, and he remembered the same thing happening when he'd been at the Embassy two nights earlier. He'd been in the dark, looking out the window just before Frank had arrived and switched on the lights. It was the garden. For some reason it perturbed him. Having a blurry form of second sight seemed like the worst of all possible worlds, and the mystery of this current aversion annoyed him, but it was strong enough to make him hesitate on the steps leading down to the stone walkway.

"Something wrong?" Lukas asked, looking back at him

"Probably, but I'm never sure." Conor waved off his anxious curiosity with a smile of apology. "Leave it, so. If the picture ever clears I'll share the news."

Within half an hour the private meeting had ended. As Kate approached across the grass with Sonia at her side, Conor could tell from her placid air of reassurance the negotiation had been a success. In this case, her instincts had been better than his own.

Sonia had responded to Kate's appeal for compassion, and to the argument that with only a few adjustments her position and Petra's might easily have been reversed. Had Sonia been the fugitive instead, begging to see her child, she would have appreciated being granted that last wish. She'd agreed to allow Petra to see Leo. Her only requirement was that she be present for the visit.

"I can't see how we've any right to refuse you on that." Conor darted a glance at Lukas, who nodded in agreement. "Will Petra object though?"

"I don't think so, at least I hope not." Sonia's pale brow wrinkled. "I believe Petra and I should look each other in the eye and acknowledge the experience we shared. We are the only two people who will ever understand what it meant, and what it cost us."

The Garden on the Ramparts sat near the western end of a long stretch of green space that ran beneath the sheer southern wall of Prague Castle. The entire system of linked parkland was known as the South Gardens. Conor had already seen a good deal of the area before knowing its name because he'd chased Sonia's would-be assassin, Karl, almost the entire length of its paved promenade from the eastern end.

He now stood in the corner of a small colonnaded portico that had been constructed directly on the ramparts. The tourists filing in and out came to snap photographs before moving down to a larger observation terrace a hundred feet away, but he wasn't looking at the view. With his back against one of the stone columns, he faced the garden and a large rectangle of crushed gravel lined with park benches. For the past fifteen minutes he'd been methodically sweeping his eyes between the three points of a triangulated area. The first point lay diagonally ahead of him—the bench where Lukas and Sonia had settled with the baby carriage between them. The second ran in a straight line beyond the two of them, where Kate was standing in a shadowed corner of the castle wall, guarding the eastern walkway. The third point was at the western edge of the garden, where Petra was expected to appeared.

This spot—peaceful, innocuous, and surprisingly public— was the one she'd chosen to surrender herself for the murder and frenzied mutilation of her husband. She'd agreed to the inclusion of Sonia, and had set the rendezvous for five o'clock. The four of them had arrived an hour early to stake out positions that would suit their purpose, which was to eliminate any possibility of Petra escaping once her visit with Leo was finished.

She arrived on time, and when Conor recognized her petite figure approaching from the west, he couldn't take his eyes off her. Contrary to expectation and her appearance the previous day, Petra looked nothing short of spectacular. Her blond hair was shining, pulled up into an elegant bun that accented a pair of sparkling diamond earrings, and she wore a short, strapless cocktail dress that fitted her like a second skin. Every inch of it was covered in arcing patterns of silver and crystal beadwork against a flesh-toned background. With all her curves in lithe, swaying motion, she looked like a newly discovered species— gorgeous and diamond-encrusted—advancing down the walkway in flat, silver sandals.

Conor stood at a distance to her right and she passed without seeing him. When she reached Lukas—also staring, open- mouthed—Petra greeted him with a deep, passionate kiss. He saw the officer stiffen and then give in, placing his hands on her waist and drawing her closer. When they separated, she turned to Sonia. A few words passed between them, and then Petra stepped forward to take her into a close embrace.

"Ah, Christ," Conor muttered nervously, earning a startled glance from the apple-cheeked German woman standing next to him. Petra had taken control, clearly having given more thought to this encounter than expected. Regardless of the fact that every one of his colleagues was armed, he was afraid they'd all brought knives to a gunfight.

Moving next to the carriage, Petra lifted the sleeping baby and held him up to gaze at him. Leo's face shrank into a prune-like grimace and reddened, but it quickly cleared when she settled him against her shoulder. She walked in a slow circle around the carriage, her hand gently caressing his head.

As agreed, they gave her ten minutes, an interval that seemed cruelly short but also dangerously long. When Conor saw Lukas glance at him with a subtle nod, he signaled to Kate. From their respective positions they each advanced in a clockwise direction, flanking the rectangular area. They stopped when they'd reached their marks—Kate on the eastern side of the walkway that stretched into the distance along the length of the castle, and Conor on its shorter western path leading back to the street. Facing each other across the wide graveled space, they stood in silent witness to Petra's final minutes cradling the child of her heart, and Conor's heart thudded painfully in his chest, nearly undone by the tears streaming down Kate's face.

Petra had her back to Conor when she noticed Kate's presence, and although still a good distance away he was close enough to hear her brief, throaty laugh. "Ah, so interesting, but not so surprising, I think." Her head moved from side to side, searching, and then as though sensing his presence she turned to face Conor and laughed again. "Yes, I thought you must be nearby. You are rarely far from her, are you?"

"Not if I can help it," he said, his own voice strained with emotion.

"Such an odd pair, the two of you. There is more to you than meets the eye, I think." She ran her eyes over Conor with a suggestive smile. "Tantalizing, since already you offer so much for the eye to appreciate. If only I had time to learn more, but I know you are here to tell me I do not. I will never be sure why you seem to be in the middle of everything, so cool and calm, keeping company with spies, but I can guess. Can't I?"

She directed this question to Lukas, who shook his head and gave a helpless shrug. Conor could only imagine the internal battle he was waging to remain in character for her—the stolid Castle Guard officer of unexceptional background who spoke no English.

Once more, she began moving around the carriage with Leo pressed snugly against her, and none of them could bring themselves to interrupt her dreamlike rotation. Even Sonia refused to intervene. She remained sitting on the bench, watchful and silent, but completely motionless. Conor didn't know how long they might have stayed frozen in place, but at last Petra stopped. She rested her lips against the baby's head for a long moment before reaching for the carriage. She pulled it forward until it stood between herself and Lukas, and after gently laying Leo inside she straightened, and smiled fondly at the officer.

"Ah, Lukas." With her hand on his cheek Petra spoke to him in English. "My noble American friend, and my royal Czech lover. No secrets between us now. I have always known you and why you came to me, but I regret nothing and neither should you. For my whole life, men have looked and taken what they wanted without seeing anything, but you gave more than you took, and you were the only one who ever truly saw me." She circled his neck, pulling him down to her face for a lingering kiss. "Forgive yourself, and try always to remember it was what I wanted."

Petra ran a hand over his shoulder and down his arm before letting it drop, and then in a darting movement of astonishing speed she turned and began sprinting away.

Although they'd agreed such a gambit would be a futile delay of the inevitable, the formation Conor and Lukas mapped out had been arranged with the conviction that Petra would try to run. Through some collective intuition they'd anticipated her strategy—it was the unexpected direction she took that came as a shock. Instead of running to the east towards Kate or heading west in Conor's direction, Petra was making straight for the ramparts and the wide, crescent-shaped observation terrace extending out from it, which offered a panoramic view over the terra-cotta roofs of Prague's Little Quarter.

Their instant of paralyzed horror gave her the only lead she needed. Although Lukas came to life first he did so with a lurch against the baby carriage in front of him, losing a step in an automatic grab at the handle to keep it from tipping over. Running from their opposite positions Conor and Kate closed in on her, but although Kate was at least ten yards in front he saw she hadn't a prayer of catching Petra.

"Stop her!" Conor began shouting at the tourists milling around in front of them. "For the love of God, will someone please stop her!"

Instead of spurring the crowd to action, his cries only made them turn and stare at him. Their curious expressions shifted to alarm as he snatched the Walther from the holster at his back—a desperate move of last resort.

"Kate, get down. Everyone get the fuck down. Now!" Kate ducked down quickly and lay flat against the ground. If everyone else had responded to his barked warning in this way Conor might have had a chance. Some did cower, but the rest scurried over the terrace in all directions, giving him no immediate opportunity for a clear, non-lethal shot. When the space finally opened, it was too late. Petra had swung herself over the terrace railing. Poised on its outer edge, she lifted her head to the sky and launched herself up into the air, arms spread wide. Conor sank to his knees, and for one breathless second before she dropped from sight, he saw the beadwork on her dress erupt in a flash of reflected sunlight.

Lukas, who had surged ahead of him, stumbled to a stop and

then continued on more slowly, passing Kate without noticing her. Rising from his knees Conor looked back at Sonia, standing with both hands pressed against her mouth, and gestured for her to stay with Leo. He continued forward to Kate, and after a tight, trembling hug they went to join Lukas, who'd already seen what he needed to and had crouched down next to the railing with his face in his hands.

Petra had chosen her spot well. A few feet to either the right or left and she might have only broken bones on a brick-lined garden or on the steeply sloping roof of a building tucked against the base of the terrace. Instead, she'd found the wedge-shaped space between both that provided an unobstructed drop of at least a hundred feet.

Below them her body lay crumpled on a patch of sand-colored cement, edging a lawn just beginning to send up new shoots of delicate spring green. There was little detail to see at such a distance, but in a cold sweat Conor had to move back from the railing. Walking a few steps away he took several deep breaths, swallowing hard while Kate followed him with her eyes, looking worried.

When he came back a crowd had gathered at the railing, full of trite remarks and ignorant speculation. Conor wanted to scream and wave his gun at all of them, but they apparently didn't recognize him as the wild man who'd done that a minute earlier. He subsided into anonymity and rested his arms against the railing, letting Kate rub her hand over his back in soothing circles. Ordinarily he wouldn't have tolerated such outright coddling, but this time he didn't object. It was helping.

"I need to go report this to the Guard duty officer," Lukas said, finally breaking the silence among the three of them. Gripping the railing, he rose from his crouched position, his face ashen. "It's going to take a while. This will likely be a shared jurisdiction between the Castle Guard and local police. I hate to ask you this, but—"

"We'll go down and stay with her, Lukas." Conor held his friend's shoulder in a tight grip. "We won't let her be alone."

Too overwhelmed to reply, Lukas nodded and quickly walked away.

"She's in a completely enclosed area," Kate said, gazing down at the pitiful scene below. "We'll need to figure out where it is and who owns the land."

Conor took her arm, gently pulling her away from the railing. "We know that already, love. It's the back garden of the British Embassy."

30

The scene at the British Embassy was in many respects a replay of the previous evening. They spent several hours alternating between meetings with now-familiar law enforcement representatives, and tedious intervals waiting for others to arrive and pose the same questions. It was close to midnight when Conor and Kate were finally allowed to leave. Sonia walked with them to the front door, and as they reached it she took Conor's arm, drawing him back with an unusual question.

"To exorcise a demon we follow our own path, yes? You are familiar with this idea, I think."

Conor nodded. "I walk it every day. I suppose we all do, in some way."

"Yes. Petra has followed hers to the end, and now I will make the journey—a different path, but I will begin tonight. One step, and then another. It's how we start our lives, yes? And how we carry on with them." Sonia gave him a warm smile. "Good night. Thank you for everything."

Neither he nor Kate registered these parting words as a final good-bye, but before long they discovered she had intended them as such. Just after five o'clock the next morning, Lukas rattled them awake with a phone call, delivering two extraordinary bits of news: Sonia and Leo had disappeared from the Embassy, along with all of their luggage, and the empty home of Martin and Petra Labut was engulfed in flames.

"Do you want to go see it?" Kate asked after the call had ended.

"Not particularly," Conor said. "Do you?"

"No, but I'm glad it's burning."

"So am I."

Conor wondered which path Sonia had decided to follow, whether it had taken her to one of the many countries bordering the Czech Republic, or only to a quieter, more obscure district of the city she loved. Wherever she was, he wished her well.

After sliding the mobile phone across the nightstand he lay on his back, hands folded on his stomach, listening to the sounds of the hotel's early risers—doors banging, toilets flushing, the rhythmic click of a roller bag and its owner, moving past their door.

"So. What should we do *today*?"

Conor smiled, hearing Kate's muffled, sleepy voice. Still only half awake, she had burrowed back under the down comforter.

He rolled over and slipped an arm around her waist. "Sleep."

"Hallelujah."

They did get up, eventually. Conor had a rehearsal with the Czech Philharmonic at the Rudolfinum for the following evening's concert, and later they took the tram to the Ram Gorse pub to pick up their travel identities and surrender their own to an express-mail envelope. The return visit was much like the first, with a few notable exceptions.

This time the bartender was a heavyset woman sporting a halo of teased-out hair dyed an electric, jack-o'-lantern orange. Possibly she was the wife of the man they'd met previously. At any rate, she was just as dour. Conor delivered his line about the Liverpool football game and she regarded him with an impassive, protruding pout.

"Is old, this code."

Conor spread his hands in apology. "It's the only one I've got."

"You are the Irish one, yes?"

"You've nailed it in one." He smiled at her puzzled squint. "Sorry. I am, yes. The Irish one."

The rest of the process followed the previous pattern, and when they walked into the small, windowless room, its arrangements looked much the same, but the woman drinking a cup of tea next to the shining brass samovar was a lovely olive-skinned brunette who couldn't have been much older than fifty. It might have been another woman entirely, except that the wheelchair—and the empty space between the seat and footplates—was the same.

"How are you, Harlow?" Conor greeted her amiably. "Sure you're looking younger every day."

She laughed. Her voice had a lower, more mellow tone than he remembered, but the breezy, quick wit was the same. "Really, this is nothing, darling. Come back next week and I'll be a teenager with spots. I *am* sorry about the passcode. Carla's quite vexed with me. I should have given you a new one when you were last here, but honestly, they're always to do with football and I think I forget them on purpose."

They had tea with Harlow, a strong brew poured from the teapot diluted with hot water she dispensed from the samovar with great ceremony. Since the Fermature and its various assets had been drawn into their mission they talked more freely this time, but as before, her time was limited, and after tea she led them to her desk for the exchange of documents.

When they stood to leave, Harlow smiled at Kate, catching

her discreet glance at the wheelchair. "Yes, that's not part of the disguise, I'm afraid, but the prosthetics are. Perhaps I'll snap those on for you, next time you visit. Although the Service always rather liked having me in the chair. They'd wheel me out during training seminars to shock young agents—a flesh-and-blood cautionary tale of how missions can take the most dreadful turns. All in the line of duty, I suppose, but I prefer my present assignment a good deal more."

"Were you wounded in Russia?" Conor asked.

"Clever man." She regarded him through half-closed eyes, as though appraising his worthiness, before nodding. "It was the Soviet Union back then, but yes, you've got it right. Perhaps I'll have more time to tell you about it some day. The tale was of some interest to a friend of yours. He came a long way to see me, just to hear it from my own mouth."

"A friend of Conor's?" Kate asked. She shot him a questioning look, but Conor shrugged, equally mystified. His circle of colleagues in the spy community wasn't wide, but he couldn't pinpoint which of them had a paid a visit to the Ram Gorse pub.

Harlow smiled at their puzzled expressions. "Come with me."

She spun around and rolled to the large safe door, which this time was already standing open. She went all the way to the end and stopped in front of a gray metal storage cabinet. Refusing Conor's offer of assistance, Harlow got one of the doors open and maneuvered the chair closer. She reached down to the lowest shelf and removed a bundle of red paisley-patterned fabric and handed it up to him. Conor accepted it, carefully unfolding it to reveal a black Makarov handgun.

Grimly, Harlow nodded at it. "At one time, that gun belonged to a Russian arms dealer. Vasily Dragonov, to be precise. I believe you're familiar with him."

"I am, but we've never met." His throat suddenly tight, Conor forced the words out in a gravelly rasp.

"Nor had your friend, I gather—not formally, at any rate—but he seemed eager for the opportunity."

Conor made no reply. He wasn't sure how to comment, or whether he should, but in his mind the pool of candidates who might have sought out this woman in her windowless bunker had just narrowed to one. Raising his head, he saw the same realization dawning in Kate's eyes.

He handed the gun back to Harlow and watched her wrap the fabric around it once again. She held the bundle in her hands, staring at it for a moment before she placed it back in the cabinet.

"My ... friend," he said, once she'd closed the door and turned her chair to face him. "Where is he, do you know?"

"I'm sorry." The Fermature was back in official mode. "I can't say any more. I've already pushed the boundaries of my position in saying this much. I only know of your connection because he told me his story as well."

Conor didn't press her on this point. He and Kate left a few minutes later and walked in silence back to the tram stop, but after reaching it they finally looked at each other, acknowledging the significance of what they'd heard.

"Where do you think he is?" she asked.

Conor gave a dispirited sigh. "Somewhere in Russia. We might have guessed as much, I suppose, but this is a stronger clue than we had before."

They had been wondering—and worrying—about what had become of Curtis Sedgwick since the last time they'd seen him, six months earlier. Given the man's troubled history, the possibilities were sobering. Although Conor had tried leveraging his intelligence connections to locate him, all inquiries had so far come up empty. For months he'd been wrestling with indecision as to whether he should get more serious about the effort to find him.

He'd been paired with Sedgwick during his first undercover

mission, when the American DEA agent had been contracted with MI6 to serve as his control officer. They'd begun their acquaintance as two halves of a fractious, mutually distrustful relationship, but they'd also traveled to hell and back with each other. As Sonia had observed earlier, with any shared experience—good or bad—it was hard to break an attachment with the only person who really understood what it meant, and what it had cost.

In the end, they'd forged a bond that was more complicated than friendship and as unshakeable as brotherhood. Vasily Dragonov represented unfinished business for both of them, but this wasn't the time or place to think about it. The tram arrived, and Conor pulled his mind back to more immediate business.

"Let's figure it out when we get home," he said, ushering Kate ahead of him through the door. "We've been wringing our hands over the eejit for months. A few more days won't make much difference."

31

"I'm sorry Officer Hasek didn't feel up to joining us this evening." Frank handed Kate a glass of white wine and took a sip from his own. "According to Eckhard he looks quite a treat in a suit and tie."

"He is a handsome man," Kate agreed, "but also a pretty exhausted one. We had dinner at his flat last night, and as soon as he'd served the coffee he fell asleep in his chair with the dog on his lap." She smiled, remembering how mortified Lukas had been, waking from his nap to find his guests had done the dishes and cleaned up the kitchen. He was grateful for their company, though—people he could talk with openly, who understood his grief and guilt and expected no explanations for his occasional long silences. She hoped they would stay in touch—they did have ancestors in common, after all.

"What's the news on Sonia?" she asked Frank. "Do you have any leads?"

"None whatsoever," he replied, smoothly. "To be honest, I've little appetite for the hunt. Oh, and in all the excitement I'd forgotten to mention she isn't the only agent who's disappeared in the last few days. Your friend Joanna Patch has gone missing as well."

"Really," Kate said, dryly. "Are you sure she hasn't just gone on bivouac with the Increment?"

He laughed. "Actually, her disappearance was reported by Colonel Albright, the thick-necked chap who engineered your kidnapping at Brecon Beacons. Insufferable man. He's been on an unpaid administrative leave ever since. He and Joanna had been having an affair."

"Does anyone know where she might be?" Kate asked.

"As I mentioned before, her last posting before Fort Monckton was Johannesburg, so there's some suspicion she's gone there, but we're not very keen on chasing after her either. She's saved us the bother of sacking her, and nobody wants to go to bloody Johannesburg." Frank looked at his watch and finished his wine. "We should perhaps consider moving upstairs, ahead of the crowd."

Kate nodded and looked down the length of the Rudolfinum's foyer, a handsome, bow-shaped hall paved in multi-colored marble. Smartly dressed concertgoers continued to stream in through the five arched entrances. The old wooden doors creaked, the glass in their frames rattling as the crowd streamed through. A flutter of nerves passed through her stomach. She might have called them sympathy pains, except at this point it seemed she was the only one having them. After a successful rehearsal the previous day, Conor had so mastered his stage fright that he'd been able to tease Kate about her anxiety on his behalf.

"I expect you're thinking I'll make a hames of it," he'd said, pretending offense. "That I'll drop the bow, or fall on my face, or pop a string."

"Stop it, you know I don't think that. You're going to be amazing. It's just that it's so many people, and … God, what happens if you do break a string?" Kate hadn't even considered that terrifying possibility.

Conor grinned. "I'll compensate. It's not as disastrous as it sounds."

"So many people," Kate repeated, now in a low voice.

"Yes, it's completely sold out, I'm told. Mostly a local audience. The symposium participants are merely a ragged remnant scattered among this crowd." Frank gave her a droll, sidelong glance. "They were meant to congregate in a pre-performance function, but the organizers have quite gone off the idea of receptions."

She laughed. "Who can blame them? Do you feel nervous for Eckhard on a night like this, Frank—when he's conducting such an important concert?"

"Good God, no. In the first place he's quite at home on the stage—hadn't you noticed? And in the second place I've rather had my fill of feeling nervous for Eckhard this week, although I believe we'll both be happy when he's safely back in Windsor having a good rest."

"Amen to that," Kate said, wistfully.

Smiling in sympathy, Frank slipped an arm around her waist and they walked to the staircase that would take them up to the Dvořák Hall. "I'm sorry to delay your own return home. Conor did explain about the meetings we'll need him for in London? It shouldn't be more than a few days, and I hope our ebullient hospitality will soften the blow?"

"He did explain, and it's fine. We're both looking forward to spending a little more time with you."

"Did he actually say as much? How extraordinary."

Conor had said as much and more, once reassured she wasn't bothered about the unexpected detour on their route back to Vermont. "Sure we've spent nearly a week with people who hated each other, in a place that felt like the inner circle of Hell. A lit match was the best thing that could have happened to that house and fair play to Sonia if she's the one who threw it, but I can still feel the film of it sticking to me. It's like that 'greaves' spread yer man gave us back at the Ram Gorse pub—an unmeltable residue you can't feckin' get rid of, no matter how hot. I'm thinking it'll be good for us to spend a few days in a house with a clean spirit and a couple of people who love each other."

Kate couldn't have put it better herself.

Once settled in the stately grandeur of Dvořák Hall her nerves began to settle, and when Eckhard appeared, his familiar face and joyous energy made her forget everything else. The first half of the program opened with a short piece by Dvořák, and culminated in the String Quartet No. 1, by Leoš Janáček. The Czech composer had subtitled his work the *Kreutzer Sonata*, and it was presented as a companion piece to Conor's performance of Beethoven's Violin Sonata No. 9, also known as the *Kreutzer Sonata*.

"Eckhard is exploring what connects these two compositions," Conor had explained, when reviewing the program with her earlier that day. "Both in terms of what you hear and what you feel. Tolstoy's novella took its name and some of its inspiration from the original sonata Beethoven wrote, and Janáček took his inspiration from the novella. You won't be hearing anything that reminds you of a peaceful afternoon in the country from either of them. The Janáček is dark and surreal, and if I play it right the *presto* movement of the Beethoven might be the most hair-raising fifteen minutes you're likely to hear in the classical repertoire." He'd tossed the program onto the bed with a sigh. "If you put the two together, it just about adds up to an orchestration of what we've lived through here—our own little novella of twisted relationships and bloody mayhem."

He was right about the Janáček. From the ominous edge of the cello's solo opening to the last poignant notes, Kate found it easy to conjure the torment and foreshadowed doom of Tolstoy's female protagonist and relate it to their own experience. It made her eager to hear what Conor would do with the Beethoven following the intermission.

When he walked onto the stage in his white tie and tails, pristine again after their third dry cleaning in a week, Kate's pulse raced. She'd never known anyone who seemed as comfortable in a tuxedo as he was in a pair of jeans covered with barn grime. His easy, athletic grace made whatever he was wearing look sexy.

"Oh my," a voice murmured appreciatively next to her, reminding Kate this was also the first time Frank was seeing Conor perform at this level.

They were seated ten rows up on the left side of the concert hall. Conor had warned her not to be disappointed if he couldn't see her, but when he turned from shaking hands with the concertmaster, his eyes went straight to her. Although he was already sinking into the fugue state that would shut everything else out, he lingered on her face for a few seconds and gave her the smallest hint of a smile.

The sonata began with a series of slow, awkward chords that Conor had described earlier as a violinist's nightmare. They were painfully emotional, a groaning wail that went unanswered, and held the audience in rapt silence. From that point forward, and for most of the remaining fifteen minutes, Beethoven let all hell break loose in his *presto* movement. The pace was explosive, the solo violin a virtuosic tornado powering the music forward and pushing the orchestra to its breathless limit. By the fourth minute, Conor and the Pressenda had fused into a single, electrifying presence.

He played without any exaggerated gestures, moving very little and never straying more than a few inches at a time on the stage, but this control of motion only heightened an air of blistering energy. Even during the brief episodes of calm it sizzled below the surface, barely contained. To Kate it seemed as if Conor was vibrating in place while a passionate, wild chaos poured out of him.

As he'd promised, it was fifteen minutes of relentless intensity. After the first movement, the sonata progressed into a series of variations on a more placid theme, but then another long, breathtaking *presto* brought the entire piece to a fiery conclusion. When it was over Kate could see that he actually *was* vibrating— or rather, trembling—as she and the audience members surged up from their seats in thunderous applause. After four curtain calls it seemed clear an encore was expected. He returned and delivered a short solo piece with a playful, swaying melody. It helped resolve the pressurized atmosphere and had the audience clapping along, and after one last curtain call with Eckhard, they finally allowed Conor to go.

"Well, yes," Frank said, turning to her with a satisfied smile. "I'd say that was rather a strong debut, wouldn't you?"

Exiting the concert hall, they followed an usher's directions down the hall to a room where the orchestra members had congregated. At the end of it, Eckhard waved a hand towel, beckoning them forward. He looked like a boxing coach who had just seen his champion through ten rounds. Conor, his face running with perspiration, looked every bit the part. He stood several feet away with his back against the wall and his eyes closed, draining a bottle of water.

"He's a bit shell-shocked, I think." Eckhard handed Kate another bottle of water with a smile. "Take him out for some air. Walk him around and make him drink more water. When he is fit for conversation, please bring him down to the Grosseto. It's the riverboat restaurant just next to the bridge. There are a number of prospective donors I would like him to charm."

Kate stepped over to him and when she took Conor's hand his eyes slowly opened. "You're right," she said. "The first movement sounded exactly like the week we just had. It's amazing how you packed it all into a fifteen-minute nutshell."

He smiled and pushed himself away from the wall. "I guess

insanity sometimes comes in small packages."

"I guess so." Kate tapped his chest with the water bottle. "Let's get out of here. Fresh air, hydration, exercise. Maestro's orders."

They left the Rudolfinum through a side door and crossed the lawn next to it, then took a walk along the riverbank while Conor dutifully drank the second bottle of water. After stopping to watch a fleet of glass-topped touring boats depart for a moonlight cruise down the Vltava, they returned along the same path and sat down on a bench by the river's edge. Conor put an arm around Kate's shoulders.

"We've one day left before we leave. Is there anything you'd like to see before we go?"

"I'd love to spend some time at the National Museum, if it wouldn't bore you too much."

Conor looked at her, mildly hurt. "Why would you think I'd be bored? I may not know a lot about art, but I'm teachable."

"I'm sorry," she said. "Are you really interested in learning about it?"

"Only if you're doing the teaching." He gave her a sheepish grin. "I suppose it's really just an excuse to learn more about you."

Kate took a breath and held it, surprised by the strength of her emotion. Such a simple observation, and he'd offered it so casually, with no premeditation or intention to impress. Just a sincere statement of fact, and it was probably the most romantic compliment she'd ever received. Shifting away from his side she turned to face him, trembling with a different kind of nervousness now.

"I learned something about you tonight, or maybe it was more about me. Can I tell you about it?"

Puzzled and curious, he nodded. "Of course. What is it?"

"It's something I suddenly realized from watching you play in a different way than I'd ever seen. I feel a little embarrassed for not figuring it out sooner. I've had this notion—a pretty conceited one really—that I was the most important thing in your life, but now I understand that I'm not."

Conor narrowed his eyes warily. "Have we not done this part already? Did I go mumbling someone's name in my sleep again?"

Kate smiled. "No. This isn't about that."

"Good. So then, tell me what, in the name of all that's holy, have you decided is more important in my life than you?"

"Maybe not *more* important, but it's at least got equal billing." Lifting the neck of the violin case he'd leaned against the bench she gave it a little wiggle.

Conor's eyebrows shot up in sardonic disbelief. "You're jealous of the Pressenda?"

"Just the opposite. I'm grateful for her." Kate rested the case against the bench and bowed her head. "I love you more than you can imagine, Conor, but some things can't be fixed with love, and there are places inside you I won't ever be able to reach. I was afraid you didn't realize it, and that you thought I had some kind of magic that would make everything whole for you again. It scared me. I felt as though you'd put me on a pedestal, and I was worried that I'd fall off sooner or later and disappoint you."

"I put you on a pedestal." Conor raised his hands and let them fall to his knees in sad frustration. "Kate, I haven't a clue what that even means. I've put you nowhere. Why would I? You're fine where you are."

"I know that now." She took his hand and held it in both of her own. "I'm not all that holds you up and you never expected me to be. The relationship you have with this violin—what it gives you, what it brings out of you—is something vital. I don't think you could exist without it, but it's completely separate from what you and I share."

"I suppose it is, yeah," Conor said. "Sure it would need to be … wouldn't it?"

Kate saw she was scaring him. For him, the idea that the darkest corners of his soul could only be accessed with a violin was so natural he didn't need to think about it. Her epiphany confused him, and because he didn't understand it he was clearly anxious about what it meant.

"Oh, sweetheart, I'm sorry. You don't get what I'm trying to say, do you? I'm telling you I'm not scared anymore. As much as I have, I'll give to you, and I know it will be enough." Kate leaned over to kiss him softly on the lips, and then moved to whisper in his ear. "You promised to ask again when I was ready."

It was such a rare treat to be a step ahead of him, to see all his extraordinary intuitions stymied while the light of understanding crept slowly over his face. For a minute he seemed unable to process it, unable to make any words come out of his mouth, until he managed to breathe one that escaped his lips in a whisper.

"Kate?"

"Properly now," she said, gently. "I know you can do it."

"I can, of course," he stuttered, "but I haven't the—I mean, I wasn't ready for—"

"It doesn't matter."

"Right so." Conor took a shaky breath and slipped from the bench onto the ground as though plunging into the deepest part of a lake. Down on one knee at her feet, he took her hand, and his eyes grew anxious, seeing hers fill with tears. "Ah, Kate. You'll have me destroyed with this."

"Never mind." She sniffed and laughed. "Keep going."

He took her hand, and ran his thumb over the back of it. "My heart, my brightest treasure, my best friend." Conor's voice caught and he lowered his head, falling silent for a moment. "My only share of the world. Please, will you marry me?"

"Yes. I do. I will. Yes. Yes."

He was on his feet by the time she'd uttered the final "yes," pulling her up with him into a kiss that steadily grew more passionate. When they finally came up for air Kate saw they'd traveled all the way to the railing along the riverbank. She pulled back to smile at him.

"That wasn't so hard, was it?"

Conor turned her face up to his, softly laughing and crying at the same time. "Jaysus, are you joking? I was never so scared in all my life."

Resting his back against the wrought-iron railing, he drew her to him, and Kate relaxed into his embrace. Safe. Content. Whole.

32

Sitting in the Prague Airport's VIP departure lounge, Conor was dressed for business. The previous afternoon, after their visit to the National Museum, he'd realized that as soon as he arrived in London he'd be going straight from Heathrow to a ministerial briefing on the Ghorbani fiasco and he didn't have a thing to wear. His tuxedo was hardly appropriate, and the jacket of the only other suit he'd brought had been rendered nearly sleeveless on one side. While the idea depressed him, the prospect of a shopping trip had raised a gleam of anticipation in Kate's blue eyes.

"Indulge me," she'd said.

The result of this indulgence was a charcoal-shaded ensemble by an Italian designer he'd never heard of, secured for an appalling price. Although he wouldn't confess it to her, it was probably the most comfortable suit he'd ever worn.

By contrast, Kate was dressed casually, in the black leggings he'd bought for her in Hřensko and a soft cashmere tunic of pale lavender. Having declined Frank's offer to include her in the briefing, she was anticipating a relaxing afternoon at the house in Windsor.

"Do I have time for a trip to the duty-free shop? I'd like to pick up a bottle of something to bring Frank and Eckhard. And maybe a few other little things."

Conor smiled at her. Still riding on a cloud of heady exhilaration after gaining the one thing he'd wanted most and feared he would never get, he felt ready to agree to any suggestion Kate might make.

"So long as it isn't Becherovka." He couldn't even look at the stuff without flashing back to the shots he'd thrown down in Martin Labut's study when he'd been trying to avoid the minister's coy invitation to carnal adventure. Conor looked at his watch. "I'd say you've about twenty minutes before I'll be telling them to shout for you on the PA. Remember what your name is, in case I do."

"How could I forget?" Kate wrinkled her nose. "Edwin and Dorothea Buckingham. I think the Prague Fermature is playing games with us."

"Well, she's no problem passing for a woman of eighty years of age. Maybe she thinks it's a skill we should develop."

After she left, he poured himself a club soda from the self-service bar and returned to his leather sofa and his perusal of the *Wall Street Journal*, the only English-language newspaper he could find. It was the first time he'd ever been allowed inside a VIP lounge (Eckhard had arranged the access), and he had to admit the experience was growing on him.

After a few minutes he glanced up to see a striking, long-legged woman in a short-skirted business suit making her way to the chair across from him. She was juggling a briefcase and purse while trying to maneuver a Louis Vuitton roller bag around his violin case, all without taking her eyes from her smartphone. Conor rose quickly from the sofa.

"Sorry, let me get that out of your way."

"Oh, thank you," she said, still focused on the phone. "I appreciate that."

American, he thought, noting the accent. She took the chair across from him, giving him a cursory glance, and then she did a double take. Suddenly she was more interested in having a conversation with him. A few minutes into it, Conor realized she'd pegged him as a millionaire, and the idea so amused him that he allowed her to continue under this delusion. He figured it was good practice for honing a covert identity.

When Kate returned, the woman looked her over and arranged her face into a mask of polite interest, but not quickly enough to hide a disdainful frown. Kate dropped onto the sofa next to him and Conor arched an eyebrow at the three bags of duty-free loot piled around her feet.

"I got a little carried away," she admitted with a mischievous smile. "I'm sorry, I didn't mean to interrupt your conversation."

"No, you're all right. This is Veronica Templeton."

The woman gave a slight start. "How did you know my name?"

"It's on your luggage." Conor smiled. "I'm Edwin Buckingham, and this is Dorothea, my—"

"Fiancé." Kate gave the woman an adorable, loopy grin. "I'm his fiancé."

"That's right, you are, aren't you?" he said, softly.

"Is New York home for you, Veronica?" At the poor woman's freshly startled expression Kate pointed at the paperwork on the coffee table. "Your boarding pass."

"Oh. Yes. Manhattan." She gave the two of them an odd look and then swept her belongings from the table. "Well, it's been nice chatting with you. I should probably be getting down to my gate now."

They held back their laughter until she was out of sight.

"That was a little mean," Kate finally said, wiping her eyes.

"Ah, go on. It was a great bit of *craic*, and she deserved it."

"She probably thinks we're grifters."

"Rubbish. She thinks I'm a millionaire who collects rare violins." Conor gave her a facetious smile. "And she thinks you're a gold digger."

"I am." Kate moved closer to him. "And I've found it."

"Me, too. I've struck gold." Conor put an arm around her, anchoring himself, grateful to be always coming home.

ACKNOWLEDGMENTS

To paraphrase Woody Allen, going from nothing to the first draft is the hardest part of any writing, but from first draft to finished product is by no means a straight line either. The inside of my head can get as tangled as the "twisted lanes of an old world city," and I am grateful to the following for serving as my compass: Claire Guare, always the first reader, for putting up with the ebb and flow of my angst; Richard "Red" Lawhern, for technical expertise and gentle corrections, and for teaching me something new with every conversation; Erik Nielsen and Mary Gibson, for musical expertise and insights that helped me get inside the head of a violinist; and Susan Z. Ritz, for her thoughtful critique, and for an open-hearted support that helps more than she knows.

Thanks also to the professionals who guided me the rest of the way: my editor, Averill Buchanan; the cover design team of Andrew and Rebecca Brown from Design for Writers; and interior layout artist, Chenile Keogh. You've all contributed what you do best, so whatever is missing is on me.

Of course, I am most grateful to all my readers and the connections I've made with so many of you. You can find me through all the social media outlets by visiting my website at **www.kathrynguare.com**. On that site you can also join my mailing list if you'd like to receive the occasional free short story and news of upcoming releases.

Or write to me at **Kathryn@kathrynguare.com**. I'd love to hear from you. About the books, or anything else!

Also Available, in bookstores and online:

Books 1 and 2 in
The Virtuosic Spy/Conor McBride Series:

BOOK 1:DECEPTIVE CADENCE

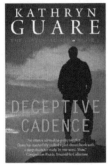

A talented Irish musician reluctantly reinvents himself, disappearing into an undercover identity to search for the man who ruined his career: his own brother.

On a journey from his farm on the west coast of Ireland to the tumultuous city of Mumbai, Conor McBride's only goal is to redeem the brother who betrayed him. But, he's becoming a virtuoso of a different kind in a dangerous game where the rules keep changing—and where the allies he trusted to help him may be the people he should fear the most.

BOOK 2: THE SECRET CHORD

Conor McBride has lost everything, and if he can't find a way to disappear in a hurry, the next thing he loses could be his life. Running from enemies he's never met and haunted by his own destructive actions, Conor needs a refuge secure enough to hold his secrets. A farmhouse inn tucked amidst the green mountains of Vermont seems ideal, but when his past catches up with him, Conor discovers the beautiful young innkeeper has secrets of her own, and that hers are more likely to get them both killed.

Made in the USA
Monee, IL
26 December 2019